Mistletoe
Mansion

Mistletoe Mansion

SAMANTHA TONGE

CARINA™

This edition is published by arrangement with Harlequin Books S.A. CARINA is a trademark of Harlequin Enterprises Limited, used under licence.

Published in Great Britain 2015
By Carina, an imprint of HarperCollins*Publishers*
1 London Bridge Street, London, SE1 9GF

© 2014 Samantha Tonge

ISBN 978-0-263-92157-1

98-1015

Harlequin (UK) Limited's policy is to use papers that are natural, renewable and recyclable products and made from wood grown in sustainable forests. The logging and manufacturing processes conform to the legal environmental regulations of the country of origin.

Printed and bound by
CPI Group (UK) Ltd, Croydon, CR0 4YY

Samantha Tonge lives in Cheshire with her lovely family and two cats who think they are dogs. Along with writing, her days are spent cycling, willing cakes to rise and avoiding housework. A love of fiction developed as a child, when she was known for reading Enid Blyton books in the bath. A desire to write bubbled away in the background whilst she pursued other careers, including a fun stint working at Disneyland Paris. Formally trained as a linguist, Samantha now likes nothing more than holing herself up in the spare room, in front of the keyboard. Writing romantic comedy novels is her passion.

www.samanthatonge.co.uk
www.pinkinkladies.wordpress.com

For Martin, Spencer and Dad – ha'way the golfing lads!

Massive thanks to my great editor Lucy Gilmour and the wonderful CarinaUK team for their excellent input, dedication and super covers. Plus thanks to my agent, Kate Nash, for her continual support.

Fellow Carina authors, you are the best and keep me sane. And Pink Ink blog gals, I couldn't manage without our hilarious chats.

I'm constantly bowled over by the support from chicklit bloggers and reviewers – your effort and time is much appreciated, with a special mention to Robyn Koshel from Elder Park Book Reviews and Tay from Chicks That Read. Plus thank you to those readers who've let me know how much my books have made you laugh – because that's why I'm in this writing business, to raise a smile (and have an excuse to go on Facebook and eat chocolate all day long ☺).

Thanks to Jo Hoddes, founder of the fabulously affordable online clothes shop Bae Boutique, (www.bae.boutique), for her support in launching *Mistletoe Mansion*, a story which features the glamorous lifestyle her customers no doubt aspire to.

Martin, Immy and Jay, I so appreciate your regular injections of perspective and confidence. You three guys make every day seem like Christmas.

CHAPTER 1

'Move your legs further apart. Tilt forwards from the waist. Rock your hips in a rhythmic motion… Nice, gently does it. Now keep that stroke light. We don't want a premature start. Remember what I said about balls…'

'Keep your eye on them,' I whispered back to the silky voice coming from the television. My jogging trousers slipped beneath my stomach as I swung my golf club (okay, broom handle). Having just chipped out of three virtual bunkers, I was practising my putting before re-doing the energetic teeing-off section.

'You still not finished, Kimmy?' asked Adam, as he came out of the bedroom, in T-shirt and boxers.

I smiled. Would the day ever come when I got tired of admiring his rock solid quads (thigh muscles to you and me)? They were like the physical representation of his personality – solid, secure, strong…

'I thought you were meeting Jess for coffee.'

'Almost done,' I said. It had been no mean feat to follow my new exercise DVD without taking a chunk of plaster out of the ceiling or knocking a bauble off our bargain-priced Christmas tree. Indoor golf wasn't the best hobby if you lived in a one-bedroom flat where you couldn't swing a cat, let alone a four foot broom.

He rolled his eyes without their usual twinkle. In fact, he'd been low in the sparkle department for several days, now.

'What?' I stopped, secretly grateful for the break. Golf may be awesome for toning bingo wings, but my back ached as if I'd played eighteen holes up Ben Nevis.

'You already had that DVD by the bird off Strictly Come Dancing,' said Adam. 'Why buy this one? You should go to the gym, like me. It'd save you a bundle of money in the long run.'

I gazed back at the screen. Just as well he'd forgotten the DVD I'd bought by the winners of Britain's Got Talent. Then there was the Hotpants Workout and the Bootcamp Bum-buster. Starchat magazine had recommended Melissa Winsford's; said it would give me "the celebrity body of my dreams".

I sighed. Her voice was all velvety and smooth, as if she lived on nothing but marshmallows and hot chocolate. With her firm boobs and flat tum, she was one of the most glamorous "Wags" (*W*ives *a*nd *g*irlfriends for those who don't know). Oops, better make that "*birdies*". Apparently Melissa hated it when "classy" golf was associated with "thuggish" football terms.

'Give me a few minutes and I'll make pancakes,' I said hoping this might raise, if nothing else, a nod of appreciation. Our usual Saturday morning ritual was a late-morning cuddle to my Hits for Lovers CD, followed by pancakes and syrup. Except today I was meeting my best mate, to indulge in festive flavoured lattes at our favourite coffee shop. And in any case, Adam hadn't been interested when I'd rolled over close for a quick snuggle-up. In fact he'd been moody all week and I don't mean in a sexy Marlon Brando way.

'You okay?' I sat down beside him, on the sofa, stomach pinching a little at the empty expression on his face. 'You've had a hard week. Let me give you a massage.'

At that moment the doorbell rang. I looked at the clock. Of course! Postie! I dashed to the kitchen worktop and grabbed a Tupperware box. It contained six rich brown cupcakes topped with dark butter icing and swirls of red and green cake glitter.

'Morning, Matt.' I grinned at his lopsided cycling hat and passed him the box. 'Hope everything works out,' I whispered.

'Thanks, Kimmy,' he said and in return handed me a brown envelope and some junk mail. He prised open the plastic box's lid. 'They look ace. Cool Christmas colours, as well. How much do I owe you?'

'Think of them as an anniversary gift.'

'What was that all about?' asked Adam, in a flat voice, as I closed the door. 'How come you're so friendly with the postman?'

'I'm on first name terms with a lot of people, since losing my job and working random temporary hours – including Dave, the window cleaner, and Sanjay who reads the gas meter.' I sat down again. 'Postie and his wife have been having problems. He almost moved out last month. Tonight he's cooking a special meal. I offered to provide a dessert that would give them a bit of, um, oomph.'

'Huh?'

'Sweet basil – it's an aphrodisiac. I disguised its taste with fresh mint which doubles as the perfect breath freshener. After a couple of those cupcakes, she'll think he's got the moves of Patrick Swayze in Dirty Dancing.'

Was Adam even listening? He stared at the brown envelope and didn't even reach out for the junk mail, to flick through for money-off coupons.

'Hungry?' I put the envelope to one side. I had to meet Jess in one hour.

'Aren't you going to open it, Kimmy?' he said, in a tight tone.

'What?'

'That envelope. It could be important.'

He was right. Perhaps it was a bill and, unlike Mum, I didn't stash my mail, unopened, into the nearest drawer. I flicked off the telly before leaning back against the beige throw. I ran my acrylic nail along the seal and tugged out a document. Maybe I'd won that competition I'd entered last month for a Hollywood makeover. I sighed. No such luck. It was an application form.

'Why didn't you just bring this home with you?' I left it on the sofa, stood up and walked a few steps over to the open-plan kitchen.

'Work has procedures. Plus there's been a freeze on recruitment. I just left your name with the personnel woman last week and crossed my fingers. I can't believe your luck.' A sparkle actually returned to his eyes.

'You want me to work full time at CountryHouse Potatoes? But I thought we'd agreed – I'd temp until the *right* job came along. Can you really see *me* sorting spuds?'

'Why not?' he asked, and raised both eyebrows.

Good question. CountryHouse Potatoes *was* a great employer. The pay wasn't bad, and from what Adam said, the staff canteen food was yummy. If the position was temporary, I'd have already been at the post box.

'I'm, um, used to working with pretty silver sugar balls and candied roses.' I smiled. 'Your average potato is uglier than my bunion.'

'Ha, ha. Come on, Kimmy. It's in catering. Put your mind to it and you could be supervisor in half the time I took. All this time you've spent at Best Buns bakery, with no chance of moving forwards… If you forgot this mad cake-making idea of yours, you could be earning real money, getting promoted…' His voice sounded even more animated than when he watched football.

'But I'm going down to the job centre again on Monday.' I opened one of the rickety cupboards and took out a pan. It was *not* a mad idea. Even the psychic I'd visited at the local Easter Fair said I was "born to bake".

He picked up the form. 'You can't go on like this forever, babe. I want to be with someone who's willing to look further ahead than next week's edition of Starchat.'

'I don't complain about your sport magazines.'

He waved his hand dismissively. 'They don't encourage me to waste money on dye kits and fake tans.'

'I thought you liked my blonde hair?' I bent down, opened the fridge door and took out some eggs.

'Wasn't your hair light brown when we first met?'

I stood up and turned around. 'Women call that "mouse".'

'For all I cared it could have been black, green, streaked with pink or shaved off. It's *you* I like, Kimmy – your contagious laugh and your… sense of right and wrong.'

I grinned. 'Like when I refused to do any housework until you agreed to go halves on a vacuum cleaner that worked?'

He gave a wry smile. 'No. I was thinking of the time you handed in that fifty pound note you found on the supermarket floor.' He shrugged. 'I don't need to be with some glamorous, hotshot business woman. Marriage, kids, decent house and maybe a Chelsea football club season ticket – that'll be enough for me.'

I put down the eggs. 'You feel pretty sure you'll have kids one day, right?'

'So?'

'I bet you've even pictured them and thought of names. That's no different to me, except that I've imagined my successful cake company, my clients, the shiny van I'll use as I drive to their homes. I even know what kind of pedigree dog I'll buy with the profits – he's called Chico and wears a leopard print coat and matching booties.'

I'd grown up with status dogs, Mum's boyfriends strutting around with Rottweilers or Staffies. They'd never let me dress them up or strategically place a few ribbons.

'And it's not just about the money,' I continued. 'Baking's my life. I even dream about recipes at night, Peanut.'

Peanut was my pet name for him, because of his one big vice: an addiction to Snickers, the nutty chocolate bars.

'But since your redundancy, you've made no concrete plans to get this supposed business off the ground.' His cheeks flushed. 'In fact, you've just given away a box of cakes. You should have charged the postman.'

'I've catered for kiddies' parties,' I said and my chest tightened. 'And it's paying off. I met Megan at her niece's do. Everyone thought the cakes I made for her wedding were awesome. At last I'm moving on to more upmarket work. The bakery taught me all I know.' I was rambling now. 'The next step is to work somewhere I can make the right contacts.'

'That's a plan?' he said. 'So, exactly what kind of job are we talking about?'

'Um… childminder to the kids of someone famous; receptionist in a top hairdressing salon…' I could just see me now, delivering cakes to some top football club. The Wags would become my best friends. The men would insist Chico become their mascot… I started beating the eggs, not wanting to catch Adam's eye. My plan sounded feeble, I knew that, but networking was my only chance. And let's face it – no one at CountryHouse Potatoes could introduce me to a chart topping singer or Olympic champion.

'The most famous person living in Luton is either dad to fifteen kids by fifteen mums or on trial for murder,' muttered Adam.

'That's a bit harsh. I thought you liked living here.'

'I do, but it pays to be realistic. Wise up, Kimmy – baking cakes is no way to escape the nine 'til five. Round here, people have to work their butts off to earn an honest living. What makes you think you're any different?'

'I don't, it's just… You saw Megan's cupcake tower – the spirals of pink buttercream icing; the ribboned gift boxes. I was up until three in the morning finishing that display.' I lifted my chin. 'And what about the selection of mini Christmas-themed cakes I made for that charity coffee morning, at the community centre, last week? Everyone went wild for the cute Stollen slices, cinnamon cupcakes and chocolate logs… ' A lump rose in my throat. 'Don't you think I've got what it takes? You know I work hard. Don't you believe I've got the talent?'

'That Megan was a one-off, babe – she got married to her boss and they moved away to London. No one else around here can afford a wedding cake that per mouthful costs more than they earn per hour. As for the charity bash, you sold those cakes at a discount price for the good cause. Your profit hardly covered your costs. Times are hard; we don't live in some crappy reality show with a quick-fix prize. However much you want it, building a successful business can take years – you ask my Uncle Ron.'

'There's nothing wrong with setting your sights high.' I bit my lip.

'So long as it's not so high that your head's stuck in the clouds.' Adam stood up. 'I'm sick of feeling as if my life's on hold. We can't plan a decent future just on my wages. The factory offers regular money, benefits and prospects. You could always do your cake thing when we've retired and got a house with a bigger kitchen.'

'*Retired?* I've only just turned twenty-one and you're only a year older! I mean… isn't that rather a long time off?' At times he reminded me of Mr Potts, my Year Eleven form teacher, who advised us to choose the most boring career we could think of because it would probably pay the most.

'I… didn't expect things to turn out like this either, you know,' he said and gave a small sigh. 'I always imagined I'd earn enough to buy a place on my own, get a new car every year and afford a two week holiday in Spain…' Adam plonked himself down on the sofa again and ran a hand through his short sandy hair, down to the back of his head. Suddenly I longed to do the same to him.

'You do great,' I said, softly. 'Not all your mates have even left their parents' homes yet.'

He shrugged. "I thought you moving in last year meant that you were ready to settle down. People like us don't get to drive sports cars or live in houses with their own tennis courts.'

'Leona Lewis does all right.' I picked up the hand-whisk and mock-mimed a ballad.

'So, now you're going to audition for the X Factor?'

'We've got years ahead of us together,' I said. 'What's the rush to cement our relationship, literally, by tying ourselves down to a mortgage?' I glanced at the oven clock. 'I've got to hurry or I'll be late for Jess.'

Adam's mouth went into a thin line. 'Look…' he said, eventually. 'Why don't we cool things for a bit? I've been thinking for a while that, well… It's for the best, babe… in the long run… Maybe you should move out.'

A ball of coldness hit the inside of my chest. No. Adam had to be joking. He couldn't mean it. We'd had a great time, ever since I moved in last summer. "Kimberley Jones has shacked up with her boyfriend" was my best ever Facebook status. Hoping I didn't smell too sporty, I walked over and sat on his lap.

'How about I find a regular bar job, to combine with the temp agency stuff? That would bring in extra money, until my baking takes off?' I slipped my arms around his broad neck and gazed right into his eyes. 'We both know you couldn't manage without me. Who else would pair up your socks or keep you supplied with clean trackie bottoms?'

His hands slipped around my waist and I leant in for a snog. However, Adam prised me off, like some rockstar rejecting a crazed fan. He reached over to the small coffee table and picked up the local paper, flicking through to the Home Search section. Then he passed it to me.

'You're serious, aren't you?' I stuttered, feeling ever so slightly sick. 'And on a practical level, how can I afford a place of my own, just like that, let alone find one a couple of weeks before Christmas? Mum won't welcome me back.' Especially as boyfriend number... I'd lost count... had just moved in. Like all the rest, he sported barbed wire tattoos and thought he was the next Eric Clapton.

'You might find a flat share,' said Adam and folded his arms. 'Makes you realise, doesn't it, how important it is to have a reliable income?'

'I've more than pulled my weight!' A wave of red-hot indignation replaced the coldness in my chest. 'Days stuffing envelopes paid for our petrol and food last month. In fact, if we ever get in at the same time, it's always me who cooks dinner and does the housework whilst you work out at the gym.'

Adam raised his arms into the air. 'But it's me who's responsible for trying to save up for our future.'

'Well maybe I needed a break from responsibility after virtually bringing up my younger brother.' My voice trembled. 'Ever had to sit your mum down and take her through the weekly budget? No. So, don't talk to me about being level-headed and practical.'

'I'd like to know what happened to that organised, sensible girl I fell in love with.'

Eyes tingling, I stumbled into the bedroom and hauled my pink case off the top of the wardrobe. Sensible? Hadn't I recently taken back the five inch high shoes I'd only bought because I saw them on Paris Hilton?

I sat down on the bed and stared at my glittery nails. It didn't make me a bad person, did it? Wanting a better life? Holidays where trees smelt of vanilla? Cars with engines that didn't take ten minutes to start? I wanted arctic white teeth; I wanted rainforest-exotic handbags. I wanted to spend my nine 'til five doing something that I loved. Wasn't it good to have aspirations? Work hard for a top lifestyle? That was what I'd always dreamed of, growing up, wearing neighbours' cast-offs. I didn't even get a brand new first bra. Mum said I wouldn't be in it that long and the money she'd save would buy a mountain of fags.

'You should have let me get down that case,' said Adam, suddenly appearing at the bedroom door. 'I didn't mean for you to leave right away.'

I swallowed. Was he having second thoughts?

'At least ring around a few friends first.'

My heart sank. 'Is there… someone else?' I said and sniffed.

'No.'

I believed him. Adam didn't do excuses. Not even if he forgot my birthday or – God help him – finished off the last tube of Pringles.

'Then give me one more chance,' I whispered. 'What's it going to take to change your mind?'

Adam hesitated for a moment before kneeling down in front of me, by the bed. He took both my hands and gently rubbed my palms with his thumbs. 'Fill in that form, babe. Then we can both look forwards.' His eyes crinkled at the corners. 'I still love you,' he murmured and kissed me softly on the lips. 'I just can't face starting the New Year without having more concrete plans for our future.'

That's what bowled me over about Adam – my gentle giant combined strength with such tenderness. The thought of life without him was unthinkable. We went together like a cupcake and cappuccino. I'd never forget feeling sick with excitement when we first started dating. Hunky Adam, with his clean-shaven cheeky smile and steadfast eyes, had asked me out. I'd never find another guy who found my "voluptuous tum" (code for pot belly) a turn on – or who, more importantly, made me feel as if the big wide world could do me no harm. Even though we'd been together for almost three years, I still treasured the things he'd bought me which showed that he really cared – not jewellery or flowers, but the emergency holdall for my car with a warning triangle and blanket inside. No one had ever looked out for me like that. When he'd bought me a personal alarm, I'd practically swooned at his feet. But all this... planning for our retirement already...

'We could window-shop for houses,' he continued, stood up and grabbed his towel. 'Suss out what sort of property would suit us. Google mortgage deals... Look into saving plans. It's never too early to start cutting back. We could eat value range food and buy clothes from charity shops.' Humming, he beamed and left the bedroom.

Mortgage deals? And had he ever tried value cornflakes? They were like cardboard confetti.

I headed into the lounge, picked up a biro from the coffee table and, still unable to take it all in, sat back on the sofa for a while. Eventually I leant forward and held my head in my hands. Adam was what my Auntie Sharon would have called "a catch" – kind, hard-working and loyal.

But why the rush to throw down roots and, in the process, throw away our freedom?

I looked up and chewed on the end of the pen, before reaching for the application form. My eyes felt wet. Every atom of me hurt. Why did he have to give me an ultimatum? With a shaking hand, I texted Jess and asked her to meet me, instead, by the bench outside Adam's flat. Then I picked up the form and slowly began writing:

SURNAME: *Dream*
FORENAME: *Ivor*
CURRENT POSITION: *Aspiring Entrepreneur*
SEX: *100% safe, please, until career well underway*
ASSETS: *Curves. Cupcakes. Ambition.*
HOW DO YOU SEE YOURSELF IN 5 YEARS:
Glossy-haired, Dior-dressed catering magnate
WHY DO YOU WANT THIS JOB: *I, um, don't.*
MARITAL STATUS: *Single, then?*
ADDRESS: *"No Fixed Abode", I guess.*

CHAPTER 2

The bus stop? Little privacy. The back of my old hatchback? No room to stretch out. The doorway of the Spoon & Sausage? I sat on my pink case, outside Adam's flat. Where on earth would I sleep tonight? How dare Adam throw me out? What a jerk. See if I cared... Yet I squeezed my eyes shut, to trap any tears, and my throat felt tight and sore – as if I'd got the tonsil infection from hell.

Perhaps I could crash in some shop's outdoor Santa's Grotto. I'd packed as quickly as I could, just finding time to brush my teeth and hair. Plus I'd squashed in some baking utensils and my novelty pig oven gloves. Adam was probably still in the shower, singing "One potato, two potato, three potato, four..."

A nearby flowering weed caught my eye. It stood upright between two paving stones. I leant forward, tugged it out and one by one yanked off its petals – *he loves me... he loves me not...* If I were famous, I imagined the sad shot the paparazzi might take of me now, the drooping wild flower stuffed through my gold metallic parka jacket's buttonhole. It would go with the headline: "Kimmy Shown Red Card by Love Rat Adam", except my Adam was more of a love-*bunny* (he'd hate me calling him that).

Shivering from the bitter December air – or was it from shock? – I nevertheless put on my fake designer sunglasses, due to the odd bit of sun. Although when the clouds parted,

Luton still looked as grey as an old pair of Y-fronts. The Greta Garbo "I-want-to-be-left-alone look" suited the occasion, don't you think, after my dramatic morning? A man in uniform walked past, spiking litter. From behind I got a whiff of something pungent – Adam's aftershave, smelt a bit like some cleaning product.

'There was no need to leave without saying goodbye,' he said to my back. 'You haven't even eaten.'

'You ordered me out.' I turned around, determined to look more cross than upset.

His hair was all wet. Like a white flag, he held up the cheap ready-decorated Christmas tree I'd bought – Adam had insisted stuff like advent calendars and fairy lights were a waste of money, so I'd had to compromise.

'You forgot this.' He gazed down at me with those metallic grey eyes. 'This is silly. At least come back for lunch.'

'Now I'm silly as well as irresponsible?' Annoyed at the tremble in my voice, I stood up and dragged my case along the street, towards the pedestrian crossing on the left. However, secretly I wished he'd scoop me up and carry me back to the flat, saying that it was all just a big mistake.

'Wait up!' he called and I slowed slightly, willing him not to drop my ace little tree. The baubles looked basic and the branches were threadbare, but it was the ninth of December, for goodness' sake, and right now my world needed a dollop of Christmas magic.

'For God's sake,' he said and easily caught me up. 'It's not that I don't understand.'

Chin trembling, I reached for my tree and gripped it by the metal base. We were in front of Clarkson's Estate Agents. He steered me to the nearby blue painted bench, where I'd arranged to meet Jess.

'I get it,' he continued. 'We all have dreams. Me, I'd kill to live like… like a top racing driver.'

I sat down, shoved my case under the bench and fiddled with a lacklustre piece of tinsel.

'Sometimes,' he continued and took a seat next to me, 'when I'm travelling back from my night shift and the motorway's empty, I hit the accelerator... But kidding myself that I'll ever race cars for a living won't pay the rent.'

'Remember that Formula One leather jacket you bought when we first started going out?' I stared across the road to the White Horse pub. 'It cost a whole week's wages.'

'Now I know better.' He leant back to avoid a kid on a skateboard whizzing past, followed by a gaggle of giggling teenagers, cheap handbags swinging, not a care in the world. A group of women in burkas walked behind them and a souped-up car, bass volume on full, zoomed along.

'There's nothing I want more than you and me together,' he said, huskily, 'even though you stick your cold feet on me in bed and leave trails of flour around the flat like some MasterChef slug. But you've got to realise that dreams are just that. During the day, it's about making the best of what you've got. This job at the factory won't come along again – they've held back on recruitment for months. When that application form dropped through the letterbox this morning my heart leapt, babe. It's the best Christmas present I could ever have, the thought that, at last, you and me would be moving our lives forwards.'

'But next week I'm baking cupcakes for my mate Nikki's hen night. I even blagged some cut-price sugar from the corner shop that's closing down. If I spend all day, every day with you, sorting spuds, I'll never have the energy for cooking after work. You're always knackered after a day at that place. And what if my business did, by some small miracle, take off and I left the factory? It wouldn't look good for you. No. It's best that we keep "us" and work separate.'

'Sounds like more excuses.' He glanced at his watch.

'Don't let me keep you,' I muttered.

'I said I'd drop round to Mum and Dad's this afternoon; things to do before that.'

'What will you tell them?' My voice wavered. 'About us?'

'The truth, of course.' He looked sideways at me. 'You know Mum. She'll blame me.'

I half-smiled. Barbara was great. Adam always joked that if he and I ever split up, she'd take my side and ask him what he'd done wrong.

'She'll have to take back her wedding outfit,' he mumbled. 'That'll teach her to buy it before we even got engaged.'

Hardly believing his words, I nodded. Telling his parents about our split meant it was final. So this was really happening? How could my lovelife have crumbled around me within the space of one hour? I took his hand, which felt icy cold. 'Just give me six months. Please. I can sense things are about to go my way.'

'You've already been temping for weeks, Kimmy.' He pulled away his fingers and blew on them with warm breath. He stood up and rubbed his hands together. 'I won't hold on for another half year.' His voice broke. 'Sorry, babe. It's over.' With that, he walked away.

I pulled the limp flower from my button hole and watched it tumble to the ground. In need of a ballad, I reached into my jeans' back pocket. Great. I'd forgotten my iPod.

'Adam! Hold on! Keep an eye on my luggage. I've left something in the flat.'

Without giving him much chance to answer, I rushed past, head down, as he sloped back to the bench. I didn't want him to see my runny nose or tears trickling out from under my glasses. My phone rang and, slowing to a trot, I reached into my front pocket. A repentant love message from Adam? No. He didn't text that fast. It was from Jess. She was on her way over and said it was just as well we weren't meeting at her place.

Hoping she was okay, I put the phone back in my pocket. Mrs Patel from the grocer's smiled at me as I turned towards the flats. If I were famous, Elton John would lend me his French villa, or I'd flee to my Barbados hideout, or (how cool did this sound) I'd *go into rehab*.

I entered the red-brick building and climbed the two flights of stairs to number fourteen. New graffiti had gone up on the whitewashed walls overnight, featuring lewd cartoons of Father Christmas. It still brightened up the place, though, and drew attention away from the missing chunks of plaster. I unlocked our front door and went in.

Stupid, I know, but I expected it to already look different. It didn't. On the left was the kitchenette, with its scratched worktop, on top of which was a Tupperware box of cranberry and orange festive cupcakes I'd made only last night, after baking Postie's batch. They were next to the tiny electric cooker and sink where a tap dripped constantly. I'd been meaning to change the washer. Mum had always relied on me to do that sort of thing. Over the years I'd picked up a lot from her boyfriends – like how to change a fuse and put up shelves. One even taught me how to pick locks, another how to hotwire cars.

I headed into bedroom and ran a finger along the furniture as I went. Adam had made a real effort when I'd first moved in; skipped the pub for weeks, eventually spending his beer money on a beech effect flatpack wardrobe and a small cabinet for *my* side of the bed. We'd also made a special trip to St Albans' market for that beige throw to cover the balding sofa. I lifted my pillow, picked up my iPod and slipped it into the back of my jeans. A photo on the windowsill caught my attention. It was me and Adam kissing

behind two plates of curry. We'd celebrated every single one
of our anniversaries at the same Indian restaurant.

'Yoo hoo!' warbled a shaky voice.

It was Mrs Burton. I took off my sunglasses and slipped
them into my parka pocket. Then I left the bedroom,
forcing my mouth to upturn. Her lined face peeked around
the front door.

'You shouldn't leave this open, dearie,' she said.

'I was just going out,' I said and grabbed the Tupperware
box of cupcakes. We moved into the corridor. I closed and
locked the door. Mrs Burton leant on her stick. Whatever
the weather, she always wore her long woollen cardigan
and secondhand Ugg boots.

'Everything all right, Kimberley? I happened to see you
outside with your luggage.'

Happened to? With her antique opera glasses and log-book,
Mrs Burton took Neighbourhood Watch to the next level.
She'd note when the number eighty-seven bus wasn't on
time and knew which paperboys were late because they'd
spent the night necking cider on the street corner.

She held up her hand, translucent skin mapped with
veins. 'No need to explain. You and your young man have
been treading troubled waters for a while now.'

'How…?'

She patted my hand. 'Not as much laughter as there used
to be. Just silence. My Bill and me used to argue a lot. Now
that's the sign of a healthy marriage. Better out than in, me
dearie, that's what I always say. But don't you worry. Men
often take a while to work out what's best for them. He's in
for a shock as to how much he'll miss you.'

'Cupcake?' I gave her a proper smile and took off the
Tupperware lid.

Eyes shining behind pink-rimmed glasses, she lifted
one out. 'It'll take a lot to improve on the walnut and fig

ones you made last week. Those beauties have kept me as regular as a cuckoo clock.'

'Thought they would.' I winked and put back the lid. Jess would be outside any minute. I kissed the old lady goodbye and went down the stairs. When I got back to the bench, Adam was pacing up and down.

'I'd better get going.' He cleared his throat. 'Where will you stay tonight?

'Um… Jess's.' I sniffed and lifted my head into the air. 'You needn't worry about me. I can manage.'

He held out his hand.

I slipped my hand into his and squeezed it tight.

'No,' he said. 'The key. I may as well have it back.'

'But there's no going back from that,' I spluttered, the inside of my chest cold again. 'Come on, Adam. This isn't you. Work's been demanding, lately. Perhaps you're suffering from stress. It's only a couple of weeks before Christmas, for heaven's sake!'

'Are you *blind*, babe?' he said. 'You haven't seen this coming? Is this all really such a surprise?'

My throat hurt again, as if I'd eaten too much buttercream icing and had a bad case of acid reflux.

'Just ring your mum, Kimmy. Ask if you can kip on the floor – she might surprise you and say yes. You can't stay at Jess's forever and we both know you'll never get a flat without proof of a regular income.'

'You've got to be joking. Her latest man's got three Alsatians. They have the sofa now.' Mum made it quite clear, as soon as I got a job at Best Buns, that I was to move out, permanently; find out for myself that life was hard. As if I didn't know that already.

As Adam strode away, my stomach cramped but I held back more tears. Life had thrown crap at me before – I'd survived, and I'd survive now too. That was the best and worst thing about getting older – each tough experience taught you how to cope with the next. I mean, one minute I'd been shooting into Melissa Winsford's ninth hole, the next I was well and truly lost in the rough…

I sat down and almost dropped the box of cupcakes. Outside the White Horse, over the road, a young couple walked along in scarves and hats, hugging each other tightly. Adam never held my hand anymore and would rather Chelsea football club be relegated than us snog in public. I used to slip soppy notes in his lunch box until he complained that they stuck to his sandwiches. Perhaps this break-up *had* been waiting in the shadows for a while.

It's funny how the things that attract you to someone eventually lose their shine – like the way he threw an arm over me during his sleep; how he insisted on using teabags twice. And I knew my liking for bowls of potpourri drove him crazy. I'd become a fan of them since living above a chip shop. It was my first flat. Dirt cheap. It had to be, on my wages from Best Buns.

From the left, a flash of red caught my eye – Jess's bobbed hair. Despite her small frame, she stood out in her tribal print duffle coat and maroon jeans. Jess didn't use peroxide, hated fake tan and wore old women's comfy shoes – in theory, we were a total mismatch. She didn't watch my fave shows like The Apprentice and Keeping Up With The Kardashians, nor did she use whitening toothpaste. Yet at school we'd both bonded through a deep hatred of sport. Except I was the lucky one, with a mum always happy to write me a letter to get out of netball or swimming; anything for a bit of peace, so that she could get back to her fags and daytime telly. It was only when I met Adam that I got into fitness DVDs. Not that he minded my squishy bits – he liked my soft curves. It was my idea to battle my muffin top. You see, I often imagined what Adam and I would look like together, posing in one of my celebrity magazines. If I could just tone up we wouldn't look half bad. We'd be the next Brangelina – the papers would call us Kimadam, perhaps. I shook myself and waved in Jess's direction.

'Kimmy?' Jess hurried towards me, eyes goggling at the Christmas tree. She carried a massive rucksack. 'Why are you sitting outside here with all this stuff?'

'And what about you, with that rucksack? I said, brightly.

'You first.' She slipped the khaki bag to the ground and sat down.

'No, you,' I said, graciously delaying my dramatic announcement that Adam had brutally (okay, slight exaggeration) chucked me out. Plus I need a few more minutes to stem any tears that still threatened. I patted her arm. 'Looks like you and Ryan have fallen out big time. Brothers… Who needs them, eh?'

She bit her thumbnail.

'What's happened?' I said.

'He called me a neat-freak; said it was worse than living with our mum.' Her chin wobbled.

'Ungrateful bastard!' I said, for one nanosecond forgetting Adam. 'You've transformed his house! Has he forgotten that his previous lodgers liked cheese and had tails?'

She offered me a stick of gum and I shook my head. Jess had taken up the habit about a month ago.

'Guess I should have knocked, before going into his bedroom this morning,' she said.

'Huh?'

Her cheeks tinged pink and instantly clashed with her hair – and her red nose. Poor Jess always seemed to have a cold through the winter months, plus hayfever in the summer – not the best allergy for someone who worked with plants. 'This morning, it being the weekend, I thought I'd do him a favour and tidy his room.'

'That was a bit keen.'

'I know, but I had this overpowering urge to clean.'

'Was he still asleep?'

'No. He, um, had company.'

'Jess!' My hand flew over my mouth. 'Was she pretty?'

'Boobs like grapefruits and a dead neat Brazilian.'

I caught her eye and we both giggled.

'So, I was wondering…' Jess glanced across at my case. 'Any, erm, chance I can crash at yours? You should have heard Ryan. Apparently it's been a *nightmare* for him, living with his kid sister, ever since Mum and Dad retired to Spain. He says he owes it to our parents to see that I'm all right, but that I cramp his style and he's sick of not having a private life.'

'What a cheek! I bet he's already struggling to work out the washing machine.'

'I shouted at him,' muttered Jess. 'Told him he was a joke and no other woman would ever move into his hovel.'

'You never shout.'

'I know.' She sighed. 'He even made some rude comment about my lentil cutlets. I mean, what decade is he in? No one makes vegetarian food like that anymore. I wouldn't have minded if he'd criticised my bean burritos or tofu chow mein. He said at least now he could enjoy a guilt-free turkey dinner at Christmas.' She nodded at my luggage. 'Please tell me you've not moved out. Have you two had one of your disagreements?'

'What do you mean?' A lump returned to my throat.

'Remember he gave you the silent treatment after your last trip to the salon?'

I'd forgotten that. He thought twenty pounds was a lot to pay for fifteen minutes eyebrow threading.

'And he didn't come out to the pub last weekend for that festive quiz.'

Nope. He was sulking because I'd turned down an interview for a permanent cleaning job.

'Do you think my head's stuck in the clouds?' I asked, voice choked up. 'Adam more or less said I'd treated his flat like a holiday camp.' I could count on Jess to be straight with me. She'd always tell you if your bum *did* look big or your new haircut sucked. I pulled the lid off the Tupperware box. Sugar was great for low moods. A bloody good cake could sort out any problem.

'You're a... a....' She sneezed and blew her nose – into a handkerchief, of course. Even tissues made from recycled paper, originally made from sustainable forests, were too environmentally unfriendly for her. 'You're a daydreamer, Kimmy; a romantic. No doubt about that. And who can blame you. Let's face it, your mum hasn't always–'

'She's done her best,' I said and bit my lip.

'I don't know why you still defend her,' Jess muttered and shook her head. She took a cake from the box. 'Whereas Adam, I guess he just looks to his parents. Marriage, mortgage and kids; the daily grind paying off...' She bit into the sponge and chewed for a moment – the only person I knew who could simultaneously munch on food and gum. 'Face it, Kimmy: you two have less in common now – you've got different priorities and have grown apart.'

'But you and me still get on, even though I hate gardening and you'd rather stare at a blank screen than follow Beyoncé on Twitter.' I took a large bite of cake too.

'But I'm not planning my future around you.' She smiled. 'No offence.'

'You'd be better suited for him,' I mumbled. Jess even had a savings account.

She shook her head. 'Have you forgotten the argument we had about recycling?'

Jess sorted through all her rubbish, composted her peelings and washed out her tins. Adam said multi-coloured wheelie bins cost the government too much money and that they'd be better off investing it in nuclear energy.

Jess popped the last mouthful of cupcake into her mouth. 'Really yummy,' she said. 'I trust it was suitable for vegetarians?'

'Of course.'

'Love that orange buttercream icing.'

'It's made with actual orange zest, instead of essence, which means...' I smiled. 'Ingredient geek alert. Ignore me.'

'Shame you used paper cases. They contribute towards the decimation of rainforests.' She opened her rucksack and tugged out a copy of the Luton News. 'Is there anyone else we can stay with?' Her mouth drooped at the corners. 'It doesn't get much worse than being homeless for Christmas. Plus I've got to get myself sorted for work tomorrow. The last thing I need, on top of this, is to lose my job. Maybe we can find a flat?'

'This late in the day?' I said. 'Have we even got enough for a deposit?'

'It won't do any harm to look through the paper. In these arctic temperatures, I for one don't want to spend tonight on the street.' She pointed to a splat of congealed sick on the pavement. 'That mess reminds me, I threw up just before I left Ryan's. Last night I had a take-away veggie burger – it must have been contaminated with meat. So, I'm a bit peckish now.'

I jerked my head towards the White Horse. 'What we need is a shot of caffeine. I might even splash out on a packet of crisps, seeing as I no longer have to justify my every financial transaction to Mr Stingy Purse Strings.'

Jess gazed at me. 'Chin up, Kimmy,' she said, softly. 'Come on. I'll treat you to a cheese toastie and chips.'

I gave a wry smile and nodded. We stood up, ready to haul our luggage to the pedestrian crossing. But then I stopped dead. What was that, stuck to the glass front of the estate agent's? Leaving Jess to drag over my case, I carried the tree and cake box over to the window. I cocked my head. The house in that photo… Wow. It was everything I'd ever dreamed of: roman pillars either side of the red front door, massive gardens, a well cute pond… I leant forwards to read the labels. Five bedrooms, a hot tub and (posh or what) croquet lawn. It even had its own games room and bar. And that kitchen! There was a big American fridge and an island to breakfast off.

'Ready?' said Jess. 'The traffic lights are about to change.' Puffing under the weight of her rucksack, she gazed at the picture. 'Bet that place costs a lot to heat.'

Why wasn't I that sensible? Instead, in my head, I was already clicking my fingers at servants whilst eating a delicious afternoon tea on the front lawn. As for that staircase! And those four-poster beds! And talk about privacy, there was room for a mid-terrace house before you came across the neighbours. I was about to step away, when underneath the For Sale caption I noticed some bold writing.

"Live-in housesitter urgently required, to maintain gardens and house until property sold. Enquire within."

'What's the matter?' said Jess. 'You look like you've just been given limitless texts.'

'Do you believe in fate?' I said.

She read the advert and stopped chewing her gum for a moment. 'Are you completely bonkers? Us? Living in a place like that?'

'Why not? Come on, you and I aren't going to be beaten by our current situation. This is the answer. Think about it – your job at the garden centre is bound to impress. And I'm well nifty with a duster and vacuum cleaner. This could be my one chance to prove to Adam that I do have a practical streak.' There's no need for him to know how wicked the setting is – just that I'm prepared to scrub and clean and work hard to put a roof over my head; that I can do anything I put my mind to, including making a success of my cake company. If I slogged my guts out to do well at this job, he'd be impressed. Then I'd wow him with my concrete business plans (um, leaflets, cooking classes, entering cake contests). My mind raced.

'You and me, together, we'll have that place sold before you can say "Mulled Wine Muffin".' I beamed, a chink of hope breaking through the storm clouds of my lovelife.

'But we haven't any experience.'

I snorted. 'You're joking? The way we've kept house for Adam and Ryan? You don't need a CV a mile long to know how to bleach a loo or polish a mirror.' I pointed to the window. '*"Urgently required"'*, I quoted. 'Sounds desperate.' I scooped my hair back into a scrunchie, unzipped my gold parka jacket and smoothed down my sequinned jumper. 'After a few days away, the two men in our lives will be pleading with us to move back.'

'I don't know, Kimmy…' Jess wiped her nose. 'What about references? How do we explain suddenly turning up like two lost tourists?' She stared hard at the photo and pointed to the right hand back corner of the lawn. 'Who do you think that is?'

I screwed up my eyes and examined the topless young man with floppy chestnut hair, leaning on a spade. He certainly had his work cut out – that garden was huge.

I fixed a smile on my face and held out my hand, flat, in front of Jess's mouth, glad she got the message but didn't actually spit her gum into *my* palm. Then she smeared on her favourite lipgloss – homemade of course, using Vaseline and food essence. I took a deep breath and pushed open the glass door. Jess caught my eye and I winked. A tiny bubble of hope tickled the inside of my chest. This dream house was going to help me win back Adam.

CHAPTER 3

'You are certainly *not* within your rights to withhold rent.'
A woman in a smart navy trouser suit and pristine blouse
looked up from her phone and gave a stiff smile. 'The
owner has been informed of the problem and we'll be in
touch shortly,' she said, returning to her call. 'Pardon?
You do realise we record some of these conversations…?
Well, maybe you'd care more if faced with eviction!'
Calmly, the middle-aged woman put down the telephone
receiver

'Are we sure about this?' whispered Jess and I nodded.

'How can I help?' asked the estate agent, in a flat voice.
Her smile had shrunk as she'd clearly worked out our
luggage was bargain Primark, not Prada. We set down
our bags and I placed the Christmas tree and cake box on
a nearby desk. The room was practically furnished with
office equipment, and talk about unfestive – there wasn't so
much as one tinsel garland.

'We're looking for, um… somewhere to rent,' I beamed.
There was no point looking too keen, and mentioning the
house straight away.

She pointed to two black swivel chairs on the other side
of her desk, which was cluttered with stationery, assorted
files and a wilted, white-flowered plant.

'It's kind of urgent.' Understatement. I sat down and
luxuriated in office's warmth. 'We're currently homeless.'

The woman's eyes glazed over and the atmosphere seemed even darker as clouds gathered outside.

'Homeless?' She raised her finely plucked eyebrows.

'It's just a blip.' I forced a laugh, which hopefully oozed confidence as if to say "of course a deposit would be no problem". As long as the rent was based on Monopoly prices, that is. I glanced sideways at Jess.

'And I'm employed at the moment,' Jess said. 'I work at… at…' She sneezed loudly. 'Nuttall's Garden Centre.'

The woman winced. Her badge said Mrs D Brown. D for Deidre? Or Dawn? Perhaps Dragon?

'We may only need somewhere short-term,' I said.

'That might make things difficult,' she said, crisply. 'Most landlords are looking for long-term tenants.'

'Tell me about it.' I rolled my eyes. 'Finding somewhere to live, in between jobs, is one of the few downsides to being housesitters – like occasionally being made homeless.'

She leant forwards a little.

'I know – it's unusual work,' I continued, innocently. 'Most people don't know the half of what's involved.' Ahem, including myself.

'I'm familiar with the job spec,' she said and tapped her biro again. 'Aren't you rather young for such a–'

'Responsible position?' interrupted Jess. 'That's what the agency thought when they gave us our first job.'

Go Jess!

'But they were so impressed with Jessica's gardening skills,' I interrupted, wondering if housesitting agencies really did exist, 'and my… um… housekeeping experience. You should have seen our last place. Overrun with mice,' I whispered. Well, it was true about Ryan's pad.

Her brow smoothed out a little. 'I bet you've seen some sights.'

'Ooh yes, um, fleas under the sofa and mushrooms in the carpet.'

Plant expert Jess shot me a puzzled look, but Mrs D lapped it up.

'And the house before that had been well trashed,' I continued.

'What happened?' The estate agent put down her biro, no longer sounding as if we were a nuisance.

'The previous sitter had, erm, secretly arranged a party and advertised it on Facebook,' said Jess. 'People stubbed cigarettes out on the walls and broke toilet seats. Personally I think those social networking sites are a danger to society.'

Her last sentence was in no way a lie – Jess didn't even have a Facebook account. I kept quiet about my four hundred and sixty-three Facebook friends and the group I once formed, "Ashton Kutcher for President". That reminded me, I didn't have Adam's laptop to borrow now, which was just as well – I wouldn't know whether to change my relationship status to single or simply post that Adam and I were… had… Oh God, eyes going all blurry again, must switch subjects in my head.

Ow! Jess had kicked me hard. She was busy playing garden doctor.

'… and don't prune them until next month, Deborah,' she was saying, 'otherwise you'll get fewer flowers next year.'

Ooh, they were on first name terms already. "Deborah" straightened a pile of paperwork and stared at us.

'I'm curious,' she said. 'There's no money in housesitting; it's normally a job for retired people who simply fancy a change of scene.'

'The agency does insist we get paid a nominal fee,' I said, not catching her eye. 'Just enough to cover food. They tell clients it's worth it to get in people they can trust.'

'Kimberley's trying to set up her own business, you see,' interrupted Jess. 'Making cakes. Housesitting gives her the free time she needs. And the smell of home cooking always helps sell those properties we look after which are on the market.'

'True – everyone loves cake.' Deborah smiled and sucked the end of her pen for a moment.

'What's your favourite flavour?' I asked.

'I don't know, um…'

'How about Madagascan vanilla cakes, with strawberry buttercream icing and marzipan ladybirds?' I said, spying a photo of two little girls on her desk. 'Or I make a mean peanut topping, decorated with toffee teddy bears. Plus currently I'm celebrating the festive season – how about figgy pudding scones? I could drop some in.'

'No! I couldn't…'

'It would be my pleasure, Deborah.'

'Well, those ladybirds do sound rather sweet.'

I jumped up to fetch my Tupperware box and removed the lid as I sat down again. Sheer ecstasy. The aroma of cranberry and orange wafted into the air. It was like a heady hit of happy pills. I took one out and placed it on her desk. Even I had to admit it looked fab, with the pretty sunset-coloured buttercream icing generously swirled on top. I'd give her five minutes tops before she succumbed.

Jess fiddled with her bracelet and I held my breath whilst the estate agent got up. She pulled out the top drawer of her grey metal filing cabinet, and after flicking through several files, drew one out.

'As it happens,' she said, 'I might be able to help.'

I fought the urge to glance over to the advert in the window.

She sat down again and took off her jacket.

'Love the shoes,' I said, cocking my head under the table. 'Designer?'

'Erm no… but thanks.' For the first time she smiled properly with her eyes, then slid a photo of that house across her desk. At the top it said Mistletoe Mansion. 'We don't usually handle housesitting jobs, but the client, Mr Murphy, is a friend of the boss. His uncle died and left him this outstanding property. He lives up north, in Manchester, so my boss said we'd handle everything to do with the sale. But we've had trouble finding reliable people to look after this place until it's sold.'

Yay! My plan was working! Here was to a festive season spent enjoying hot tubs and playing billiards. I swallowed. Christmas without Adam? It just didn't seem real. Jess kicked me again and with a jolt I focused again on the photo.

'It's a large property. What exactly are the terms and conditions?' asked ever-practical Jess.

The woman peeked at the cupcake before looking at another sheet of notes. Was it my imagination, or did she position her hole-punch to cover something written in red?

'You would be expected to keep all the rooms spotless,' she said, 'the bedrooms with ensuites, the kitchen, receptions rooms, the Games Room and its bar. Also to maintain the gardens… Not mowing at this time of year, obviously, but keeping track of weeds, digging over the borders regularly – doing everything to keep it in tip-top shape. We're hoping it won't take much longer to sell – there have been a couple of bites lately, despite Christmas approaching. You would forward any post on to Mr Murphy and deal with service contractors such as the window cleaners. And, of course, show around prospective buyers and generally keep the place secure.'

'Are we given notice to leave?' asked Jess, whilst I returned to my fantasy of mirrored dressing tables and walk-in wardrobes.

The estate agent skimmed the piece of paper. 'The position runs from week to week with no notice required if the property sells.' She looked up at us. 'It's for one person but if you maintain the garden, Jess, I might be able to persuade Mr Murphy to let you both stay. Like I said, landlords are looking for long-term tenants, you'll be lucky to find a place to rent for just a few weeks. So maybe this arrangement could be beneficial to both parties?'

'It sounds great!' I said. 'I mean… Yes. Mistletoe Mansion seems suitable. Nothing we can't manage, after some of our previous jobs.'

'Which brings me to references,' Deborah said and reached for her biro.

'Ah, look at the state of this,' said Jess, exchanging glances with me before she picked up the wilted, white-flowered plant. She fingered some yellow leaves, before sticking her finger in the soil.

'Even kitchen herbs die on me.' Deborah smiled. 'So, ladies, references please.' She picked up the cupcake and took a bite at… four minutes and thirty seconds! I knew she'd give in.

'It's a bit awkward,' I said, as a faint "Mmm" escaped her lips. 'The agency we're registered with, um, wouldn't appreciate us moonlighting elsewhere.'

'Tightly run, are they?' she said, a blob of orange icing sticking to the corner of her mouth as she took another bite.

We both nodded. She was an estate agent. Pilfering staff from somewhere else wouldn't bother her.

She gazed at me and then Jess, who was still examining the plant. She looked at her notes; took another bite of cake; moved the hole-punch. What *was* written down there?

'Mice, fleas, mushrooms… Nothing much fazes you, am I right?'

'We're professionals,' I said, evenly. 'Nothing has ever made us quit a job.' And let's face it, what could possibly make life difficult at Mistletoe Mansion? Too many party invites from loaded neighbours?

'Why didn't the previous sitter see the job through to the end?' asked Jess.

'Oh, erm, personal circumstances.'

'How long has it been on the market, then?' I said.

'About six months – it went on just after the uncle died.' She cleared her throat. 'Times are hard, so that's not unusual. When could you start?'

'Tonight,' we both chorused.

'Really?' said Deborah.

'We're always keen to get started on a new job,' Jess gushed and put back the plant.

'Fair enough. If you're sure. Just let me make a call. Delicious cupcake, by the way,' she said, and disappeared out the back.

I eyed the hole-punch. Maybe I could just nudge it, accidentally on purpose, to see exactly what that red writing said.

'Mushrooms in carpets?' hissed Jess. 'Don't you feel just a teensy bit guilty about making all this stuff up? It's a bit over the top. Her boss won't be happy with her if it doesn't work out. We're bound to be rumbled.'

'Look, they need a housesitter. We need somewhere to live… And we're going to do our best to sell that place. No one's going to lose out.' I reached for the hole-punch. 'And I'm sure we can persuade this Mr Murphy guy to let us stay there for Christmas week, even if it happens to sell super-quick.

'What are you doing now?' whispered Jess.

'She's hiding something; if I could just read what's underneath.' Carefully I pushed the hole-punch across. Scrawled in red biro, surrounded by smiley faces, it read,

"*Must love Gh–*". Deborah's heels click-clacked back into the room. Damn! I hadn't managed to read the last word. What could it say? "Gherkins"? Perhaps "Ghosts"! A haunting could be wicked if it involved me and Adam, Whoopi Goldberg and a sexy potters' wheel. I must have misread the writing – maybe it said "Gn" and the previous owner had a hideous collection of gnomes.

'Well, ladies,' Deborah said, sitting down, 'Mr Murphy is delighted to have you on board. Normally he'd be more particular about references, but seeing as the situation is urgent he's agreed – on the understanding that I drop by now and again, to check things are running smoothly.'

'Awesome!' I said. 'I mean, that's great. And he'll pay our… expenses?'

'Yes, but he's impatient for a sale now, so he's relying on you. So am I.'

'We won't let you down,' said Jess and wiped her nose.

'I hope not – Mr Murphy has been quite fair. He's agreed to pay you a nominal sum to cover food. He'll add it on to the weekly budget he gives you for cleaning materials and butcher's bones.'

'Bones?' Jess and I chorused.

'Didn't I mention his old uncle had a dog? Mr Murphy isn't sure what to do with it, so…'

'He just left it there?' said Jess. 'What happens when there's no sitter?'

'Luke Butler calls in. He used to be the uncle's handyman and has helped us maintain Mistletoe Mansion.'

Of course! "*Must like G…*" That red writing had to be about a breed of dog.

'This Luke… Is he the half-naked guy in the photo?' said Jess.

Deborah blushed. 'Yes. It was a very hot day. I didn't like to ask him to put his shirt back on.'

Can't say I blamed her. He'd looked pretty hot. Not that I'd be interested in another guy for a long time.

'Why doesn't he housesit?' I asked.

'Initially Luke moved in but didn't… how can I put it… have the best manner when showing prospective buyers around. And I don't think housework was his forte. So he agreed to keep an eye on the place from afar and do general maintenance until the place sold.' A small sigh slipped from her berry red lips. 'Have to say, he is very good with his hands…' Jess glanced at me and I bit the insides of my cheeks, trying not to laugh.

Deborah slid over some paperwork. 'Here's the address, Mr Murphy's phone number, and a comprehensive list of your duties. The house is in Badgers Chase, a private cul-de-sac. It's very picturesque.'

I glanced at the papers. Badgers Chase was on the St Albans side of Harpenden, near where Jess worked. Harpenden was a well posh village with continental cafés and fancy boutiques – the complete opposite of Luton.

'I haven't been to Harpenden for ages,' I said. 'Mum used to take us there to play on the common.' Or rather, left us there whilst she met her fancy new man in town. Once she spotted comedian Eric Morecambe, its most famous resident. Not that celebrities impressed her. "Lucky buggers who don't live in the real world," she called them.

'The nearest bus stop is about half an hour's walk away,' continued Deborah. 'It's a very exclusive area, not far from a golf club. Isn't Nuttall's Garden Centre also that side of Harpenden, Jess? The one with the large bronze acorns outside?'

'Yes. Getting there should be easy. I cycle everywhere – unless it snows.'

The estate agent tapped her pen on the desk. 'Are you sure it wouldn't be better to delay moving in until morning?'

We shook our heads. She hesitated. 'Okay. I'll call you a taxi.'

'I've got a car,' I said. 'But doesn't someone need to show us around?'

'I've only been to Mistletoe Mansion a couple of times. It's not strictly within my duties. Lovely place though. Luke can answer all your questions. If you just wait a minute I'll ring him. He's very flexible. I'm sure he'll be able to pop round tonight.'

Her eyes dropped to the hole-punch and that writing. It was clear that whatever the prospective housesitters "*Must love*", she didn't. I racked my brains for breeds of dog beginning with G: German Shepherd, Golden Retriever, Greyhound... Oh my God! Perhaps it was a Great Dane! And come to think of it, that second letter after the G did kind of look like a fancy R. Wow. There was no need for Jess to know. You'd need a dustbin bag for the poop you scooped and giant dog hairs might prove as irritating for her as pollen.

We moved our stuff to the window, whilst Deborah made us a coffee and got distracted by trying to sell a one bed mid-terrace to a young couple with twins and three cats. The toddlers were well cute and liked the baubles on my little tree. They were even more interested in my box of cupcakes, and I was going to offer them one until their mum looked daggers at me. Eventually they left and Deborah rang Luke. He was out. She left a message and finally he called back to say he'd drop by the house.

Jess waited whilst I collected my hatchback from the small car park behind Adam's block of flats. I tried not to look up at his window, but couldn't resist, irrationally hoping he'd be there, beckoning at me to come back. With a sigh, I got into my car. It was white with flecks of rust and not remotely glamorous. I'd done my best inside, to

Adam's disgust fitting a furry pink steering wheel cover
and matching dice. I pulled up outside the estate agency
and beeped the horn, hoping the police wouldn't pass by
and see me parked on double yellow lines. When Jess
came out, I left the engine running to help her haul our
luggage into the boot. The sky had darkened to slate and
the air had slightly warmed. Perhaps it was going to rain.
Deborah took the tree from Jess, as my best mate got in
the passenger seat. I gazed out of my side window. Luton
looked blander than ever, like a cherry cupcake missing
the fruit.

'Good luck,' said Deborah, after we'd fastened our
seatbelts. She leant in on Jess's passenger side, passed her
the tree and held her hand over the wound-down window.
I revved the engine politely. 'It's not too late to change
your minds,' she said. 'I mean… If it was me, I'd wait until
tomorrow. The afternoon sky is so dark, it'll be as if you're
unpacking in twilight.'

'Don't worry about us,' I smiled. Jeez – what was her
problem? Did this Great Dane turn into a werewolf at
midnight?

'See you soon,' said Jess and began to wind up her
window. 'Thanks for sorting us out.'

Deborah pushed a bunch of keys through the
ever-decreasing gap. 'Luke's headed out to get you some
bits for the fridge.' She pointed to the sky. 'Just as well
he's saved you a trip to the shops. A storm's brewing,' she
called as we drove off.

'Phew! You're bonkers!' Jess said and unwrapped a
piece of gum, as the tree balanced on her lap. 'I can't
believe I let you talk me into that.'

'But we pulled it off. Sorted ourselves out – as
I knew we would.' Traffic lights loomed and I applied
the brakes.

'Ryan's not going to believe I've already got somewhere else to stay.' She chewed vigorously for a moment. 'Do you think Deborah will find us out?'

'As what? We're perfectly capable of looking after that place. I reckon we'll do a good job. Here's to living in the lap of luxury, I say.' And getting that place sold; impressing Adam.

'Has Deborah got a crush on this Luke or what?' said Jess. 'Did you hear her on the phone? No one should flirt with someone they could have given birth to.'

Now and again, Mum dated younger men. She even went off on holiday to Spain with one and left fourteen-year-old me alone, to look after my younger brother, Tom. Auntie Sharon had dropped in when she could, but wasn't there when Tom twisted his ankle or the lights blew.

'One had better put together a rota for the chores,' I said, in a posh voice. 'I'll clean during the day. You garden after work. A cosy supper will be served at eight sharp. One will be expected to change. Mistletoe Mansion has standards.'

'Idiot!' Jess grinned at me. 'It all seems too good to be true. There's got to be a catch.' Spit-spots of rain hit the windscreen. 'Have we got time to stop off at Ryan's to get my bike? There should be room for it if we put down the back seats.'

I nodded as the lights switched to green and we pulled away from the estate agents – from lacklustre Luton; from my life with Adam. I blinked quickly, thinking that only that morning we'd been curled up under the same duvet. Just as I steered around the corner, my sombre thoughts were interrupted by a shriek of 'Wait! Stop the car! There's something you should know!' I glanced in my rearview mirror whilst Jess, oblivious to the shouts, fiddled with the radio dial. It was Deborah, running towards us, high heels in hand and cheeks purple!

CHAPTER 4

'Get ready to run for your life' I said to Jess, as we drove
onto Mistletoe Mansion's drive. Badgers Chase was a
T-shaped cul-de-sac and our new home was right at the
bottom of it. Lightning had just struck the middle of a field
on a distant hill and disaster was imminent – if we didn't
get inside right this minute, the rain would turn my hair,
still straightened from yesterday, into candyfloss.

Jess put the small Christmas tree in the back, next to the
bike and our luggage. Wow. As we passed the well cute pond
on the left, I gaped at the Roman pillars. After parking up,
I got out and was distracted from the amazing scenery for a
moment as a juicy splat of water hit my head. I could count
on one hand the number of people who knew my hair had
a natural curl. My eyes tingled. Adam and I shared lots of
secrets, like me knowing his bank pincode and him keeping
schtum about my girl crush on famous chef Delia Smith.

'Well established borders, aren't they?' called Jess, in
gardening mode. She inspected the right hand side lawn
and yanked out a handful of weeds from the borders
crammed full of various shaped plants, with spikes and
berries. Jess was muttering in Latin. How come only
doctors and gardeners got to speak a classical language?
I took a deep breath, feeling as if I was on some epic film
set. Any moment now a voice would shout "action" and
some heartbreaker hero – hopefully a clone of Adam –

would appear, perhaps in classical dress. I would allow him to accompany me for a walk, then his love rival would turn up with a shotgun and... I sighed. This cul-de-sac oozed romance. The houses stood so far apart – whereas I'd never lived anywhere that wasn't a bowling ball's roll from a fish 'n'chip take-away or betting shop. At the foot of the leafy, winding road which led here was the nearest bus stop, a thatched pub called the Royal Oak and a post box.

Despite the menacing clouds, I walked down the drive to join Jess. Woody scents filled the air. Where was the stink of exhaust fumes? Or the litter? Or the sound of Mrs Patel shouting at a late newspaper boy? Or the roaring engines of planes leaving Luton airport? I slowed down to a stroll and imagined the photo if paparazzi snapped me now. Maybe I'd look like some Hollywood star in one of those awesome perfume adverts, in some lush setting, the breeze blowing my hair... Good decision Kimmy, not to tell Jess about Deborah running after us. Nothing was going to stop me moving into this place. No doubt the estate agent had heard the weather forecast and was simply going to warn us about the storm.

'Ooh, nice.' Jess said and pointed to a border running along the fence, right near the house.

I admired the plant, with its sprinkling of small, cream flowers.

'*Lonicera fragrantissima* – unusually it flowers in winter.

I shrugged.

'Winter honeysuckle to you,' she said and grinned.

I headed over and plucked a small spray of the flowers. Mmm, what a lovely sweet scent. I tucked it behind my ear.

'Not as festive as holly,' I said and jerked my head towards a prickly plant next to the honeysuckle, 'but less painful.'

Jess shook her head at me and then gazed around. 'We'll have to get some white wine vinegar to get rid of all these weeds.' Jess didn't believe in chemical products, something she kept from Dana, her sales-mad boss at the garden centre.

Another splat of rain landed on my head and I hurried back to the car and grabbed my pink case and Christmas tree. I'd pull Jess's bike out of the hatchback later. There'd be room for it in the massive double garage. Like an evacuee from a city, I hovered in front of the cylindrically carved white pillars either side of the front door. There was a brass lion's head knocker right in the middle. On the red brick wall to the right was a fancy gold plate, saying *Mistletoe Mansion*. My eyes ran over the classy Georgian windows and moss-free grey-slated roof.

'Come on,' I called, 'let's get in before this rain does more than spit.' On cue, thunder rolled. The car door creaked as Jess fetched her rucksack. Seconds later she stood beside me and took the keys out of her pocket.

'Maybe we should knock first,' she said and chewed her gum more slowly for a moment. 'I thought I saw someone at an upstairs window. That Luke might be inside.'

'Hopefully filling the fridge,' I said, and realised all I'd eaten today was that cranberry and orange cupcake. I smoothed down my hair, grasped the knocker and rapped hard. The sky was charcoal-grey now and a shiver ran down my spine. Maybe I should have rapped quietly in case some giant dog really lived here. Yet there was no barking, just the pelting of rain. I reached for the knocker once more.

At that moment, the door swung open but no one appeared. Prompted by a small yap, Jess and I glanced to our feet.

'Aw, what's your name, buddy?' said Jess and knelt down.

You had to be joking! Who could be afraid of this tiny brown and white mutt? With those chocolate button eyes, it wasn't the slightest bit fearsome. In fact, it would have looked well cute in a little tartan jacket.

'Scoot, Groucho,' said a flat voice. From around the side of the door appeared the man from the photo, wearing a lumberjack checked shirt with fawn cords.

I rubbed my ear as my eyes swept over his frame. Cords and a checked shirt? That was the uniform of granddads. Except he somehow made them look fashionable, and as for his chestnut bedroom hair and half-shaven face... A frisson of something stirred in my belly. Huh? That had to be a hunger pang. I'd only just broken up with Adam. It couldn't be anything else.

I hauled my case over the doorstep and he watched me drag it into the ginormous hallway, unlike Adam who would have insisted on carrying it for me. His almost old-fashioned manners were one of the things that had attracted me in the beginning – the way he'd always be the first to buy a round at the pub; how he'd offer to drive, if he and his workmates went out on the razz. I took in the arrogant stance of this Luke, with his hands shoved in his pockets. Would I ever meet another bloke like Adam?

'Groucho's an unusual name,' I said, as Jess followed me in. At least there wouldn't be any poop-scooping up after a Great Dane. I gazed around. Oh my God. That staircase was amazing. You'd build up an awesome speed, sliding down those banisters.

'Walter Carmichael – Mike Murphy's deceased uncle, the guy who used to own this place – he bought Groucho at the turn of the millennium, the year he gave up the evil weed,' said Luke. 'It was his idea of a joke.'

Groucho... Marx. Of course, that ancient comedian with a bushy moustache and eyebrows, and a fat cigar always between his lips… *Must love G*… So, I was right, those red scrawled notes were about the dog, but the G stood for his name, not his breed. I looked down as he cocked his head sideways. What possible harm could this Groucho cause, especially with those little grey hairs sticking out from his chin?

'Does he, um, behave himself?' I asked, as the white-tipped tail vanished around the side of the staircase.

'He's toilet-trained and doesn't bite, if that's what you mean,' said Luke, staring at the flower in my hair. 'But he's a Jack Russell – nosy; always into everyone's business.'

'You must be Luke?' said Jess and smiled as she closed the front door. 'I'm Jess and this is Kimmy.'

She held out her hand but he shoved his hands deeper into his trouser pockets, which irked me as it made me focus even more on the great things about Adam I was missing.

'There's milk, eggs and bread in the fridge. Help yourselves to anything else you find. The last housesitter quit this place in a hurry.' He smirked. 'The kitchen cupboards still have some food in them.'

I set my Christmas tree down on the laminated floor, next to a mahogany coatstand, and took a good look around. The winding staircase really was well impressive, with its oak banisters and burgundy carpet. At the top it branched out, to the left and right, past several glossed white doors with gold handles, on both sides leading around to the front of the house. On the cream walls hung brass-framed paintings – I squinted – of foxhunts and deer and fishermen. All this place needed was a tinselled pine tree much bigger than mine – it would be the perfect family home to live in during the festive season.

'Wow. Impressive,' I muttered, head back as I gazed up towards the high ceiling and a waterfall effect crystal chandelier. Downstairs were more paintings and to the right, a watercolour of Mistletoe Mansion, in the far corner, above a door – perhaps that was a loo. On the same side, near the front of the house, was an open door leading to the poshest lounge. I walked over to peek in and admired the sage green armchairs and sofa, the long oak coffee table, matching dresser and mega fireplace. On the mantelpiece was a photo of a friendly-looking old couple.

'Mr Carmichael liked his paintings,' I said and came back into the hallway. Jess was still gazing at the chandelier.

'Yep. Murphy's already sold some of them off.' Luke stared at a portrait, to the left of the lounge door. It was of an old man, serious looking apart from a twinkle in his eyes – the man from the photo on the mantelpiece.

'That's him? The uncle?' I asked.

He nodded and then pointed to behind the staircase. 'Groucho's gone to the kitchen. The patio doors in there lead onto the back garden and there's access to the dining room which is at the back of the lounge.'

Not really listening, I looked out of the front windows and the torrents of rain. Wind rocked the honeysuckle and the weeping willow shimmied like… like seaweed caught in a stream. Listen to me – I'd gone all high-falutin', thanks to this place. It was even more impressive than I'd expected and felt homely – kind of lived-in, not grand or imposing. Not what I'd expected for the empty house of a dead man. My chest felt lighter than it had since me and Adam split.

'What's through there?' asked Jess, looking left to a heavy mahogany door, next to a white hallway desk.

Luke consulted his watch. 'See for yourselves. I'm off.' He tugged his thumb towards the desk. 'Murphy's phone number's in an envelope on there, along with other stuff like a daily "to do" list with my phone number on, and things like how to work the boiler. Also there's the remote control to open the garage.' He grabbed a thick jacket from the coat stand and opened the front door. An earthy, musky smell of aftershave wafted my way – so different from Adam's favourite fragrance that smelt like clinical air freshener. 'Just one more thing – a couple of bedrooms are locked. Don't try to force them open.

'As if we would!' protested Jess.

'They're full of the Carmichaels' personal stuff,' he continued. 'Murphy hasn't sold much of that yet. He won't sort through it until he has to, I reckon, when the house sells. So, just keep out.'

No "Nice to meet you" or "Good luck, I'll pop in tomorrow to check you're okay." Adam would have at least told us to lock the windows at night and taken us through a fire drill. Not that I needed a man to look out for me, but his attentive ways made me feel all fuzzy inside. After a childhood spent practically fending for myself, Adam's caring nature had initially dazzled me.

Whereas my initial impression of Luke was the complete opposite of considerate Adam. Whistling, the handyman upturned his collar and slammed the door as he left. Groucho appeared and after several minutes of tickling jumped up as if to say "I'll show you the place," but a sharp crack of thunder saw him skedaddle under the white desk. Jess picked him up and he licked her nose.

'Let's take a quick look behind that mahogany door and then find something to eat.' She turned the handle and we went in. Wow: this was the Games Room with… I couldn't believe it! Only what I could describe as a mahogany *throne* in the corner! That was it. From now on, in my head, this room would be named after my favourite show of the moment, Game of Thrones! I'd have to plait my hair to enter and create a cocktail called Sex in Westeros!

Polished, rich brown panels covered the left and far side walls, with the rest painted racing green. In the middle stood a full size billiards table and on the right was the small, but well stocked, bar. There was lager, and cola, and a professional-looking line of spirit bottles hung in front of mirrored tiles. As the mahogany door creaked shut behind us, I tiptoed across and bent over the bar. This would be perfect for Adam, I thought, gazing at the different shaped glasses, the small sink and silver ice bucket. After a hard day at work he was often too tired to go to the pub.

Jess pointed to a dartboard at the end of the room, fighting to keep hold of Groucho whose legs pedalled mid-air. Eventually she put him down and, yapping, he ran back to the door. 'I don't think I'm the only one who's hungry.' Jess threw her gum into a small bin.

I walked over to a window. It was almost dark now and rivers of rain down the glass warped the view. I pulled on a cord which closed the curtains.

'Picture us,' I said, 'sipping fancy drinks, eating Pringles... And getting handyman Luke answering our every beck and call.'

Jess pulled a face. 'He's hardly Lady Chatterley's lover.'

'What, our bit of rough?' I grinned. 'His manners are almost as bad as my brother's.' Tom never ate with his mouth closed, and wiped his nose on his sleeve. Mum let him do what he wanted – eat pizza in bed, not tuck his shirt in for school, drink juice straight from the carton.

We went back to the hallway and I stopped by the desk, impressed at how the sound of rain resounded around the big hallway. A dog lead lay curled up, next to a bunch of letters and I flicked through, looking for the "to do" list Luke had talked about. A scrap of paper caught my eye and I pulled it from the pile. Scrawled across the front in red it said *"IMPORTANT! NEW HOUSESITTERS READ THIS ASAP!"*

Lightning flashed again and Jess pulled the hall blinds shut. I unfolded the piece of paper – the words looked as if they'd been written in a rush. With the chandelier light now flickering, I read the note out loud:

"*Leave now. Don't stay a single second. If I told you why, you wouldn't believe a word. Just trust me; this is the worst job I've ever had – especially when it's dark.*"

'It's probably a joke,' shrugged Jess.

'Must be,' I said and smiled brightly, the hairs standing up on the back of my neck as I thought of Deborah chasing us, purple in the face. As if on cue, an ear-splitting clap of thunder rang out and all the lights went off. Groucho's claws, on laminate, scratched and skidded to a halt, no doubt under the desk.

'We need to work out where the fuse box is,' Jess shouted.

Thunder clapped again, as I felt my way into the lounge and looked out of the windows. Forks of lightning lit up the garden – the bushes looked like crouching figures and the weeping willow like hanging rope. Perhaps a zombie-like White Walker from my fave show might appear…

'Any luck yet?' I called and searched the shadowy lounge. When I got back to the hallway, she'd opened the blinds but there were no nearby streetlamps to help. Jess switched on her phone and, using it like a torch, headed towards the Games Room.

'Wait! Did you hear that?' I hissed, my skin prickling from head to toe.

'What?' she said and hurried over to me.

'That thud?' There it was again – from upstairs. My heart raced as Jess switched off her mobile.

Arm in arm, we stood at the foot of the staircase. Now, through the rain, I could make out a dragging sound. It was too early in December for Santa, dragging his sack, I told myself, trying to keep my mood lighthearted. However, thoughts of zombies flashed into my mind again and I swallowed. At least in Luton I could blame any strange noises on the flatmates above.

'It could be a tree brushing against an upstairs window,' said Jess, uncertainly.

Lightning flashed once more and lit up a shape, at the top of the stairs.

Did I scream? I wasn't sure. All I could focus on was a man. He was carrying a body over his shoulders. Thunder muffled something he was trying to say as he dumped his load and made his way down. What I wouldn't have done, right then, to have had a Great Dane to protect us, big poops or not. Thanks to another flash of lightning, I spotted my little Christmas tree and grabbed it. Javelin had been soooo boring at school, but then I'd never had the incentive of warding off some murdering lunatic.

The figure came nearer and with a deep breath, I drew back my shaking arm. One, two, three... now or never... I hurled the tree as hard as I could, towards the bottom of the stairs.

CHAPTER 5

'What the…? Why the *hell* did you do that?' shouted a male voice.

'I've found the fuse box,' hollered Jess, and apart from the chandelier, the lights flicked back on. Dim rays filtered through from the kitchen and Games Room. Rooted to the spot, I squinted back at the bottom of the stairs, finally able to make out this freak's face.

'You?' My clenched fists uncurled a little.

Luke glared at me and rubbed his head. Jess came over from a cupboard behind the hallway desk.

'Careful,' I muttered to her and stepped backwards, as we didn't know him well.

'For God's sake,' he said. 'Who do you think I am? Some Rural Ripper? This is sleepy Harpenden, not the East End.'

He wanted to try living in Luton, where crime practically began in the crib. Only last week the bloke living below us caught a nine year old, snooping through his flat, armed with nothing but a stink bomb and Star Wars sabre.

My heart raced as I pictured the tabloid headlines, if I was famous: "*Courageous Kimmy Scuppers Stalker.*" Well, Luke had met me briefly, and that's all it took for those weirdoes to become obsessed. A story like that would win Adam back. The magazines would feature our reunion. The police would provide me with panic buttons and a cool bodyguard…

'Who were you carrying?' I said in a half-whisper.

'Why don't I show you,' said Luke with a sinister grin.

Groucho could have at least bared his teeth or found a phone and punched in the number for the police, with his titchy paw. My mouth went dry as Luke went back upstairs and dragged the body along the landing. He flipped it over his shoulder and came back down. I gasped, took a larger step backwards and prayed that my legs wouldn't give way. My fists clenched tight once more. What kind of monster was he? That body was headless.

'Let's go!' I screeched to Jess. Startled, Groucho scampered into the kitchen and let more light into the hallway as he pushed the door open.

'Kimmy, wait a minute,' said Jess.

More visible now, Luke stood at the bottom of the staircase. Blood trickled past his eyebrow and one arm was draped casually around the shoulders of…

'A dressmaking dummy?' My mouth fell open.

'Who's the dummy now?' he scoffed.

His smug look made me almost wish it had been some murder victim instead.

'Is this your idea of a joke?' I straightened up and folded my arms.

He took a handkerchief out of his pocket. 'That your way of saying sorry?' He wiped the blood from his head.

'What are you doing with that thing? Whose is it?' said Jess.

'It belonged to your predecessor. I agreed to pick it up for her – she refused to come back to Mistletoe Mansion.'

'Why?' I asked.

His mouth twitched. 'Pleasurable as this has been, ladies, it's time I was off.'

'Try knocking next time,' I said, blocking out thoughts wondering whether it would scratch to kiss his bristly face.

No, I wouldn't apologise for his injury. He was to blame. And so were his sexy hair and sardonic smile, for making me think the unthinkable – that, in time, there might be other men out there who could turn my head. No, I wouldn't consider that. Adam and I were meant for each other and this… this arrogant, rude, unfriendly handyman just proved how important it was for me to win back my decent man.

'Didn't want to disturb you.' He shrugged. 'Thought I'd be in and out. It might have been safer, though. Didn't know I'd come face to face with such a drama queen.'

'You've bent my tree!' I said, picking up the now lopsided Christmas decoration.

'How inconsiderate of me. Next time I'll duck.' He shoved the doll under one arm and approached me, leant forward and slid the honeysuckle from my ear, his fingers gently brushing against my scalp. 'Don't think Mr Murphy would appreciate you picking the flowers.' And with that he left.

I stared out of the front window as he swaggered down the drive. The rain had calmed to a rhythmic patter and the weeping willow hung limp, like my hair after a swim. 'I didn't think I'd ever meet anyone ruder than my younger brother. Fancy barging in unannounced, without the slightest concern for scaring the crap out of us?'

Jess shrugged. 'Suppose he was doing someone a favour. Guess he's used to popping in and out as he likes.'

'You're defending him?' My eyes narrowed.

'Per-lease, Kimmy, he's not my type! Anyway, I'm a man-free zone. It's all too soon after…' Her voice broke. She'd ditched her last boyfriend a month ago. He was older, kind of distinguished and spoilt her rotten. It shouldn't have been a surprise when the bozo let slip to straight-up Jess that he was married with no immediate plans to leave his wife.

'Come on… Don't know about you but I'm so hungry I could eat a Groucho-sized nut roast,' she said, and gave a half-smile. 'Let's eat and sort out who's sleeping where. Then we need to write a list – prioritise jobs for tomorrow… I need to search out the recycling bins and find out on which day they're emptied.'

I put down the plastic tree, hoping to mend it later, and followed her into the kitchen. Oh my God! The big American fridge with double doors! Jess found some biscuits for the little dog, whilst I pulled out eggs, butter, a small slab of cheese and milk. I'd never used a halogen hob before and ran my fingers along its shiny surface. To the right of the sink were the French patio doors. Arms full of ingredients, I teetered over and took a quick look outside. There, on raised decking, big and round and covered in a green cover was the hot tub – a very cool Facebook status immediately came to mind!

Within fifteen minutes, we were sitting at the granite island in the middle of the kitchen, eating omelettes and drinking milk.

'Here's to us,' said Jess, as she raised her glass and drank the contents down in one. 'At least I've worked out why this place is named after a parasitic plant.'

I raised an eyebrow.

'Out the back…' Jess jerked her head. 'Right at the bottom are apple and poplar trees – plus that willow at the front… All are the perfect hosts for mistletoe. I bet the owners have suffered constant infestations over the years.'

'Great, let's hope, in daylight, we can spot a mass of the stuff to help decorate this place. It's hardly festive.'

Jess wolfed down the omelette.

'You *are* hungry.' I grinned.

'Well, we've only been here a couple of hours and already rescued some torso and committed Grievous Bodily Harm.'

'Did you see Luke's face when the lights came on? What a shame my tree's now wonky.' And I supposed it was a pity that its metal base cut his head. Would he need stitches? Okay, perhaps now I was feeling a titch guilty. 'Beat you upstairs,' I said to Jess and slipped off the stool. 'I'm going to bagsy the best bedroom.'

'We're not in Juniors now, you know,' she said, but nevertheless broke into a chase as I charged into the hallway and upstairs. The chandelier's bulbs must have blown, so the landing was dark. Therefore I slowed and edged my way around to the very first door on the left, at the front of the house. It was locked, so I edged my way back, to the next door down. I opened it and switched on the light.

'Hello Magazine eat your heart out,' I murmured.

Transfixed, we entered the sumptuous room. Bang opposite the door was a huge four poster oak bed, with silk crimson sheets trimmed with gold, and a row of pretty cushions embroidered with red and purple flowers, leant up against the headboard. A lavish dressing table with carved feet stood at the end of the room, by the huge back window which boasted generously cut crimson velvet curtains hanging to the floor. I peeked out onto the back garden and could just make out the trees Jess had talked about. I pushed open the top window and shivered as I listened for a moment.

'Did you hear that shouting?' I said and quickly closed the window. 'Sounds like a couple on this street is having one humdinger of an argument.'

'Maybe life in Harpenden isn't so idyllic after all.'

Next to the bed, on the left, was a huge oak wardrobe and further around, a door, no doubt leading to an ensuite. Sure enough, I glanced in. It couldn't be more feminine, with the delicate pink smudged tiles, cream bathroom units and gold accessories. A showerhead stood over… was that a whirlpool bath? A floral design decorated the toilet seat and even the loo roll had a rose imprint on it.

In a trance I headed for the bed and flopped down, just imagining myself in one of those fancy lifestyle magazine photo shoots. Groucho jumped up next to me and snuggled up. I gazed at a rich oil painting of a vase of poppies.

'I can see you two aren't going to budge.' Jess grinned. 'In here's too posh for me anyway. Let's look at the other rooms.'

Reluctantly, I heaved myself off the super sprung mattress, longing to squidge the lush carpet between my toes. In fact, I kicked off my boots and socks and padded around for a few seconds. It felt like the softest clover-filled lawn; it felt like I'd just had one of those fish pedicures.

'Come and look at this!' called Jess. After a quick peek in the wardrobe, I hurried onto the landing. I walked to the next room and tried the handle. It was locked. Jess was in the next one along and I went in. With a whoop of joy, I headed straight for a black laptop and sat down in a swizzle chair. How had I managed almost a day without social media?

'Wonder why he needed an office,' said Jess, her gaze jumping from the immaculate cream blinds, to the beige leather sofa and shiny laminated floor. On the right hand wall was a massive plasma television. 'Let's hope the last two rooms aren't too small, Kimmy, otherwise I might be sharing your bed.'

'As long as you don't talk in your sleep, like Adam.' Or dribble on the pillow. Or throw the duvet off every time I pull it up. I bit my lip. Sleeping alone tonight was going to be weird.

The next door led into a mint green bathroom with a gleaming walk-in shower and shiny silver accessories.

It even had a bidet! And was that a waterproof telly? I'd seen one on an old series of MTV Cribs. The tiling was understated and the streamlined accessories classy.

Jess dragged me out, and along the landing to the last room at the front of the house. It was a modest size with a full bookcase.

'Stieg Larsson, Audrey Niffeneger…' murmured Jess, flicking through. 'All the modern greats.'

I squinted. Hmm, couldn't see any of Kim Kardashian's novels and you didn't get more modern than that.

'You happy in here?' I asked and took in the terracotta walls, peach bedcover and minimalist furniture. The room also had its own ensuite with gigantic mirrors. On the right, a big window faced the front garden. With its distinct lack of knick-knacks, this room was probably for guests. That meant one of the locked rooms must have been the master bedroom – probably the first one I'd tried to get into, on the other side of the landing, at the front.

'Sure am,' said Jess. 'I left my novels at Ryan's.' She took a weathered-looking book off the shelf, sat down on the bed and yawned. 'It's been quite a day. Think I might get an early night.'

'But we haven't been in the hot tub yet,' I protested. 'Or played at least one game of darts.' I didn't want to go to bed and, in the black of night, have to face thinking about my break-up with Adam this morning.

'Some of us have got to be up for work tomorrow.'

Claws scratched against the door which opened slightly. Chocolate eyes appeared. Groucho squeezed himself through the gap and cocked his head.

'I bet our instructions include taking him out for a late-night pee,' said Jess and gave a wry smile.

'Leave it to me,' I said, with my most martyr-like expression.

Jess grinned. 'Don't worry. I'll stay up so that nosy you can tell me what you discovered about the neighbours.'

'I don't know what you mean,' I said innocently.

'And I'll have a list of things to do tomorrow ready for when you get back.'

With Groucho shadowing me, I trotted downstairs and into the kitchen. I grabbed my gold parka and slipped it on. Then I fetched the dog lead from the white desk in the hallway. I fastened it to Groucho's collar and stopped by my pink case for a moment, wondering if I should change into something more fashionable. I wanted to make the right impression and it was good practice for dealing with all those fancy clients I'd have on my books when my business took off.

Except I was pretty tired. It was dark. And somehow it wouldn't feel the same without Adam there to tell me I looked nice. He still did that, even though we'd been going out for two years and eight months – longer than any of Mum's boyfriends had hung around. Just as I'd get to the point where I'd hug her latest bloke longer than he'd hug me, there'd be some massive argument between him and Mum and he'd leave – whereas Adam had sticking power…

'Come on, boy,' I said, and we headed to the front door. I shivered. Was someone behind me? Don't be stupid, I told myself. Don't let that Luke spook you out. The air smelt grassy and fresh as I locked up behind us. I squinted through the darkness. No one was around. Where were the drunken shouts? The screech of bus brakes? The empty kebab wrappers? Ah yes. I'd left them, back in Luton.

'Don't tempt me!' yelled a distant voice.

Hmm. I spoke too soon. I was right, when I heard shouting outside, on opening the window of my new bedroom – some couple was having one hell of a row.

I glanced down at the tiny Jack Russell. The last time I'd walked a dog it had belonged to Mum's boyfriend before last. One and a half long years Rick had stayed, with his roll-ups, his mechanic's oily nails and his Pirelli calendars. The plus was, he'd found my little car cheap and done it up. Also, he owned Stud, the gentlest of Staffies, with a tickle-stick tongue and shiny mocha coat. As soft as putty on the inside, if you gave him a biscuit, he held out his paw to say thanks. But he had the neck of a boxer and eyes of a jackal – I never felt scared walking him out, at night. Whereas Groucho stared up at me as if he rather hoped I might growl if anyone dodgy walked past.

'Let's track down this argument,' I whispered to him and zipped up my jacket, hoping the evening dampness wouldn't curl my hair. We veered left at the bottom of the drive and eventually a house even bigger than Walter's loomed into view. That was proof of money – owning a place in a road where the homes are all different designs. I'd only ever lived in a terrace or block of flats.

I squinted. A huge conservatory was attached to the back. This house was set further forwards than Walters's and the brickwork looked centuries old. The left hand side was a wide turret. The massive front door was oak and had a huge chrome knocker, in the shape of… an eagle. Ivy climbed the door and in front of the turret was a double garage and… Wow! A parked silver and blue… I strained my eyes… Bugatti! I'd read an article on them and recognised the elegant shape, the spoiler and the distinctive two-toned bodywork.

In the middle of the right hand lawn stood a grey water fountain and – another bonkers thing about this place – it was in the shape of a bag of golf clubs! Water ran from the club heads, poking out of the top. This house belonged to a sports-mad pensioner, no doubt. As we carried on, something black darted down from the trees. Was that a bat?

'Don't walk away from me, when I'm talking,' shouted a woman's voice. I crouched behind a bush in the front border. The Bugatti had been parked at an angle, as if the driver had been in a hurry to get inside. All the downstairs lights were on. A door slammed and seconds later a man and woman appeared in the top bedroom. Their outlines seemed strangely familiar.

Groucho sniffed a nearby shrub and I evil-eyed him. Don't you dare cock your leg just inches from my face! I stared again at the Bugatti. Adam would have killed to give that a test run…

Suddenly the front door flew open and I ducked down further, behind the bush, inhaling the smell of wet leaves and damp soil. I could see frosty white mist escape my mouth, as I breathed in and out. Willing Groucho not to yap, I peered through a gap in the plants. At the sound of footsteps on the drive, and thanks to the porch light, I got a clear view of the man's face.

What? No, it couldn't be. My heart skipped a beat, before I took a quick double take. The number plate said JON 45. I was right! IT WAS GOLFING STAR, JONNY WINSFORD!

CHAPTER 6

It's official: miracles do happen; fantasies come true. My new neighbour was the hottest talent on the UK golfing circuit, known as The Eagle. That explained the door knocker and the bonkers water fountain. And that woman... I put my fist in my mouth. She must have been Melissa, she of the velvety voice who, only this morning, on the telly, had taken me through my putts and tee offs.

Me? Living just along from the Winsfords? Who cares that I left my fitness DVDs in Adam's flat, because now I had the real 3D version of the instructor living right next door. Not that Adam would be impressed. He reckoned golf was a sissy's sport and that any bloke who promoted moisturiser was "a right muppet".

I bet he secretly fancied Melissa, though, with her full lips and pert bum. She'd single-handedly sexed up British golf – and her trophy-winning husband certainly put the *pwhoar* into plus fours. Between them, the Winsfords had brought golf to the nation and even increased sales of those naff jumpers with diamonds printed on. After their weekly appearances in the glossies, even I'd picked up lots of golfing terms, like a "slice" meaning a shot curving to the right, like a "bogey" – yuck – meaning a score of one over par.

The bass beat of Jonny's – I'd already decided we'd be on first name terms – radio pulsated loudly as he got in and revved the engine. As he reversed down the drive, Melissa raced out of the house. Unsteady on her feet, she wore a sexy nightie and screamed at him to stop. On a frosty patch of tarmac, she slid to a stop, then yanked open the car door, grabbed his... phew, *belt*, and pulled him out.

I wanted a nightie that clung to my nipples; I wanted a car that didn't need a bump start. She stabbed his chest with her finger and then shook her fist. In response, he stroked her hair, moved in closer and lifted her up. Wow. She looked even more glamorous, spread-eagled, across the blue bonnet. Maybe posh cars needed a *hump* start?

'Let's go.' I whispered to Groucho, as Jonny lifted Melissa up again and carried her indoors. They were obviously one of those passionate couples who, like in the movies, had great make-up sex. Unlike me and Adam. He'd just sulk for days whereas I should copyright my selection of flounces and dramatic sighs. We were well-matched in that way and would jokingly vie for the Brownie points of apologising first.

Wait until Jess heard about our glam neighbours, although glitzy sporting types weren't really for her. She liked men with hidden depths and meaningful stares, like crossbow-armed Daryl out of zombie series The Walking Dead. God knows why she'd fallen for shallow Phil.

'Lost something?' asked a husky voice.

Aargh, talk about zombies! Maybe I should've followed Adam's advice – he never approved of women going out on their own after dark. I jumped up and gulped with relief not to find myself facing a member of the maggot-infested Undead. Instead I stared at a double chin and friendly eyes topped with defined grey brows. The old man wore a bright yellow cap and an even brighter anorak, tightly zipped up around his rotund front. Groucho wagged his tail and the man picked him up.

'Hope I didn't scare you. Let me introduce myself. I'm Terry.' He gave a little bow. 'I live the other side of Walter's.' He ruffled Groucho's ears. 'I spotted you earlier – you're the new housesitter? Just settled in for the festive season?'

'Yes. The name's Kimmy,' I said, heart pounding. Jeez! First headless corpses carried down stairs, and now strangers creeping up on me in the dark… So much for Groucho alerting me of danger. 'And there's my friend, Jess – she's housesitting too. I… um… thought I heard some money fall out of my pocket, that's what I was looking for.' I smiled and tucked my hair behind my ears, wishing I'd checked my make-up. No doubt this was an Important Person. You had to be, to afford a place in Badgers Chase. The man wore tartan trousers and – oh my God – over his shoulder had a brown leather man bag. LOL! I mean, funny. Must stop thinking in abbreviations. That's the trouble with spending so much time on Facebook. 'Did you know Mr Carmichael well?' I asked, politely.

'Walter?' His sparkly eyes dipped at the corners for a second and he put Groucho back on the ground. 'We've both lived here for… ooh, nearly two decades. Lily, his wife, died five years ago. They were the sweetest couple. She'd been ill for a while but seemed to have turned a corner. They even booked a cruise but, one night, she passed away, right out of the blue.'

'That's so sad.'

Terry nodded. 'Took it hard, he did, as you'd expect – for a long time talked about not wanting to keep Lily waiting.'

'Huh?'

'They didn't have children. It was only the two of them. She'd promised to wait for him if she went first, at the Pearly Gates.' He smiled. 'I told you they were sweet.'

'How did he manage on his own?' I asked, as we headed back to Walter's.

'As well as anyone can. Eventually he cleared the house of her things; even her fab pashminas and hats. Then he got a new kitchen fitted. She was a great cook – made a wicked lemon meringue.' Terry sighed. 'He couldn't bear to spend time in the old kitchen – too many memories. He even got rid of her beloved Aga.'

'Didn't he keep anything?'

'A few bits. She had this amazing recipe book that listed all her favourite cakes. Lily won lots of local competitions and there was a bit of a scrabble to find it after the wake, when her so-called friends from the Women's Institute visited.' He shook his head. 'Not very dignified. Anyway, they were the kindest couple – traditional to the core. She never mowed the lawn and he never filled the kettle.'

'You must miss them… ' I liked Terry. He wasn't at all what I'd expected – not stuffy nor snooty. I had wondered whether the neighbours might blank me, like that posh designer clothes shop owner in St Albans, who'd evil-eyed me when I'd ventured inside during the sales.

'Walter introduced me to his golf club,' he said, 'and recommended me for membership, even though some of the other members were a bit… well… didn't approve of...'

'What?'

'Me. Strange isn't it, seeing as golf is one of the campest sports in the world – what with the bright colours and plus fours, the silly club covers and all those jokes about holes-in-one. The first few games were a riot. My opponents hardly dared bend over to pick up their balls.'

I grinned.

'Walter always had a great sense of humour, though. I'd never have got through my Ken's… departure last year, without him.'

'You've also, um, lost, your partner?

'We were fifteen years together. And I didn't *lose* the bastard, he buggered off with a twenty-year-old shelf-stacker from BargainMarket – you know, the frozen food shop.' He caught my eye and chuckled. 'I'm trying to see the funny side now. At least he left me with a stocked freezer. Last count I still had forty-five mini pizzas, seventy-two sticky chicken skewers, ninety vegetarian spring rolls and a hundred and eight jumbo tempura prawns. Walter used to call in before his dinner sometimes and we'd share a plateful with a bottle of Merlot.' He pulled a face. 'Ghastly food.'

'So, why don't you throw it out?'

'Now it's just me, what else am I going to put in the freezer? And Walter would turn in his grave; said I should at least donate them to some soup kitchen for the homeless.'

'He sounds like a good bloke.'

'The best.' Terry smiled at a middle-aged lady who walked past with her Dalmatian. She wore a glossy fur (was that real?) hat and matching gloves. 'Anyway, listen to me blathering on,' he said as we arrived at Walter's drive.

'Did you know the last housesitter?' I said. 'Luke… he's the handyman–'

'Helpful lad.'

Really? 'He was around earlier collecting her stuff – seems she left in a rush.'

We reached the drive.

'She was, er, a pleasant enough woman. So was the one before her.' He looked at me and shrugged. 'Walter was always happy here, whereas everyone since…'

'What?'

He fiddled with his manbag for a moment. 'It's getting late. I never know when to stop chatting. You get off, to unpack. Why don't I call in, some time, erm, in the daylight? I know Walter's house inside out and could show you around. Luke can sometimes be a bit... He's a busy man, but his heart is in the right place.' Terry cleared his throat. 'Only if you two girls want, though – an old fogey like me might cramp your style!'

'*You* cramp *our* style?' I said, with a wink.

Terry clapped me on the back. 'I'm going to enjoy living next to you.'

'That would be great if you could show us where everything is. Thanks... Terry.' I tugged my head towards the Winsfords' place. 'Must be cool for you, living two doors down from a golfing legend.'

'Legend? That would be Greg Norman or Seve Ballesteros. Whereas this rookie...He's done okay. Bit flash, though. But his wife's brought a breath of fresh air to the sport. Some of her clothes are just fabulous.' His face lit up. 'And I'm sure I saw that pushy brunette from morning telly at their house the other day, for some sort of interview. Then there was the time Antonia... '

'Not *Antonia Hamilton* who won last year's Strictly Disco?'

He clasped his hands together. 'Yes! She visited. I think she took time off from her tour to help choreograph Melissa's fitness DVD. I looked through my backlog of Starchat and sure enough, they both went to school together. They'd been photographed together by the paparazzi at some school reunion.'

'You keep a backlog of Starchat magazines too? My boyfriend never understood why I did that.'

'Neither did Ken.'

'And Infamous magazine?'

'Shh! It's our little secret! We really ought to be reading some more upmarket coffee table magazine in Harpenden.'

I grinned again.

'You'll have to come round some time, Kimmy. Now must go. Frazzle will be wondering where I am.' He tilted his cap. 'Ciao, sweetie! Any problems, I'm just next door.'

Frazzle? Was that a nickname for some new boyfriend? He paused for a few seconds to look at Mistletoe Mansion, opened his mouth as if he was going to say something, then changed his mind.

Mrs Winsford! Antonia Hamilton! Living here was going to be so cool. Maybe I'd become good mates with Melissa, we'd go shopping and she'd tell me the latest gossip about her famous chums. Perhaps she'd advise me on keeping your man, and help me win back Adam.

Humming quietly, I led Groucho up the drive, when he suddenly ground to a halt. His chocolate button eyes stared right up at the locked front left room. I followed his gaze and the hairs stood up on the back of my neck. In that top window, staring straight back, appeared a... a strangely illuminated, transparent face. Every millimetre of moisture drained from my mouth and my legs felt wobbly. I squinted as it darted from side to side, my heart racing and hands feeling clammy. OMG! Not only did we live next to a celebrity – now we had our very own ghost.

OF COURSE! The G word that Deborah had managed to hide... That red writing, under the hole-punch... The *Gh* must have meant... I swallowed hard: *Must Love Ghosts.*

I'd always wanted to appear on Most Haunted, that programme where they investigated spooky goings-on. Now I had my own live show. Stumbling slightly, I scooped up Groucho and looked around for Terry, but there was no sight of the bright anorak. I forced myself to gaze up at the window again and jumped back – it was still there.

'Cooee!' I warbled and waved with a trembling hand. Appear friendly. Don't show you're scared to death (unfortunate use of words, there).

The face stopped still for a minute then darted manically. My stomach scrunched. Perhaps I'd upset it. Who knows what other ghouls were in this place? With a deep breath, I charged towards the house. There was no time to lose. Practically wetting myself with fear or not, I had to get in the house and warn Jess.

CHAPTER 7

Go on, you beast, do your worst. Turn into some incisor-flashing, blood-drooling werewolf... Try and take a bite. I'm not scared.

It was no good. My attempts at telepathy were useless. Groucho merely rolled onto his back, batting his chocolate button eyes for a tickle. Clearly he'd be no help fighting against some spirit risen from the dead. I was trying to convince Jess that there really was evil afoot in Mistletoe Mansion. 'Officially nuts' – that's what she thought I was.

'A ghost?' she'd eventually said. 'You've been watching far too much Most Haunted.' Just because I'd tried to impress her with what I'd learnt from the show and talked of *light anomalies* and *residual energies*. But she didn't laugh out loud until I suggested asking this *astral being* I'd spotted to knock three times to prove it was there. Tears had run down her face as she'd waved me out of her room. 'It's late,' she'd said, and giggled. 'I've got work tomorrow. And no, this isn't Blue Peter, so I'll decline your request to help you make a Ouija board out of cereal boxes and loo roll.'

Still spooked, I'd then played dirty and questioned her love of a certain supernatural zombie series. She'd shaken her head. Didn't I know those shows were fictional?

Squinting at the shafts of morning winter sunshine, I dumped my shopping on the kitchen floor and made an extra strong coffee. Last night I'd hadn't slept a wink, due to all my senses being on red alert, homing in on every suspicious creak or thud. Yet when Jess popped into my room before work – with my first caffeine shot of the day and with the daily to-do list Luke had mentioned (Jess had edited it of course, and written on several other things she thought were important) – we had a good laugh. Maybe she was right. The face I saw could have been the moon's reflection. As if a cut-throat estate agent would believe in, let alone jot down notes about, ghosts.

Not that Jess was happy when I finally told her about Deborah running after us, trying to stop our car. She worried there might be something wrong with the tyres or exhaust. Not likely. Adam gave my car a thorough check-over, once a month.

Tucking my slightly frizzy hair behind my ears, I gazed out of the kitchen window, onto the sweeping back garden and the cloudless, crisp December sky. A smile inflated my cheeks. I had to update my Facebook status to "*Kimmy Jones is…*" What's that expression? Living the life of Riley? No, living the life of *Kylie,* more like! After the shock of Adam dumping me, my stomach still twisted when thinking of him, but the waves of nauseous hurt were now alleviated by my belief that me helping to sell Mistletoe Mansion could bring me and Adam back together.

It was great to be back in this bubble of luxury after my quick trip to the supermarket. I'd been tempted to drive into Harpenden and explore the upmarket food shops. But I'd found some cash for our expenses, in with the list of instructions, and it wouldn't stretch too far. So, I'd headed to my usual store and bought the essentials (Pringles and Oreos) before buying baking ingredients and other groceries. I'd also picked up some cheap garlands of tinsel, to drape over the pictures and portraits, otherwise – my broken tree apart – no one could tell Christmas was only two weeks away. Despite the storm, my car started straightaway, after its first ever night in a garage. What fun I'd had with the remote – at the touch of a button: garage door up, garage door down.

I finished my drink, put away the shopping and ticked off the first entry on Jess's list ("Stock up"). What an awesome kitchen, with its pristine cupboards that opened properly and shiny worktops. And what an array of utensils, some of which looked surprisingly old. Walter must have kept more reminders of his wife than Terry knew about. There were Tupperware boxes, pastry cutters, jelly moulds, pie funnels, whisks and spatulas... Yet the inside of the double oven was spotless. After Lily's death, Walter must have eaten out every day or nuked ready meals for one, in the microwave.

The doorbell rang. I put away the last bottle of milk and yawned as I headed for the front door. Truth be told, I wouldn't have slept last night anyway. Apart from the shower dripping every sixth second (I counted), the bed was well big without Adam. I'd stretched star-shaped, burped out loud, done all those things I'd fantasised about doing if I ever slept alone. But it wasn't much fun and I felt even worse when Groucho reminded me of an amorous Adam, by waking me up with a nudge in the back (except the pointy body part Groucho used was his paw).

The doorbell rang again and I looked at my watch – it was almost time for a sandwich. Suddenly I stopped dead. My heart raced. What if that was Melissa, inviting me around for a sushi lunch? Or maybe she just drank that maple and cayenne pepper diet formula all the celebrities swore by. She was so slim, I bet she never ate a bacon butty or double cheeseburger with extra large fries.

I dashed into the hallway and wished there was a mirror to check my appearance. Feeling judgy, I glanced down at my legs, squished into discount skinny jeans. At least I was wearing my new black top with a silver sequinned stiletto on the front. I sucked in my stomach. What would I say? Pretend not to know her? Or gush about her talented husband?

'Just coming!' I politely called, at the last minute remembering my – what did the French call it? – *pièce de résistance*. I couldn't resist buying it, whilst out at the shops. I legged it back into the kitchen and grabbed a cute pink canine sweater with glitter trim off the worktop. I tore off the tag and knelt down by Groucho's bed. 'Good boy,' I said and made him stand up. Well, they didn't have it in blue, and weren't dogs supposed to be colour blind? Wrestling his front paws, I managed to pull it on snugly and adjust the shape. 'Aren't you handsome?' I cooed. Melissa probably had a Toy Poodle or Chihuahua. 'Naughty, don't pull back your top lip. Pink is soooo your colour.' Feeling like Paris Hilton or Britney, I carried him (squeezed as if my arm were a vice, to be honest). Talk about ungrateful – he did his best to tug off the new outfit.

I opened the door to a wall of icy air and felt the smile drop from my face. 'You again?' Oops. That sounded a bit rude. Terry thought Luke was okay, so perhaps I should try to see his better side. It wasn't his fault that he'd made me realise not all men were as thoughtful and considerate as Adam.

'Ten out of ten.' Luke eyed Groucho's sweater. 'You going to invite me in? After all, I did ring the bell this time.'

'Can I ask what for?' It's not as if this Luke owned the place; he couldn't just call by for no good reason.

'The chandelier bulbs blew during that storm, yeah? Of course, if you'd rather fix them yourself…'

'Erm, okay,' I muttered. He was wearing those light cords again with a blue shirt, under his unzipped anorak.

The skin on his chest (what little of it I could see) was tanned and his profile straight and solid. Yet he didn't seem the gym bunny type, like Adam, whose muscular shape was well-defined. Luke bobbed out of view for a moment, and then came in carrying a step ladder and toolbox.

'What's with the jumper?' He nodded at Groucho.

Groucho barked and I released him to the ground. He rolled on his back, paws scrabbling at his stomach.

'Think he's trying to tell you something.' Without asking, Luke bent down and pulled the jumper off.

'Why did you do that?' Honestly, forget my good intentions. He could have at least asked first.

'He'll overheat indoors, let alone be the laughing stock.' He ruffled Groucho's head. 'That better, mate?'

Annoyingly, the little dog ruffed.

'He has been taken out this morning, hasn't he?'

'There's no need to check up on us,' I said stiffly. 'We found the list of instructions. It's not rocket science.'

'How about a cup of tea then, Jess?' He leant forward towards me. Once more I smelt his musky aftershave that made the word "sex" pop into my head.

'It's Kimmy,' I muttered.

'Huh?'

Arghhh! This man really was soooo annoying!

'I might put the kettle on,' I sniffed, 'if you have a look at the shower in my room. It's dripping. Or leave me a large pair of pliers and I'll unscrew it later. I reckon the washer's damaged.'

He stared at me for a second. 'No. It's okay. I'll take a look. Where are you sleeping?'

'At the back of the house, on the left.'

'Lily's room.' His face softened. 'She suffered from insomnia; preferred her own space so she could do her embroidery in the night, without waking up Walter.'

Luke must have known the Carmichaels well. He made them sound more like relatives than former employers.

'Milk, no sugar, thanks Jess,' he beamed.

I glared, turned three sixty degrees and made my way back into the kitchen. Scraping my hair back into a ponytail, I ignored his irritating whistling. I seized some flour, sugar butter, eggs, rummaged around for a sieve and mixing bowl, then grabbed the fab silicone cupcake pan Jess had bought me for my last birthday. There was nothing better for stress than beating cake batter – apart from eating it of course, once it had been baked, iced and sprinkled. Mmm.

Three quarters of an hour later, six naked cupcakes stood on a wire rack, almost cool and waiting to be dressed. I'd mixed the batter with a generous dollop of mincemeat and was just finishing off the brandy buttercream icing, which I piped on top. Then I delicately added a green marzipan holly leaf and red berry to each one. Just as well I'd subbed our expenses money to pay for my baking ingredients. I grinned to myself. This was the kitchen I'd always dreamed of. Film crews could tape my latest series here: Kimmy's Sixty Minute Meals (I wasn't as quick as Jamie Oliver).

'All done,' said a voice behind me.

I turned around and to my annoyance my cheeks burned. He'd taken off his anorak, unbuttoned his shirt a little and had rolled up the sleeves. Determined to find a distraction from his appealingly toned skin, I focused on a scab above his eyebrow.

'Um, your cup of tea, I forgot…'

'Let me.' He brushed past me to wash his hands before filling the kettle. He reached for the packet of tea bags and my eyes ran over his lean back. He was lankier than Adam; looked as if he kept himself in shape without really trying.

'How's your head?' I said, when the drinks were ready. We sat down at the breakfast table and he helped himself to a cupcake. Deep breaths. Must be nice, because apart from anything else I wanted to quiz him and find out why some of the bedrooms – particularly the one where I'd seen the moon-face – were locked.

'I'll live.' Luke shrugged. 'You not having one?'

'It's lunch time.'

'But you might have poisoned it; perhaps you still think I'm the Harpenden Ripper.' He took a knife out of a nearby drawer and cut the cake into four. He offered me a quarter.

'Thanks.' Why did I say that? After all, I was the host and he was the guest. Although nothing made me happier than watching someone stuff their face with my cake. It made me feel like I'd won the lottery or magically fitted into a size ten.

'Not bad.' Crumbs fell from his mouth and I felt an inexplicable urge to run my finger along his top lip, which was covered with the brandy buttercream icing. Not that there was any need as, seconds later, he slowly licked it off with his tongue. I touched my throat. No surprise that he didn't use a napkin like Adam. Good, reliable, straightforward Adam, who knew my name was Kimmy and didn't break into houses to cavort around with headless dummies.

'Lily made amazing cakes,' he said. 'A rich fruity one with brandy was one of her specialities.'

I took a bite and then another. Mmm, great, the sponge was lovely and light, despite the mincemeat. The sugar soon worked its magic and made me think that maybe Luke wasn't so bad after all. Another bite. I mean, here we were, drinking together, making chit-chat…

'Yes – I've heard about her secret recipe book that some of her so-called friends have been trying to get their hands on,' I said.

Luke picked up another quarter, leaving me the slice with the marzipan holly.

'So, Miss Cake-baker, what's the story? Why are you really here?'

I almost choked. 'Pardon?'

He lolled against the back of the stool. 'We both know you two girls aren't housesitters.'

'And what makes you say that?' I said airily, and tried to keep my cool.

'For a start, you've picked holly out of the garden and, along with that gaudy tinsel, decorated the house. Then I spotted a framed photo of you and some bloke out on show, in your bedroom. The first day here you're baking and worried about a slightly dripping shower as if you hope to stay here for a long time. Then there's that god awful dog sweater.' He took a swig of tea. 'You've even bought potpourri for the lounge. All of these things say to me that you see Mistletoe Mansion as some kind of home, rather than a job. Housesitters don't become attached like that. They bring the minimum amount of stuff and leave half of it packed.'

'I'm… a bit of a homebird,' I waffled. 'What's wrong with trying to make a place cosy, especially at this time of year? Anyway, what is this? Oprah?' His eyes flashed as he grinned and for some reason part of me enjoyed the banter.

He smirked. 'Bet the reason you're here involves a man. That guy in the photo?'

'I'm a professional woman.' I cleared my throat. 'This job is not some knee-jerk reaction to Adam and me… It's just another contract.'

'Whatever you say.'

'And anyway… This place, I can't explain it… it's got a good feeling,' I said and shrugged. 'It doesn't feel empty. It feels like a home.'

He stared at me for a moment and ran a hand through his hair. Fighting thoughts of how I'd like to do that – just

because, um, it would be pleasant sensation, of course –
I stared fixedly into his eyes.

'Best cupcake I've ever tasted, by the way,' he said.

My chest glowed. 'Thanks. Have another one.' I still
needed to ask him about the locked rooms.

'Better not. Things to do. The summerhouse door needs
mending – I've been putting it off for days, what with
recent rain. It won't take long and then I'll be out of your
way.'

Summerhouse? How cool was that! I grabbed my gold
parka and followed him and Groucho into the back garden
and hung back for a second as winter sun rays tickled my
face. As well as Luke whistling, birds chirped and far away,
young children giggled and shrieked. A distant aeroplane
streaked the blue sky. I strolled past a large shed and
impressive patch of wildflowers swaying gently. Further
on, bushes bulged with white berries... This place was
pretty enough now – in the summer it must look awesome.
This was one huge garden. Surely if Adam were here, right
at this moment, he would understand why I aspired to a life
so much bigger and better than the one I had?

Luke's whistling stopped as, towards the bottom of
the garden, he examined the door of what looked like the
poshest Wendy house, just in front of the poplar and apple
trees. It was shaded by a weeping willow which was almost
as big as the one in the front. I caught him up and peeked
through the windows at a wicker table and two matching
chairs with embroidered pillows. Talk about a private beach
hut. I could just imagine myself lounging on the decking
at the front, in designer glasses and eating a skinny ice
cream... I could see the tabloids' paparazzi photos of me
sitting in the shade, reading some movie script, wearing
shades and one of those Greta Garbo turbans, with Luke,
topless, fanning me with a palm leaf...

'Aren't you supposed to be cleaning the house? This isn't a holiday park,' muttered Luke, back to his former unfriendly self.

Daydreaming ruined and my sugar rush having worn off, I stared at him – why run hot and cold? Airily, I walked on a little, to admire a regimental-looking vegetable garden. A little overgrown, but... wow! Those looked like leek tops and various other lines of green leaves... Jess wouldn't believe her luck.

With a glare at Luke, I made my way back inside. What was it with him? I was making an effort, even though we'd got off to a bad start. With a sigh, I walked through the kitchen, on my way picking up some nibbles I'd bought for the Games Room which I took in and stashed behind the bar. Dust covered all the bar's glasses and with the sun shining on the panes, I could see that the inside of the windows needed a good scrub down.

However, riled by Luke saying I needed to start cleaning, I delayed and picked up the darts. One by one I threw them at the dartboard. Triple twenty! I hadn't lost my touch. One of Mum's boyfriends had been a pub team champion. I took three more shots.

Several goes later, I yawned, left the Games Room and went to check my shower, unable to face another sleepless night. As I went upstairs, I cocked my ear to listen for dripping water but instead heard a strange noise, like... a blowing gale. There it went again. I ran up to check in Jess's room. Perhaps it was some of that New Age stuff she listened to, like the tide breaking or the mating call of whales. But there was no CD player; her iPod was missing. The office was very quiet too.

The spooky image from the night before jumped into my mind and within seconds my hands felt clammy. But ghosts didn't haunt houses this modern, I told myself, sternly. You only had to watch Most Haunted to know they hung out in historical buildings and graveyards. I went into the ensuite in my room. The dripping had stopped. At least that Luke had done something right.

I came back out into the bedroom and picked up the photo of me and Adam. Sunday morning – normally we'd still be in bed, him reading the paper after I'd pinched the supplement to read the celebrity stories. Then we'd head over to his parents for a traditional roast. I'd take dessert. My chest tightened. Life with him was comfortable. I enjoyed chilling with him – enjoyed curling up cosily at night, with someone who accepted me for who I was.

I shook my head. Thing was, since yesterday, I'd been questioning whether that was really true. Adam asking me to leave confirmed what I'd refused to consider for a while now – he didn't truly "get" the real me, who had ambitions and aspired to running a successful baking empire. Yet this realisation didn't stop me missing my ex – there, I managed to say that word without choking or going through a box of tissues. Perhaps I should phone him. Plenty of couples stayed together happily, despite not fully understanding each other… right? I reached into my trouser pocket for my mobile…

Urgh. No. I pulled back my hand. Stay strong. Best to wait a couple of days, by which time he'd work out that the toilet didn't clean itself. I glanced up. Funny, I hadn't heard the bedroom door close – a draught must have pushed it shut. I gripped the gold door handle. Hmm. It wouldn't budge. I grasped tighter and pulled it hard. Still no luck.

Heart thumping, I again recalled the spooky face from last night and hurried over to the window. Down on the lawn, Groucho swaggered up to a blackbird. It looked like Luke had gone. Maybe if I shouted through the open top window, that friendly man Terry or Melissa would hear and raise the alarm. But their houses were so far away, not like the mid-terrace I'd grown up in where the neighbours could probably hear my disgusting teenage brother break wind.

What would they have done on Most Haunted? 'I mean you no harm,' I eventually said, voice trembling. 'Show me a sign that someone is here.'

At that exact moment, a sweet-smelling cloud of smoke edged its way under the door. What now, a fire? Had I left the oven on? Yes, that must be it. My chest relaxed for a second. All these shenanigans had to be due to something logical like that – except that… that… the smoke smelt kind of sweet and the whooshing wind noise increased in pitch. Oh shit! I swallowed hard.

'Show me your presence,' I stuttered, mouth dry, like I'd scoffed a whole packet of wafer crackers.

Brave Kimmy Flees Fire – I could see the headline in OK Magazine. And a photo of me and Adam, arms around each other, him declaring his love since I'd almost died.

I sat on the bed and picked up the list of instructions I'd been reading that morning. There was no other option; Luke was nearest. I'd have to find his number and ring for his help. The police was a no-no. If Mr Murphy got to hear of any damage, from me having potentially caused a fire, he'd probably blame me and I'd be out; I'd lose my chance to impress Adam. I had to keep any funny goings-on in this house well under wraps. Ghost or no ghost, Mr Murphy had to think my stay was running smoothly.

My finger ran down the page, to Luke's number. I slid my phone out of my trouser pocket and dialled.

'Luke? It's me, Kimmy… The housesitter. I'm trapped, in the bedroom. Talk about odd noises… and I think something's on fire.' I lowered my voice. 'Someone's in the house, I'm sure of it. Can you come back? I wouldn't ask if there was anyone else.'

Apparently Luke was in his car and about to drive off. Finally, with a sigh, he said to shut myself in the ensuite, just in case the smoke was dangerous. Not that I needed his advice. I laid a damp towel across the bottom of the bedroom door. It reminded me of the time Mum lit the barbecue with petrol and the flames instantly spread to the lawn. Hands flapping, she'd run around the garden, whilst I got the hose and put it out.

After a few minutes, a voice shouted, 'Kimmy? You in the bathroom?'

Legs feeling wobbly, I pushed open the ensuite door and there Luke stood, by Lily's bed, chestnut hair all tousled. Slowly I left the bathroom.

I looked around. 'Was it, um, the oven? Have you put out the fire?'

'This your idea of a joke?' His lips pursed. 'It's not my job to play your silly games. Mr Murphy pays me to do handy work. That's all. I've got another job to get to.'

'Games?'

'Smoke, an intruder, sounds of a blowing gale…? What next? Voices coming out of the telly? Crockery moving on its own?' He shook his head. 'And as for your door being locked…'

'I could have been burnt to death!'

He laughed. 'I know it's a boring job, minding the house, but really – if you need company, go visit Terry next door, he's a sound bloke. I'm flattered, don't get me wrong, but…'

'You think I *fancy* you?' My top lip curled. Who the hell did he think he was?

He folded his arms. 'Why else would you pretend the shower was broken? Ply me with cupcakes? Ask me to come back and put out some imaginary fire?'

'That dripping kept me awake all last night!'

'All the showerhead needed was a good clean. Any idiot could see that.'

'Well, for your information, I'm not romantically available,' I said, through gritted teeth. 'That photo you spotted is of–'

'Adam?' he smirked.

'Yes. My boyfriend… well my ex… But we're getting back together and I'm not looking for a replacement and even if I was, you would hardly be–' I stopped. Did someone just scream?

This whole cul-de-sac was bloody bonkers, what with shagging on Bugattis and smoke under doors; what with dogs that didn't understand pooch jumpers were the in-thing and big-headed handymen who thought a leaky shower was an excuse for seduction. Luke eyed me for a second, as if he might say something else, but instead charged downstairs. I followed. There was another bloodcurdling scream and we legged it onto the drive.

CHAPTER 8

'This is a matter of life and death!' screeched a female voice. 'You can't do this!'

OMG! My recent scary experience forgotten, I instantly recognised the back of that beautifully coiffured head. Melissa Winsford stood on the pavement at the bottom of Walter's drive, shouting into a phone, wearing the shortest, tightest blue dress, which showed off every inch of her size six legs, plus a tailored black leather jacket and what looked like a real crocodile skin handbag. The sunglasses (totes unnecessary) had a Chanel C on the side. I could tell that, under the flesh-coloured tights, her caramel tan was perfect, with no streaks or blotches of orange – unlike my legs, which had the odd razor cut and patch of stubble. On the pavement just behind her, I stood panting, next to Luke. We'd practically sprinted the length of the drive.

'Don't think you'll get away with this!' she yelled. 'I'll spread the word – make sure you never work south of Watford again!'

She stuffed the phone into her bag and something like a sob escaped her lips. Maybe her doctor had misdiagnosed some fatal illness. Or her accountant had fiddled the books.

'Are you okay?' I asked and subtly tried to brush flour off my jeans. Pity I hadn't had time this morning to re-straighten my hair.

She jumped and turned around. 'How long have you two been there? Do tell your editor that there's nothing to report and if you've taken any photos, darling,' she said to me in a more velvety voice, 'delete them and I'll provide you with some shots that'll really sell.' She unzipped her leather jacket and subtly pushed out her double D cups. What a pro!

'We're not the press. I'm Luke. Last month I unblocked your upstairs loo, as a favour to Mr Winsford. He saw me mending Mr Carmichael's roof.'

'How nice for you, darling.' She stopped posing, whilst I chuckled as she visibly shuddered at his cords. If only I'd thought to grab Groucho, complete with his new glitter-trimmed sweater. 'Are you the cleaner?' she asked me. 'I'd have thought they'd have sold this place by now.'

'No, I'm…' My cheeks flamed up and I felt toasty warm, despite being out in the arctic air without a coat. What was my name, again? Deep breath, in and out… Pull yourself together. 'I'm Kimmy. The housesitter. Can I just say, what a fan I am, Melissa? Is it okay to call you that? I follow all your fashion tips in Starchat. Did…'

She held up a hand. 'Cute. Drop by my place later; the housekeeper will give you a signed photo.'

'We thought you were in trouble,' said Luke, a long blade of grass now in between his teeth. 'Obviously we needn't have bothered dropping everything to run to your side.'

She fished in her handbag and pulled out a crisp twenty pound note. 'That's for your time.' Luke shook his head and, whistling, strode back up the drive. 'Is he gay?' she whispered. 'He's certainly got the body for it. And with some top products he could have great hair. Although his whistling would give me a headache… Why can't he just wear an iPod like any normal person?' She passed me the twenty, instead. 'You take it.'

'Um, thanks!' I just couldn't turn down the chance to hold a banknote that had once belonged to someone famous.

Melissa still wore her glasses. Maybe her eyes were red and swollen. 'Is there anything I can do to help?' I asked softly. 'That phone call… I couldn't help hearing…'

She removed her glasses. Were those false eyelashes? And tattooed eyebrows were so cool.

'Have you ever been let down badly, Kimmy?'

'Yes, there was that time–'

'Hurts, doesn't it,' she continued. 'It was going to be one of the most important days of my life.'

'What was? I hid my hands behind my back, wishing I'd redone the nail varnish before breakfast.

'I'm having a little get-together this week, for some of the golf wives from the local club. Nothing flash – not like the parties I have with the national *birdies*. But still – I want to make an effort. Jonny and I have lived here for over a year now, and… I don't feel like I know them much at all.' Her smile nearly blinded me as the winter sun caught her Osmond white teeth. 'Not that I'm bothered, you understand, I'm a busy woman. But the golf on a local level, the social life, it's still important to Jonny…'

Really? If the tabloids were right, her husband spent most of his time abroad, or in Woburn or London. Perhaps she got lonely out here in the sticks, where the theatre was hardly West End and the common was no Hyde Park. Although Harpenden was only half an hour away on the train from the capital, not that I expect she ever took public transport.

'I've pretended it's a fundraiser,' she continued, 'told them to bring their cheque books. But the real reason, the real surprise…' She clapped her hands. 'I've arranged for them to all have Botox! A few injections and I'll be their new best friend.'

'But I thought you hadn't had anything done… In all your interviews you say…'

She gave a bright laugh. 'Some of these ladies are older than me – it's a favour to them. It goes without saying, I don't need it yet.'

I raised my eyebrows.

'Okay, maybe I've had it done once,' she said and gave another small laugh, 'as an experiment, nothing more.'

But she'd only just turned thirty! I gazed at her rosebud lips. Maybe she also had fillers and collagen; perhaps dermabrasion or a chemical peel. I studied her face with interest. Reading the gossip magazines practically qualified me to carry out most procedures.

According to *Infamous*, the top players' wives didn't approve of her glamour. She'd only met Jonny a couple of years ago, and they still thought her under their league. Clearly they didn't know class when they saw it. You only had to flick through the magazine spreads of the Winsfords' wedding to see that Melissa had good taste. It had taken place right at the beginning of December and was Christmas themed. Melissa wore mini-bauble earrings and a dress trimmed with fur. The vicar let them spray the length of the aisle with fake snow. At the reception there was a whole turkey on each table, with crackers. As for the cake, it was an almost life-sized chocolate Christmas log, decorated with fake robins. Perfect.

'Has the doctor let you down, then?' I asked. Perhaps she'd booked some dodgy East European medic you see on those documentaries called things like "Plastic Surgery Holidays from Hell: How My Nipples Fell Off".

'Doctor? No, my lovely nail lady, Sandra, is doing it.' She sighed. 'Don't know what I'd do without that women, she's more like a counsellor, the problems she's helped me talk through whilst she's filed and buffed. Anyway, no, it's far worse than that. The top-notch catering I'd ordered – a small exclusive company run by a chef who used to work at Claridge's… He's pulled out.'

'Oh.' Naughty of me, wasn't it, to feel disappointed that her upset wasn't caused by a more sensational story? But I was used to her living her life in the headlines. I wanted the excitement of affairs, drug problems, surgery gone wrong or – every girl's nightmare – cellulite, weight gain and spots. 'That's bad luck,' I said and tried to sound sympathetic. Adam would have told her to get a life and do the cooking herself.

Melissa shook her head. 'People nowadays, it's all me, me, me. Just because his mother died suddenly last night. I mean, I'm only asking for one afternoon out of the week.'

Footsteps approached and Luke walked past with his toolbox whilst I digested her news. Er, she did sound just a bit insensitive. I squirmed, trying to ignore the possibility that one of my favourite celebrities wasn't perfect after all.

Melissa scrolled through the contacts on her phone. 'There's no way I'm cancelling. It took me long enough to get some of those wrinklies to agree to come.' She caught my eye and gave a nervous giggle. 'I mean, those lovely ladies are so busy with their charity work and families, they don't have time to look after themselves properly,' cooed her velvet tones. 'I was thrilled to finally find a date they could all make. I'm trying to move them into the twenty-first century and make them more on trend.

On trend. I loved that expression. Yet if I used it I'd sound like Eliza Doolittle trying her luck at being the Speaking Clock.

'God knows it took long enough to get the national birdies to wear matching jackets, like the Americans,' continued Melissa. She sighed. 'The Ryder Cup will be here before I know it. I'll have to start my pre-tournament diet. You know, the last fancy lunch I went to was at the house of the team's brightest new player, Jason Lafont. His wife…'

'Alexandra?' I'd seen her in one of those more traditional magazines full of recipes, short stories and adverts for clothes with elasticated waists. Mrs Lafont was a more natural version of Melissa, with strawberry blonde waves and natural curves. Much as I admired Melissa's dedication to her appearance, I'd never have implants, not since reading they could burst on an aeroplane or if you sneezed really loud.

'Yes. Alexandra,' she said, as Luke appeared at the front door. 'She put on miniature fish 'n' chips in specially made newspaper cones. It was salmon, of course, with sweet potato wedges, balsamic vinegar and pesto ketchup on the side. It was all anyone talked about for weeks afterwards.'

'Try Kimmy's cupcakes,' said Luke, as he strode past, heading towards his van. 'They're up there with Mr Kipling's; *exceedingly* good.'

Huh? So now he was being nice?

'I don't think so.' She pressed dial on her phone. 'Hi Charlotte,' she said. 'Did I ever phone to say those canapés we had at your Wimbledon party were out of this world? Hmm. Yes, really super. In fact, I was wondering, what's the name of your caterer? Really?' Melissa pulled a face. 'Gosh, clever old you! Oh, my taxi's arrived, must dash. Let's lunch some time. Byeee!' She ended the call. 'Ghastly woman,' she muttered. 'Teeth as yellow as custard. I can't believe she does her own baking.' She fanned her face as Luke started the van's engine and drove off.

'Why don't you come inside?' I said. 'I've just made a fresh batch of cakes. I cater for parties and can do any flavour you like.'

'You run your own cupcake company?'

'Yes,' I said, with more confidence than I felt. Well I did. I'd been paid for my work and I was the boss. 'I've catered widely for children's parties, weddings…' Okay, only one, but still. Adam would be proud – here I was, pushing my business forward. Except Melissa was looking at her phone again… I took a deep breath.

'Our current, um, specials are all to do with Christmas. Like Cranberry and Orange, Merry Berry and Mouthwatering Mincemeat,' I gushed. 'There's also a, um, skinny range for the health-conscious.' Did I sound entrepreneurial? I hoped so – this was the chance of a lifetime. Imagine me, catering for the Winsfords? Perhaps OK Magazine would do a photo shoot. I'd have to get some business cards done. If Jess was off work, she could waitress and… Another deep breath. 'Then there's our regular alcoholic range,' I continued, 'including Pina Colada surprises topped with Malibu flavoured buttercream icing and popping candy, and coffee cakes decorated with, um, Baileys whipped cream, plus festive Port and Orange. Then there are the fun ones,' I said, thinking back to the kids' parties I'd catered for, 'decorated with green and red sprinkles, marzipan Santas and snowmen…'

'I suppose a look wouldn't hurt.' The phone went back into her handbag. 'After all. I am desperate.'

My knees shook. I'd invited the star of all my magazines in for a coffee and cake and she'd said yes!

CHAPTER 9

'I wish now I'd put a dress code on the invitation: no sleeveless blouses.' Melissa shuddered. 'A couple of the golfers' wives don't even shave under their arms.'

I waved at Terry as I turned to close the front door. He was driving past in his cream Beetle.

Melissa craned her neck to look into Walter's lounge. 'Cute. Very homely.' Her tone shouted "boring and bland".

I pointed past the staircase. 'The kitchen's through there.' As she led the way, I ogled her thin thighs. 'Do you do your DVD every day?'

'Mine? You've got to be jok… Ahem. Yes, of course I do.' She turned around and beamed. 'If I'm not too busy. What with my massage appointments, nails and hair, then there's the sessions with my personal trainer, three times a week – and that's only if I'm not speeding up to London to have lunch with Lucy Locklove.'

Lucy Locklove! She was only my all-time fave TV presenter!

'It's hard work being a national sportsman's wife. Even on holidays I have to be well turned out, because of the paparazzi. For our last spring break in Barbados I bought ten bikinis.'

I pointed to the breakfast table and scraped my hair back into a scrunchie that was in my jeans' pocket. Melissa brushed some crumbs off a stool and sat down. Didn't she have just the perfect life? The golfer's wife had matched all my expectations about celebritydom. I couldn't wait to see inside her home.

'Do you see much of the national birdies?' I said as she rested her bag on her lap. I put one of the mincemeat brandy butter cakes on a plate and passed it over.

'Only when the tournaments are on. I'm still a bit new to the group. Luke Donald doesn't live far away, though. His wife's really into art…'

'Diana Donald's gorgeous-looking,' I muttered. During the Open, Starchat had done a page on the best-dressed golfers' wives.

'It's her Greek roots,' said Melissa and shrugged. 'Ian Poulter's wife, Katie, is okay too; used to be a nurse.'

'They sound… normal,' I said. 'Not like footballers' wives.'

'I suppose most are – although Sam Torrance's wife used to be a film star. Another is a show jumper.'

I wondered what Melissa used to do. The magazines never spoke about that.

'Napkin?' she said.

'Of course.' Oh dear. Kitchen roll would have to do.

She picked up the cake and smelt the buttercream icing before prodding the marzipan holly leaf with a long nail. Then she took the biggest bite ever and, in slow motion, chewed. I took this opportunity to scrutinise, up close, the first celebrity I'd seen for real. She had a smooth forehead, no crow's feet, manicured nails, non-existent roots, tattooed eyebrows in an immaculate arc and spotless skin, as well as full lips, perfectly outlined and glossed. What a goddess. The camera *didn't* lie, not if you had access to all the top cosmetic procedures and products.

'Try this,' I said and passed her one of the Cranberry and Orange ones I'd made at Adam's. But I almost dropped it

upside down when she put the kitchen roll to her lips and…
Did she spit out my cake?

'Is there a bin in here?' she asked and I pointed to one
of the cupboards. Had I been fooling myself? Were my
non-celebrity friends and family too kind to tell me that
actually, my cooking was pants?

She helped herself to another piece of kitchen roll and
took a big mouthful of the Cranberry and Orange one, then
did exactly the same again – chewed slowly, before spitting
it out.

'They are fabulous – with the light texture, irresistible
flavours and so pretty.'

'But you… I mean I thought… You spat them out!'

'Spat?' she looked shocked. 'Goodness, no! That's a
trick I learnt from the American wives. It's just a different
way of eating – none of the calories but all the taste.' She
sighed. 'I love those girls, over the ocean. What amazing
lifestyles… They've all got indoor cinemas and outdoor
barbeques the size of your average council flat. The
captain's wife, Tulisa, has just got planning permission
for an underground nightclub at their ranch. And talk
about great hair, sensational nails… Rumour has it, they
all even co-ordinate their underwear. Whereas the English
birdies…' She grimaced. 'Once we were trying on some
free jogging outfits, a sponsor handed out – a couple of
them don't even match their own bras and knickers.'

'Really?' I gasped. Surely everyone followed that rule?
They needed to buy my bible, Cut-Above-Couture. God
forbid they wore tights with open-toed sandals or black
with navy or brown.

'They haven't even all had Brazilian waxes,' she
continued. 'How unhygienic is that? But then I suppose
they've had an uphill struggle, this side of the Atlantic.
I try to tell myself it isn't their fault, if they think we

should look inconspicuous. It's all that British tradition, all that Old Boys stuff.'

'Huh?'

'Women are to be seen but not heard at the golf club. It's a haven for the men. Some still won't serve anything in a skirt at the bar, unless it's tartan and hiding more than a frilly thong.'

'Well, I'm sure the local golf wives will love the Botox.' The most generous thing I'd laid on for my friends was a night of chick flicks and face packs.

Melissa half-smiled. 'I'd better get going. Jonny's bringing his son home for supper.

'His ex-wife lives near, doesn't she?' I said, hoping my knowledge would prove myself a real fan.'

'Jeanie?' Melissa's voice went funny. 'Yes. Lovely lady. Done, um, a great job of bringing up Eddie. He's very polite for a teenager.'

All the magazines said how well Melissa got on with the first Mrs Winsford. Amazing, really, since Jonny left Jeanie for her.

'Anyway, must go, darling. They'll be home toot sweet.'

Ooh, I wished I could speak French like that.

'So,' she said. 'Tomorrow? Are you free?'

Oh my God. She was going to invite me round for lunch!

'Um…'

'Get your people to speak with my people,' she said.

'That would be great!' I said and beamed. Oops. Reality check. 'Um, except that I don't have "people" – I… I prefer to sort stuff out myself.'

'Really?' She pulled a face. 'Okay. Let's say half past nine sharp. My guests will be here at ten.'

How exciting! What would I wear? And… Huh? Guests? Ah. I got the impression that didn't include me. But yay! Cue a mental image of me jumping up and down! That meant I'd got a catering contract, for a bunch of ladies being treated to Botox. But boo! It didn't give me long to prepare.

'How many are going?' I asked, forcing my voice to steady.

'Six wives.' She yawned. 'Let's see if I can remember all the details: the captain's wife, Vivian, sixty-ish… one of the few wives who plays golf. Her best friend Pamela, who's also heading for retirement…' I listened as Melissa gave descriptions of all the guests. 'And finally Saffron…' She wrinkled her nose.

'Saffron?' I grinned. 'Haven't cooked with that for a while. You don't like her?'

'Bit of a bitch. In my position, three types of ordinary people step into my world: those *in* awe, those *in*different and those *in*sanely jealous, like Saffron. Her boyfriend, Steve, is a new member. They recently got engaged. He gets on well with Jonny. She's a receptionist, in a car sales room, I think, and always loaded with some snidey comment. At the Centenary Ball last month she praised me loudly for wearing last season's shoes, what with the recession. Then she questioned what I did all day, whilst most of the other wives work. I only invited her tomorrow because the others seem to like her. She's very young; brings out the older women's maternal instincts. Jonny thinks I mad for asking her.'

'Why?'

'He must have heard her digs about me not having a proper career. He knows how much time it takes networking and supporting everything he does.' She beamed. 'So, enough about her. I'm looking forward to a good selection of cupcakes – and yes, a Christmas theme would be fab. Maybe a few skinnies. Everyone's driving so cut the alcohol.' She put on her shades. 'Although, no –

why should I miss out? Those Pina Colada ones sounded good. Nothing beats the flavour of a cocktail. Maybe call them Santa Coladas…'

'But I haven't told you how much they cost…' I said, practically clapping my hands.

She peered over the top of her glasses. 'Money is no object. By the way, what's your baking company called?'

'KimCakes Ltd.' I'd seen this name a million times, on the side of my imaginary delivery van.

'Let me write down my landline and mobile numbers for you – I'd rather you ring than call at the house, if you've any questions.'

I grabbed a notepad and biro Jess had left on the kitchen unit and gave them to her.

'That's awesome writing,' I said, as her delicate hand expertly guided the pen.

'Thanks,' she said and stood up. 'I once did a course in calligraphy. It always impresses when writing out party invitations.'

We went into the hallway and I opened the front door.

'I don't need to say to look smart… Ciao.' Catwalk-style, she and her size six legs sauntered off, down the drive, crocodile handbag swinging from side to side.

I closed the door and did a little jig around the hallway. Tonight I'd Google cupcakes and find out the going price. I glanced at my watch: one o'clock – I had to get back to the supermarket, there was no time for lunch. I hurtled into the kitchen, grabbed the last Cranberry and Orange cupcake and scrabbled around for my car keys, accidentally knocking Jess's list of jobs onto the floor. I'd tidy up later. Taking a large bite of sweet yumminess, I headed outdoors.

By three o'clock I'd returned and after letting Groucho out to kid himself he could catch a pigeon, I set out my extra ingredients: flour (wholemeal and plain), sugar (icing and caster), butter (low-fat and normal) and eggs (large). Then there was a tub of glacé cherries, chocolate bars, a bottle of Malibu, marzipan… a whole variety of toppings and flavours.

Phew! I rolled up my sleeves, grabbed the mixing bowl from earlier and studied the array of items for a while, before weighing out the ingredients for the first of five small batches. The completed menu would include:

Miniature dark chocolate logs cakes, filled with a rich chocolate cream and dusted with icing sugar.

Skinny Stollen slices, made from a light fruity dough and topped with low-fat almond buttercream icing.

The rich mincemeat cupcakes, topped with brandy buttercream icing and a green marzipan holly leaf with red berries.

Uncomplicated wholemeal cinnamon and spice muffins, for any guests who suffer from indigestion.

The Pina – I mean, *Santa* – Colada Surprises consisting of pineapple juice flavoured cake, filled with popping candy with Malibu buttercream icing and a sprinkling of "snow" (dessicated coconut).

Three hours later, I gazed around the kitchen, my work finished, face sweaty and arms tired. Flour had showered down my clothes and across the floor. I could feel butter around my ear and suspected my lips might have been stained with dark chocolate. But then, a good chef always tastes .what they're cooking. The breakfast island was cluttered with open jars and packets, plus a puddle of almond essence and red colouring. The sink was stacked high with dirty cutlery, pans stained with melted chocolate and measuring jugs smelling of Malibu. Before I could tackle any tidying up, I needed a strong coffee.

Ten minutes later, I sat down on one of the stools and gazed at my cakes with pride. A burst of music interrupted my self-congratulations and I walked into the hallway. The festive notes floated down from upstairs… Wait a minute. It was that classic song, White Christmas… It made me feel all dreamy myself, although it set Groucho off as he ran around the hallway, wagging his tail and yapping.

I crept upstairs. It was coming from the left hand front room. I tried the door handle which was well and truly locked. I shivered. The air had turned cold, as if the heating wasn't really turned on. As the music faded, I returned to the kitchen. Whatever. I hadn't got time to investigate Mistletoe Mansion's strange happenings. The black clock ticked to six and the front door slammed. I went back into the hallway. Jess wouldn't believe the day I'd had. And it hadn't finished yet. I still had business cards to make. Tomorrow I had to network, network, network!

Except Jess didn't look like she wanted to talk… And that wasn't just because of her red swollen nose and streaming eyes, still suffering with a cold. Instead she threw down her hessian carrier bag, slipped out of her trainers and let her thick winter coat drop to the floor. She sank down onto the bottom of the stairs. Muddy stains streaked her jeans and dust covered her bottle green "Nuttall's Garden Centre" shirt.

'Drink?' I asked.

She shook her head.

'What's the matter?'

'Ry… Ry….' She sneezed loudly and blew her nose. 'Ryan came into work; told me he'd stored a lot of my stuff away in the loft.'

'That's a bit quick.'

'Apparently some bloke from his work is moving in. Ryan says he's about to live the bachelor life he's always dreamed of. You know, bin overflowing with empty beer cans, take-away pizza boxes piled high and used as foot rests.' She shrugged. 'This housesitting job has really got to work for us, Kimmy. We need to stay here long enough to sort something else out. I've rung a couple of friends but one's got her sister staying with her at the moment and the other said her landlord would go mad if she let anyone stay longer than one night.' Jess plucked some sticky seeds from her sleeve. 'At least you're here all day, to keep things running smoothly and work through our lists of jobs. If Mr Murphy has no complaints, we should be here for at least a couple of weeks.'

Ah. That list of jobs. I wasn't even quite sure where it was.

'Although Deborah's message was a bit worrying,' said Jess and wiped her nose. 'But then we owe it to her to do our best.'

'Huh?'

'You know – I jotted it down for you, on the list. It was on the answerphone this morning; those prospective buyers coming around as soon as tomorrow, after lunch. That's why I wrote down for you to clean the Games Room and lounge – close up, both are dead dusty. Then the dining room table needed polishing and all of the bathrooms needed a going over. The last housesitter clearly didn't stay long – parts of this place haven't been touched for weeks.'

I fixed a smile to my face. Surely she'd understand; I'd been too busy – this was my business at stake. And how long would it take anyway, to do a bit of tidying up?

She got to her feet. 'Time to keep my end of the bargain now, anyway, and give both the borders a going over, get outside and tidy up the straggly weeds. I hope that shed out the back is unlocked.' Her eyes scoured my clothes for a second. 'You've been baking? You should have done that tomorrow morning, the smell might have helped sell this place.' She turned and headed into the kitchen. 'Good thinking, though. I'm starving. So, what is it today? Chocolate? Nutty? Dolly Mixture?'

She gasped as we entered the kitchen.

'Um… It won't take me long to tidy up. You see I was talking to Melissa – she's got a party tomorrow – needed someone to take over the catering. She tasted my cupcakes and well… how could I say no? It… it was urgent. And we want to get on with the neighbours, don't we?'

Crimson in the face, Jess glared at me. 'Are you crazy? Does this mean you've done none of the jobs?' She bobbed forwards and picked something off the ground. It was her list. 'You haven't even stocked up properly, I mean just look at all these items – how the hell did you pay for this stuff?'

'Out of my own pocket. I'll earn it all back tomorrow and more. She said money was no object.'

'This do, tomorrow, it's for charity, then?' she muttered.

'Kind of…' I shuffled from foot to foot. 'Well, that's what I'd call it. She's offering some old biddies free Botox.'

'You've jeopardised our first proper duty in this house, showing people around, so that a bunch of women can inject poison into their wrinkles?'

'It's not like that… This was too good an opportunity to miss! You understand don't you, Jess? Think how impressed Adam will be if I make some real money and contacts and bring in more orders–'

'How impressed do you think he'll be if we get thrown out before we've started the job?' She shook her head. 'So now, after a day on my feet, not only have I got to garden front and back, I'll have to help you clean all those rooms? It'll take ages to sort all this out into the relevant recycling bins.'

'I can manage.'

'What? In between hobnobbing with the neighbours and making marzipan berries?' She jerked her head towards the puddle of red colouring. 'Have you any idea how difficult that is to get off?' She banged her fist on the breakfast table. 'Maybe Adam was right! You're totally irresponsible! If we lose this place we'll be out on the street. How could you be so selfish?' she gulped.

'Jess, calm down,' I stuttered. I'd never seen her like this before.

'Calm down?' She picked up a half-empty bag of flour, plunged in her fingers and lobbed a handful at my head. 'Hey, this is fun, isn't it? Let's make as much mess as we can.' She brandished the bottle of red food colouring.

'No... not my... hair,' I screamed, in between spitting out flour. Too late. And peroxide was so absorbent. Jess picked up one batch of perfect muffins, rushed to the patio doors, slid them open and–

'No, Jess! You may as well put a gun to my head and shout pull!'

She gazed at me. Her lip quivered. Was that a *sob*?

'What's the matter?' I hurried over and prised the wire rack from her fingers. I put it on the worktop. We both sat down. A fat tear plopped onto her shirt and I tucked a random strand of hair behind her ear. 'Is it Ryan? Or work?' My voice sounded alien due to the flour having dried it out. 'You can tell me, Jess,' I said, softly, chest squeezing. I'd never seen my bestie this upset before. 'Whatever it is, I'll help you sort it. That's what best friends are for.'

'How?' she sobbed. 'Can you wind back time?'

'What do you mean?'

Her shoulders shook. 'You'll think me so dumb, Kimmy. I'm pregnant!'

CHAPTER 10

Breathe, Kimmy, breathe. In and out. Inhale, exhale...
Look at me, already practising to help Jess with her
contractions. I stared at my best mate, a crumpled mess.
Jess. Pregnant. As a baker, there had to be some witticism
I could make about a bun in the oven. But joking was the
last thing on my mind. My heart pounded at the thought
of a baby growing inside her stomach. This was serious,
grown-up stuff. Life-changing. I opened my mouth to talk
but words wouldn't come out. Instead I reached out and
squeezed Jess's arm.

'It'll be okay,' I said, eventually. 'We'll get through this.'

'How?' she wailed. 'I couldn't afford a week's nappies,
let alone a cot or pram on my current wages.'

My eyes filled at the sight of sensible, level-headed Jess
sobbing like I did at the wrong time of the month. I shook
myself. Get a grip, for Jess's sake. I focused, for a second,
on the rows of cakes I'd made for Melissa. Like a herbalist
or naturopath, I decided which was the best to lift Jess's
spirits.

Which to choose? The Santa Coladas? No, not alcohol,
in her condition. And was popping candy even safe, in the
early stage of the pregnancy? Maybe Jess would be better
off with the plain, un-iced cinnamon spice ones. After
all, lots of women got bad indigestion when expecting
a baby.

'Here…' I guided Jess to one of the stools and put the plate in front of her. She opened her mouth to speak.

'Shh!' I said. 'Don't talk. Just eat for a moment.'

She sniffed loudly and, like a small child, did as I said. After a few mouthfuls, one solitary tear trickled down her cheek. But cakes were a girl's best medicine – whether it was to comfort a broken heart or ease nerves before an important appointment. I poured myself a glass of water. I'd never seen Jess so angry, chucking flour into my mouth and colouring into my hair. At least it was red and not some way out colour like green or blue or … Blue? Wait a minute – had she even done a pregnancy test?

There had to be some mistake, I thought, as I watched crumbs tumble down her chin. This was the girl who'd grilled Miss during school sex lessons and asked if two condoms were safer than one (the answer's "no", due to more friction). I passed her a square of kitchen roll as she ate the last mouthful.

'You're more in need of a tidy up,' she said and wiped her mouth. 'Sorry. I … don't know what came over me.'

I forced my lips to upturn before sliding the red food colouring down to the other end of the table. 'Just in case.'

She half-smiled back.

'Have you done a test?' I asked, gently.

'Yes. I nipped to the chemist on my lunch break and bought one of those fancy kits that tells you how far gone you are – eight weeks, it said.' Her voice wobbled. 'I was sick again this morning at work. Thought nothing about it until Dalek gave me the evils and asked if there was something I needed to tell her.'

Jess and her colleagues called Dana, their boss, Dalek behind her back, because, like those monsters from Doctor Who, she spoke in a flat, monotonous voice and made everything sound like a threat.

'You were sick yesterday morning, right? But I thought that was some veggie burger you'd eaten?'

'Obviously not. And I've taken up chewing gum the last month, because recently I'm always hungry. Then I remembered Mum saying that you're supposed to get that pregnancy nesting instinct, when you go mad cleaning, towards the end, not the start like she always did.'

'So?'

'Me, cleaning Ryan's bedroom on a Saturday morning? Usually not even I'm that keen. I obviously take after Mum.'

'Right…' Mustn't ask about the dad; not yet. Don't do it.

'So now you know why I lost it… This house is more important than ever at the moment. When it was just me living at his, Ryan found it too much. He won't want a mini-me hanging around as well. In any event, that bloke's moving in and–'

'You know I'm here for you. We'll get through this. Together.'

She shrugged. 'I can manage on my own. I'll have to.'

'Don't be silly. That's what best friends are for.'

'I said I'm fine,' she snapped.

I bit my lip. Okay, she was still in shock – as was I. A pit formed in the centre of my stomach. This was what Adam wanted – kids, a domestic future together. But even if I was married, with a regular job and mortgage to boot, the thoughts flashing through my mind of how Jess's life was about to change, made me realise… I just wasn't ready for any of that. An unsettling flutter in my chest made me question… Much as I wanted Adam back, in the long run, was it for the best?

'Of course I'm going to help,' I said firmly. 'Haven't we always looked out for each other? Like the time Mum was rushed into hospital with stomach ache. You met me there and supplied me with coffees whilst I listened to the doctors…' They told her, for the hundredth time, to clean up her lifestyle.

Jess's voice broke. 'Like when I broke up with Phil…'

Hmm, her latest boyfriend and, I guessed, the imminent father.

'You dropped everything and came round to Ryan's. We spent the whole night talking, watching rubbish TV and eating popcorn.' She bit her lip. 'But this is different… My mess… I… I must stand on my own two feet.'

'Well, I'll always think of myself as the kid's slightly bonkers aunt-in-waiting. Unless… I mean, you've still got options…'

Jess bit her thumbnail.

'There's no need to rush into anything,' I continued, gently, 'but if–'

'I'm having it.'

As I knew she would. Jess kept stick insects as a child and, to her mum's annoyance, wouldn't even throw out the masses of eggs before they hatched.

'Then, I'll be with you every step of the way – even if you use those eco-friendly reusable nappies.'

'I'll be a very environmentally-friendly mum – especially as, on my budget, most of the baby's stuff will have to come from secondhand shops.' She gave another big sniff. 'You don't want a best mate who's carrying a kid around the whole time. Admit it. You think I'm a joke.' Her chin wobbled.

I got up and put my arm around her, shards of pain piercing my chest as her eyes swelled, all red. If only I could wave a magic Harry Potter wand and turn back time a couple of months, for her. 'This is hormones, Jess. You aren't thinking straight. The rational you knows I'm one

hundred percent behind you. And what about the dad…?'
Okay, I know I wasn't going to mention him but the sooner
Jess faced the realities of how she was going to manage
financially, the better. 'Whoever he is, I mean, not that I'm
expecting you to confirm anything, but…'

'*Whoever he is*? I can still reach that red food colouring,'
she muttered.

She had a point. Phil was the only bloke it could be.
Jess only slept with guys she'd fallen for and it wasn't
long since she'd split with Phil, the married bastard who'd
promised to leave the wife when his twins grew up – they'd
just started pre-school.

'Will you tell your mum and dad?' I asked.

'Not yet.'

'Ryan?'

'No way!' She stood up too. 'Look… Can we drop the
subject for the moment? I… I need to get my head around
it – weeding the borders will do me good. You tidy up in
here – don't forget to sort out all the bits for recycling
but… thanks, Kimmy.'

I smoothed down her rumpled hair and leant forwards –
cue an awkward hug that hopefully made her feel a titch
better. Then the doorbell rang. Jess escaped out onto the
back patio and I scooted to the front. My eyes tingled. Poor
Jess. The way her chin wobbled. Her blotchy red eyes.
With a sniff, I opened the door.

Diamond shapes printed on a pink jumper and a coral
cap greeted me. Terry had just about managed to tuck his
top into his tight grey slacks.

'Oh my God!' I said. 'Aren't you just the cutest thing?
With those tiny legs, that snub nose and such small, perky
ears… You're so well-groomed!' No, I wasn't hitting on
Terry, I was talking to…   'Frazzle?' I asked. 'You named it
after bacon crisps?'

His eyes twinkled.

'It's so tiny!' I looked down towards the end of the red lead.

'Yes – that's the point; *she*'s a *micro*-pig.'

I ran my hand along the black skin and gazed into the huge, trusting eyes. This was living the high life! Back in Luton, Frazzle would have been ribs on the barbeque before you could say oink. She was hardly bigger than my novelty pig oven gloves.

'Now the introductions are over, may I ask, is everything is all right? There was, um, some yelling earlier – I couldn't help overhearing something about putting a gun to someone's head.'

Heat crept up my neck as I swung back to Terry. 'Soz about that. Me and Jess – a little argument. And we've got all this work to do, before some prospective buyers arrive tomorrow.'

'Anything I can do?'

'Oh, no thanks,' I said unconvincingly, thinking about all the chores ahead of me, before bed – like scrubbing the kitchen, vacuuming and dusting. Then there was bathroom after bathroom to clean…'

'Come on, Frazzle,' Terry said and barged past me. 'Let's help these two girls settle in.' From under his arm he took a folded up magazine and waved it in the air. 'I brought you that copy of Starchat. It's the one that talks about Melissa's school reunion.' He winked. 'There are also some pretty hot pictures of Jonny. Page twenty-three.' He stood still for a moment and breathed in. 'Something smells good. Wow.' He'd reached the kitchen and took off his coral cap to reveal a bald head, carefully avoiding any spillages as he put it on the table. He let out a low whistle. 'Someone's been busy.'

'I'm cooking for Melissa. She's invited some wives around from the local golf club. The party's tomorrow and the caterers have let her down.'

'You're a professional cakemaker?' he asked.

'Yes,' I said. The more times I told people that, the more it seemed true.

'What a pity it's not the real birdies coming.' His eyes widened. 'Wouldn't you just love to meet the latest girlfriend to join the crowd, Tracy Clifford? Did you see–'

'Last week's Infamous?' I interrupted. 'I know – that white dust around her nose looked a bit suspicious.'

'She insisted it was face powder.' Terry grinned. 'She won't last long on that stuffy circuit. Ah well, I still expect all the goss. There might be someone famous there so I want all the details – what they wear, how much they eat.'

'Melissa showed me this trick,' I said and started to put the cakes into Tupperware boxes. 'It involves chewing food for just a few seconds, then spitting it–'

'Kimmy?' Jess appeared at the patio doors and frowned at Terry.

'Nice to meet you, sweetie,' he said and stretched out a podgy arm. 'I live next door. The name's Terry and this is my better half – Frazzle.'

Jess's tearstained eyes lit up as soon as she spotted the miniature pig sniffing some flour on the kitchen floor.

Terry picked up the animal and handed her to Jess. 'She gets on well with Groucho and if you tie her to Walter's weeping willow, she'll be as happy as a pig in… well…'

Jess tickled behind Frazzle's ears. 'I'll start the borders,' she called over her shoulder and disappeared outside.

'Nice girl,' said Terry and helped me force down a Tupperware lid. He glanced sideways at me. 'Is she all right? I'm a good listener, you know.'

I shook my head, not daring to open my mouth in case I broke Jess's confidence and the whole pregnancy thing slipped out.

'Well, if you change your mind…'

'Thanks, Terry – I appreciate it,' I said, managing to leave it at that.

He fiddled with something underneath the base of a cupboard. Suddenly classical music blasted into the room. He re-tuned it to some disco channel.

'Cool radio,' I said.

But Terry didn't hear. Dishcloth at the ready, his ample hips rocked jerkily to some retro soul groove. As he filled the dishwasher and scraped remnants of butter and sprinkles into the bin, his breathing became laboured. I tried to work out his age. Late fifties perhaps? It was difficult to say as there were hardly any wrinkles on his chubby face. Certainly not much older than the oldest of Mum's boyfriends.

I offered Terry a random chunk of chocolate from the worktop, but he mouthed the words "no" and "cholesterol". Then he continued to fill the machine, doing the John Travolta point in between each item, stepping side to side and jiggling his bottom.

Glad to see Jess digging outside, with a more cheerful face, I headed upstairs to the bedrooms with a bucket of cleaning products, kitted out to clean my shower, the mint green bathroom and Jess's ensuite. By the time I'd rinsed out the last sink, my arms ached and I needed a cold drink. It had been quite cathartic and I'd kind of put Jess's bombshell into perspective. Every day women got pregnant. That was life – messy and unpredictable with shiny jewels of happiness sometimes coming out of the darkest spots. She and me, we'd manage somehow. I'd be the best aunt I could. We'd get as much equipment as we could from charity shops and fingers crossed my baking earnings would help.

As my eye caught sight of the laptop, when I passed the office, I bobbed in to enjoy a quick social media catch-up. Waiting for me on Facebook was one poke, as well as three messages. Someone had also sent me a puffer fish for my virtual aquarium. Adam had always refused point blank to become a member; said it was childish and a waste of time.

My eyes scoured my homepage. Susie had got tickets to see Bruno Mars! Mandy was still recovering from that hen weekend. Callum had lost his wallet, Zoe was eating a sandwich in Oxford Street and Chelsea had changed her profile picture. But best of all… I could hardly believe it… India off Celebrity Chastity Challenge had accepted me as a friend!

As the vacuuming downstairs stopped, I wondered what news to share with my online friends. Normally my Facebook status would include some link to my favourite cute animal YouTube clip, a new cupcake recipe or the latest celebrity goss. However, this time my friends would be well impressed. Quickly I typed: "Am baking for Melissa Winsford!" I snapped shut the laptop and headed towards the top of the stairs. Terry shouted my name and feeling pleased with myself, I breathed in the fresh smells of bleach and ceramic cleaner, wafting out of every room.

I was about to go down when… Oh God… That White Christmas music played again. I shivered and goosebumps broke out on my arms. Although there was no smoke or sound of whooshing gales…

I know someone's there and I'm not frightened, you know, I said in my head, even though, chest heaving, I was rooted to the spot. Racking my brains for phrases from Most Haunted, I concentrated hard. *Knock three times if you mean no harm.*

'Kimmy?' called up Terry, from the Games of Thrones Room (still think of it as that). I paused, mouth dry, eyes wide open. Then bolted towards the staircase, down to the comfort of human company. The music had stopped now, anyway.

I opened the door and there amidst the racing green walls and mahogany panels sat my new neighbour and Jess. My shoulders relaxed. They were at the bar, drinking… some yucky muddy drink. Terry slid a murky cocktail down to the stool next to Jess.

'What's in this?' I asked, making my way around the billiards table. At least it had one of those brollies in that I'd bought.

'Half orange juice and half… half…' Jess sneezed. 'Cola. We were thirsty and Terry suggested this. It's called a Muddy Water.'

'I tried to persuade Jess to let me nip home for some champagne,' said Terry and took out a handkerchief to wipe his perspiring cheeks. Frazzle was curled up at the foot of the stool. Groucho was standing guard, ready to be the first to claim any fallen crisps. I shoved a Pringle in my mouth. They were Adam's favourite flavour. We used to challenge each other to eat them sideways.

'How about you, Kimmy? A spot of champers?'

'Better not, Terry – I've still got to sort out the hallway and downstairs loo and maybe give the windows the once over too.' I looked out of the front window and right at the bottom of the drive spotted two cute copper-coloured dogs trotted past on leads, long hair shimmying from side to side. 'Borders look good, Jess.' The sun was setting. Sunday night. Adam would have just got back from the gym, ready to sit next to me on the sofa and watch his favourite detective series.

'What time are these buyers arriving tomorrow?' asked Terry.

'One o'clock,' said Jess. 'Deborah, the estate agent, is coming this time too. Just to see how we've settled in. Spying for Mr Murphy, I guess.'

'Great dress sense, that woman,' said Terry. 'I've seen her several times. Fabulous shoes.'

'Did you see much of Mr Murphy, Terry?' I asked. 'He must have been close to Walter, to get this place. Is he married?'

Terry sipped his cocktail again. 'No. Single – Walter mentioned a long-term relationship that broke down. I met him a few times, during those last months. It's a long way to come from Manchester – his mum, Walter's sister, moved there when she got married. He seemed a decent sort – took Walter out to country pubs and would shout him a round of golf. Walter and Lily didn't have any other younger relatives – Mike was their only nephew. Not that there was much of a family resemblance. Mike was a bit flash for the old man's taste – you know, chunky jewellery, dyed hair. But they discussed politics and world news together.' Terry grinned. 'Right until the end, Walter was as sharp as they come, despite his series of strokes.'

'Strokes?'

Terry ran a hand over his bald head. 'The effects of them were largely physical. No one ever took Walter for a fool. I remember the week before his last funny turn, he gave the postman a hard time for leaving a parcel out in the rain.' Terry shrugged. 'Eh, listen to me wittering on... So, I wonder if Jonny will be at this Botox party tomorrow morning, supporting his wife.'

'I don't think so.' Which was such a disappointment. I could have sneaked a photo of him on my phone. Uploading that onto Facebook would have guaranteed me a hundred friend requests... Jonny topless from the shower, Adam furious when the photo got leaked to the press... The headline would read: "Jealous Ex accuses The Eagle of preying upon young housesitter, Kimmy."

'I've got to be at Melissa's for half past nine,' I said and shook myself back to reality. 'I'll get up early to give the place the last once-over. It's your day off tomorrow, Jess, right?'

She nodded.

'Well, you have a lie-in, I'll make sure everything looks spotless before I'm off. I should be back before twelve and then I'll cook you–'

She glared. 'I'm fine.'

Terry flicked through some CDs behind the bar. He rolled his eyes. 'One of the few things Walter and I disagreed on was our taste in music. Give me Michael Jackson or The O'Jays any day. Whereas Walter was into classical and what he called cosy "Fireside music". Terry cocked his head. 'What was his favourite now…' He picked up a Christmas Greats CD. 'That's it: Bing Crosby dreaming of a White Christmas. Jeez, he used to play that song at all times of the year. It may have been easy-listening for him, but not me!'

I almost dropped my Muddy Water. Oh my God – the music upstairs.

'He did like Bond music as well, though,' Terry continued, as he came across a CD with Sean Connery on the front.

Jess bit her thumbnail. 'Phil, my, um, last boyfriend… He was dead keen on all those Bond soundtracks and films. Plus he loved the old greats like Bing Crosby too.'

'Have you played that Christmas CD whilst we've been here, with the White Christmas track?' I asked Jess, a shudder running up my spine.

'You really think I want to remind myself of that married jerk?'

'Oh. Yeah. Sorry.' I swallowed hard. That only left one person – or entity – who could have played it, then.

'Everything okay, Kimmy?' Terry asked. 'You've gone a bit pale.'

I nodded and knocked back my drink, on automatic. So, the ghost, spook, astral being, whatever you wanted to call it, was Walter Carmichael. I shivered. How could I have not suspected this before? *Walter was haunting his own house.*

'Anyway, here's to you two girls,' said Terry and raised his glass. 'Hope you stay longer than your predecessors.' He glanced at his watch. 'I, um, hadn't realised it was so late. Better get going, girlies. Come on Frazzle. It's time for your sow nuts and then I'll make us both a nice fruit salad. Good luck tomorrow, girl.' He gave me a wink.

'Let me cook you something here, as a thanks for all your hard work,' I said, still digesting the revelation that Walter hadn't moved on to the next world. I followed Terry into the hall. Why was he suddenly in such a rush? It was as if he didn't like being out – or at least near this house – as night-time approached.

'Much, erm, as I'd like to, Frazzle doesn't like staying out late. It's been my pleasure though. Remember, I want all the goss from the Winsfords.' He took out a small golf pencil and marker book from his back pocket and scribbled down a number. 'Ring me when you get back.' Then he tucked Frazzle under his arm and quickly disappeared into the chilly evening air.

I closed the door and glanced towards the kitchen. I could hear Jess pottering about. She'd switched the radio back to classical. I tiptoed halfway up the stairs and stared at the front, locked bedroom. Dare I try to provoke Walter to show himself, just like they sometimes taunted spirits on Most Haunted? Last night's polite request for three knocks hadn't worked. Perhaps it was time to get tough. But what if he'd been turned evil and stole my soul or possessed my body? Knuckles white on my clenched fists, I gave it a go.

'I know who you are now, Walter,' I said, in a trembling voice, a wave of nausea rising up the back of my throat. 'Show yourself. What are you afraid of? Stop hiding behind your… your cheesy music and silly smoke screen. Why try to frighten me and Jess? Cos, newsflash! It isn't working. I've felt more startled by children calling at Halloween; more horror-struck by my hair after five minutes in the rain. Come on, Walter… Throw chairs around. Smash crockery. Do your worst! It's time to man up!'

CHAPTER 11

With an ear-splitting scream, I tumbled down the stairs. My back smacked onto the floor. Metallic-tasting liquid – blood obviously – trickled out of my mouth. Wind whirled around the hallway. Jess charged out of the kitchen and spotted me in a twisted heap, limbs lying at funny angles. White Christmas played loudly and thick smoke filled the air. 'Have mercy on me,' I begged, as ominous footsteps descended the stairs…

Nah. Not really. No such excitement. But that was what I imagined might happen, if this spooky Walter had any guts. Instead I was still talking to him in my head, a couple of hours later, stretched out, star-shaped, underneath silk crimson sheets, wishing I was wearing some equally exotic negligee, instead of my tatty old Hello Kitty pyjama bottoms and T-shirt. I didn't mention my revelation about the ghostly happenings to Jess – or the fact that I'd been locked in my room and nearly burnt to death. I figured she'd already got enough on her mind – a few minutes ago I crept onto the landing, to investigate some loud sniffs. But she must have heard me from her room, because when the floorboard creaked it went quiet. She'd cried again earlier, despite me cooking her favourite tofu and nut stir fry. The Jess I knew rarely did tears.

'It'll be okay,' I'd said, willing my eyes not to water as I brushed back her red fringe. The last time she'd blubbed like that was when her pet rabbit died in Year Five. Even then she'd put on a brave face, her designing a memorial plaque for the coffin (shoe box), me singing word-perfect *I Want You Back*, by N Sync.

'How will everything be all right?' she'd sobbed. 'There's no crèche at work. As it is, I barely earn enough to pay rent. Mum and Dad are enjoying retirement in Spain – I can't ruin everything for them. And Ryan can hardly look after himself, let alone a nephew or niece.' Then she'd gone all independent again – told me not to worry, and it was her problem, she'd sort it herself. Why, oh why, was she shutting me out?

I yawned and gazed around my – Lily's – bedroom. *Walter, maybe you could ditch the Christmas tune and play something more to Jess's taste*, I said in my head, all fear gone as he was clearly a figment of my imagination or too chicken to answer back. I pictured him as my fantasy Grandpa, seeing as I'd never had one all these years. He'd be smartly dressed, in a golf shirt of course, smell of cigars and perhaps wear a flat cap. He'd want to know all about my cake-making dreams, sit me down and dish out helpful advice.

Arms still aching from all that cleaning, I got up and plaited my hair. What luxurious surroundings, I thought, for the hundredth time, with the fancy carved dressing table and velvet curtains… I gazed at the oil painting of poppies before switching off my bedside light. I still wasn't used to the complete dark of Badgers Chase and missed the glow of street lamps and take-aways that always crept into Adam's flat. I'd done well to resist texting him, to resist begging him to take me back. Nor had I ruined my surprise by telling him about KimCakes Ltd finally taking off. No, I'd wait until tomorrow night when I could inform him, in business-like tones, of exactly how much I'd earned at Melissa's.

I yawned again and closed my eyes, missing the sound of Adam's heavy breaths. Yet, annoyingly, images of Luke crept into my mind. His floppy hair, those god awful cords, the way they showed off his… okay, he had a nice bum. Mmm, musky-smelling Luke, with his bristly cheeks, in a tight white vest, muscles flexing as he carried me out of a burning Mistletoe Mansion – me as light as a feather (I had to be dreaming), armed with a first aid kit full of cupcakes…

Wow! I woke with a jolt. That was some freaky dream. I sat up and leant against the luscious pillows and threw off the silk sheets and duvet. Perhaps I'd become too hot… Yeah, that was the only rational explanation for imagining moody Luke as some hero figure. Eyes wide open, fingers gripping the duvet, I strained to listen to every noise – was that an owl? There was a distant bark… I snuggled back down. What had woken me up? In Luton it was usually a low aeroplane or car alarm going off.

It was eerily quiet and despite my bravado about speaking to Walter, the night blackness spooked me a bit. I sniffed. What was that familiar sweet smell? I sat back up, suddenly cold with the December night air. The hairs stood up on my arms at the unexpected sound of rushing wind. According to my phone, it was half past twelve. I grabbed one of the purple embroidered cushions at the foot of the bed and gave it a big hug. Maybe Walter was a little bit ticked off at my earlier comments. *Come on, um, Mr Carmichael, I was only joking, play that Christmassy tune again, it's, um, kind of cool.* But that sweet smell only got stronger. I switched on the light. Uh oh – it was the smoke from earlier today, once again billowing under the door.

Every molecule of my being springing into action, I threw the cushion onto the floor and jumped out of bed. My phone fell onto the mattress. Again, like earlier, the door wouldn't budge. Yelling to wake up Jess, I pulled on the handle, hard. Then I heard banging noises from the adjoining front room as if someone – or something – was moving around. My heart knocked furiously against the inside of my chest.

'Fire! Jess! Wake up!' I called in a shrill voice.

'Kimmy?' called a distant voice. 'Is that smoke coming under my door?'

'Yes! Stop it with a damp towel. Be careful,' I shouted back. Then, without warning, my bedroom light flicked off. I gasped and stood statue still for a moment before feeling my way back to the switch. On the way I collided with a chest of drawers and tears sprang to my eyes. When I finally found the switch, it didn't work.

In the pitch black, I climbed over the mattress, searching for my phone. If I could just get to the window and shout for help... But... Oh no... Please tell me this wasn't happening... My body went into spasm as something or someone curled their fingers around my foot. Instinctively, I kicked to and fro, imagining all kinds of gruesome scenarios and a weird noise escaped my mouth, like a cross between a wail and a sob. Finally, my leg broke free. Gulping, I dived to the floor and dropped my phone. It skidded under the bed. Astral beings were never so bold on Most Haunted. I must have really wound Walter up.

Yet could that really have been the grip of some ghostly elderly man? And according to Terry, Walter was a sound bloke. Plus White Christmas hadn't played since I'd woken up. I swallowed hard. Only one thing could explain this: there had to be *two* spirits – gentle Mr Carmichael and some evil demon that got up to mischief and blew smoke.

'Stay away!' I hollered, as heavy breathing came from the other side of the bed. Slowly I got on my knees, turned around and peeked over the bed. My mouth went dry.

Standing by the chest of drawers was a tall figure, its arms flailing around. All I wanted to do was curl into a ball and hide but I couldn't – not now I had Jess and the little one in her belly to protect.

'Leave me alone!' Did this evil spirit have an axe? What about a machete? Perhaps a drill? At least if I was famous, I could have assumed it was just a fan waving an autograph book. "Mysterious Murder of Kimmy Jones – Police Grill Ex-boyfriend" would be the headline. Adam would feature in all the celebrity magazines, saying he was innocent and had been about to take me back. Then they'd arrest a crazed fan of mine, a previous offender, whose fingerprints were found on the front door handle…

The figure's arms dropped and it strode towards the bed. With a whimper, I ducked down and scrabbled frantically under the bed for my phone. Man up, I told myself; time to put into action those karate moves Adam taught me, after I once got pickpocketed. Hands shaking, I forced myself once more to peep over the bed. Phew. It had gone. Perhaps Walter had somehow scared it off.

I leapt to my feet, opened the window and screamed for help, feeling even more spooked as a bat flew past the cloud-veiled moon. At least I'd stored Luke's number in my phone. With bionic speed I searched for his name and pressed dial.

'Luke! Is that you?' I whispered, voice shaking.

'What? Who is this?' he mumbled.

'It's me. Kimmy.'

'Huh? Have you any idea what time it is?' he whispered back.

Maybe someone was sleeping next to him.

'Please… I… Come over,' I stuttered, managing to suppress a sob. 'I've just been… It might come back… And the smoke…'

'Slow down.'

'There's a…' Ghost would sound stupid. 'A burglar about and the lights won't switch on. There's that smoke again too… He got hold of my leg and–'

'For God's sake,' he said. 'Not that nonsense again. It was nothing last time. You're a capable woman. Just check through the house for fire hazards. If you're really worried, call the fire brigade or police.'

'No! We might lose our jobs, if there's a fuss. Please Luke. Please come round just one more time.'

'Look, I know you like me, Kimmy, but please save your sad ploys to catch my attention to a reasonable hour of the day.'

'I beg your pardon?' I said, his arrogance helping me forget, for one moment, that my life was at stake.

'Your cooking's not bad, though,' he said. 'If you want to impress, forget these silly stories, just bake me some coffee and walnut cakes.'

'Might have a problem using the oven gloves, if my arms have been hacked off by some weirdo,' I hissed. 'Look, I'm sorry to bother you…' Which was the absolute truth. How I hated asking for help, like Mum had over the years, bugging neighbours and various boyfriends to wire plugs and put up shelves. 'It, the burglar, whatever, they're stronger than me and I haven't got a pepper spray, gun or bat. If not for me, then… then come round for Jess. All this upset won't do her any good,' I said.

'What do you mean?'

'She's… not well.'

He sighed down the phone. 'This better not be another false alarm. If it is, I'll ring Murphy myself.'

'Oh don't worry – I really am at risk of being murdered.' I snapped. 'And for the last time, you're the last bloke I'd have a crush on!'

A phut of exasperation floated down the line. 'What is it with you housesitters? What's so difficult about looking after a property and getting it sold?'

The line clicked dead. I sunk to the floor and hugged my knees. If I'd have rung Adam, there'd have been no questions – he'd have been here in a flash, armed with his quads and biceps. Unless… unless he was over me already. After all, it was over twenty-four hours since we'd last spoken and he'd obviously been fed up with me for weeks prior to that. Although I had to admit, just occasionally, Adam's protective nature felt suffocating and in a funny way it had felt good to hear Luke say I was capable – that he didn't feel the need to rush around to fight my battles. Which was a messed up way of thinking because I totally loved caring Adam, didn't I? Whereas Luke's unprovoked rudeness was TOTALLY, definitely, unquestionably off-putting – even though I just knew his earthy smell and teasing mouth must make my pupils dilate (nature's giveaway that something's got the potential to turn us on).

My mind raced and I blocked out inquisitive thoughts about what Luke would be like as a boyfriend. Something dug into my side as I leant back against the wall – a pair of my high heeled shoes – perfect, to gouge the eyes out of anything that came near. Every centimetre of my body froze as the door creaked. Someone entered the room. It was too soon to be Luke. Stiletto in hand, I stared across the room.

'Aarggh!' I hurled myself over the mattress and lashed out with the shoe.

'Ow! What the hell…' someone shouted. Firmly, the thing prised my weapon out of my hand, then backed me up against the drawers. The demon or whatever it was felt solid and blew warm breath onto my neck, as if I was standing under a tropical shower. I sniffed. Hmm. A musky smell teased my nostrils. A firm hand slipped around my back and covered the pointed drawer knob, as if to stop it digging into my back.

'Surprise, surprise, you're all right,' muttered the voice and flicked on the lights.

'Luke?'

He was still pressed against me. Wow. What amazing moss green eyes. How come I hadn't noticed them before?

'Y… you didn't take long to get here,' I stuttered.

'I was already walking nearby. Couldn't sleep, so reckoned I'd get some fresh air and check on Walter's house. It's been empty for so long, guess that's become a bit of a habit.'

I squirmed uncomfortably. 'You can back off now.'

'Are you sure? You won't attack me again? First a Christmas tree and now…' He glanced at the floor. 'A shoe.' He stepped away and rubbed his chest. The hood of his jacket fell onto his shoulders. It was spotted with rain.

'Sorry,' I mumbled. 'It's just you looked like… Is Jess okay?'

'I came to you first. Just in case this was another trick. Talking of which, where's the smoke this time?'

'It's gone again. But Jess'll tell you…'

I followed him onto the landing and towards her room.

'It's only me, Jess,' I called.

She opened the door, Groucho standing on her feet, her face as white as his tail.

'Maybe *you* can tell me what's going on?' he said. 'Everything okay? Kimmy said you weren't well.'

'I'm fine,' she snapped. 'Was there really a fire?'

He shook his head.

'You saw the smoke, right?' I asked, willing her to say yes.

'Thought so, but it was dark. Things always look different at night.'

'She saw smoke,' I said, confidently to Luke. 'And something… someone came into my room. It grabbed my leg. I was worried you were next, Jess.'

'I heard you scream,' she said. 'My door wouldn't open, otherwise I'd have tried to help. And there was this dead strange noise, like a whirlwind. We should call the police.'

'And say what? I've seen a spooky face, there's the sound of wind and some well weird smoke? The police don't deal with hauntings, do they?' Oops. There. I'd said it.

Luke burst out laughing. 'You think there's a ghost? And I was hoping you two were more sensible than your predecessors.'

'Why? Has something like this happened before?' asked Jess.

'And what's all this about a…' he smirked, '…spooky face?'

I shrugged at both of them. 'Laugh if you want but I'm convinced there's a spirit stuck in limbo here.' Best not to mention Walter. They'd probably get me sectioned. I thrust my hands in the air. 'Why didn't anyone warn us about these ghostly goings on?'

'Because this place needs to get sold and Deborah wasn't going to jeopardise that because of the witterings of a bunch of housesitters. Sure they all mentioned noises in the night, but ghosts are for kids at Halloween.' He put his hands in his anorak pockets.

So I wasn't the only person to have suspected supernatural goings-on. Suddenly Jess put her hand to her mouth, darted to the bathroom and threw up.

'Just as well you're off work tomorrow,' I said to her when she came back and collapsed on the bed. Groucho snuggled up to her side. 'Don't worry. I'll deal with Deborah and her clients.'

'She's coming tomorrow?' said Luke and passed Jess the glass of water from her bedside table. 'Cancel her. You've both had a shock. Get her to re-schedule the appointment.'

'We can't,' said Jess, weakly.

I gazed at the black rings under her eyes. 'It might be an idea,' I said. 'I'm over at Melissa's in the morning and without your help, I'm not sure I'll get this place spotless in time. It's Deborah's fault anyway. She knew about this ghost thing. I'm sure that's what I saw written in her notes.'

'That red scrawl could have said anything,' said Jess.

'Time I left this nuthouse,' muttered Luke and disappeared onto the landing.

'You aren't going?' I called after him. 'What if that thing is still here?' I caught him up in the hallway, downstairs. He turned around by the front door.

'What, the spooky ghoul?' He smirked. 'Make a cross out of two wooden spoons and sleep with that above your bed.'

'Can't you at least open the room at the front, upstairs? I'm sure I heard movements in there.'

'Chill out.' Luke went to leave. 'Whoever it was is unlikely to come back. And, as I've found out the hard way, you're good at defending yourself.'

Tears pricked my eyes. I wasn't crying really. Not in front of him. I was tired, that's all; in shock. 'Whatever,' I mumbled. 'Thanks for coming.' I headed for the Game of Thrones Room, wishing there really were some helpful warriors in there. Sitting at the bar, I grabbed the tube of Pringles and shoved in a handful, sideways on.

'That is one wide mouth.' Luke appeared at my side. He helped himself to a crisp. 'Okay. I'll kip on the sofa in the office upstairs – that's if you control your attraction to the Adonis that is Luke Butler.' He took another crisp and chuckled.

I was still spluttering with indignation an hour later as I took six cupcakes out of the oven. We all needed something to calm us down and what could be better than a mouthful of fresh, fluffy sponge, dolloped with melt-in-the-mouth buttercream icing? Comfort food at its best. Luke had said coffee and walnut was his favourite flavour and so I'd obliged, finding some nuts left over from Jess's tofu stir fry.

As the sugary aroma floated upstairs, Jess had surfaced. Her nausea passed and she looked just like she needed a midnight – well, okay, two o'clock in the morning – snack. The topping, to suit my best mate, was made with decaffeinated coffee. But when it came to decorating Luke's cake, a little bit of that demon spirit must have infiltrated me and I added some extra-strong caffeinated stuff I found in a cupboard. With any luck, that would keep him awake all night and he'd see smoke and scream in terror when a hooded figure clutched *his* leg.

However, by the time I'd changed, flossed and moisturised, irritating snores had replaced the whistling escaping from his room. Once again I lay star-shaped, under the crimson sheets and snug duvet. I turned towards the window and gazed through the chink of open curtain. The cloud had cleared. The light rain must have stopped. In retrospect (could say this now that the imminent danger had passed), the evening had been a thrill! I'd always wanted to see a ghost and better than that, I'd actually made physical contact.

At that moment, the familiar tune of White Christmas drifted into my room and I didn't feel scared, convinced that the old man had helped protect me from the evil intruder, before. *Walter, you're here again? Did you get rid of that other spirit for me? Why is it in your house? Perhaps it lived on this land, years before you appeared. Is it keeping you here against your will? Let me help.*

The music got louder and I sat up in bed. I could either wake Luke, to prove that I wasn't lying, or grab this chance to communicate with the old fellow.

'Knock three times if you're there, Walter,' I said, out loud to the moonlit room, deciding that maybe the spirit couldn't read my thoughts. 'You don't scare me. I know now why this house feels like a home. It's because you're still around. You were – are – a good person. So, why haven't you joined Lily at the Pearly Gates? I know it's not you trying to harm me. We could be friends. Just let me know you're here.'

OMG! There were three low thuds.

CHAPTER 12

My KimCakes Ltd venture was almost over before it started as:

I got up late – having hardly slept after Walter's thuds. It was too tempting, you see, not to ask him everything I'd always wanted to know about ghosts: "Can you still eat chocolate?", "Do you spy on people having sex?", "Can you walk through walls?" and "Have you seen Michael Jackson or Elvis yet?" Strangely enough, there was no further response. I'd try again soon and find out why he was hanging around Mistletoe Mansion.

Once up, showered and hair blown dry, I then wasted time trying to decide what to wear. By the sounds of it, the local golfers' wives were a conservative bunch. I didn't own many outfits that hid my knees or covered every centimetre of my boobs. Then, by chance, I stumbled across an apron in the kitchen, draped over a chair, as if it had been especially left out. It was navy with white stripes, your standard butcher's job. Tied around my black skirt and white top, it really made me look the part of *professional caterer*. To add the final touches, I pinned my freshly straightened hair into a bun. Instead of my bronze foundation and purple shimmer lipstick, I plumped for a brush of translucent powder and smear of Vaseline.

It's what Cut-Above-Couture's style guru called the "chameleon effect": sometimes, rather than stand out, it was better to blend in.

I had to ring Deborah to tell her the appointment with her clients was off. Her voice lost its warmth until I mentioned the terrifying ordeal of the night before. Cue apologies from her that we hadn't slept well – guilty conscience or what? She duly bumped the appointment to eleven o'clock the next morning. I raced upstairs to tell Jess the good news but – asleep or not – she was hidden under the covers. I hadn't the heart to wake her up.

Luke, on the other hand, got up early and sat in the kitchen like a bed & breakfast guest, so I rustled up soft-boiled eggs with toast. No doubt he'd spent ages trying to look so effortlessly appealing, just to wind me up. I did my best to ignore him swaggering around in nothing but boxer shorts, sitting really low on his flat waist, and a man's dressing gown he'd found upstairs, which he left deliciously – I mean *annoyingly* – undone. There was something so basic about him… Almost dirty. My cheeks flushed. I certainly didn't, in any way, feel the urge to run a hand, fleetingly, across his thighs. If the paparazzi guys were around, and IF (that's capital letters) I fancied Luke, this scene might just grab Adam's attention, coupled with the headline: "Handy Hunk Dips his Soldier into Kimmy's Yolk."

I still had business cards to make, so put something simple together on the laptop and cut them out. Each was a small rectangle of paper with "KimCakes Ltd" written at the top, my full name underneath, then my mobile number.

Worst of all, Melissa rang me (although that's best of all too, I mean, how cool is that?) to remind me to set up at half nine and – get this – to 'not forget the savoury nibbles'. Huh? When I hinted that we'd only spoken about cakes, the velvet tones disappeared and she suggested I sort it out toot sweet. 'No problem, see you soon,' I'd cheerily replied, before screaming silently on my fist.

'Thanks, Terry, you're a lifesaver,' I said and stood back as he came into the hallway. I'd rung him as soon as I put the phone down on Melissa. Thank God for my brainwave. Laden with packets of frozen food, we hurried into the kitchen. The worktop was covered with an array of herbs and salad items. That was the good thing about sharing with vegetarian Jess – there was always plenty of fresh stuff in the fridge and cupboards.

'Are you sure about this?' said Terry. Today he wore a pea-green jumper over tight, tan plus fours. 'I'd stay to help, but despite the poor weather forecast, I'm due to tee off in half an hour.'

'You've done enough already. I've just got time to make this lot look presentable.'

He sniggered. 'Just imagining Melissa's face if she knew her savoury nibbles were actually my leftovers from BargainMarket.'

'It's not funny! My reputation's at stake.'

'You'll be fine.' He patted his portly stomach. 'Once they taste those cakes, those women will be in sugar rush heaven and won't want to eat anything else.' A whistling attracted his attention. 'Luke's here?'

I stifled a yawn.

'Late night?' He winked.

'You think me and Luke…?' I pulled a face. 'I'd rather become a nun.'

'Kimmy! Have you seen his pecs? And from behind, in just the right pair of trousers…'

We both giggled.

'Honestly, Terry. He acts as if he's some megastar and I'm his groupie.'

'What's he doing here, so early?'

'Last night… I couldn't sleep. There were noises… smoke.' My stomach scrunched as I recalled that thing grasping my ankle. 'It's a long story.'

His cheeks burnt red.

'Terry?'

'Really must go, now,' he muttered.

'You *knew* about all this? Why didn't you warn me?'

'Um…'

'This house… Sometimes… strange things happen,' I said. 'How long has this been happening?'

'Apologies…' Terry shrugged his well-rounded shoulders. 'You're right. Once night-time falls, I know from the other housesitters that scary stuff happens… Ever since Walter died, this funny business has been going on. It's held up every sale. I hoped this time would be different. New, permanent neighbours would be great.'

'You know, something grabbed my leg last night.'

Terry bit his lip. 'Jean, the last woman, said it clasped her arm and tried to pull her out of bed. No one's ever been badly hurt though – just shaken up.'

I thought for a moment. 'Did she ever mention random smoke or… or Christmassy music?'

'No music, but yes, smoke, locked doors and a bizarre noise of a blowing gale. How about I fill you in properly later? Who knows, maybe if you stick around for long enough, whatever this thing is will get bored and disappear.'

Blimey. So I really was living with something paranormal. I didn't know whether to gasp in fear or jump with joy.

'Do you believe in ghosts?' I said and followed him back to the hallway. 'Luke thinks I'm bonkers.'

'Ever watched Most Haunted?'

'I love that show!' I said.

'Me too! Aren't the celebrity episodes hilarious?'

I grinned. 'But Walter's house isn't ancient. And according to Luke, before Badgers Chase was built, there was nothing here but fields and rivers. No cemetery. Or jail. Or psychiatric hospital.' I shuddered.

'It's a mystery.' Terry ran a hand over his bald head. 'Anyway, got to go. All the best for this morning. I look forward to hearing the details!'

I closed the door behind him and raced back into the kitchen. First things first: heat up the frozen goodies – most only took twenty minutes. Whilst they were cooking, I prepared the garnishes. When the buzzer went I took out the snacks and laid them on platters.

I reached for a jar of black olives. I could scatter those with some flat-leafed basil, in between the pizza and cheese bites. As for the mini hot dogs… I quickly fried up some chopped onion and put a spoonful on top of each with a squirt of mustard – that looked well cute. I'd lay the tempura prawns out on a bed of lettuce and sprinkle cherry tomatoes and slim cucumber sticks on top. Natural yogurt, another of Jess's favourites, would help make yummy dips.

I looked at the time: nine o'clock. For good measure, I'd also take a couple of tubes of Pringles. Well, these guests weren't celebrities.

I to-ed and fro-ed with all my boxes and plates, stacking them in the hallway. Hands on hips, I surveyed the pile. I'd just have one last check of the kitchen, where I stopped dead at the door. There, on the worktop, stood a couple of silver cupcake stands. They were beautiful, with silver wire swirls to hold the cakes, the stands in the shape of trees. Where on earth had they come from? What an exquisite, beautiful design. It was as if they'd been left there on purpose, just like the apron.

Feeling more like a professional than ever, I carried them into the hallway. Luke rushed past, said he had to go. If that was Adam, he'd have insisted on staying to help me get my stuff over to Melissa's. Three quick journeys on foot I'd need, to dump everything outside the Winsfords' house. By the time I'd made my last trip up the drive and past the garages and golf club shaped fountain, it was bang on half past nine – and the gathering grey clouds had turned black. Rain was becoming a bore. With Christmas exactly two weeks today, I was dying for at least a sniff of snow.

I rapped the eagle knocker, which was in the middle of an amazing Christmas wreath, made from miniature gold and white baubles, interspersed with glittery fake bronze holly. Jonny's Bugatti wasn't on the drive and I was kind of relieved not to meet him for the very first time in my sexless outfit. As for my make-up free face, I had no intention of meeting such a hot celebrity guy as nature intended. Shivering without a coat on, I smoothed down my hair. The Winsfords' gardener wore an out-of-season man-from-Del-Monte hat and smiled as he trimmed the hedges at the front of her lawn. I smiled back then flicked a fly away from the tempura prawn platter. Tasty smells escaped the foil cover and my stomach rumbled.

The door opened. Wow. Melissa had theme-dressed for the occasion. Her hair was twisted back in a conservative chignon and she wore modest cream plus fours with a beige, diamond-print jumper. And as for that demure pearl necklace… Ten out of ten, I thought. It was all very modest.

'Kimmy, darling... Glad to see you on time!' Melissa led me into the hallway.

I didn't see the assassin. I'd been murdered, right? That was the only way I could have died and gone to heaven. I mean, OMG! I'd officially walked into a virtual Hello! magazine spread. Was the décor romantic, or what, with the damson chaise longue and delicately carved telephone table running along the right side of the stairs?

'That's an amazing chandelier,' I murmured, eyes raised to the high ceiling. It had silver effect leaves curling around each glass candle and a hundred times more crystals than on Walter's.

'Imported. Cost a fortune,' said Melissa as she repositioned a large vase of white lilies, mixed with gossamer light feathers, on the window sill at the front.

On the far wall, as you entered, was a large framed quote on a white background:

"Nothing is too beautiful,
Nothing is too expensive."
Ettore Bugatti

'And all those trophies,' I said, in a daze, staring at a glass cabinet straight ahead, behind the chaise longue.

Both of us went over. Melissa opened the glass doors and talked me through each one. She knew exactly when and where each prize had been awarded and carefully lifted them out, one by one – the big silver cups with enormous handles, bronze figures in the middle of a swing, glass golf balls perched on gold tees, a silver golf bag inscribed with the number one, and shield after shield. They were all on full view to potential burglars. No doubt they were protected by some laser beam alarm system, like in Mission Impossible.

Next to the cabinet was a six foot Christmas tree. It was artificial silver, with co-ordinated tinsel and baubles in black and sparkly grey.

Set in the wide turret on the left was the kitchen, and Melissa called the gardener to help me carry in the food. For a moment I stood transfixed by the black circular breakfast island and matching stools with gold legs. In the middle was a black vase filled with exotic black roses, intermingled with gold-sprayed leaves. Another chandelier, in gold, hung from the pointed ceiling.

'Feel free to use the fridge-freezer,' said Melissa, graciously, showing me to an industrial-sized fridge even bigger than Walter's. There was plenty of room inside for my BargainMarket platters. In fact, it didn't look like Melissa and Jonny ate in much at all. There were some diet colas, low calorie ready meals, chilled champagne, a half-eaten bar of king-sized chocolate and various jars of cosmetics. And… oh my God, I'd seen pictures of that in magazines: a shallow sky-blue and gold tin of Beluga caviar. Next to the fridge was a tall gold rack filled with wine bottles. I stared at a door on the right, at the end.

'The dining room's through there,' said Melissa. 'Take a look. We really ought to use it more often.'

As instructed, I peeked my head in. It was sumptuous – all mahogany, buttercream and fuchsia pink, with billowing curtains that looked like ships' sails. To one side was a smaller Christmas tree, in the more traditional colours of green and red. In the middle of the table stood a pearl shell vase filled with candy-coloured fake tulips. At the back of the room was part of a simple, white conservatory; it must have stretched further across, out of sight, to the back of their lounge.

I turned back to the kitchen and gazed out of the sparkling windows. Huh? Little greens and bunkers?

Melissa shook her head. 'Don't ask. Jonny wanted a mini golf course landscaped into the back garden.'

'Is that…?' I pointed to a massive looking shed. It was well smart, with a flag on the top and…

Melissa nodded. 'His own little clubhouse. It's got its own bar, a snooker table, juke box… What more could a man want?'

I could just imagine Adam and myself living in a similar place. Infamous magazine would make us their lead story: "Reunited cake magnate Kimmy and partner show us around their lush lovenest…" Luke would be the hired help and I'd make him obey one of those wacky celebrity rules where he wasn't allowed to look me in the eye.

'You'll serve the food in the lounge, darling,' said Melissa's velvet tones. I followed her into the room on the other side of the hallway. It was bigger than Adam's whole flat, especially with the other end of the humungous conservatory at the back. It was ultra modern, unlike Walter's which was filled with various bits of traditional furniture which didn't necessarily match. Everything here was co-ordinated, right down to the colour of the drink mats. There were no cosy touches like Walter's dog-eared books or Lily's needlework box with multi-coloured threads hanging out. Even the little row of gold Christmas socks, hanging from the mantelpiece, looked brand new. Plus there was a third Christmas tree, again perfectly co-ordinated, this time in plum and gold. No homemade baubles dangled from its branches, no wooden ones or clip-on fake robins… Everything looked as if it was there for effect. Inwardly I chuckled. What *would* Melissa think to the little one I'd hit Luke over the head with?

She chatted about a small table she'd set up by the window, for the cakes, but I hardly listened. It was as if I'd dived into my favourite celebrity homes TV show.

I gazed at the velvet red curtains and glistening glass coffee table, the fragrant bowls of purple and red potpourri, a wicked gold ornamental birdcage and massive, gilt wall mirrors... Two armchairs matched a plum, curved sofa, and ornate ottoman, and on every seat in the room was a palatial cushion, neatly positioned into a diamond. As for the carpet, it was even more luxurious than the thick pile in Lily's bedroom. If it was green, Jess would have said it needed a damn good mow. If only I had time to text Terry – he'd be well jealous.

'When the ladies arrive, darling, make the coffees toot sweet. After a drink and one of your creations, I'll introduce Sandra, my nail lady, and she can get out her needles. Whilst she's knocking off the years, nearer to lunch time, you can fetch the savoury food.' The front knocker rapped. 'Shirley, the ex-captain's wife cancelled, by the way.' Melissa's mouth sunk a little. 'Apparently she's woken up with a headache.'

We walked into the hallway, and she opened the door to a tiny, plump-ish lady with bobbed grey-blonde hair in a short-sleeved white medical coat. Her perfectly pink painted nails curled around the handle of a plastic case.

'You must be the caterer. Lovely to meet you,' she said to me, before air-kissing Melissa. 'Where shall I set up?' she asked.

'The conservatory,' Melissa said. 'It's airy and cheerful and should ease the nerves of the Botox virgins.'

Sandra placed a hand on Melissa's arm. 'I'm sure it will be a great success. I've brought my varnishes and files too, thought I could throw in a free manicure, have them leaving here looking really glam.'

'What would I do without you? That's a fab idea!' She linked her arm with Sandra's. 'Make yourself at home in the kitchen, Kimmy,' she said, as they went into the lounge.

Minutes later, the phone rang and after a short conversation echoed into the hallway, Melissa's face appeared around the kitchen door. 'Pamela's cried off now – something about a domestic emergency. So that's four of them left. Although Sandra says not to worry, that'll give her more time to do the manicures.'

What was wrong with those women? Weren't they dying to see the house of someone famous?

Melissa looked at her watch. 'Hadn't you better switch the coffee machine on?' She nodded towards a contraption on the unit, just along from the wine rack. Next to the compact black and silver machine were stacked china cups and saucers, white with black flowers.

Close up, it looked like something out of a spaceship's control tower. Adam and I thought we were posh when we bought a percolator, but this… And just look at that stack of cute little sealed coffee punnets! I picked one up – oh, pardon *moi*, they were actually called "Disc Beverage Pods". I'd be able to take individual orders, such as a Latte, Espresso, Medium Roast and Cappuccino, then Macchiato (huh?), Chocolate and – get this! – Tiramisu flavour!

Having whetted my own appetite, I switched on the machine and filled it right up to the two litres mark. I unpacked the cake stands and took the lids off the cake boxes. The rich mincemeat cupcakes and Santa Coladas looked awesome staggered up one silver tree, the Malibu buttercream icing easily overpowering the scent of those black roses. On the other stand, I carefully balanced the dark chocolate logs and skinny Stollens, then found a large serving plate to set out the cinnamon and spice muffins. I placed everything perfectly on the lace cloth in the lounge, having managed to find plates to match the cups and small silver forks. Melissa had left out some fancy holly and ivy paper cocktail napkins.

The doorbell rang and I stood to attention, feeling like the kitchen maid out of Downton Abbey.

'Vivian!' Melissa said. 'So glad you could make it.'

I peered around the door and saw a busty women in her sixties barge in, black patent handbag (her court shoes matched) clasped to her chest, blue silk blouse bolstered tightly into a beige skirt. Her tanned, wrinkled face revealed a lifetime of golf and cigarettes – she was clearly the perfect candidate for Botox.

'And Denise. Hello. How are you?' asked Melissa.

She was the doctor's receptionist, married to one of the pros, with two kids at secondary school. Middle-aged, with short mousy hair and no make-up, Denise wore a military design grey dress with buttons all the way up. Her slim legs cried out for stylish shoes but instead she'd chosen a flat trainer type. She wore what looked like one hundred denier flesh-coloured tights and on her back hung a mini rucksack.

'Good morning, Melissa,' said Denise stiffly, and looked around. 'Rather isolated here, isn't it? Give me the hustle and bustle of an estate, any day.'

Vivian was already over by the trophy cabinet. 'You should see my Geoff's collection of prizes; takes me a whole day to polish them. It's just one of the responsibilities of being the captain's wife.'

'Ladies, what would you like to drink?' Melissa said, her smile already looking a little fixed, like those actors at the Oscars who've just found out they haven't won. 'Cappuccino, Espresso…?'

'Got anything straightforward,' said Denise, 'like black tea?'

'Why don't people sell coffee in English any more?' said Vivian's clipped tones. She turned to me. 'White coffee, please dear.'

By the time I took their drinks into the lounge, the doorbell had rung again and two younger women were in there too, chatting. One had her hair tied back in a scrunchie and wore sporty culottes, a cute pink hooded cardigan and cute stud snowman earrings. She had to be Kate, who, Melissa said, had two toddlers and worked in a gym. Melissa liked her best. That meant the other was Saffron, with hair as yellow as her name and a tan which clearly didn't come from one of those exotic holidays the Winsfords enjoyed. She'd given Kate a lift and had just slipped her keys into her Louis Vuitton handbag, which I subtly scanned. It was fake, just like the one I'd bought off St Albans' market. You could tell because there was no monogrammed LV on the zipper pull. Saffron stared around the room, lip-lined mouth open, kohl-rimmed eyes like saucers. Her nails were turquoise with red jewels and her frilly dress was both higher at the bottom and lower at the front than any of mine. I could have sworn I'd seen that exact dress on sale last week in one of my favourite discount shops in Luton.

'Thank you, dear.' Vivian took her coffee from me.

'I'll have one of Melissa's lovely Macchiatos please,' said Kate.

'Got any green tea?' said Saffron. 'If not, I'll have a black coffee, ta. Got to watch my figure – otherwise the men won't, know what I mean?' She smiled smugly. 'Although I couldn't do nothing so energetic as Melissa. All that sweat. Don't you get bored of your own exercise DVD, babes?'

'I'm with Saffron,' said Denise. 'And I couldn't sit through all those manicures and hair appointments, either.'

'I see it as my duty, as one of the national birdies,' said Melissa, in a tight voice. 'People expect me to look my best at all times.'

Vivian was on her feet, studying a portrait of the golfing wife.

'It's very brave to hang that up,' said Saffron, innocently. 'Was it drawn before you went on a diet?'

'Just look how the artist's captured Melissa's fine bone structure and glossy hair,' said Sandra firmly, as she passed by and winked at Melissa. 'No amount of weight loss could achieve those two things.'

Saffron wrinkled her nose.

'Kimmy, isn't it?' said Kate to me, as I tried to make my escape. 'The cakes look delicious.'

'Yes, maybe you could hand them around, Kimmy,' said Melissa, in a measured voice. '*KimCake Ltd*'s products are very exclusive.'

'Never understood people paying for fairy cakes,' said Vivian.

Denise nodded. 'Especially us mums. Having kids makes you your own expert on icing and sprinkles. And just because they cost the earth doesn't mean they're the best quality. We had a patient in the other day who'd ordered some fancy ones online. They'd taken a big bite and almost choked on a plastic twist tie.'

'These are rather special though, and Christmas-themed,' said Melissa, through gritted teeth. She glared at me.

'Um yes,' I stuttered, and gave them a tour of the two pretty stands. Kate clapped her hands when I mentioned the mincemeat cupcakes' brandy buttercream icing. Vivian sniffed and said she'd try the Santa Colada, only because Denise was driving. Saffron, in between gazing at Melissa's lush furnishing, interrogated me as to the number of grams of fat in each skinny Stollen and said I should really offer gluten-free, as that was a very trendy diet. Modest Denise said she'd try a cinnamon and spice muffin, as that was the least fancy. So I served their requests onto the delicate china plates and left the room. At least whilst they ate, it went quiet.

I mean, jeez! Friendly Wysteria Lane of Desperate Housewives it wasn't! I'd always thought that being a celebrity meant people would like you, or at least pretend. But Saffron was obviously jealous, Denise unimpressed, Vivian competitive... Thank God for Kate. If anything could bond this mismatched bunch together, it would be eating cakes with the melt-in-mouth buttercream icing and kick of sugary sponge.

When I went back, Vivian was onto her second Santa Colada and Denise was asking Melissa if she could have a plain biscuit instead of another cake. Kate gave me the thumbs up and wiped some brandy buttercream icing from around her mouth. Saffron was playing with her healthier skinny Stollen, a tortured look on her face as she refused to let herself eat it. Melissa should have shared her tip about chewing it then spitting it out. But there was no need as Saffron finally put down her plate. Then she ran her hand over the expensive sofa.

'Have to say, I am rather impressed, young lady,' said Vivian to me and raised her cupcake, a popping candy fizzing noise coming from her mouth. 'This Malibu icing is delicious and the dessicated coconut's texture just sets off the richness.'

'Same for the brandy buttercream icing,' said Kate and licked her thumb. 'Good thing I'm not driving home.'

'Don't know what's wrong with simple flavours nowadays,' muttered Denise. 'Go to buy a chocolate bar and you have the choice of about ten versions. And it's impossible to understand the list of ingredients. One of our patients has a nut allergy and is always coming in with Mick Jagger lips, after eating something that's been cross-contaminated and not clearly labelled'

'Kimmy has an impeccable record,' said Melissa, in her velvet tones. 'I was lucky to find her.'

'Who else have you catered for, dear?' asked Vivian.

'Um, most of the national team,' I said, with an air of confidence, despite crossing my fingers. 'And some footballers.'

'Really?' Saffron sat upright. 'That's mental!'

Vivian shook her head and smiled, as if to say the young woman would eventually grow out of being impressed by celebritydom.

'I'm holding a hen night for my big sis this Friday,' continued Saffron. 'We're having a buffet – you know, finger food, like on those frozen food supermarket adverts. You could give me your card. It's not too late, is it? I'm thinking pink and glittery with her name on, and all the better if you have a recipe that's low-cal... I saw one in Starchat last month for chocolate fudge cupcakes. They done a list of all the celebs eating healthy at the moment. Gluten-free cupcakes are the latest must-have,' she said and shook back her bouffant blonde hair, as if she'd just made some important announcement.

Blimey. She sounded just like me yakking to Adam about the latest celebrity gossip. I passed her one of my, ahem, business cards – they were tucked in the pocket at the front of my apron.

'It's my niece's seventh birthday in a few weeks,' said Kate. 'I'd love a boxful to take along, if you could theme them around Disney Princesses.'

'Um... of course.' I handed out another paper slip, successfully containing my excitement until I got back to the kitchen. Adam would be well impressed with this.

'Open a bottle of champagne, will you, darling,' said Melissa, as she appeared right behind me. 'Everything okay?'

She'd caught me jumping on the spot, clapping my hands.

'Just a bit of cramp.' I grabbed a bottle out of the fridge, whilst she put some glasses on a tray.

'I think these ladies need loosening up a bit before I bring out the Botox.' Melissa grinned.

I carried the filled glasses through and Melissa encouraged them all to have at least a few sips.

'Far too early in the day for me,' said Denise and put down her glass.

'Never too early, as far as I'm concerned,' joked Kate.

'So tell us, dear,' said Vivian to Melissa, in a booming voice (maybe I'd overdone the Malibu). 'Which charity are we supporting? How much would you like us to contribute for every cake we eat – or…' she eyed the remaining Santa Coladas, '… buy to take home?'

Melissa cleared her throat. 'You've probably been wondering who Sandra is, to-ing and fro-ing in her white coat.' She nodded towards the conservatory at the end of the room, where the nail lady had just finished setting up.

'I assumed she was your cleaner,' said Denise. 'We'd already met the gardener. It must be nice to have so much help.'

'No. I mean I do have a cleaner but it's her day off. Sandra's… well perhaps she should explain.'

'Is she a nurse?' said Saffron. 'You trying to help her raise money for new hospital equipment?'

Melissa waved to Sandra, who made her way past the gold birdcage and over to the plum sofa and chairs where the guests sat. I stood in the doorway, ready to bolt to the kitchen for more champagne if required.

'Um, this isn't exactly a charity fundraiser,' said Melissa and beamed. 'I thought I'd do all of you hardworking wives a favour instead. Sandra?'

The tiny woman gave a warm smile. 'Good morning, ladies. I'm the answer to your prayers. Ever looked in the mirror and wondered who that was looking back? Ever bought a new outfit, had your hair done, and still felt inadequate? From behind her back she drew out her hand, her long red-nailed fingers grasping a needle. 'Botox, ladies,' she said. 'It's the easiest way to get the face that reflects the real you.' She jerked her head towards Melissa's portrait. 'By the time I've finished with you, you could look almost as glamorous as the lovely Mrs Winsford.'

Smugly, Melissa folded her arms. This was her *pièce de résistance*. Er, yes, resistance, all right. Denise's eyebrows knotted across so far they almost became one. Kate and Vivian's mouths fell open.

'Botox?' they gasped, in horror.

CHAPTER 13

'You've got to be joking, Melissa. You brought me all this way under false pretences so that someone could inject a toxin into my face?' Denise shook her head. 'This isn't as exciting as it might seem,' she said to Saffron, who had sat bolt upright, eyes all sparkly.

'Toxin's a misleading word,' said Sandra. She went over to Denise and put a hand on her shoulder. 'And we all enjoy a few glasses of wine, but that's not supposed to do your liver any good – what's the difference? We can do it right here if you like. Just lean back and relax, deep breaths…'

Saffron glanced at the other ladies and her shoulders sagged. 'Um, of course. Denise is right,' she said and shook back her hair. 'Anyway, who's to say all of us need it, know what I mean?'

'And even if we do,' interrupted Vivian, 'it's cost me a lot of air miles and packets of Silk Cut getting my wrinkles. That's quite an investment. Who wants to see the face of a twenty year old on the body of a gran?'

'Might be a few sessions before we could knock that many years off you,' muttered Sandra and brandished the needle.

'It's only a bit of fun,' said Melissa. 'Kate… You're up for it?'

'Sorry, hon, but how will I tell the kids off, if I can't even frown?'

'One of our patients had too much and it spread,' said Denise, flinching as Sandra raised her needle. 'It gave her temporary facial paralysis. Her cheek muscles were so badly affected, she couldn't eat properly for weeks.'

'She lost weight as well, then?' said Melissa. 'Bonus! Come on, ladies. It's my treat and doesn't hurt a bit. I mean, not that I'd know, but so I'm told.' Her cheeks tinged pink.

'Just relax,' said Sandra to the doctor's receptionist. 'You'll hardly feel a thing.'

Denise's eyes narrowed. 'Are you even properly trained? I don't fancy placing my face in the hands of a nail technician.'

'Like you've got a lot to lose,' muttered Melissa.

'I've been treating Mrs Wins... um, I mean, lots of clients, successfully for months,' said Sandra.

Saffron did a poor job of suppressing a smile. 'Wow, Melissa, babes, so the rumours are true. You must be even older than I thought if Botox is your best bud.'

'You look great on it, hon,' said Kate in a loud voice. 'I guess it's just not for everyone. But...' she glared at the others. 'It was very generous of you to think of us.'

Denise grabbed her rucksack and stood up. 'Speak for yourself, Kate. I'm a busy working woman with a family to look after. If this isn't for charity, then I'm wasting my time.'

'And I don't want to end up with lips like obese caterpillars,' said Saffron. 'No one would ever kiss me again.'

'It's collagen that does that,' I said.

'Whatever,' she replied airily and picked up her handbag.

'It was just... I thought you'd be pleased,' said Melissa, eyes looking all shiny. 'Your average woman doesn't get the chance to go to a Botox party.'

'Are you calling us average?' said Saffron, drawn-on eyebrows arched.

'Botox parties are for people with too much money, if you ask me,' said Vivian. 'Or too little sense. Whereas we all live in the real world...' She flicked some crumbs off her silk blouse and wavering slightly, stood up. As she walked past, she patted my arm. 'I'll get your number. Those Santa Coladas would be a huge hit at my Bridge Club.'

I smiled but didn't feel like jumping quite so high as before because Melissa's shoulders slumped as her guests left. Sandra was back in the conservatory, shaking her head as she packed away her stuff.

'Ring you later,' said Kate to Melissa, and mouthed "sorry" before following on the heels of Saffron who, with a flounce of her frilly dress, teetered out of the room.

'What went wrong?' Melissa sank onto the plum sofa. She swilled back a mouthful of champagne and asked me to fetch another bottle and a glass for myself. By the time I got back, she was ready for a second glass.

'Here,' I said and passed her one of the rich mincemeat cupcakes. 'This'll make you feel better.'

'Whatever do you mean? The morning was a success. They enjoyed the food. I'm sure they thought me very generous.' But her mouth downturned and she took a huge bite. 'Sod the calories. Take one yourself. At least we know how to enjoy ourselves. Saffron hardly ate one mouthful. And as for Denise... She's always got some medical horror story to tell.'

I took one of the dark chocolate logs before sitting next to her, on the sofa. Who would believe I was sipping champagne in Jonny Winsford's house? I felt another Facebook status announcement coming on: "Champers to celebrate as business is booming."

'Do you want me to stay for a while, Melissa?' said Sandra in a soft voice as she stopped by us, holding her case. She'd taken off her coat to reveal a pastel skirt and smart magnolia blouse. 'Don't you worry about those ladies. They wouldn't know a favour if it pinched them on the bottom.'

'No. Honestly. But perhaps you could come round later in the week to do my nails. Your cheque…' Melissa muttered, words slightly slurring now.

'Don't worry, dear.' Sandra squeezed Melissa's shoulder. 'We'll sort that out next time. I'll show myself out.' She disappeared into the hallway and the front door opened and closed.

'She seems nice,' I said.

Melissa topped up our glasses. 'My manicure sessions are a godsend. Sandra always has really good advice. She's shown me this facial exercise routine that's supposed to produce results better than a facelift. And once I opened a bottle of champagne for lunch whilst she was here to celebrate sales of my DVD. I'd forgotten I was supposed to drive to meet Jonny in Harpenden for some fundraiser. Sandra insisted on giving me a lift there and wouldn't let me order a taxi.' She took a large sip. 'What a wasted opportunity. Those women don't know how to make the best of themselves.' Her words were less velvety and strands of hair had slipped out of her chignon. 'And we never got to try your savoury nibbles. I'll keep them if you like. Jonny's agent's visiting tonight.'

'Really?' That sounded important. I wouldn't want to let Melissa down. Not after the humiliation she'd faced this morning. 'Um… I'm better at baking cakes than making canapés. Honestly. I'm sure he'd prefer some of your home cooking.'

She giggled. 'Darling, Jonny didn't marry me because I know how to hold a whisk. We eat out a lot and if people come to dinner, I get in caterers. Just tell me how to heat them up. In fact, why don't you come back later and–'

'I was thinking the, um, prawns looked a bit off.'

'But you were going to serve them to the ladies.' Melissa looked at me sideways, then got up and wended her way into the kitchen. I followed. She yanked open the fridge door and lifted the foil on a platter of mini hot dogs. Her eyes narrowed. 'They all look exactly the same – more factory-produced than handmade.' She slammed the door and hiccoughed. 'What's going on?'

'I… I thought you only wanted cakes. When you mentioned at the last minute about *savoury nibbles*, I panicked and…'

'Bought them?' Melissa shrugged. 'I hope you used that new deli in town.'

I swallowed hard. 'They came from BargainMarket.'

'Oh, BargainMarket, yes well…' She gasped. 'BargainMarket! I wouldn't feed a dog from there. Wasn't it recently investigated by the Health and Safety Watchdog?' She glared at me for a few seconds before her eyes twinkled and she laughed. 'Can you imagine Vivian's face if she knew?' she spluttered. 'And as for Saffron, she'd die at the levels of salt and unsaturated fat. And no doubt squillions of Denise's patients have lost their lives to cheap, mass-produced savoury snacks!'

'I have tarted them up,' I said and chuckled. 'I think we'd have got away with it.'

'Good thing I didn't waste my caviar on them.' Melissa glanced at me. 'Although it does need eating up. Ever tried it?'

I shook my head.

She opened the fridge door, took out the tin and fetched a teaspoon. 'Wish I had some crackers,' she said, and prised off the lid.

'I've got tubes of Pringles,' I said and rummaged in one of my bags. With a flourish I dragged a tube out, opened it up and set it on the table top.

'Pringles?' Melissa giggled. 'Why not? Hold one out.' She spooned a teaspoon of dark grey pearly eggs onto it.

I stared at the crisp for a moment.

'Go on,' she soothed.

Deep breath. Mouth open… Mmm. The smooth pearls burst on my tongue and tasted like a breath of sea air, just before the cheesy aftertaste of the Pringle kicked in.

A screech of wheels cut through our conversation, then a key turned and the front door opened. OMG! It had to be Jonny – the golfing god himself. Melissa jumped up and hurried into the hallway.

'Honey?' I heard her say. 'You're home early.'

'Have you been drinking again?' said a male voice. 'Where is everyone? '

'They had to get off. Busy women. But they loved the cakes. The caterer's still in the kitchen. We were just…'

'You invited Saffron after all.'

'How did–?'

'Just saw her husband down at the club. Steve said she'd be coming. Get rid of the caterer,' he said. 'God knows why but the bloody paparazzi have trailed me all day again. So, if you open the door – try to at least stand straight.' Footsteps disappeared upstairs.

Feeling a bit woozy, I hurtled into the lounge to fetch the cakestands. Then Melissa helped me carry all my stuff onto the front doorstep. She'd shoved the tin of caviar into my bag and handed me a folded cheque.

'Thanks, Kimmy. This is the going rate, I reckon. Let me know if it's not enough. Got to go. Ciao.'

'But the savoury nibbles…? And I've written an invoice…'

'I'm not fussed about the paperwork,' she said and glanced up at the stairs again. 'And those mini pizzas didn't look too bad after all.'

She slammed the front door behind me and I was left staring at the golf fountain, before noticing a long lens peer at me from the bottom of the front garden. This was awesome! I was being papped! If only I was wearing more make-up and trendier clothes. How typical that for my first appearance in Starchat I was dressed like a butcher.

I made my first journey back to Walter's house, strolling past the silver Bugatti and trying to ignore the photographer in muddy combat trousers. How important did I feel! Even though I walked quickly, the bloke soon caught up and grabbed one of the cakestands.

'Let me help yer, love,' he said, a cigarette drooping out of one side of his mouth. Puffy bags hung under his eyes. 'Jonny and Melissa seem okay? Some fancy celebration was it? Yer know 'em well?'

'They seem very happy, which is all I'm prepared to say,' I said, in my poshest voice. 'You can quote me on that, if you like. The name's Kimmy Jones.'

He snorted. 'Not unless yer provide me with some dirt.' He thrust the cakestand back in my arms and slipped a silver card into my apron pocket. 'Give me a ring, if yer catch anything going on. Me or someone else from the agency can be here in minutes. There's good money in it.'

Ew! I didn't like him. He wasn't what I'd expected from the paparazzi at all. Where was the cool bike, leather jacket and wavy mop of Italian black hair? With his chunky lily-white legs sticking out of stained shorts, his sweaty face and receding hairline, I wouldn't want him shadowing me everywhere. I'd always imagined if I was famous, the paparazzi would be my friends. We'd laugh together and

I'd hand them cups of tea. In the press I'd be known as 'The Paps' Sweetheart'.

Not long later, I lay on my bed, apron off and bun undone. The photographer's silver card was on my bedside table. It had an oily fingerprint on it. Ugh. Jess was out. The house was quiet. It was just me and Groucho, cocking his head and looking all cute, cos he knew it was his dinnertime. On the little table next to me was the empty blue and gold tin of caviar. How decadent was that, me eating the food of the gods in bed? Clearly I was made for the celebrity lifestyle, as not everyone could enjoy raw fish eggs.

I gagged slightly and rushed to change the subject in my head. Now was my chance to try speaking to Walter again. I mean there were no rules, were there, that said ghosts only communicated at night? First things first though. Relaxed and calm, it was time to unfold that cheque. I took a deep breath. Fifty quid perhaps? My cakes were worth that. I squealed as my eyes scanned Melissa's fancy writing. Surely there was some mistake? Hands shaking I reached for my phone. For a few hours' work, I'd just earned three hundred pounds. An amount like that would blow Adam away!

CHAPTER 14

'Take that!' I said, not referring to Auntie Sharon's favourite pop group. I glanced at the clock: nine already. Deborah and the prospective buyers would be here in two hours. My arms ached, my palms stung and my chest heaved up and down. Had I just had a fight with that arrogant Luke or Jess's ex or that obnoxious photographer outside? No. The target of my aggression was some butter and a few innocent-looking eggs.

The reason? My lip quivered as I flexed my weapon (a silver hand whisk). It was Adam's fault. He'd eventually answered his phone yesterday evening, after I'd spent the afternoon tidying up the house. I'd hardly stopped for breath to tell him about Melissa's cheque and the other bookings, namely Saffron's hen night, the cakes for Kate's niece's birthday and Vivian's bridge club. His reaction? On the positive side, his first words were:

'You okay then, babe? Where are you staying?'

On the negative side? Where to start? I'd gone on to tell him about Mistletoe Mansion – you know, hot tub, fancy neighbours, micro-pig called Frazzle. He didn't think I'd taken on board his plea for me to keep my feet on the ground; didn't give so much as a grunt of interest when I'd babbled on about how my business was taking off.

'So, when does this holiday come to an end?' he'd muttered.

'Holiday? Hardly, what with running this house, keeping it clean and tomorrow I'm showing potential buyers around as well as baking my (fake designer) socks off.'

'And what happens when you move back to Luton? You still don't get it, do you? It's an unworkable dream. These people you're mixing with are giving you fanciful ideas.'

'Three hundred pounds, Adam – for a few hours' work – plus half a tin of caviar!'

A sigh whooshed down the phone. 'Look, gotta go.' He rang off.

I poured the batter into the silicone moulds. These were the vanilla and strawberry ladybird cupcakes I'd promised to make Deborah. The front doorbell rang and I closed the oven door, before heading into the hallway. I pulled out my scrunchie and hoped my hair didn't look too much of a mess.

Eyes alert, Groucho sat under the table in the hallway, as I opened the door to… a red-nosed, shivering Terry. He wore orange and brown checked plus fours and an apricot anorak. I loved his colourful ensembles.

'Not stopping long! I just came over to see how yesterday went.' He stared at my face. 'Did you get any Botox?' He put Frazzle on the ground and Groucho scooted over for a sniff.

'Poor Melissa,' I said. 'No one was impressed. When they found out the coffee morning wasn't for charity, they all left, wrinkles intact.' I gave him a run-down of the details.

'Poor Melissa. What's her house like?' he asked.

'There's a massive birdcage in the lounge and the kitchen's done out in black and gold. You should see this cabinet full of trophies. And the décor was co-ordinated down to the last thread of cotton and shelf bracket…' On and on I went, Terry lapping up every detail. 'Then there's the carpet – it's higher than Jedward's quiffs. And I counted at least three Christmas trees.'

His eyes widened. 'Ooh, wonder if I can get the name of her interior designer. By the way, why all the paparazzi outside Melissa's place? The last time they had that much attention was when Jonny made that joke about the Scottish, whilst up there playing the Open. Remember that picture of him in Starchat?'

'How could I forget!' It was of Jonny in a sporran (sexy legs or what), telling some offensive joke about Glaswegians and bagpipes. I shrugged my shoulders. Who cares why the cameras were there? All that attention was exciting.

'Got to fly,' said Terry, and picked up the pig, 'if I want to get nine holes in, without freezing my fingers off. The weather's decidedly chilly today. By the way, do you watch Celebrity Snippets? It's on tomorrow at seven. There's supposed to be new revelations about Zac Efron.'

'I love that programme! Look…Why don't you come here to watch it? We'll have something to eat. Maybe go in the hot tub?'

'Sure you young girls want me around?'

'Who else can I talk to about what Melissa's house and clothes are like? And you won't believe how the Winsfords have landscaped their back garden. Jess isn't interested and Groucho isn't really one to gossip.'

Terry grinned. 'It's a deal. I'll bring my costume and something fizzy to drink.'

I closed the door. It was awesome to finally find someone who could match my fascination for celebrities. The girls at Best Buns bakery bought the magazines to glance through at lunch, but didn't pore over the outfits and accessories like me. Sure, they'd daydream about living like Cheryl Cole, but I actually worked on how I could achieve that by myself. A bit like Mum, my colleagues just hoped one day Mr Right would come along and simply hand them a perfect life. They didn't even collect and categorise the magazines like me and Terry. I mean, what could be more inspiring than flicking back a few years to remember just how far your fave celeb has come?

I dashed into the kitchen to take out and check the cupcakes. Pressing them gently, I found that each sponge sprung back exactly the right amount. So, I left them to cool whilst I prepared the topping, with butter, icing sugar and thawed out mini frozen strawberries. The icing blushed just the right shade of pink and smelt all sweet and summery, despite the time of year.

Twenty minutes later, the cakes were iced and crowned with marzipan ladybirds. I put them in a Tupperware box, before wiping up the mess from the black and red food colouring. I didn't want to provoke one of Jess's hormonal rages again. It had gone ten and I pulled off my apron. It was time to check the house one last time, before Deborah got here.

The lounge, despite Walter's clutter, actually looked tidy. The Games Room was immaculate. So were my and Jess's bedrooms. The bathrooms sparkled, even the doortops were dusted. I slipped into the office. Pristine. There was nothing left to do so I just had time to log onto the laptop and check Facebook.

Oh my God! Leah's new profile photo made her look like a vampire with that red-eye. Aw, Rosy from Best Buns had set up a fan group for her new kitten. Lucy from secondary school had invited me to do a quiz on my underwear – which would, apparently, unlock secrets about my personality. I scrolled down my homepage. Poor Becca had splashed bleach on her new trousers.

Yet again I had something exciting to report, other than what I'd eaten for breakfast. After clicking onto my status,

I typed: "KimCakes Ltd is finally taking off – orders are flying in!" The doorbell rang and I shut down the laptop.

Groucho beat me to the hallway and barked loudly when I opened the door. Deborah wore a cream high-necked blouse, brown tailored trousers with a matching jacket and high heels with the cutest button straps. A couple in their forties stood behind her, properly wrapped up for the weather, in smart winter coats over office clothes – they had obviously taken time off work.

'Hello, Kimmy,' said Deborah, crisply, without quite looking me in the eye. Well, she must feel sheepish for failing to tell me I *must love ghosts*.

'This is Mr and Mrs Davis,' she said and turned back to them. 'As I promised, this is an impressive property. Lovingly cared for and maintained, this house has everything you're looking for – space, real character and the perfect location which is rural yet on the commuter belt. Shall we start in the Games Room?' She pointed them to the left. As they went in, she held my elbow. 'Watch and learn,' she whispered. 'In the future, you'll show buyers around on your own.'

'If I'm still here,' I whispered. 'Why chase after our car? Forget to tell us something, did you?'

She fiddled with her watch. 'Erm… yes, I'd had second thoughts and was trying to catch you up to say that maybe I should chase your references.'

'Rubbish! You *knew* why this place was taking so long to sell. I think you were going to warn us about Mistletoe Mansion.'

'I don't know what you mean,' she said and her mouth took a firm line. 'You wanted the job, didn't you? Looked pretty desperate, in fact. I did you a favour. It's my neck on the line, if this place still fails to sell.'

'And it could be my neck, literally, in the noose, if whatever's in this house turns out to be a hangman.'

'You said nothing fazed you – mushrooms and mice…'

'That didn't include supernatural beings! You withheld vital information.'

'You weren't exactly honest yourself. Or shall I press you for the name of the agency you work for?'

'Um, no, you see, as we said–'

'You get to read people pretty well in my job. I always know when someone's lying – like so-called buyers who just want to snoop around or rival agents bullshitting about how much commission they're on.'

'Hellooo?' called Mrs Davis.

'We'll talk later,' said Deborah and headed into the Games Room.

I followed her in.

Wow. She was good. Awesome as this room was, only an estate agent could make it sound like the welcoming front room of an aristocrat's house – a much better idea than my intention of schmoozing clients by saying that it was the perfect place to act out some bloody battle or sexy seduction from Game of Thrones (well, doesn't everyone watch that show?).

'Bedrooms, next?' she said and I led them upstairs, disappointed to hear Deborah explain that the two rooms full of Walter's stuff needed sorting before you could get a real sense of their space. They wouldn't be unlocked unless the Davis's wanted a second viewing.

'You'll adore this room,' Deborah said to Mrs Davis, 'it's wonderfully feminine and lush.' Gingerly, she pushed open the door to where I slept.

I gasped. How did those cushions get on the floor? Why was the ceiling lampshade hanging loose? Who'd thrown my rouge onto the walls and pulled the paintings well crooked? Groucho lay in the middle of the bed, innocently licking his paws. If he was a Great Dane he might have done some of the damage but I could hardly blame a ten inch tall Jack Russell.

'I, um… don't understand,' I muttered as the buyers raised their eyebrows.

Deborah bit her lip. 'Perhaps we should move along,' she said in a stiff voice, 'to the room once used as an office.' We walked past the locked room opposite the top of the stairs to the one where'd I'd just updated my Facebook status.

'I was just in here two minutes ago!' I said in a high pitched voice and gazed around at the knocked over swivel chair and papers scattered across the beech desk. 'Look, um, let's go down to the kitchen,' I said. That would impress them and maybe a fresh cupcake would make them forget all this mess.

'I hope we aren't wasting our time,' said Mrs Davis, in a tight voice as we all walked along the landing. 'We're very busy people.'

'I can't apologise enough,' said Deborah. She caught my eye as we followed the couple down. I shivered. Maybe the mean spirit – the one that had grabbed my foot – was back.

With bated breath, I led the way into the kitchen, praying I wasn't about to walk into puddles of food colouring. I sighed with relief. Everything was as I'd left it, the cupcakes neatly in their box, utensils draining, flour and other ingredients presumably still in their packets. Deborah ushered the couple to look out of the window. Despite the low winter cloud, the garden still looked magnificent.

'… and you must see the hot tub.' Deborah led them to the French patio doors. But eyes narrow, jaws set, they stopped by the glass. Tossed to one side was the cover and clumps of flour floated on the water, along with jet black pools, just like the marzipan ladybird dots.

'Is this some joke?' said Mr Davis to Deborah, looking around, perhaps for some hidden camera. 'What sort of amateurish outfit do you work for? We won't be using you again.'

'Wait, please…' she spluttered and hurried after them into the hallway. It was no good. The couple slammed the front door behind them. Deborah swore under her breath and we went over to the front window to watch them leave. Luke was at the end of the drive and they were talking to him. A man carrying a large camera walked past them, heading for Melissa's house.

'I would say sorry for the mess.' I stared at Deborah. 'But you know it wasn't my fault.'

She threw her hands in the air. 'Happens every time – an angry couple ring me, followed by the housesitter on the phone swearing blind they *had* tidied up.' She sighed. 'I know. I should have told you, that this place is… But it sounds so stupid… Have you seen the smoke? Heard the strange gale?'

'Yes. And the White Christmas tune.'

Her brow furrowed. 'That's a new one on me.'

Inside I felt kind of warm. So Walter hadn't revealed himself to the previous sitters. Perhaps he could relate to me because I baked like his wife. Or perhaps I'd picked up psychic abilities by watching so much Most Haunted.

'What about the lights going out?' she said. 'And has anything, um, physically made contact?'

'You mean grabbed me? Yes. I could have been seriously injured. You should have warned us this place was haunted.'

'Sounds mad, doesn't it?' said Deborah. 'But what else could explain this mess? I've cherry-picked the housesitters so far – all reliable, sensible sorts. In fact, you two have been my biggest gamble, with no references and you're quite young.'

'Come on. I reckon we both need a cupcake,' I said and we headed for the kitchen. 'I made a batch of those marzipan ladybird ones I promised for your kids.'

'Sod the kids.' Deborah smiled.

Twenty minutes later we were sitting in the green velvet armchairs in the lounge, coffees on the low oak table, a plate with a cupcake on each of our laps.

'Have you told Mr Murphy why the house won't sell?' I said and took a large bite.

'What would I say? Word would get back to my boss. If anyone got to hear I thought a ghost was in one of my properties, my reputation would be in tatters.' She took a mouthful of sponge. 'That reminds me. Mr Murphy's down here on business the day after tomorrow – said he'd drop by here in the morning. So it goes without saying…'

'I know. I'll make sure everything's spotless and hope no astral being messes it up.' I'd have to do an early tidy up on Thursday morning, as Terry would be around the night before for telly. Walter would be pleased to have his nephew visit.

Deborah licked strawberry buttercream icing from her top lip. 'Mmm.' She sighed and slipped off her shoes. 'Do I really have to give the rest to the children?'

I grinned. Perhaps the viewing wasn't so bad I thought, taking another mouthful. There'd be others. I was determined to get this place sold.

'So what exactly have you told Mr Murphy?' I asked.

'The same excuse I gave you – that times are hard and that pre-Christmas is a notoriously bad time for the market. I suggested he should lower the price if he wants a quick sale. He said another agency had told him the same – that's his way of letting me know he might take his business elsewhere.'

'But you found him housesitters!'

'For the commission on a place this size, any agency would do the same, whether he's friends with the boss or not. You and Jess… Are you definitely staying? You won't run off in the middle of the night?'

'No.' I wanted to help Walter. In any case, what choice did I have? Adam was no nearer to taking me back and more importantly, pregnant Jess needed stability for at least a few more days.

A sudden rapping on glass came from the kitchen. Deborah looked at her watch. 'I'd better get going – appointments to keep, piles of paperwork to plod through…'

'I'll just get you the rest of those cupcakes. Come round again and I'll make you those toffee teddy bear ones I mentioned, with peanut butter icing.' I grinned. 'For the kids, of course.'

The knocking became more frantic and whilst Deborah slipped on her shoes and went out of the front of the lounge, I dashed to the door at the back, almost skidding around the corner into the kitchen. Outside stood Melissa, leaning against the patio doors – hair bedraggled, black, gold-trimmed velour tracksuit grass-stained. Perhaps she and Jonny had, ahem, sunk a few holes on their mini golf course. I opened the patio doors and a gush of cold air breezed in. A little unsteady, she held out a jar of black olives.

'Hello, darling,' she mumbled. 'You left these behind, yesterday.'

I sniffed. That was some "perfume". I recognised the alcoholic bite to it straightaway. It was from the same range as Mum's – let's call that Eau de Cider. Melissa's smelt slightly classier – Eau de Prosecco, perhaps. The golfer's wife half-smiled, then promptly tripped over the patio frame. The olive jar and England's number one birdie – appropriately – went flying.

CHAPTER 15

'Don't move. I'll be back in a minute,' I hissed to Melissa, as she got to her knees and clung to a stool. I grabbed some ladybird cupcakes, put them in a Tupperware box and carried it in to the hall where Deborah was waiting.

'Everything all right?' said Deborah and undid her umbrella. 'What was that crash? Did you know there's a load of photographers at the end of the drive?'

'They're always hanging around Badgers Chase, what with the Winsfords living here.'

'Imagine living your life in the spotlight, like that.' Deborah shuddered. 'Right, well, I'll be in touch,' she said and took the box. 'Thanks for these and, um, I hope things settle down here, for everyone's sake.'

As soon as the front door was closed I hurried back to the kitchen. Melissa was searching through the fridge. Luckily the jar of olives hadn't smashed and I picked it up.

Melissa shook her head. 'What is wrong with you people? This fridge is full of food. Where's the champagne?'

'How about a coffee?' I said. 'And a cute ladybird cupcake?'

She sniffed. 'Okay. Don't normally drink at lunchtime, anyway. It's those bloody parasites with their cameras outside, every lens focused on my window. It's like I'm some little metal duck on a funfair shooting range. Every time I move they're ready to pop their corks.' Her usual velvety voice had hardened.

I put the kettle on, as she sat down at the breakfast island. 'Must be great, though, having your face in all those magazines? And it's well good publicity for your DVDs.' I sighed. 'I wish the paparazzi were interested in me.'

Melissa snorted. 'You don't know what you're talking about. One of the first ever photos they printed of me was taken when I popped out to the shops, without any make-up.' She took a cupcake and picked off the marzipan ladybird. 'Even if I'm only off to the gym, I always have to make an effort – hair sprayed, clothes ironed, polished nails perfectly filed…'

'But that's good, isn't it?' I poured out the drinks.' You set high standards, living like a princess…'

'Yes, all on my own most of the time, like Rapunzel – except no one's going to rescue me from my tower. And knowing my luck, if some saviour climbed up my hair, the extensions would break and they'd fall to their death.'

Melissa wore extensions? That had to be the best kept celebrity secret of the year!

'I love children,' she said softly, and gazed at the ladybird before biting its head off.

Wow! Another exclusive? Was Melissa Winsford trying to get up the duff?

'Jonny wants us to wait before we have any,' she said, with no further prompting, 'until his career is more established.' She lifted the chunky mug to her lips and sipped, before pulling a face. 'I didn't know you could still buy instant coffee in Harpenden.'

'I don't get it,' I said, ignoring the jibe. 'Isn't Jonny's career already well underway?'

Her cheeks tinged pink. 'He's already got a son, Eddie… Maybe he doesn't want to make babies with the second

Mrs Winsford.' She glanced down at her clothes. 'Mind you, can't say I'd blame him, the way I look at the moment.'

'Climb over the fence, did you?' I grinned.

She groaned. 'One of the paparazzi shouted out to me, just as I fell over the top of it. They must have broken all the rules and gone onto our drive. I was only trying to avoid them, but they'll probably make up some story about me taking a roll in the grass with… with that whistling friend of yours.'

'Luke? The huffy handyman?'

'You don't like him? With well-cut clothes he could be pretty hot, along with the right moisturiser and tweezing. What he needs is a man-over.'

'Perhaps,' I said, trying not to think of his deep moss green eyes and the way his mouth twitched at one corner when he made a joke. Or the top of his boxer shorts sitting invitingly low on his flat waist, yesterday morning after he'd stayed over…

'Or else they'll make out you're my lesbian lover,' she said and nibbled her cake.

Just imagine that headline! "Double Birdie for Kimmy and Melissa. Indignant Jonny and Adam say their Exes had Always Been a Few Strokes Under Par."

'I could cause a diversion, if you like?' I said. 'We could swap clothes. I'll distract them whilst you could go back the way you came.'

'That's sweet but I'm not sure you could pull it off. It's taken me years to develop my taut bum. You'd stretch these tracksuit bottoms. They cost a fortune.'

How come I didn't feel offended by her unintentional insults? Probably because they were just that – she was too wrapped up in her own problems to think her remarks through.

'We've got more or less the same colour hair,' I insisted, 'and we're about the same height. I've got some big bug sunglasses, like Victoria Beckham's. It'll be fun!'

'Your bingo wings might give you away.'

Melissa clearly had an expert eye as she'd been able to spot them through my winter clothes.

'No one will notice them under your tracksuit top,' I said. 'Plus it's spitting with rain. I'll hide under an umbrella.'

She took another mouthful of sponge, chewed slowly and actually swallowed it for once. 'Okay,' she said, her smooth tones returning. 'Just don't talk to them. Your Luton twang would be an absolute giveaway. But have you got anything else I can change into? No offence, but those skin-tight leggings are very last season – and not terribly flattering, even with my pins.'

'So why are so many photographers here, today?' I asked.

She shrugged. 'Probably some tart has made up some kiss 'n' tell story about Jonny. There's no major championship for a while, so they're looking for personal, newsworthy stuff. One of those slimy bastards did shout out something about a mystery blonde.' She shook her head. 'It's all so clichéd. And amazing how many of those bimbos go quiet when you threaten legal action.'

Five minutes later, she was upstairs with me, sorting through my wardrobe. You'd think she was choosing some outfit to attend a fashion show, finally selecting white jeans with a designer (okay fake, but she was kind enough not to comment) leopard-print shirt. Then, in front of me, she stripped off and I almost gasped out loud at her washboard stomach and perfectly round boobs, clearly visible through a skimpy lace bra.

'Jonny bought them for me,' she said and wiggled her chest. 'They were a first anniversary present.' She handed her stained tracksuit bottoms and top over to me.

'I'll, um, just get changed,' I muttered, and scuttled into the bathroom. I slipped on the velour tracksuit bottoms and rubbed the waistband between my fingers. Wow. They were so silky, I could hardly feel them on. I came out of the bathroom and smiled at Melissa. She lay on the bed, next to Groucho.

'You'd think I could at least have a dog,' she said, 'but Jonny's allergic.'

'What would you get?' I asked. 'A tiny one?'

'Oh no. Handbag mutts are sooo not on trend. Whereas a Corgi, that's classy. If it's good enough for the Queen…' She stood up and cleared her throat. 'Thanks for the help, Kimmy. To return the favour, why don't you let me sort out that muffin top? I'll send my personal trainer round; treat you to a couple of free sessions.'

She did have a point – I'd hardly managed to pull the tracksuit trousers over my size twelve hips. It would be nice to look toned, although I'd keep a few J-Lo curves. I'd be one of those celebrities the magazines praised for "keeping it real".

Melissa eyed me for a moment. 'Maybe carry a magazine in front of you. Otherwise they'll think I've had a breast reduction.' She stood up and headed for the door, but something silver stopped her dead in her tracks. She reached down to my bedside table. 'I've seen those cards before. It belongs to one of the paparazzi.' Her cheeks flushed. 'I should have known better. You're just like everyone else – not interested in the real Melissa Winsford, just after some dirt to sell.'

Surely she didn't really believe I could be that low? 'Accuse me of anything but that, Melissa – I don't know why I kept it. The guy's a creep.' I snatched the card and tore it up.

'Why should I believe you after the number of times I've been let down in the past? Like the nurse who told the papers about my varicose veins or the beautician who took a photo of me on her phone whilst I was having my top lip waxed.'

Hmm, I remembered that picture – not a flattering look. 'Melissa, you don't know me well, but I'm a loyal friend – just ask Jess. And the easiest way to insult me is to suggest I'm out to make a quick buck. I have long-term plans to earn money through my cake business – not get paid for selling secrets about people I like.'

She stared at me for a moment, and then shrugged. 'I just don't get it – all this interest in the trivial parts of celebrities' lives. Imagine knowing if Audrey Hepburn had cellulite or Marilyn Monroe suffered from spots.' She shook her head. 'Tell me. What's the appeal of reading about stuff like that?'

I thought for a moment. 'It's good to know that despite fame, people are still human, you know? Not much different to the rest of us. That way, maybe my life isn't so bad. That way, maybe it's possible that one day I'll get me a life full of glamour and designer clothes and second homes abroad.' I shrugged. 'Anyway, if you're a true fan, any news is totes interesting – what your favourite star eats for breakfast, how they met their boyfriend or girlfriend...'

'But it's gone too far nowadays. Let's face it – James Dean wouldn't be such an icon if we'd seen lots of photos of him with his fingers up his nose. But apparently it's a two way thing – if I want coverage of my new DVD then I've no right to any privacy.' She pursed her lips. 'I'll delete your phone number. Don't call me again.'

'I'd never contact those slimeballs outside!' I followed Melissa onto the landing. 'If that was my game, don't you think I would have done so by now?'

'With what story?'

'How about finding out that you do use Botox? The magazines have been asking that for months now, quizzing specialists, asking for readers' verdicts.'

She paused at the bottom of the stairs.

'You can trust me,' I said in a soft voice, and smiled. 'Come on. Tell me your favourite cupcake. I'll make some for tomorrow night. Terry from next door is coming over to watch telly and go in the hot tub. It'll be just a cosy neighbourly night in.'

'I don't think so,' she said, stiffly. 'Jonny's been away at some charity event and is back tomorrow. He'll want to catch up – maybe take me to dinner.'

'Suit yourself, but it could be a laugh.' She looked like she needed a good night out. 'My mind's boggling at what Terry's swimsuit will be like. Let's pray it's not an Ali G sling bikini!' I shuddered. 'Or one of those new one-sided thong swimsuits...'

Melissa caught my eye and despite herself, half-smiled back. 'Suppose I could pop over for an hour.'

'And the cupcakes?'

She sniffed. 'How about a Christmas one, to get me in the festive mood? I've had to do all the decorating at home... Jonny's not interested.' Melissa bit her lip. 'Christmas... Really it's about kids, isn't it?'

'Yes – us big kids as well,' I said, gently. 'How about... ooh... gingerbread ones, with nut and chocolate buttercream icing on top – a skinny recipe, of course?'

Melissa licked her lips and nodded.

'Vivian rang for your number, by the way,' she said, as we headed back to the patio doors. 'I gave her your mobile number. If you really want your business to do well, though, you should enter the cake competition at the Harpenden Christmas Market. Jonny was the guest of honour last year. It's not as big as the July Highland Gathering, or Christmas lights' switch-on, but still, lots of local companies and farmers get involved – it's a last-minute chance to buy food and gifts for Christmas. There are various craft-makers demonstrating their art, a big raffle, lots of festive food to buy... Mulled wine on sale, and lots of ideas for presents.' She shrugged. 'It's not a bad afternoon out, as long as the weather holds. The guy who owned this house, Walter, his wife won the cake competition several times. And apparently a few years back, someone trying to launch their own cake-icing company entered and on the back of winning got loads of orders.' She yawned. 'The wives at the golf club were going on and on about it at the last dinner we went to.'

'When is it?'

'Saturday after next. The twenty-third, the day before Christmas Eve. Jonny's agreed to launch the balloons that kick it off.'

That gave me, ooh... ten days, to think of a winning idea, practice it and... 'Aren't I too late to enter?'

'Guess I could swing a late registration for you, if you like.'

At that moment the front door clicked open and I nipped into the hallway.

'Jess? You're home early. What's happened?'

Chest heaving, Jess darted into the downstairs loo. I hadn't heard retching like that since the time macho Adam tried to show off that he could stomach a Vindaloo curry.

I dashed in after her and held her hair away from her face as she bent over the sink, but she pushed me away.

'I can manage,' she croaked.

'At least let me get you a glass of water.' Minutes later, I returned with a tumbler-full. Melissa was in the kitchen, scrutinising her reflection in the patio door windows before following me. She waited in the hallway as I went into the loo.

'Kimmy? Are you ready?' she called moments later.

Jess raised her eyebrows as I passed her a sheet of loo roll to wipe her nose. It was the pleated stuff, with flowers on and softer than a powder puff.

'It's Melissa. I just need to see her back to her house. Don't ask!' I whispered. 'I won't be long and then I'll tell you all about Deborah's visit. You get yourself to bed. How on earth did you cycle home? You should have called me to pick you up and–'

'Stop fussing,' she said, in clipped tones.

'I'm only trying to help.' What was it, with her?

'Someone got a bit of a hangover?' said velvet tones. 'I know just how you feel... Nessie, isn't it? Cheap champagne. That always does it for me. What's your poison?'

'Human Chorionic Gonadotropin, if you must know,' Jess barked as she met Melissa in the hallway. 'And the name's Jess. Not Nessie, nor Bessie, nor Tess.'

'Oh, um, okay, Jess,' said Melissa. 'Not sure I've heard of that cocktail.'

Jess shook her head, and muttered something about an airhead. Although to be fair, not many would know HCG was the pregnancy hormone. Jess was clever like that and shone at pub quizzes. She knew what DNA stood for and could even spell that place in Wales with the longest name in Europe.

'I'm shattered; going to lie down,' mumbled the brainbox. She kicked off her trainers and with heavy footsteps made her way upstairs. Her bedroom door slammed. I shrugged at Melissa and we headed back to the patio doors.

'Take this,' said Melissa, after staring at her wedding finger for a moment. She slid off her famous yellow diamond ring. My stomach tingled as she passed it to me.

'You're not serious?' I muttered and held it in the air, tilting it from side to side. The pear shape gem twinkled like the insides of a golden kaleidoscope.

'I dropped hints to Jonny after seeing the film...'

'Breakfast at Tiffany's,' I said.

Melissa half-smiled. 'You really *do* read all the magazines. Yes. As soon as I saw that yellow Tiffany diamond on Audrey Hepburn, normal diamonds never quite looked the same. Put it on. Flaunt it at those cameras.' She cleared her throat. 'Look after it for me.'

Wow. This rock was worth more than… than the average semi in Luton. I curled my fingers tight so that it couldn't possibly fall off. Melissa glanced sideways at me.

I grinned. 'Worried I'll run off?'

'Like to see you try, with all the paparazzi's motorbikes waiting outside!' She smiled. 'See you soon. Ciao.'

I left the kitchen for the hallway, shoulders back, head high. Now I felt like a real celebrity – special, different, somehow taller. I put on her trainers (ooh, weird sole, they looked like those fancy weight loss ones), grabbed my big bug sunglasses from the kitchen table, picked up a magazine from the hallway table and stepped out of the front door. I hoped no one saw me briefly stumble. In the weird trainers, I felt like I was walking on a wobble board. Plus it was hard to resist the urge to pull down the tracksuit bottoms. They'd wedged right up in between my legs. I held my lips in a "blowing up a balloon" position, in the hope that they'd look more plump.

'Melissa! Woo hoo! Over 'ere love! We thought we saw you leg it to your neighbour's a while back.'

'Yo! Melissa!' yelled a man's voice. 'Look up, love! Give us a nice smile! Where's Jonny?'

Sexy walk? Check. Flaunting ring? Check. Superior celebrity expression on face? Hmm, perhaps I should lose the balloon lips. Even though it had virtually stopped raining, I put up my umbrella and ducked underneath. Yikes, if only Melissa had been wearing a coat, it was freezing. And to match the winter temperatures, I must have looked extremely cool, as I sashayed down the drive, as if on a red carpet, approaching the clicking cameras and shouts. So what if they didn't know who I really was? At least I might finally get my picture in Infamous.

Talking of which, I held the magazine over my modest B cup chest. The sound of snapping shutters and pong of cigarette smoke overwhelmed me as I turned left. The Winsfords' place wasn't far but with these men crowding around, poking their lenses under my nose, the short walk began to feel like a marathon.

'Give us a quote, Melissa. Anything. Come on, love, then we'll leave yer alone.'

'Why don't you take off those glasses?' called a voice.

'Or get out those tits,' sniggered someone else.

I pulled the umbrella down further, like a shield. Mustn't perspire in Melissa's top. Mustn't trip. Mustn't talk. MUSTN'T LOSE RING. Hey, so far I was doing pretty good.

'Stuck-up bitch,' someone muttered.

'You look a bit rough,' said a nearby voice. I glanced to my right and spotted muddy combat trousers. It was the photographer who'd given me his silver card.

'Understandable, though,' he continued. 'All this talk of Jonny fooling around with another blonde. Likes playing twosomes away, doesn't he? Everyone knows golfers are the new footballers. Do yer trust him or is yer marriage under par?'

Melissa had been right. This was all about another false kiss 'n' tell.

'Don't you worry about letting yerself go though, love,' he continued. 'I think it's admirable that yer happy to put on some weight – you were a lot slimmer the last time I saw you this close.' He blew smoke in my face. 'In fact, yer arse looks almost big enough to pinch. If it goes to print, it might inspire yer to get into shape before the big tournaments kick off, in the spring. Can't have the cute little American golfing Wags seeing yer look less like a petite birdie and more like an albatross.'

Cheeks flaming, I quickened my pace but a couple of men appeared from nowhere, on the pavement in front. I dodged them and put my head down further, praying I wouldn't fall off the kerb or walk into a lamppost.

'What's yer problem, love? All we want is one good shot.'

'We're starving – got any posh nosh?'

'Show us a bit of cleavage. Where's your sense of fun?'

Ignoring the insults, I pushed forwards, heart racing. One of the quieter photographers growled at the men to move out of my way and pushed me gently onto Melissa's drive. 'Haven't you got daughters or sisters?' I heard him mutter to the others and then something about how they should be ashamed. Gratefully, I charged towards the house. Being trailed by the paparazzi hadn't lived up to my fantasy at all.

At the garage I dropped my umbrella and hurried up to the front door. A funny noise came from around the left of the house. I crept around to the side. There it was again. Was that a sob? I walked down to the back garden, past the kitchen, *at last* (was I really saying that?) out of sight of the cameras.

'Melissa?'

Head in hands, she sat on the grass, next to an upturned wheelie bin.

'What's wrong?' I threw down the magazine and took off my sunglasses. 'Vandals? Foxes?'

She looked up at me. 'No. Another kind of vermin.'

My brow furrowed. 'I don't think rats are strong enough to–'

'Those bastard photographers have gone through my bins. Usually they wait until dark.' She bit her lip. 'They must have got a whiff of a really juicy story out there if they're this desperate.' She gazed around at the mess. 'Jonny will go mad.'

'But what are they hoping to find?' I stared at the cardboard boxes and crumpled kitchen roll. 'Don't you shred the important stuff?'

'Yes. Anything with our personal details on and all the post, of course. But…' She sniffed again. 'I've a nasty feeling I threw some empty tablet boxes in here yesterday. Jonny's on prescription drugs for a bad back. He hates the press finding out anything that might hint he's not on form.'

'Come on. Let's tidy up,' I said and swallowed. Poor Melissa. 'Maybe they're still amongst all this rubbish.'

She shook her head. 'I've already looked. He'll go ballistic if news creeps out. Also, I… I threw out a pregnancy magazine I couldn't resist buying last month.' She sighed. 'At least they left the bottle bin alone. Last month some story surfaced about how many bottles of champagne we drank a week. Jonny didn't speak to me for two days. Said it reflected badly on his wholesome, healthy golfer image and made him look unprofessional. He could hardly say it was me drinking all that fizz.'

Shaking her head, she stood up, whilst I pulled her ring off my finger.

'That made me feel ten feet tall,' I said and handed it over, with a wry smile.

'You fooled them then?'

'I think so – although they thought you'd put on weight.'

'What do men know?' Melissa said and stroked the diamond before she slid it back onto her finger. She stared at me for a minute. 'Come upstairs to my changing room, Kimmy. I guess one good turn deserves another. I've got something that could really make you feel sky-high.'

Changing room? Was that another word for drugs den?

'I... um... don't even drink much,' I said and followed her through the kitchen and upstairs. 'I wouldn't want to get high on...'

'Nearly there,' she said as we reached the landing and entered a room almost straight ahead. I walked in. Rubbed my eyes. Opened them again. On the left was a wall covered in the biggest, gilt-framed hairdresser's salon mirror. On the far wall was another mirror, above a wide shelf covered in an array of toiletries, make-up and brushes. There were two pink stools in front of this. Across the length of the right hand wall were two wardrobes with pull open doors. Cherry red wallpaper made the room look so extravagant. The carpet was fluffy and I felt an urge to bend down and give it a cuddle.

Melissa pointed to the left hand wardrobe. 'My clothes are in there. But in here...' She pulled open the right hand one. I almost blacked out. Was this a dream? A walk-in shoe wardrobe? Shelves ran down either side and right at the end was a full-length mirror. As the doors opened, a trail of ceiling lights lit up.

'Go on, Kimmy. Take anything you want. What's your favourite colour?'

Goggle-eyed, I walked up and down the shelves of shoes, like an officer inspecting a parade. There were stilettos in red, gold, black, blue, and two whole rows of strappy sandals! I pointed to a pair of pink and gold golf shoes.

'I had those made specially,' she said. 'I'm taking lessons behind Jonny's back. It's going to be a surprise when I challenge him to a match on his next birthday. The teacher's a lovely guy.' She smiled. 'He calls me a right little hooker.'

'What?' Sounded like an insult to me.

'I *hook* the ball when I swing, although I've still no idea what that means.'

'Jonny will be impressed. It's a great idea,' I said and gawped once again at a shoe shop selection of wedges and platforms.

'Your feet are about my size, aren't they, darling? A five?'

I nodded. When it came to measurements, our shoe size was the only thing we had in common.

'How about these? Cute but practical. I've only worn them once.'

She handed me the most amazing pair of, ooh, five inch high gold platforms, with intricate white leather flowers across each strap. My hands trembled. Perhaps this was a turning point in my life – I'd never held genuine designer shoes before.

I bent over, slipped off Melissa's trainers and slid my feet between the soft leather straps. Then I stood up and looked in the mirror, towering over Melissa now. My legs looked all model-like and somehow thinner. They were summer shoes really, but who cared!

'Thanks,' I stuttered.

'No problem.' She headed for the landing and I followed her downstairs, praying I wouldn't trip and fall.

'By the way,' she said as we reached the kitchen. 'I caught sight of Jess just before I left yours and offered my congratulations. She was making herself a hot drink.'

'Congrats? Um…'

'The baby.'

'You knew?' I said.

'Straightaway. One of the golfing wives had bad morning sickness, plus I've read every book ever published on pregnancy. The name of that "cocktail" she mentioned was actually the pregnancy hormone.'

'What did she say?'

'Jess got very angry; thought you'd told me; said people should mind their own business. I didn't know it was some sort of secret. Anyway, the last thing she did was throw down her tea towel and announce she was leaving Harpenden.'

CHAPTER 16

Smeared green bile where rouge should be – not an attractive look. Not that Jess usually wore make-up, and if she did it had to be made from base ingredients that had never been tested on animals. I'd taken off my new shoes and hurried across the fence and back garden, into Mistletoe Mansion. Carefully, I'd laid the designer shoes on my bed, then found Jess in her ensuite, throwing up into the toilet.

'Who else have you told?' she muttered and pushed me away as I brushed strands of red hair from her face.

'No one! Honest. Melissa just guessed. You gave it away with that cocktail name. You're not leaving, are you?'

'Haven't got a choice, have I?' she muttered. 'Nowhere else to stay.' She stood up, ran the cold tap and bent over for a drink and wash. I passed her the towel and she snatched it from me. 'I can manage,' she said.

That was it. I locked the bathroom door and stood in front of it, arms crossed.

'Right,' I said. 'Spill.'

'What do you mean?'

'Ever since that pregnancy test result, you've refused any help. We've always been there for each other, haven't we? Like... like me taking revenge on Dan at school for asking if your surname was Weasley.'

'Thanks for reminding me of that,' said Jess although she half-smiled. 'Dan reckoned the only reason he failed his maths GCSE was because of that itching powder you slipped down his back.'

'And what about the time I lost my favourite headband on that cross country run neither of us could get out of? You walked the length of the route again with me, after school, in the rain, 'til we found it on a bush. I was well chuffed.'

Jess wiped her nose. 'This is a little more serious than that.'

I put my hand on her arm but she shook it off.

'What?' I said. 'Jess. It's me. Kimmy. The girl who's borrowed your toothbrush and knows you've secretly got the hots for middle-aged gardening expert Alan Titchmarsh. Come on… What's bugging you?'

'You mean apart from me having ruined my life?' She sniffed.

I folded my arms.

'Okay, okay,' she mumbled. 'It's just… Perhaps I deserve all this. Your mum…'

'What's she got to do with this?'

'I… I know you think I've always given her a hard time – it's because I've seen how difficult things have been for you, because she was careless enough to get pregnant so young, without a regular boyfriend… I felt angry on your behalf.' Jess rambled on. 'Maybe this is karma; the universe punishing me so I find out how truly difficult single parenthood is. I always thought I was too sensible for it to happen to me. I feel…' her voice wavered, '…stupid.'

'But why push me away?'

She gulped. 'You must hate me. After all my critical comments, now I'm in exactly the same position as her. I'm such a hypocrite.'

'No you're not. You're a great friend. I know it was only cos you cared about me that you said those things.'

Jess used to get fired up – when Mum forgot parents' evenings and non-uniform days and sent me to school in a shirt stained with tomato ketchup from the night before. 'Mum is Mum,' I said. 'And certainly not a mascot for all single mothers. Lots of women get pregnant and left in the lurch. It doesn't make them stupid or a bad person. Just unlucky.'

'But still, everything that happened when you were at school… That time your mum turned up to the end of year play drunk…'

I bit my lip. Yeah, I sure had some memories that would be best well and truly buried.

'Who's to say she wouldn't have been like that if she was married, in the suburbs with two point four children?' I said, eventually. 'Having kids, under whatever circumstances, doesn't completely change a woman's intrinsic personality. And remember Chloe Pritchard's mum? Always volunteering for school trips, on the PTA – she chose to be single and Chloe's dad came from a sperm bank. You'd never meet a more upright, organised woman.'

Jess gave a wry smile. I squeezed her hand. Although my bestie did have more in common with my mum than you'd ever think. I'd never forgotten, the night I got my GCSE results – they weren't bad. Mum was so proud. Over a can (or six) of strong lager, she talked properly, for the first time ever really, about how her parents – or rather her dad – had thrown her out when the bump showed, but like Jess, she was determined to carry on with the pregnancy. Grannie kept in touch though, and without fail sent me a card and five pound note for every birthday. 'I was never going to give you up, girl,' Mum said to me. 'You and your brother, Tom, you're the best things I've ever done. You've got the good bits of me. Don't waste them, like I have.'

'Come on – meet you in the kitchen. Let me rustle up something to eat.' I raised my eyebrows. Jess stared at me for a moment, sniffed and then nodded.

Half an hour later, over pasta, I gave her a full explanation of why the house was so messy. With every mouthful, Jess became more like her old self.

'Here, let me get you another orange juice,' I said. 'How do you think your young-hearted mum will cope with the news that she's going to be a gran?'

She looked at me and we both laughed.

'How will *your* mum react?' asked Jess, in a small voice. 'We've never really got on. She'll have a field day, I bet.'

I passed Jess her drink and sat down again. 'You'd be surprised. All these years, she's always told me how lucky I am to have such a loyal friend.'

Jess flushed red and changed the subject by asking what our famous neighbour had been doing here and why on earth I'd invited her over the next evening. Then she headed off to bed, saying she didn't know why I was hurt by the paparazzi's mean comments; that if they'd compared my arse to the size of an albatross's (golfing term!), compared to hers in nine months it would look like a goldcrest's (the smallest bird in Britain, apparently – Jess knew random stuff about nature, like that).

She was right. I needed to get some perspective. Mentally, I stuck out my tongue at the paparazzi and headed for my apron and oven gloves. Two hours later I'd made a batch of Melissa's skinny gingerbread cupcakes and a batch of one of my favourites: succulent black cherry (tinned ones made the batter so juicy), topped with a generous buttercream icing swirl and dark chocolate shavings – my retro Black Forest Gateau cupcake. Okay, so not Christmassy, but gorgeous at any time of the year.

I checked my phone and replied to several messages – Saffron had rung. She wanted twenty girly cupcakes for Friday's hen night, which gave me three days to brainstorm my designs. Luke also texted. He asked how the house viewing had gone and, when I told him about the mysterious mess-making, offered to clear my cooking ingredients out of the hot tub before Melissa and Terry came round tomorrow.

Funny. Why would he do that? I'd tried, over the last day or two, to figure out why he ran hot and cold. From the start he'd been rude, which had put me on my guard. And even though he was as arrogant as they came, I couldn't help wondering if that was just a thin veneer. Clearly he'd been fond of – and looked out for – Walter and Lily. Plus he'd done the decent thing the other night, and stayed over after the evil spirit attacked me in my bedroom…

I sighed. Whereas Adam… I knew him inside out. Okay, him dumping me had come as a shock, but if we got back together I figured the future would be pretty much mapped out. Which was good, no? He offered me all the security I'd missed as a child. Yet since we'd split – since I'd moved into Mistletoe Mansion – I… I couldn't help wondering if my relationship with Adam – my safety blanket – was holding me back.

Increasingly confused, I headed upstairs, and after a quick shower, got into bed and sat, plaiting my hair. I plumped the floral cushions behind me, then stared blankly around the room. Talk about Mum always made me feel heavy inside. If Adam was here he would have given me a big hug or nuzzled my neck – whatever mood I was in, that always made me laugh. I pulled up the luxurious crimson duvet. Perhaps I was the stupid one. There was Jess, up the duff and on her tod, whereas Adam was practically begging me to put down roots with him for a secure future.

A remedy was required, to clear my muddled mind and cheer me up. My mouth watered as I reached across to the bedside table and picked up my self-prescribed cure – a ginormous Black Forest Gateau cupcake. Mmm. I closed my eyes, partly to avoid Groucho's begging eyes, partly to savour every mouthful as the cream caressed my tongue and the sponge slowly disintegrated, releasing the moistness and slightly sharp richness of the cherries.

I took another bite. The house was so quiet, all I could hear was the dog's breathing. I still wasn't quite used to living in a rural cul-de-sac, half-expecting, at any time, to hear a car roar past or someone's bass-beating music. A detached house was perfect. No arguments coming through the walls – nor the neighbours' latest video game or telly programmes. And what bliss not to hear the constant tip-tap of footsteps above me. The couple in the flat above Adam's had laminated floor fitted and I could have sworn the woman lived in stilettos.

Eventually I opened my eyes and put the empty plate back on the bedside table. Groucho lay down against my side. I bet Lily never ate in bed. I imagined her stretched out there, with gloves covering hands slathered in Pond's cold cream and rollers in her hair. Although she could probably afford to have her hair done daily at a salon, prior to lunch in a fancy bistro with Walter. What a happy couple they must have been. I felt heavy inside again. Was I doing the right thing, refusing to settle down with Adam?

My shoulders sagged and I leant back against the cushions and felt my mouth downturn. Then I jumped. What was that? It felt as if something had tickled my feet. A cold ball hit the inside of my chest. What if it was the evil being that had grabbed my leg? Feeling sick, I gingerly pulled up the duvet and sheets to look. Groucho sat next to me, wagging his tail.

Nothing was there, but a cool breeze snuck around my neck. The familiar White Christmas music started to play. Groucho's tail still looked like a top-speed metronome. It must have been Walter trying to make me smile.

'Walter!' I sat bolt upright, chest now airy and light. 'Was that you?' I looked around the room. 'Um… if it was, tickling my feet, hmm, that's a bit random!' I giggled. The music got louder. 'Walter!' My feet felt ticklish again. Perhaps I should have freaked out but was too excited at the prospect of him wanting to communicate.

The air became draught-free again now and as still as a Botoxed forehead. There was no hoot of owls, no overhead aeroplanes heading for Luton airport. I cleared my throat. Perhaps I could find out exactly how the house got so messy today. I needed some answers off the old man – or rather ghost. So I had to word my questions carefully.

'Walter?' I said softly.

Groucho sank down onto the lush bedcover again but his chocolate button eyes were wide open.

'It's me here – Kimmy. But then you can see that, can't you?'

Nothing.

'I want to help. You can't be happy, stuck down here whilst Lily's waiting at the Pearly Gates.' I smiled. 'Terry told me all about you two. Said you were "the sweetest couple". Knock three times, Walter. Knock three times to let me know you're definitely here and then we can try to sort things out.'

Hardly daring to breathe, I waited. Oh my God. My head felt dizzy. Three low thuds came from the wall between my room and the front locked one.

'Thank you,' I whispered, and took a deep breath. 'Knock three more times if you made that mess today.'

Three more thuds! I gasped. This was easier than expected.

'And again if… if…' I thought back to my favourite episodes of Most Haunted and rubbed my hands together. '…if you were really murdered and won't leave until the culprit is brought to justice.'

Nothing. Okay. Suppose that was a long shot.

'Were… were you secretly sick of being upstanding in real life, and just want to have some fun before you pass on?'

The dreamy Christmas music wafted into the room and it felt kind of comforting, as if Walter was encouraging me to carry on with other suggestions. I shivered. What a pity ghosts weren't more tropical.

'Let's go back to basics, then. Knock three times if you understand that…' I swallowed hard. '…That you're dead.'

I almost clapped my hands as he gave three thuds again. Groucho's head cocked. This reaction from Walter was a good result. At least his haunting, for want of a better word, wasn't because he still thought he was alive and cross about strangers moving into his home. So, next…

'Are you finding it hard to leave here because this place reminds you of happy times?'

No reply to that.

'Okay… um…' He'd been a charitable man, according to Terry. Perhaps he was here on some mission of goodwill. 'Have you a message for someone? Is a friend you knew in trouble? Do they need your help?'

Clearly not.

'Are you plotting to take revenge?' I said desperately, finding it difficult to imagine this old man caught up in anything dodgy. Yet the music got a little louder, almost as if to say I was on the right track. "Revenge", perhaps that was a bit strong... 'Walter – have you got *unfinished business*?'

Three low thuds. A grin spread across my face. What a feature this would make in Starchat. Perhaps the famous me would be given a supernatural problem page to write, called "Supernatural Solutions – Kimmy Counsels your Dead".

Right. Concentrate. Unfinished business, what could that mean? He'd been retired, but dealt with charities and was active in the golf club. I fiddled with my plait.

'Knock again, Walter, if you owe someone money.'

Nothing.

'Or someone owes you?'

Silence still, apart from the air around my neck turning positively arctic.

'The will?' I said lamely. 'Knock three times if you aren't happy with the will.'

Three *loud* thuds! Wow! But he hadn't got any kids. Who else would inherit apart from his nephew? The nostalgic notes of White Christmas stopped suddenly and I felt warm again. Walter had gone.

My hands shook a little, but I didn't feel scared. If only he'd stayed longer, I had a zillion questions in my head. He'd been fond of his nephew, hadn't he? Plus, according to Terry, was *compos mentis*, until the end. He wouldn't have signed anything without reading the small print.

I stared into space, different scenarios running through my head. If Mr Murphy wasn't supposed to get everything, then who else would benefit? Oh my God… Perhaps Walter and Lily weren't such a perfect couple and he'd had a lovechild who the old boy had originally provided for. Or maybe the couple had been brainwashed by some religious cult and had intended everything to go to them.

After what seemed like hours of thinking, I could only conclude that, behind closed doors, Mr Murphy was a bully and had forced Walter to sign a new document –

or had forged a new, secret copy. Perhaps he'd charmed Walter into altering the will and now the old man could see Murphy for the conman he really was…

I clapped my hands. Of course. Thursday morning the nephew was visiting – the perfect opportunity for Walter to show his true feelings and for me to find out more!

CHAPTER 17

I looked across the wicker table at Terry and shook my head. He sucked in his cheeks, for one moment making his chubby face look almost chiselled. We both knocked back a mouthful of tea as a fly circumnavigated the inside of the summerhouse before deciding my buttered toast wasn't interesting enough. Jess's bicycle was gone so she'd obviously made it into work. Terry had rapped loudly at the front door just after nine and woken me up. Following my late night chat with Walter, I'd still been asleep. Groucho had disappeared from my bed and when I came down his chocolate button eyes had begged for a plate of biscuits.

I pulled up my blanket. Terry did the same. We grinned at each other. I'd insisted we breakfast outside, even though it was December, as once I'd left Badgers Chase there'd be little opportunity for me to dine "al fresco" (listen to me!).

'Poor Melissa,' I said and stared once again at the tabloid before my eyes. The morning breeze crept in through the open doors and lifted the top corner of the newspaper. I adjusted the pretty embroidered cushion behind my back, feeling nice and comfy in my jogging trousers and one of Adam's jumpers I'd, ahem, "accidentally" packed. I looked up for a moment. Plants swayed in the full borders and a posse of nearby starlings chirped. Everywhere was green. The air smelt fresh. My ears homed in on nature's sounds.

In that moment, Luton and Adam could have been in another universe.

I gazed at the article again. Jonny? In the back of a taxi? Snogging some mystery blonde? Terry had brought over his morning paper, bursting with how he'd had to pick his way through the crowds of journalists and clicking cameras all around Badgers Chase. For once, the paparazzi rumour mill had got it right. For the hundredth time, I focused on the photo of the young woman who was partially hidden as the golfer, back to the camera, kissed her. Her arm was wrapped around his neck and from her wrist hung a silver bracelet with two charms – a mini Eiffel Tower and an engraved heart.

'Just look at those headlines,' I muttered, stomach squeezing at the thought of Melissa upset. They'd come straight from the stuff nicked out of Melissa's wheelie bin: "Jonny on Drugs for Extra-marital Bonking Backache" and "Pregnant Melissa's Curvy New Figure". At least there was no photo of her falling over Walter's fence. Nor any of me in disguise – what a shame.

'More toast?' I asked. Terry had eaten my breakfast.

'Apparently the photographers have spotted him with this woman before,' said Terry, still glued to the newspaper, looking kinda cute in a rainbow coloured bobble hat. 'Do you think Melissa knows who she is?'

Before I could answer, footsteps approached from the garden path. We looked at each other. Maybe that was her.

'Quick! Shove that paper behind your cushion,' I said and hurried out of the summerhouse and onto the lawn. Groucho almost tripped me up as he stopped chasing an imaginary cat and ran to greet...

'Luke?'

'Very perceptive,' he said and bent down to stroke the dog.

I failed to think of an equally sarcastic reply.

'Late night?' He stood up and came nearer to me, the corner of his mouth twitching. He turned up the collar of his anorak. I willed myself not to look at his appealingly tight jeans that asked the question, how difficult would they be to get off?

'The side gate was left open,' he said. 'One journalist wouldn't leave me alone – told her cameraman to zoom in and asked me to take my top off. Can't say I blame her.' He grinned. 'You're not going to throw something at me, are you? At least there aren't any plastic Christmas trees in the back garden. I thought I'd be safe, unless you've armed yourself with a spade.'

'Ha, ha,' I said and tried to smooth out the creases from my jogging bottoms.

'Morning, sonny.' Terry waved at Luke as he walked past, manbag over shoulder, colourful bobble hat slightly crooked.

'Hi, Terry. Noticed your front guttering is hanging a bit low. Could have been that storm we had the other night. Would you like me to check it out later?'

'Really? You're a diamond.' He clapped Luke on the back. 'Better get going, Kimmy. See you tonight, seven o'clock sharp. Don't worry, I'll show myself out.'

Luke headed towards the bottom of the garden. 'Not too much milk in my tea, Kimmy. I'll be at the vegetable patch.'

I followed him to the well-ordered patch, and admired the neat row of poles and plants. 'This isn't some motorway caff, you know.'

'Oh well, if you don't want me to clean out your hot tub for your party tonight…'

Ah yes. I'd forgotten his odd offer to help me and my chest warmed a titch. He bent over to uproot a couple of leeks and handed them to me. There was that weird friendliness again – but I was grateful for the veg and might make soup for lunch. Then I headed back towards the kitchen, but something grabbed my leg and wound itself around my ankle. My leeks fell to the lawn with a thud as I tripped and fell. A piercing pain shot through my foot.

'Get off me!' I shrieked to whatever it was. Perhaps that evil spirit had morphed into a snake. If only I could grab a leek and whip the demon senseless.

'Jess must have pruned back those overgrown roses,' said Luke, already by my side, on his knees. 'You've trodden on a small branch and your foot's bound up in the middle of a pile of hose. Didn't you see it?'

Before I knew it, he helped me stand up. To steady myself, I reached down and leant on his head. The tousled bedroom hair slipped between my fingers whilst, still on his knees, he untangled me. It was silky smooth and long enough to grab hold of.

'A couple of large thorns have gone through your sock, into your ankle,' he said. 'Where are your tweezers?'

'It's all right.' I limped towards the patio doors. 'I can manage.' But he caught me up and slipped an arm around my waist. His fingers gently spread around my ribcage and for some reason, my stomach fluttered. We went through the patio doors and into the kitchen.

'In your bedroom, are they?' he said and eased me onto a stool.

'On the bedside table,' I mumbled. Much as inflexible me hated to admit it, I found it difficult enough just to paint my toe nails, so Luke's assistance would be useful. Within minutes Luke had returned and knelt on the floor again. Gently, he dug out the thorns and massaged the skin with his thumbs. Tingles ran up and down my legs. Thank God I'd shaved again recently, otherwise he'd have been the one in pain.

'Done,' he said, finally. 'I'd wash your ankle, if I were you; kill off any bacteria.'

'Yes, Dad,' I mumbled. We smiled at each other and he headed outside again. So, today it was friendly Luke, not the one who was as irritating as nettle rash. Quickly I showered, changed into jeans, a better fitting jumper and my gold parka. Then I returned to the summerhouse, hair curled from a night's sleep, loosely tied back. Whilst washing, a slight panic had set in. I needed to brainstorm ideas for Saffron's hen party on Friday. The bottom of the garden was as good a place to clear my head and work as any, and Luke was busy dealing with the hot tub now.

Once settled, I gazed around. Utter heaven. The nearest you got to fresh air in Adam's flat was opening the front windows onto a road reeking of take-aways and petrol – whereas the smell of Walter's garden reminded me of a nature trail we once did at school.

Pen in hand, I stared at the blank piece of paper in front of me. Hen nights – "pink", I wrote down. "Girly". "Saucy". "Fun". My pen hovered for a moment before I roughly sketched some willies and boobs. I could make little black whips out of liquorice, and marzipan handcuffs. I reckoned Saffron would love them – unless, for appearances' sake, she'd like to come across as more classy. So as well, I jotted down "roses", "glitter", "hearts" and "chocolate". Saffron wanted a personal touch, so I'd spell out her sister's name in icing – the word AMY was just short enough to fit on one bun.

Yay! That seemed like a plan. I chewed on the end of my pen. Now I could concentrate on brainstorming exactly how to find out what was troubling Walter about his nephew.

'A man could die of thirst in this place.' Luke stood in front of me, forehead perspiring. He wiped it with his arm. 'The tub's done. I drained it and refilled. It's all in working order.'

'Thanks,' I said, as he grabbed the other wicker chair and sat down next to me, stretching out like a cat in front of a fire. S'pose he deserved a mug of tea and maybe one of my Black Forest Gateau cupcakes. I headed indoors. By the time I'd returned, his drink and plate in hand, he was chuckling. Aarggh! Beam me up, Scottie! I'd forgotten to hide my sketches.

'Remind me never to ask you to cater for my mum,' he said.

My cheeks flamed. 'I've only got until Friday night to come up with the right recipes and bake them. I'm catering for one of Melissa's friends – well, acquaintances. Whatever. It's a hen party.'

'Don't reckon you can go wrong with body parts. In my experience, even posh girls have got a dirty sense of humour.' He took a large bite of cherry sponge. Cream and chocolate shavings stuck to the corners of his mouth. I fought the urge to stretch out my arm and gently wipe them off. 'It's a gift, being able to bake like this,' he said and wiped his mouth himself.

I raised one eyebrow and waited for the punchline – the rude insult.

'No. Really. I mean it. And as you know, I've been lucky enough to eat Lily's creations, so I know what I'm talking about. How long has KimCakes Ltd been up and running?'

He remembered the name! I knew it would catch on! But how to answer? I could lie, say the business was established, ooh, months ago, had been a great success and I now had a well impressive client base. But I had the feeling he'd see right through me if I didn't tell the truth and then I'd feel even more stupid. I picked up the pen. Why would I want to impress him, anyway? 'Three days.'

He coughed violently, crumbs tumbling onto his lap.

'Melissa was my first proper customer,' I said, quickly, not giving him chance to diss my dreams. 'Apart from a wedding I did in Luton. It's always been my goal to run my own cupcake company. And this job could help start things off. Then two of Melissa's other friends want me to cater for them and–'

He put down his cake. 'Good for you. It takes a lot of guts to break out on your own.'

I stared at him, having expected the negative comments I was used to, from Adam.

'What's the matter?' he asked and ran a hand through his chestnut fringe.

'You don't think I'm mad?

'Has someone said you are?' His moss green eyes stared right through me.

I blushed.

'We all have to start somehow and as long as you can deliver the goods, blagging is as good a way as any. It's refreshing to meet a kindred spirit – someone who wants to get out there, and grab a bit of the good life for themselves.' He shrugged. 'For my first handyman job, I wrote a false reference from some imaginary customer. The old lady was a bit picky. I didn't like deceiving her, but knew I could do a good job for her at a decent price. Afterwards, she recommended me to all her friends. I still do the odd job for her.'

'How long before your business paid enough to do it full time?'

'A few months. But I learnt quickly that I had to diversify. I do a bit of gardening and, for the customers who know me well, like Walter, I keep an eye on their house whilst they are on holiday – water plants, check the pipes in the winter, that kind of stuff.' He popped in the last bit of cake. 'Just need another drink to wash that down,' he said.

Without thinking I stuck my tongue out at him and he burst out laughing.

'You don't like me, do you?' he said, once he'd stopped.

'You've hardly welcomed me to Mistletoe Mansion with open arms!' I spluttered. We grinned. Wow. It almost felt as if we were getting on. Mind you, us, kindred spirits? I think not.

His face softened for a second. 'Don't take it too personally,' he murmured and leant forwards to brush a random curl out of my face. Heat flushed up through my neck. Why had he done that? And why did it make my pulse race?

'What do you mean?'

The twinkle disappeared from his eyes. 'Look, erm, forget the drink. Busy day. Washers to change. Shelves to put up.' He scraped his chair back and picked up his toolbox.

'You can't say something like that and just disappear!' I said and followed him across the lawn, but there was no reply. 'Anyway, I should be out of your way soon. There's another viewing Friday morning and I'm determined it'll go well.' That told him. Moody bugger. Just in case he still thought I was hoping to hang around here forever cos of some supposed crush. Although truth be told, a tiny part of me hoped the viewing would be a flop. I needed to work out what was bothering Walter, before Mistletoe Mansion sold and Mike Murphy got his hands on the inheritance.

'Last time I checked, I was all grown up and allowed to say what I want.'

I caught up and touched his arm. Tingles pitter-pattered from my fingers, up to my shoulder.

'Just remember what I said.' Luke smirked and turned around. 'Black whips and handcuffs; dirtier the better, that's what ladies want...'

'Don't change the subj–'

'Kimmy?

I gasped and looked behind Luke. Adam? Standing one metre away? How did he get here?'

Luke's mouth twitched. 'I'm Luke. Pleased to meet you.'

'This is Adam,' I stuttered, heart racing faster than ever now. Peanut had come! He must have missed me! Perhaps he was impressed with my Botox morning earnings after all.

'Think you were just leaving, mate,' said Adam, grey eyes steely as he took a step forwards. He stared at my hand which was still curled around Luke's arm. I jerked it away.

Luke grinned. 'Remember, Kimmy, great big boobs and long wi–'

'I get it,' I said, through gritted teeth.

Luke shot me a glance, then looked at Adam. 'No need to worry, *mate*,' he said. 'We're discussing Kimmy's cake business and the designs for her latest booking.'

Oh my God. I couldn't believe Adam was here. That was great! Fab! Brill! Everything I wanted! Then why... I dunno, did a tiny part of me sink, as if weighed down by a record-breaking anchor.

'Kimmy's very talented,' Luke continued. 'Cupcakes are big business nowadays. She'll do well to set up on her own.'

'And what would you know about Kimmy?' said Adam, looking at Luke's toolbox. 'You reckon this is a good time to be setting up a business? During the recession?' Adam shook his head.

'Doesn't take me long to get the sum of someone, that's all... ' Luke turned to me. 'Cheers, Kimmy. Thanks for the snack.' He headed for the leeks I'd dropped on the lawn. 'These will do nicely for my dinner.' Whistling, he strode towards the house. He disappeared around the side. The gate clicked shut.

I laughed nervously at Adam. 'This is a surprise. How come you're here? I mean, shouldn't you be at work?'

'I'm on a late shift today. Great to see you too,' Adam said, brow still furrowed. 'Although it doesn't look as if you've missed me much. Who was that? You two seemed pretty cosy. You didn't even hear me cross the lawn.'

'That guy's a jerk,' I said, telling myself not to cave in and throw my arms around my hunky boyfriend's – ex-boyfriend's – broad shoulders. 'But then it's none of your business – not since you threw me out.' Stiff upper lip, girl, I told myself. Calm down. Don't show him you're chuffed to bits that he's here. Which I was… Even though I stood more upright and felt myself get all defensive about the business; even though I had to slide into the old familiar – and unpleasant – self-justification mode.

'Thought I'd check you were settled okay.' His mouth downturned a little. 'Seems like I needn't have bothered.'

Oh bum. I melted and took his hand. 'Come on – let me show you around the house.'

'Just look at this kitchen!' I said, moments later. He didn't flinch as I opened the huge fridge doors, nor mumble a word as he followed me up the staircase, me chatting about the paintings. I pointed out the chandelier. Still no reaction. So I led him into the fancy bathroom and switched on the waterproof telly. At last, some response – he muttered something about "More money than sense". Surely the Game of Thrones Room would cause a flicker of excitement? I hurried downstairs and waited impatiently for him as he strolled after me, expressionless.

'This room is awesome!' I pushed open the mahogany door. Adam trailed in behind me and stared at the dartboard and snooker table. He ran his hand along the bar.

'Amazing, isn't it?' I grinned and pointed to the throne. 'Fancy role-playing a little warrior on queen, one-on-one?'

His shoulders gave a little movement up and down. 'S'okay, I suppose. A bit flash. I mean, what's wrong with going down the pub?'

'Nothing! But it means you can invite your friends over. In fact tonight I'm having the neighbours over for a small party, including Jonny Winsford's wife from next door. Why don't you stay? We're going to use the hot tub.'

Adam stared at me in a strange way.

'What?' I asked.

'You sounded so serious on the phone about seeing this job through and making some extra money baking – I almost felt like giving you a second chance. But you've obviously spent all morning drinking coffee in that ridiculous outdoor Wendy house and tonight you're living it up.' He shook his head. 'I should have known better. All of this... For you it's just one big laugh.'

My chest tightened. 'Adam... You've got it wrong. Jess and me, we're totally serious about...' See? Me having to justify myself again – being away from him had made me realise just how often he forced me to do that.

'Save it!' he said and headed past the mahogany door and into the hallway. He gazed at the chandelier again. 'It's all too over the top for me.' A muscle in his cheek twitched. 'But then some people like to show off that they've got money.'

I grabbed his hand again. 'We could have a place this big, one day, if you'd just let me chase my dream. You could furnish it how you wanted. Even build your own gym. The bookings I've already got could be just the beginning...' Uh oh – I was rambling.

'People like us don't belong in houses like this.' He sniffed. 'I like Luton. It's real and if it's good enough for my mum and dad… I mean, I just saw a man outside dressed up in clothes brighter than a fruit bowl, carrying a bloody weird-looking dog under his arm.'

'It's a micro-pig – called Frazzle,' I said and gave a nervous giggle, despite feeling as heavy as the Titanic inside.

'I rest my case.' He sighed and ran a finger under my eye. 'It doesn't suit you here, babe. You're hardly getting any sleep.'

The kitchen patio doors banged and he jumped.

'That's because… I know it sounds bonkers, but this place is haunted,' I whispered. 'I've made contact with the ghost. It's…'

'A ghost?' Adam snorted. 'Listen to yourself! What planet are you on? Too many trashy magazines and rubbish telly, that's your problem.'

'I was, um, joking,' I stuttered. Aarggh! I shouldn't have mentioned Walter – Adam didn't believe in astrology, let alone the supernatural. 'Don't go! We can sort this out. The money from the hen party I'm catering for will pay our food bills for a month.'

'Hi Kimmy!' said Luke, emerging from the kitchen.

Oh great.

'Didn't think you'd mind me letting myself back in,' he said. 'I left something in your bedroom.'

Adam's face flushed purple.

'It's not what it sounds like,' I said to Adam. My throat hurt as he turned to go.

'Goodbye, Kimmy,' said my boyfriend – my ex – in a tight voice. He yanked open the front door and slammed it shut after he left.

CHAPTER 18

'Why are you trying to cause trouble,' I'd hollered at Luke, fists curled, seconds after Adam stormed off.

I sighed and blocked out the memory, trying instead to focus on my party evening. Hot tub? Ready. Hair straightened? Yes, even though the steamy water would frizz it within seconds. Lip gloss applied? Of course, despite the imminent onslaught of snacks and fizzy drinks.

Alone, I waited for the guests to arrive, my mind – my aching chest – incapable of wiping out Adam's disastrous visit, hours earlier. There'd be no point discussing it with anyone. Jess and Melissa had problems of their own and if I kept it to myself, it was easier to pretend it hadn't happened. My chin quivered. All my plans to impress him had been for nothing.

'What is it about me that you hate?' I'd said next to Luke. 'Because clearly you're well intent on ruining my life. You run hot, you run cold... I can't keep up. Why deliberately cause trouble between Adam and me?'

'Don't be so dramatic,' he'd calmly replied, whilst I considered baking him cupcakes "accidentally" made with yew seeds (they're poisonous, according to Jess).

'I recognised him straight away,' Luke continued. 'He's the guy from the photo in your bedroom. I bet he's the one who thought you were mad setting up your own business. What with his symmetrical, safe haircut and uptight voice… You're better off without him; I know his type and bet he's never taken a risk in his life.' He wrinkled his nose. 'And he smells like toilet cleaner.'

'That's his aftershave and no he doesn't!' I snapped, a titch annoyed that I'd kind of felt relieved at Adam's departure – it meant I could be myself again. Not that I'd stop loyally defending my boyfriend to smug Luke. 'Honestly, you've only met Adam for a few minutes, how could you possibly have a clue what he's like?' Toddler-style, I felt my bottom lip jut out.

'Solid. Reliable. Afraid of change. My sister's husband is similar and always tried to put me off striking out on my own. Now I work for myself whilst he's still slogging his guts out at a supermarket.'

If only Adam had turned up when I was cleaning the house from top to bottom – or even better, showing some prospective buyer around.

'You all right?' asked Jess as she came into the kitchen. 'Your face looks all funny.'

'Never better,' I said, brightly, even though, inside, every fibre of me flinched as I recalled Adam's disdain. 'You sure you don't mind this get-together? If you're not up to it, I can phone Terry and Melissa. It's not too late to cancel.'

'I'm fine. As long as we get tidied up in time for Murphy's visit tomorrow morning. The last thing I need this week is to find myself homeless again.'

'Has Dana been on your back all day?'

'Yeah, more than usual. I was amazed that she let me off half an hour early for the doctor's.' Jess had just stepped out of the shower and her bobbed red hair was wrapped up in a towel turban. I wrinkled my nose. She'd clearly been using her homemade vinegar and lemon shampoo.

'Did she want to know what was wrong, every time you threw up?'

'I've just let her assume I've caught some kind of bug. She had the cheek to ask if I'd been out boozing last night.'

I neatened a plate of sandwiches and popped a festive sage and onion flavoured crisp into my mouth. 'You've got to put her in the picture sometime,' I said, softly. 'Why didn't you tell me about your appointment? I'd have come too.'

She half-smiled. 'Maybe you could come to the first scan – although you'll have to go out if they want to prod my bits.'

'Talking of which…' I grinned. 'Take a look at these.' I opened a Tupperware box and shoved it under her nose. Inside was an array of hen party cakes, some bearing marzipan willies and liquorice whips and handcuffs.'

Jess grinned back at me. 'Classy.'

I put the lid back on. 'Have you got a due date?'

Jess sat down at the breakfast island, looking, if anything, slimmer than normal, in a knitted burgundy dress. The only indication that something was different was the pronounced bags under her eyes. 'I won't have an exact one until my first scan, but the doctor reckoned it would be around the twenty-fourth of July.'

'Wow.'

'I know. It's really going to happen, isn't it? A date makes it so much more real.'

'I thought of a great way to choose a name, you know – combine your favourite author with your lucky number like the Beckhams did for their daughter, Harper Seven. You could call your kid… what's that author you like? Stieg something. And you were born on the sixth – there: Stieg Six.'

She snorted in disgust.

'It's a good idea if you get stuck for names,' I said, airily. 'Although I can't decide which works best for me…

Snooki – or Jordan – Four… What about naming the baby after fruit like Gwyneth Paltrow? She chose Apple, so how about Kiwi? Or Guava! Talk about exotic. Or Blackberry? Hmm, yes, even better, name them after some cool phone. LG Cookie sounds awesome.'

She stared at me as if I was from another planet. 'It was only an idea,' I said hurriedly, glad that at that moment the doorbell rang.

Jess headed upstairs, muttering something about hot tub parties wasting energy – all that water, all that heat…

For her sake, I waited until her bedroom door closed. A potentially hysterical Melissa recovering from the day's tabloids, was the last thing Jess needed. I opened the door.

'Terry!'

My neighbour strolled in, carrying a plastic bag of clinking bottles. He took off a long burgundy mac to reveal a bright turquoise shirt and sky-blue trousers. I couldn't wait to see his swimming costume. A holdall hung over his shoulder, presumably containing his trunks and towel.

'Is she here, yet?' he whispered.

'Melissa? No. Maybe she won't come after all,' I said and hung his mac on the mahogany coatstand.'

He adjusted his golfing cap. 'Does my head look bald in this?'

I grinned.

'I only ask, because those paparazzi fellows were clicking away. Got to look my best if I'm going to appear in *Infamous*.'

Giggling, I led him through to the kitchen.

'I'll open the champers,' he said and pulled a bottle out of the plastic bag. 'It's chilled, and a great vintage.'

The doorbell rang again and we raised our eyebrows at each other. Perhaps those cameramen wanted a close-up of the Winsfords' trendsetting neighbours? The photo's tag-line could be: "Melissa seeks solace with the trend-setting Harpenden Set."

I rummaged around in a drawer and drew out a corkscrew, then handed it to Terry. Deep breath. I straightening my halter bikini top, underneath my sparkly cardigan, and headed into the hall. I pinched my cheeks to give them a good colour. Apparently that's what girls did in the days when they weren't allowed to wear make-up, according to this racy old-fashioned drama on the telly.

Pout in place, tummy pulled in, I opened the front door. So much for having my photo taken. Melissa knocked me to one side as she barged past. She wore diamante-edged sunglasses, a sporty cap pulled down over her face, tight grey jeans and a sequinned pashmina. From the bottom of the drive, the photographers hollered at her to give them just one decent shot.

I shut the door and exhaled, muffin top back in place. She'd already dumped her sports bag and headed for the kitchen. I followed her in.

'Melissa, this is Terry, he lives at–'

'I know, darling. Number ten. Cream Beetle. Funny-looking dog. We've never actually said hello.'

'She's a micro-pig,' he said and beamed, staring at Melissa, looking as if Christmas had come several days early.

'Sounds technical,' she said. 'Robotic toys look more lifelike every year.'

'No… micro as in small,' Terry said.

'Nice,' she said in a flat voice. A small sigh escaped her lips. 'Any chance of a drink, and I don't mean coffee or tea?'

There was a loud pop and I held the glasses as Terry filled them up. Melissa knocked hers back in one and held out her glass for a top-up. Terry raised an eyebrow at me, as he gave her a refill.

'So, Kimmy,' he said to me, 'are we watching TV first?'

I nodded and carried some nibbles into the lounge, with my new friends following.

'Love your watch, Melissa,' said Terry, as we sat down, him in one of the green armchairs, me and Melissa on the sofa. 'Gucci?'

She put her glass down on the long oak coffee table. 'Here.' She took it off. 'I don't want it anymore. You have it.'

Terry took off his golf cap and ran a hand over his head before taking it from her. After fingering the smooth face, he handed it back. 'Did Jonny give it to you?' he said, gently.

A tear rolled out from under her sunglasses.

'Ken, my partner of fifteen years, he ran off with a twenty-year-old shelf-stacker last year,' said Terry. 'The local charity shop did really well. How was I to know he hadn't wanted me to donate his favourite suit or gold-plated cigarette lighter?'

Melissa took off her glasses. Her eyes were puffy; nose swollen.

'We're so sorry about this latest tabloid story,' I said. 'How's it going? What's Jonny said?'

'We had a big row,' she gulped. 'He couldn't believe I'd been stupid enough to throw out his medicine boxes and that pregnancy magazine; said I should have more trust, that he was only comforting that bimbo in the photo, a caddy's girlfriend who'd just been dumped. Jonny offered to see her home as she was in such a state. He always was a gentleman. It's one of the first things that attracted me to him.'

A gentleman? Since when did chivalry include sticking your tongue down someone's throat?

'He reckons I drink too much, nag about having kids and most of the time look miserable as hell. How could he say all those things, after everything I've done to support him? I tried to explain it was hard to make friends. Apart from Kate, the local women believe I'm up myself, whereas the top birdies don't think I'm good enough.' Her voice wobbled. 'I've really tried hard – since we moved here, I've thrown countless coffee mornings, themed dinners, fundraisers... Ask me anything about booking caterers and venues, I'm you're woman.'

'Well, *we* like you,' I said and squeezed her arm. 'It can't be that bad, surely? Perhaps you just intimidate the women at the club?'

She shrugged. 'If only Jonny was around a bit more. We could socialise as a couple. I can't even get any sort of job as I'm expected to drop everything and be there with him on all his tours. That's one reason I did the DVD. It's something I've achieved. On my own.'

'What about Jeanie, his first wife?' I said. 'Couldn't she help you make new friends? She lives near doesn't she? And you get on so well.'

Melissa gave a sarcastic laugh. 'You still believe everything you read in the gossip mags? Infamous twists the truth, darling. Jeanie hates me. Can't say I blame her.'

'No!' My mouth stayed open.

'Have you told Jonny how you feel?' said Terry. 'I still don't know to this day the real reason Ken left. Sit your husband down. Talk it through. Perhaps you can work it out?'

'I've tried – but every time I complain about the smallest thing, he goes mad. Says I should be grateful, that I'd be nowhere without him. Says he bought my parents a new house, helped my sister through college – makes me feel ungrateful.'

Blimey. Whoever knew money could cause so many problems. My stomach twisted as I thought of Adam – the only thing he wanted to do was work his guts out to look after me and our future together.

'How did you meet him?' I asked.

She sipped her drink. 'I wasn't bright enough to go to university and had no clue as to what to do when I left school. There wasn't much work around, so I went to stay with relatives in Ireland – my aunt there found me a job waitressing at a nearby golf club. They hosted some minor charity tournament. Jonny was visiting and we fell head over heels.' She smiled. 'I thought he was a caddy to start with.'

'Can't believe I've never heard that story before,' said Terry.

Come to think about it, I'd not seen much in the magazines about Melissa's past.

'You know, Jonny started off his career by shagging, for a really modest wage.'

My drink went down the wrong way and I spluttered.

'That's what they call collecting the balls from practice areas. He never let on about his success until our first kiss.' Her eyes misted over. 'I didn't believe him when he said he was some hot-shot international golfer.' She half-smiled. 'I don't talk much about my life before Jonny. Unlike some of the other wives, I… I haven't been to public school, or college, or had any sort of career. I'm not an actress or model… I'm not even a mum. All I am is Jonny Winsford's wife.'

'That's not true!' exclaimed Terry, chubby cheeks flushing with indignation. 'Melissa Winsford is a fashionista!'

'You're a DVD goddess,' I said. 'The fittest birdie out there! Infamous' "Hottest Celebrity Legs of the Year 2013".' I squeezed her hand. 'Come on. Let me get you a plateful of food and we'll switch on the Celebrity Goss.

Maybe you can give us the insider's view if any of your mates are on it?'

'I'm not in the mood for a programme that laughs at the lives of people like me. Not today anyway. Not when everyone must think I'm the biggest joke of the hour.'

She had a point. Stupid me. I hoped my foot wouldn't spend the whole evening in my mouth.

'I wouldn't even know if Jonny was having an affair,' she mumbled. 'He's always on his phone and is away for days at a time on tours. Talk about opportunity.' She looked me dead in the eye. 'What do you think? You follow celebrity break-ups. Does he seem innocent?'

'I…'

'Flashdance is on the other side,' said Terry, smiling. 'Why don't we watch that and then drown our sorrows in the hot tub?'

'S'pose I've got nothing to lose,' she said. 'Beats fighting my way back through the paparazzi, just to return to an empty house. Jonny stormed off; sounded like he burnt rubber doing so. Pity he didn't knock over a couple of those parasites.'

'All right if I help myself to the buffet?' asked Jess. She was at the lounge door, wet hair hanging limply, book in hand.

'Of course! Want to watch telly with us?' I asked.

'Fetch me a plateful will you, darling,' Melissa said to Jess.

'Fetch it your–'

'I'll get a selection of goodies, shall I?' I said, quickly interrupting my housemate. 'Terry, you put on the telly. Melissa, another refill…?'

Two refills, four sandwiches, five mini chicken kebabs, two handfuls of Pringles, three Oreos, one Christmas gingerbread cupcake and a several of hours of flash-dancing later, I sprawled out in the hot tub, hair curling like gift ribbon. Terry squatted opposite, eyes shut, bald head perspiring, champagne glass steamed up. I ducked down so that the water rose to my shoulders. How awesome was this, soaking outside, all warm and toasty up to my neck, despite the freezing night air?

A breeze tickled my ears. Perhaps Walter was watching, reminiscing about parties he and Lily had thrown. At least Melissa had brightened up. She sat in between me and Terry, in the most amazing tiger stripe swimsuit. Terry didn't disappoint and wore Hawaiian trunks, with a gold medallion. As for Jess, in her condition she wouldn't come in. Instead she'd disappeared upstairs, having done a good job of keeping schtum every time Melissa moaned about her less than perfect life. I could understand how the birdie came across as ungrateful and spoilt, what with her amazing house, bags of money and enviable model looks. But Jess won't have noticed the way Melissa's bottom lip trembled when she asked me to put her Gucci watch somewhere safe when we got in the tub.

'What time is it?' asked Terry. Something barked. A fox, perhaps? Groucho, asleep on the patio next to us, cocked one ear.

I glanced through the patio doors to the kitchen clock. 'One o'clock.' Hey, this was the life! It wasn't even the weekend! Dreamily, I gazed back at the night sky, admiring the white crescent of moon.

"Kimmy Living the High Life Without Lowlife Adam!"– I could see the headline now. Well he was low for disrespecting the amount of money I'd earned from Melissa's coffee morning – and for hardly batting an eyelid at this awesome house.

'Lily said this hot tub did wonders for her arthritis.' Terry yawned and stretched out his arms. 'Hey ho – reckon the paparazzi are bored yet?'

Melissa shook her head. 'They're like the undead,' she said. 'They don't eat, sleep or piss, darling. They just stalk.'

'I feel like the undead with these raisin fingers.' The skin on my hands was wrinkled from soaking too long. 'Let's get out. Finish off with a coffee.'

'No! I hoping to sweat off a few stone yet,' said Terry.

'Don't think we've got that long,' said Melissa and examined her nails. She leant over and patted his belly. 'You should buy my exercise DVD. You'll soon find another man if you follow my instructions to the T.'

'"Tee". Very funny. Good golfing joke,' he grinned. 'Won't Jonny be wondering where you are?'

She shook her head and leant back. I tried not to stare at her huge, pert boobs which emerged from the water like a pair of buoys. 'When we've rowed before he stays out for the night; sleeps over at his agent's house.'

His *agent's* house? I looked at Terry and knew he was thinking the same as me.

A flash of red appeared in the kitchen and Jess came over. She opened the patio doors.

'Has one of you been smoking inside?' she mumbled, hair dishevelled, pillow creases indented into one of her cheeks.

'Ghastly habit,' said Melissa and reached for a bowl of strawberries. 'Don't people realise it yellows teeth and gives them premature wrinkles?'

I glared at Jess, willing her not to make some sarcastic comment like "oh yes, that's far worse than the fact it rots your lungs." But I needn't have worried as she shushed us. 'Listen. I also heard…' Jess shot a look at me, '… a funny wind noise.'

I stared back at her. Was that troublesome spirit back? Perhaps Jess was scared and needed some company upstairs.

'I'm shattered,' she continued. 'Why don't you lot call it a night?'

'No wonder you're bushed, darling,' said Melissa. 'Little one kicking yet?'

Jess evil-eyed her.

'What?' said Melissa.

Terry sat up. 'I didn't know you were preggers, Jess.'

Melissa picked up another strawberry. 'Sorry. Forgot no one else knew. But you're hardly hiding it by eating a whole packet of ginger biscuits tonight. Ginger is a classic cure for nausea, plus no one eats a whole packet unless they're pregnant or bulimic – and no offence, Jess, but you're clearly not interested enough in your body image for it be the latter.' She stepped out of the water and reached for her towel. 'You're very lucky,' she said eventually, in a small voice. 'Guess we should quieten down. The bump needs its sleep.'

At that moment, the lights went out.

'I'll sort out the fuse box,' I said, and jumped out of the water. Quickly I dried myself down and grabbed my cardigan, whilst Melissa bombarded Jess with advice about folic acid. I felt my way to the cupboard behind the hallway desk and... presto! The lights switched back on. But there was thick swirly smoke coming from upstairs. It didn't smell of burning, just that familiar sweet odour. Oh God. A coldness iced the inside of my chest. That thing was back. What if it grabbed me again?

'Jess! Quick!' I called, in a wobbly voice, and the others hurried into the hallway. Nervously, Terry looked up at the smoke.

Melissa giggled. 'Spooky! Don't tell me – this place is haunted.'

'Yes!' I blurted out, shivers tickling my spine. 'That's why it's not selling; that's why the housesitters never last long.'

'Has it ever hurt you?' asked Terry, wrapping his humungous towel tightly around his tum. He bit his lip and stared up the stairs once more.

'Something grabbed me the other night,' I said. 'It tried to drag me across the room.'

Melissa beamed and clapped her hands. The whole episode seemed to have cheered her up no end.

'Aren't you scared?' I asked her, as we hurried back into the kitchen.

'Me? Afraid of some spirit? When, daily, I have to deal with those lens-shoving leeches outside? Then there's the bitchy comments from other women and patronising questions from journalists… No, I can deal with something that won't make a pass at my husband or point at my cellulite. But what if it attacks Jess?' She tutted. 'You've got a child to think about now.'

Jess folded her arms, just before the lights went out again.

'Back in a second,' I muttered, body shaking. Walter would look after me. I'd be all right. But where was his White Christmas music? Come on Mr Carmichael, how about some teamwork.

Eyes wider than those belonging to cute Beanie Boo toys, I felt my way along the kitchen wall, out of the doors, around the front of the staircase, towards the hallway desk and… Oh God! I stood rooted to the spot. Breathing came from behind me. Someone, something, must have been waiting on the stairs. *Walter, help!* But there was still no music. My heart pounded. Should I turn around or dive under the desk? This dilemma was solved when it lunged and with a hideous cackle, pushed me towards the cupboard. I let out a scream and before I knew it, I'd been bundled in, next to the fuse box.

'Come out or make a noise at your peril,' said a raspy voice. The door closed in my face. Teeth chattering, I sat as still as I could. Please don't let that thing come at me again. Please, make it go away... A sob was just about to escape my lips, when... What was that scratching sound?

It went on for several moments and then nothing – until footsteps got louder and Jess called out my name. A gasp of relief shot from my lips. She opened the door, switched the fuse and jumped as she saw me huddled up, in a tight ball, at the back of the cupboard.

Jess stood back to let me out. My legs still trembling, as we passed the desk I looked down. Scratched into the surface of the wood was one word: "LEAVE." I swallowed hard.

We rushed back to the kitchen. Terry was refilling the kettle, whilst Melissa picked chopped nuts off one of the Christmas gingerbread cupcakes.

'They weren't cheap but did the job,' said Melissa, to Terry. She looked up at me. 'Just talking about a celeb acquaintance of mine who had problems – a poltergeist I think. Paranormal investigators got rid.'

'Like the ones on Most Haunted?' I rubbed the bottom of my back, which hurt where I'd been shoved onto the floor. Jess offered me a stick of gum and after a few minutes of manic chewing, my heart finally slowed from a canter to a trot.

Melissa nodded. 'SpiritShooters they were called. I can get their number. If it were me, I'd get them around without delay.'

I sniffed; looked at Jess; gazed at her stomach. Nothing would make me leave this job unfinished, but things were getting dangerous.

'They banish bad spirits?' I said. Walter wasn't evil. What about him? I didn't like the name Shooters, but perhaps my spooky friend would know to keep a low profile whilst they were around. He mustn't get moved onto those Pearly Gates until I'd helped him sort out his will.

'Yes. I believe they can even arrange an exorcism.'

I nodded. Thank God Mr Murphy was visiting in the morning. I'd be honest with him; see if he'd pay for these ghostbusters. Blow what Deborah thought. As soon as he got here, I'd tell Mr Murphy the real reason Mistletoe Mansion wouldn't sell.

CHAPTER 19

As hard as I could, I slapped Mr Murphy on the back.

'Drink this water,' I said, and passed him a glass. He sat at the bar in the Games Room – his favourite place in the house, apparently – tears running down his face. He'd almost choked on a mouthful of chopped nuts, whilst eating one of the cupcakes left over from the night before. Why? Because I'd told him about the haunting. Clearly his mind wasn't open to the paranormal. Good thing I hadn't accidentally given him one of the hen party cakes. A large marzipan willy down his throat might have proved lethal.

'A ghost?' he said, finally, and put down the water. It had dripped down his suit, which was navy with dark grey stripes. He wore a shirt which looked too tight around the neck. He wiped his eyes, took off his jacket and loosened his wide tie. On his little finger was a huge gold signet ring.

'That's priceless,' he said. 'Where on earth did Deborah get you from, love?' He shook his head. 'No wonder this place isn't selling if she entrusts it to neurotic young women.'

'Here's proof!' I said and showed him the note the previous housesitter left for me and Jess. 'This was a warning from a sensible, retired lady who was into dressmaking. Don't you think it explains why no one lasts here longer than it takes to say *Boo*?'

Mr Murphy rubbed his receding hairline. The little hair he had left was dyed just a bit too black. 'You want me to fork out good money to pay some loony organisation – what is it called, SpiritShooters – to look around? As if trying to sell this place isn't costing me a fortune, already. Plus I'm going to have to pay to have that scratched word removed from the hallway desk. In fact I might not bother. The house-clearers can have it.'

The doorbell went and, inwardly sighing, I got up. I hadn't even had time yet to question him, to find out why his uncle was unhappily stuck in limbo. I'd tried to make a good impression by tying back my hair and wearing my most serious outfit – the black skirt and blouse I'd worn to Melissa's Botox party. Although I got the impression Mr Murphy was a man who'd appreciate more leg and cleavage.

I opened the front door. Wow. Melissa was glammer than ever. Mr Murphy's desires had been granted. Clearly she'd dressed up for the photographers, in the most gorgeous purple and silver bandage dress. It looked just like one I'd seen on my favourite celebrity-inspired shopping website, Bae Boutique. Her hair was sprayed to within an inch of its life and her make-up fashion-shoot perfect. An open aubergine suede jacket and silk scarf completed the ensemble.

'Morning, Kimmy,' she said, just the hint of dark circles under her eyes.

'Feeling better?' I said, softly.

'Yes. Don't know what you put in those cupcakes, but I woke up determined to pull myself together and show the world that I wasn't bothered by those stupid rumours.'

I grinned. As usual, there was no grim situation a bit of sponge and icing couldn't brighten.

'We've made up.' Melissa pointed to her necklace. 'Like it?'

'Cool.' What's not to like about platinum and diamonds? 'That must have cost him a packet.'

'Jonny said you couldn't put a price on my trust.' She cleared her throat. 'Thanks for, um, last night, by the way. It did me the world of good. How's it going with Walter's nephew?'

'He thinks I'm totally bonkers,' I whispered. 'Deborah had been right not to tell him anything spooky. Charm had oozed out of him, until I'd mentioned the word "ghosts".'

She straightened her skirt. 'Let me talk to him and work the Winsford magic.'

'He's in the Games Room, to the left,' I said and closed the door. What had I got to lose? At this rate, Mr Murphy was about to make me and Jess homeless.

'Now I haven't got all day, missy,' said Mr Murphy, standing up. He turned around. His mouth fell open. 'Mrs Winsford… What a pleasure!' He flushed as red as the festive tinsel I'd trailed along the bar.

'The pleasure's all mine,' she said in her most treacle-like tones. Melissa minced towards him, hips swaying, hand outstretched. What an entrance! 'Walter always spoke very highly of you.'

What a liar! She'd never even spoken to her elderly neighbour. Cold air suddenly engulfed me and I smiled to myself – clearly Walter wasn't happy with that lie.

'Really?' Mr Murphy pulled out a stool for the golfer's wife. 'He was a decent uncle. I was just so sorry when…'

Melissa sat down and wrapped her hand over his. 'Mr Murphy, isn't it? May I call you…?'

'Mike.' He smiled like a schoolboy who'd finally accessed the Red Hot Dutch TV channel, his eyes saying "you can call me whatever you want".

'It was terribly sad about your uncle,' she purred, 'but he would want you to move on; would want this place sold. You should listen to Kimmy. Everyone in the cul-de-sac knows about the Mistletoe Mansion Ghost.'

'Pah, what a lot of…'

But he stopped mid-sentence as Melissa opened a jar of cocktail cherries, took one out and sucked on it hard. I bit the insides of my cheeks in a desperate attempt not to giggle. He reminded me of Groucho, who stopped dead if he smelt my favourite beef burger flavour crisps. In an attempt to control my laughter, I rearranged the snooker balls.

'Love your suit, by the way,' said Melissa and lightly brushed his knee with her hand. 'I like a man who takes pride in his appearance. Just look at your watch.'

It was impossible not to notice it. Large, shiny, rather like a compass.

Mike loosened his tie further.

'Harpenden is a small village,' she said. 'Close-knit. If word gets out of Badgers Chase about funny happenings here, you'll never sell. But then you're a clever man. I'm sure I don't need to tell you that.'

He wiped his forehead with a hanky, before standing up and pacing the room. 'You've got the number?' he said. 'For these…'

'Paranormal investigators?' said Melissa.

Mr Murphy nodded. 'Reliable, are they?'

'Ooh yes,' she cooed. 'They always give one hundred percent satisfaction.' Slowly, she uncrossed her legs. 'I think it takes a real man to admit that he needs help.'

'I like to think I'm broadminded.' Mike went back to his chair next to her and sat down. Immediately he jumped up and his eyes bulged. He rubbed his behind. There, on his chair, was a fork upturned. I looked skywards. Walter?

'I'll ring my friend now,' said Melissa and took out her state-of-the-art phone.

'Another coffee?' I said to Mr Murphy.

He nodded. 'And one for Mrs Winsford.'

By the time I got back, Melissa was playing snooker with Mr Murphy, splayed forwards across the table, legs parted.

'Ooh… Aahh,' she murmured as she concentrated on the shot.

Mr Murphy followed her every move, in that tight dress.

'Why don't you ring that number now, Mike?' She stood upright. 'Then we can finish our game before you head off for your meeting. Don't you think Kimmy and Jess have been saints to stay here so long, in view of the frightening circumstances? Unlike the other housesitters, they haven't let you down.'

'Indeed. Apologies, Kimmy. Clearly there's a problem here. I should have been informed.'

Whilst he dialled, Melissa and I headed over to the window with our coffees and I gazed at the sky which – yippee! – with all that sea-foam low cloud, looked as if it might snow.

'Thanks,' I whispered.

'My pleasure… almost,' she said and we giggled, before going over last night's events.

'Done!' announced Mr Murphy. 'They're coming tonight – from what you told me, they felt the situation required immediate attention. They'll be here at eight o'clock, a few hours after it's got dark.'

This was exciting! I'd have to change my Facebook status to: "Meeting totes real ghostbusters!"

'Talking of the time,' said Melissa, 'I've just remembered a very important appointment. Sorry Mike, I'll have to take a rain check on that game.' She gave me one of her snowdrop white smiles. 'I'll see myself out. Good luck tonight.'

Mr Murphy stared after her. 'Shame she had to go. Classy bird, that one.'

I sat down at the bar, desperate to quiz him. I didn't have long to find out more about his true relationship with Walter.

'Did you ever see her when you visited your uncle?'

He sat down next to me. 'No, love. The old man and I didn't hang around here much – we ate out at pubs or walked in the countryside.'

'You must have been very fond of him.' I said and wished Walter would leave off the cold air, which was freezing enough to let it snow indoors. He was obviously close and keen to hear every syllable that came out of his nephew's mouth.

Mr Murphy nodded. 'I wasn't expecting to get such a large cut of his estate. But then we were family.'

'Close, were you?'

'The son he never had, reckon that's how he thought of me.' He shivered and rubbed his arms, as if he were outside. 'We were always on the phone,' he said, not catching my eye. 'My mum and dad have passed on. He hadn't got any other relatives.' With a gasp, he jumped up and turned around. 'I could have sworn someone just poked me...' Nervously, he scrutinised the room. 'Look, um, I'd better get going. Let me know how the investigations go. I'll be on my mobile. I'm travelling back to Manchester this evening.' He picked up his briefcase and hurried into the hallway, 'I've just got one condition about tonight – Luke must be here. No offence, missy, but know I can trust him. He's sorted out problem after problem at Mistletoe Mansion and will be able to show the investigators around properly. Aarggh!' he jumped again before striding to the front door and yanking it open.

Walter! How could you torture your nephew like that? Clearly you and Mr Murphy weren't as close as he suggested. A cold draught blew around my neck in agreement. So why, oh why, had Mike lied?

CHAPTER 20

'What was that?' asked Luke, unlit torch in hand, as he rushed into the lounge. He'd just been playing darts with Jess in the Games Room, along to Terry's Disco Anthems CD left from the hot tub party, at full blast. I jumped up from the armchair. The three of us were waiting for SpiritShooters to arrive. Concerned some mischievous ghost might again go for me, I brandished my torch like a knife.

'Only kidding.' Luke chuckled and collapsed onto the sofa.

'Very funny,' I sniffed. Damn. I'd broken my resolution to give him the silent treatment. I still hadn't forgiven him for upsetting Adam yesterday. My inner toddler wanted to call him some stupid nickname – puke rhymed with Luke. Pukey Luke. Yes, I liked that. Pukey Luke with his stupid, cryptic comments like the one he threw at me yesterday, about not taking things personally. What could that mean?

Determined not to waste anymore of my brain power on him, I sat down and went over Mr Murphy's visit again, still trying to work out why he'd bigged up his relationship with Walter. I glanced sideways at Luke, in his faded jeans and white shirt. He opened his mouth to speak but at that moment Jess came in. She offered us each a stick of gum. I took one. Pukey Luke declined.

'Tell me again why Murphy wanted me here,' he said, and ran a hand over his unshaven chin.

'He trusts you, apparently.' I said, annoyed at a primeval urge in me to touch that bristly skin. Adam's face was always as smooth as armpits after a good dose of Veet. 'Plus you've got the key to those locked bedrooms.'

'I'm surprised Murphy's happy for them to look through all of Walter's private stuff.' He stood up. 'I'd better go up and unlock them and check there's at least walking room around all the boxes. Honestly. This is a complete waste of time. The Carmichaels lived here happily for years and never complained of mysterious ghouls, with raspy voices, grabbing them…' He shook his head at me. 'Are you sure you didn't just… I don't know, trip over Groucho and fall into that cupboard?'

'No! Anyway, how do you explain that word scratched into the hallway desk?'

'It could have been there before and no one noticed,' he said. 'You don't need a degree to work that out.'

'You don't need a degree to do much, as far as I'm concerned,' said Jess.

He shrugged. 'Might get you a well-paid job.'

'Yeah, so you can spend the rest of your life in debt to the State,' she replied.

'Friends of mine, neighbours, a few years older, I watched them all leave uni with a loan, unable to get a job because of the recession. Then I met Adam…' I shrugged. 'He agreed with me that it was a waste of time.'

'And you're happy with your job, Jess?' said Luke.

I smiled. 'Jess was always going to work in a garden centre. As far back as I can remember, you had your own vegetable patch, didn't you?'

She blushed.

'Remember when we all took sunflower seeds home to grow in Juniors? Yours grew into giants. My seedlings shrivelled and died.'

'I want to do a landscaping course one day,' she said.

'Sounds sensible,' said Luke, on his way out of the room. 'A gardening friend of mine did. I can get details of it if you want.'

Jess and I raised our eyebrows at each other. There was his helpful side again. I was tempted to say something sarcastic when the doorbell rang. I smoothed down my top, which had a sequinned skull on the front – a suitable choice for the imminent spook-chasing evening. What would these SpiritShooters be wearing? A smart, special ghost-repelling uniform made from high tech material that protected them from being possessed? I couldn't wait to take a look at their equipment. Be careful not to get caught, I said to Walter, in my head. Otherwise you'll be banished to those Pearly Gates, leaving behind your unfinished business.

Followed by Jess, I went into the hallway and opened the front door. I could have jumped up and down as delicate flakes of snow now tumbled to the ground! Under the porch light stood three people in thick anoraks, carrying rucksacks and sleeping bags. Hitchhikers, perhaps, who'd got lost and were wondering if they could camp in the garden, before a potential blizzard.

'Sorry, this is private property,' I gushed. 'You could try pitching your tents on Harpenden Common.'

The youngish man in smart trousers raised his eyebrows at the blonde lady in, ooh, her forties. An older man, in creased beige chinos, leant forward and held out his hand.

'Mike Murphy called us,' he said. 'SpiritShooters at your service.'

'Oh. I thought you'd be wearing… um…' I stuttered.

The younger man in the suit grinned. 'Alien-looking protective space suits, or dark glasses like Will Smith in Men In Black?'

I smiled sheepishly.

'You must be one of the housesitters?' said the older man.

'Yes. I'm Kimmy. This is my colleague, Jess.'

'Age, please?' he said and got out a notebook. 'Nationality? Marital Status?'

'Doug!' said the woman and shook her head. 'He's a retired police officer, in case you hadn't noticed. I'm Barbara, a medium and psychic.'

Talk about top-to-tail in conservative clothes, with her sensible skirt and shoes. She could have at least spiced things up by carrying a crystal ball or wearing some exotic turban.

'And this is Rob.' Doug pointed to the younger man who stepped forward and smiled.

'I'm a private detective,' said Rob. 'More to the point, I'm the team sceptic.'

'The team sceptic?' said Luke, coming down the stairs. He beckoned to the three of them to come in. 'I'm Luke by the way – a friend of the owner.'

The three investigators entered the hallway and put down their rucksacks. I closed the front door and indicated to them to hang their anoraks on the coatstand.

'Yup, cynical as they come, that's me,' said Rob. 'You won't catch me talking of spirits stuck in limbo or lost souls tormenting the living. I deal with facts and proof. I'm the voice of reason.'

'Luke's our sceptic.' I said. 'He thinks all of this is complete nonsense.'

Doug, the retired policeman, licked his pencil. 'I'll need dates, times of strange occurrences – witness statements, perhaps fingerprints…'

They picked up their bags and Jess and Luke led our spooky guests into the lounge whilst I headed into the kitchen. Pity I hadn't had time to bake, I'd been too busy tidying up for the viewing tomorrow. I knew some great Halloween recipes and cupcakes topped with devils and gravestones would have created an awesome atmosphere.

By the time I arrived in the lounge with coffees – okay, I admit to first of all standing by the back patio windows for ten minutes, barely containing my childlike glee at the parachuting snowflakes – Doug was talking intently with Jess and, by the looks of it, had already written several pages of notes. Barbara wandered around the lounge, picking up various ornaments and running her hand along furniture. Rob chatted to Luke, both of them shaking their heads and tutting. Their conversation stopped when I handed them mugs.

'Kimmy…' said Rob and stood up. He swaggered up and down the room for a moment before taking a swig of his coffee. 'Tell me precisely… What have you seen that offers up proof of a ghost?'

I chewed gum for a moment. Don't let slip about Walter, the White Christmas music or low thuds. I didn't want him exiled to the edge of eternity or imprisoned in some airless jar or whatever these investigators might do. No, it was the violent spirit that I wanted them to get rid of.

'On several occasions the house has filled with smoke,' I said.

'Luke says you called him over but he never found hard evidence of anything strange. Perhaps it was neighbours, burning rubbish in their garden, on the sly?'

'In the middle of the night?'

'Well, they'd need to be discreet as this neighbourhood is in a smoke-free zone,' said Rob. 'Or could it have been your breath, as you exhaled? It's been extremely cold lately…'

'I'd need a mouth the size of a foghorn to create that much white air.' I evil-eyed Luke, daring him to make some insulting comment.

'You also believe it made physical contact, on several occasions?' Rob raised his eyebrows.

I sat down on one of the sage green armchairs. 'Yes, in the bedroom. Then, last night, it pushed me into the downstairs cupboard. I've got a massive bruise, to prove it.'

Luke's brow furrowed at that comment, almost as if he was concerned.

A smirk crept over Rob's face. 'But what about in the garden? Didn't you think something had grabbed your foot?'

I glared at Luke. Why should it surprise me that he'd tell Rob about the hose and embarrass me like that?

'Wasn't your foot tangled up in garden equipment?' continued Rob.

'So?' I muttered.

'All I'm saying is, you wouldn't be the first person to mistake something perfectly earthly and rational, for something supernatural.'

'How well do you all know Mr Murphy?' asked Doug.

'Luke probably knows him best,' I said.

Luke shrugged, 'Seems like an okay bloke. Walter liked him.'

'Terry next door says the uncle and nephew seemed to be quite close at the end,' I added. 'But I'm not convinced – I'm surprised Mr Carmichael left him the house.'

'Why?' asked Luke, with an intent gaze.

'He never really visited until the last few months. Just seems a bit odd.'

'Do people know the nephew well around here?' said Doug. 'Is there anyone who might hold a grudge and not want the property to sell?'

We all shook our heads.

Jess wiped her nose. 'As Mr Murphy might have mentioned to you, he lives in Manchester.'

'What about the agency trying to sell this place for him,' continued the retired policeman. 'Perhaps you could give me their number. Could be someone trying to ruin their reputation.'

'Or,' said Barbara, in a soft voice, 'there could be a spirit here, angry and confused, trying to make their voice heard…' She smiled at me. 'Think about your senses, dear girls. Since living here, what have you smelt, felt, heard?'

Cold air when Walter was around. His music, that made me feel relaxed and happy… But all of that was my little secret.

'Scared to death.' I said, 'what with lights going out and doors suddenly locking. Plus the smoke… It has a sweet smell.'

'Sometimes a loud wind blows, but you don't feel anything with it,' said Jess. 'And once Kimmy saw a strange face at the front window.'

'Probably the moon's reflection,' said Rob. 'Happens all the time.' He rubbed his hands together and glanced at his colleagues. 'I don't think we'll be here long tonight. Let's get this show on the road.'

But by the mantelpiece, Barbara had picked up the photo of Walter and Lily holding hands. For the first time I noticed the psychic's long, painted nails and as for her rings! Each finger bore a different jewel – a silver band punctuated with amethysts, a gold ring bearing a large green gem… Clearly she didn't read Cut-Above-Couture. Didn't everyone know, not to mix metals? She gazed at the photo for a few seconds before closing her eyes tight. Everyone stared at her for what seemed like hours, then she finally opened her eyes again.

'Ready, Doug?' she said, in her soft voice.

'Uh huh.' He skimmed through his notes.

Rob pulled open his rucksack and took out some talcum powder. 'Show me this desk with the scratch.'

We led him into the hallway. Barbara and Doug followed. Rob ran his finger over the scratched word, *LEAVE*. Then he took a piece of paper from the letter rack and picked up a pen we'd left there. He searched in his pocket for a moment and brought out a ten pence coin, which he placed in the middle of the piece of paper. He drew around it, then sprinkled talc all over the floor and far around the desk.

'No one tread on the talc or come near this area,' he said. 'We'll see at the end whether the coin has been moved. And if there are footsteps printed in the talc around it – that'll give us a clue of what we're dealing with.'

'How?' I said.

'If the person…' he glanced at Barbara and sighed, '…or *being* that's moved the coin is a man, woman or child.'

'Or dog.' Jess grinned. 'I'll find Groucho and lock him in the back garden.

Doug put his notebook into his rucksack and pulled out some sort of gadget, about the size of a camera. It had a dial and a meter with a red hand. This was more like it! I bounced from foot to foot, still wishing Doug and the others wore some special uniform.

'Rob, you'll take the EMF detector?' said the ex-policeman.

Rob nodded and caught my eye. 'It measures electromagnetic fields,' he said. 'Spirits supposedly give off high levels of electromagnetic charges.'

'Could one of you go around and check that all the windows, and inside and outside doors, are firmly locked and closed,' said Barbara. 'And turn off the heating, so that we can hear the slightest noise.'

'Sure,' said Luke and whistled as he circumnavigated the talc and went upstairs.

Barbara opened her bag and took out some wind chimes and string. 'I'll find some good spots to hang these,' she said and disappeared into the kitchen.

Rob handed Doug a torch and then took a strange-looking camera out of his bag. It had a wide lens and behind, at the top of its long, red handle, was a screen. 'Thermal imaging camera,' he muttered, as Luke came back.

'To show up hot or cold spots?' I said, chuffed that hours of watching Most Haunted had paid off.

Rob nodded. 'It can reveal areas of heat that the human eye can't see. Some people believe spirits absorb energy and therefore lower the temperature of the air directly around them.'

That explained Walter's icy presence. Ooh, I felt another Facebook status coming on: "I'm delving into the spirit world with machinery at the forefront of science."

Slightly out of breath, Jess came back to the hallway. 'So, Rob, you don't believe in any of this spooky stuff, yet Melissa Winsford's friend was dead happy with the results of your visit and felt their supposed poltergeist had been banished. How do you explain that and the supposed success of SpiritShooters?'

'Good question,' said Rob. 'In short, most people are so desperate by the time we arrive, that they are willing to believe anything they think will help. I'm always honest with them. I've never yet come away from a job and believed I've really come into contact with the dead. Often, just having us say that and them seeing our tests puts their minds at rest; they stop seeing every shadow or hearing every noise as proof of life beyond the grave.'

'You've *never* seen or sensed a ghost?' I asked. 'Not once?'

'Sure, we've picked up stuff on our equipment, but I can't say I've ever been truly convinced. You're a good example of what happens when people start to believe there's something from another world in their house,' he said. 'By the time that hose trapped your foot, you'd already been spooked a few times and your mind was set to think the worst of everything. That's what happens. Paranoia is a powerful emotion.'

'So, you're earning money under false pretences,' said Luke.

'You've got to remember,' said Doug. 'That's just Rob's opinion. More often than not, Barbara and I feel we've communicated with some lost or confused spirit. We feel we've helped them to move on.'

'Either way,' said Rob, 'if the customer's happy, I reckon we deserve our fee.' He sniggered. 'Believe me, I'm as disappointed as anyone. What wouldn't I give to take a spirit on?' He made a gun shape with his hand and pretend fired.

I swallowed, fearing for Walter's safety.

Barbara came out of the lounge, hands empty, wind chimes obviously in place.

'Let's turn out this hallway light. On with the torches,' she said. One by one we went up the stairs, in the dark.

'Keep away from the talc, people,' said Rob.

'As quiet as you can, please, everyone,' said Doug. 'Now, let's separate. Barbara, why don't you take Kimmy into her bedroom, seeing as that was the first place there was *an event*?'

'Luke, you show me the locked rooms,' said Rob. 'I'll switch the EMF detector on.'

Unfair! I wanted to take a peek at Walter's stuff.

'Jess, could you show me the office and your room, please,' said Doug. 'Explain exactly what you heard last night when everyone else was downstairs, in the hot tub? I need to know precisely where the sounds seemed to be coming from, how long they lasted, whether they were high or low pitch... Then you and me, Rob, we'll scout around downstairs.'

Everyone mumbled their agreement and fell silent.

'What's that noise?' said Luke.

Oh, here we go again, funny ha ha, except... Everyone listened. Aarggh! It was faint music. Walter? Hush! Barbara will find you out. The hairs stood up on the back of my neck. Was that because I was cold? Scoot, Walter, quick as you can, escape.

'I'll go down to investigate,' said Barbara.

No way! I had to think fast.

CHAPTER 21

'Let me check it out,' I said. 'Honestly Barbara. It's probably nothing.'

Was that by accident she shone her torch towards my face? I held a calm, polite smile for a few seconds before making my way downstairs. Luke followed.

'Don't want you injuring your back, again,' he said.

'Whatever.' I hurried into the Games Room. Phew. Panic over. 'It's Terry's Disco Anthems CD. You and Jess must have left it on.'

I went to the bar and switched it off. On turning around, I almost collided with Luke's chest, not realising he stood so close.

'Fearless, aren't you,' he murmured. 'After everything you've experienced... Didn't you worry that there might be a sinister being in here, waiting to throw you in the cupboard again – or worse... make you a target on the dartboard?'

'Is that supposed to be funny?' I said, resisting the urge to spread my palm against the firmness of his torso.

'How *is* your back?' he asked, in unfamiliar gentle tones.

'Um... fine.' I tried to get past but he put his hands on his hips and didn't budge. Ooh, this was all a bit Game of Thrones like, with him being stubborn and macho.

'Did you hear that?' he said.

Mirroring him, I put my hands on my hips and shook my head.

'The phantom hose,' he whispered back. 'It's slithering and sliding, coming to get you again.'

'Yeah, thanks for showing me up by telling everyone about that.' I couldn't hold back a smile.

'Just trying to get to the bottom of what's going on,' said Luke, acting all innocent, his quirked up mouth giving away a mischievous nature. 'Look... I'm sorry, okay? About yesterday... Adam's an idiot, but I didn't mean to upset you.'

Wow. An apology? This was unchartered territory.

'Anyway, you get back upstairs,' he said. 'I'm going to check the windows – I forgot to take a look in here. Make sure you don't walk in the talc and...' he smiled again, as I rolled my eyes, '... I know. You're not stupid. I'll shut up now.'

Upstairs on the landing, Rob was waiting for Luke. 'Well?'

'Just a CD we left on,' I whispered. 'Is Barbara in my room?'

He nodded and signalled for me to go in. Gently, I pushed open my door. Moonlight half-lit the room as Barbara was by the window and had opened the velvet curtains. Outside, the flakes of snow were now big and clunky, looking far too heavy for the delicate way they wafted down.

'When the spirit made contact – clasped your leg – did the room feel especially warm or cold?' she asked.

'Um, I don't think so.'

'And downstairs, under the cupboard? You say the spirit spoke to you? What exactly were its words, dear?'

'"Come out or make a noise at your peril".'

'No temperature changes? No draughts?'

'Just that windy noise – and the scratching from the word it etched on the desk.'

'It's odd,' she said, 'because ever since I entered this house I've felt... welcome; relaxed. Not threatened in any way.' She fiddled with one of her many rings. 'Some buildings I walk into, straight away I'm on my guard, I can just sense that there's a negative spirit waiting for the opportunity to make trouble.' She closed her eyes and breathed in deeply. 'There is the whiff of anger but... and this is going to sound odd...' She opened her eyes. 'It's almost smothered by an aura of politeness. You know, old-fashioned good manners, not wanting to upset people who are innocent bystanders...'

Mouth dry, I sat on the bed. Wow. She was good. But another reason I couldn't risk telling her about Walter was that Mike Murphy was paying her fee. Whatever I said about the old boy needing more time here, she might move him on, to close the case and keep her client happy. Or trigger-happy Rob might do something more ominous. Or Mr Murphy will find out his uncle isn't happy and be more careful with his lies about how well they got on.

'Kimmy?' she said, quietly. 'Is there something you want to tell me?'

Without looking her in the eye, I shook my head.

Barbara pulled her cardigan tighter and shone her torch at the photo of me and Adam and smiled. 'He looks nice. Your boyfriend?'

'Um, no. We're not... You see...' And before I knew it, I was telling her all about the break-up – then meeting Deborah, helping out Melissa... Aarggh! I even let slip about Jess's pregnancy.

'It's been quite an eventful week then,' she said.

Tears pricked my eyes and I chewed on the gum manically for a second. Where did all that emotion come from?

She squeezed my arm. 'You're sensitive. That's why, perhaps, you've connected with something astral, here...?

I said nothing.

'Kimmy?'

'There's a bad spirit here.' I stared her in the face and folded my arms. 'That's what you need to work on. It assaults people and scares them with smoke.' I stood up and paced around for a moment. 'SpiritShooters – that's quite an aggressive name.'

'I know. Personally I'm not happy with it, but the men – they both own guns. Boys and their toys – I was outnumbered when it came to a vote. Really, what it means is "troubleshooters" – we go into a situation and sort it out. It doesn't mean we're out to eliminate any sort of lost soul… And of course not all souls want to depart this mortal coil. Not until they're ready. Sometimes they have to find closure.'

We looked at each other and inexplicably my eyes felt wet again. Could she sense Walter's concerns? The door opened.

'What's the verdict, Barbara?' said Rob. 'Luke's shown me the two locked rooms – nothing much in there, apart from old furniture and knick-knacks. The EMF meter didn't spring into life, either.' He glanced at me. 'There was no sign of a spooky face near the front window. I had a preliminary scout around downstairs, in the lounge and Games Room.' He shrugged. 'Zilch there.'

Just visible through the darkness, Jess, Doug and Luke appeared on the landing.

'Nothing to report,' said Doug. 'Haven't heard your wind chimes either, Barbara. No knocking, gusts, cold or warm patches. Nothing came up on the camera.'

I looked sideways at Barbara and shivered, wishing we could put the heating back on.

'I think you might be right on this one, Rob,' she said and glanced back at me, through the moonlight. 'Kimmy's been under a lot of stress lately, and could perhaps have imagined things… like with the hose.'

Jess's voice cut through the shadows. 'There's nothing wrong with us. Whilst I'm not convinced there's anything paranormal here, don't forget all of the previous housesitters have scarpered, cos of strange goings-on.'

'Don't worry,' said Doug. 'We've the whole night ahead of us. Who knows what might happen. And even if we rule out a haunting, that's only the beginning – Rob and I will then come into our own and investigate, try and work out if anyone is sabotaging the attempts to sell this house on purpose. You and previous sitters may be the victims of a cruel joke – some sort of elaborate hoax.'

As we followed the others downstairs, Barbara held me back for a moment.

'If there's anything you want to tell me – anyway I can help – just ring our number. Ask to speak to me. I could come round on my own one night with my Ouija board.' Her voice lightened. 'And I don't own a gun.'

I muttered my thanks. Luke switched on the lights and we all made our way downstairs. I almost collided with Barbara as she stopped dead at the foot of the stairs and stared at the coin on the hallway desk. Oh my God! It had moved. I followed her gaze down to the talc. Wow. No footprints. So how had something got to the desk without walking? Surely Walter wouldn't have bothered moving the money – which meant that at last the other spirit was putting in an appearance. Rob could blast that one with a paranormal Kalashnikov, if he wanted.

Rob turned off the lights again and took out the EMF meter, whilst Doug immediately lifted up his thermal imaging camera. But whilst we all skulked around downstairs for another hour or so, nothing else happened. Eventually Barbara flicked all the lights back on and

I prepared soup and sandwiches. Then the ghostbusting team set up camp in the lounge, for the night. Once more Luke was to sleep next to my room, on the sofa in the office.

'Night, Jess,' I called from the landing, as she disappeared into her bedroom. Luke hovered by my door. 'So, Kimmy, do you still believe in your ghost?'

I shrugged and avoided his eye. 'I just hope SpiritShooters don't leave too much mess. Prospective buyers are visiting tomorrow morning. Then I've got some last minute cooking to do for the hen party in the evening.'

'I had a job on, but it's been cancelled,' he said. 'I'll nip home to change, first thing in the morning, then come back and help you tidy up, if you like; stick around for when the buyers are here – make sure no funny stuff goes on.'

I met his gaze. 'That's very…' Surprising. Yet I wasn't sure whether to accept his offer. Deborah herself had said he didn't have the best manner when prospective buyers visited.

'It'll make things easier all round,' he said.

'I suppose…' My eyes narrowed as I took in his cocky, teasing smile.

'You're at a crucial stage with KimCakes Ltd. You need to be on form tomorrow night – up for networking. Making contacts, that's your priority.' He shrugged. 'And if the investigators come up with nothing, it won't hurt to have a big, brave man around the house.'

I snorted. 'Who would that be?'

He chuckled and I joined in. Then I stared at him for several seconds.

'Is the ghost behind me?' He grinned.

'No, it's just…' I stuttered. 'Guess I'd better get some sleep, then. See you in the morning.'

He touched my shoulder. 'What's the matter?'

'You're the first person – apart from Jess – to really take my business seriously.'

'What about The Boyfriend?' he asked.

'Ex,' I corrected.

'Didn't Adam want you to set up on your own? Why'd he turn up if you're no longer an item?'

'None of your business.'

His amazing moss green eyes crinkled.

I sighed. 'He wants me to get a "proper" job with a pension, benefits… He's thinking mortgage and savings and I'm…'

'You want to make a name for yourself?'

'Exactly! Not that I'm against settling down. But first of all I want to give my dreams my best shot. Live the High Life. Get that big house, go on holidays abroad…'

'Yeah, right…' He smirked.

'What's wrong with that?'

'I'm all for running my own business – being my own boss, setting my own agenda – but as for earning megabucks… I've worked around here long enough to see that money doesn't buy happiness.'

'You mean Melissa?'

'She puts on a brave face but the paparazzi give her a miserable time. And take the woman at number fifteen – she sleeps with the window cleaner because her husband is some big CEO and always at work.'

Blimey. I pulled a face. That sounded just like Mum's new neighbour who had a mysterious bald visitor every time her husband worked the factory late shift. Being rich clearly didn't protect you from everyday problems.

'Then Cynthia at number five is being treated for a shopping addiction,' continued Luke.

'I should have such problems!' I scoffed.

'I doubt it – her husband's divorcing her because of all the lies.'

Ouch.

'Then Bill at number twelve doesn't speak to some relatives because he's sick of lending them money and not getting it back. And number twenty, well, they're about to declare themselves bankrupt. Gambling, I think...' He shrugged. 'I could go on.'

Wow. Who would have thought this idyllic cul-de-sac was filled with such misery and screwed-up folk? It made me think of lottery winners I'd seen in the papers who declared their winnings had brought them nothing but heartache.

'But goals, they're good, right? I have a dream – there's nothing wrong with that.'

'Couldn't agree more, and I can tell you're determined to make it happen,' he said. 'I feel like that about my business. The only difference is I picture the customers and staff I'd eventually take on – not the fancy clothes and stuff I'd buy with the profits.'

'So, you don't approve?'

'I didn't say that. As long as you don't let your happiness become dependent on how much is in your bank account. Nothing wrong with aspirations as long as you're prepared to work hard for them and don't expect anyone else to hand them to you on a plate – that's what I reckon. Self-respect, a sense of achievement, everyone should aim for that. Just don't expect working for yourself to be easy.'

'I'm not that naïve,' I said and lifted my chin.

'Never said you were. You might want to consider doing an online business course, like I did – whether you need to know about sales and marketing, customer service or financial management... Or perhaps someone in your family has business experience they could pass on. Your mum or dad?'

'Not Mum.' Understatement of the year. 'Never met my dad.'

Those green eyes stared into mine.

'Mum had a one night stand with a biker when she was sixteen.' Why was I telling him this?

His tone softened. 'Must have been hard for you – and her.'

'She got council housing. Then later, Tom – my brother – his dad stuck around for a while. Mum does her best. She's... kind of fragile.' I smoothed down my top. 'Anyway, I had thought about doing a business course – perhaps at evening school.'

'Go for it,' he said. 'It can only help if things take off and you ever need to go to the bank for a loan.'

'A loan?'

'Yeah – to help you expand the business. You might need premises or kitchen equipment or money to back an advertising campaign.'

'You mean, think big?'

'Why not? A lot more work came my way, once I invested in some electric hedge trimmers and a shredder.' He shrugged again. 'So, I'll make sure I'm here tomorrow morning?'

'Yes. Um... that'd be great...' I eyed him suspiciously. 'Why are you being so helpful? I just can't make you out.'

'Does it seem so unbelievable that I can be a good guy?'

I raised an eyebrow.

He gave a wry smile. 'I've been in a similar position to you, that's all – went out with a woman for a couple of years. Last spring we broke up. She...' His cheeks flushed. 'Kat didn't understand how I was willing to live on the breadline for a while, until my business took off. She wanted me to go into finance, like herself. Kat had no ambition to find a way to do a job she really enjoyed – she found banking boring but stuck it out because it paid well.' He bit a nail. 'I'd rather spend my life renting a one-bedroom flat, if it meant I can still work outside in the fresh air, and be my own boss. Although don't get me wrong… I've got every intention of making my business a success.'

I studied his face – the eyes serious for a change, those firm lips. Perhaps we had more in common than I'd initially thought. I mean, yes, I liked the finer things in life, but the bottom line was – I wanted to spend my life baking. Suddenly a yawn escaped my mouth. Luke yawned back.

'You like me after all,' I said, unable to hold in a smug chuckle.

'Huh?'

'You yawned after I did. Scientists have proven you only do that if it's someone you approve of.'

'Now *I* fancy *you*?' he said with a grin.

'I doubt you have time for anyone else, what with your ego!' I said, hotly.

'Don't be mean,' he teased. 'Otherwise I might not come next time you call me in the middle of the night. Where would that leave you?'

Suddenly the lights went out and Doug called up to keep everything quiet. I tried to reply but it was difficult… what with those firm lips of Luke's pressed against mine! How did this happen? My heart raced and my eyes closed tight. It felt so… Oh God. Tingles everywhere. I pulled away for a second, to subtly swallow my gum and hoped the claim that it would stay in your stomach for seven years was nothing but an old wives' tale.

He pulled me close again. Why didn't I draw back, all melodramatic, like in the movies, and tell him off for assuming that I was interested? Instead, I stood up on tiptoe. Without realising it, my arms had wrapped around his neck. My face brushed against his bristly cheeks and with no sense of control, I pulled him tight. Luke had a sharp edge to him. I liked that. It made every cell in my body pulsate with desire. Plus the way he kissed, tenderly across my lips at first and then deeper... It felt animalistic and made me respond in a way I never had with more conservative, regimented Adam. It was no good. I could no longer fight the surge of chemistry that ignited between us and caused explosions of pleasure to wake up unknown parts... But, but... I had to get off this rollercoaster and remind myself I was only at Mistletoe Mansion to salvage my relationship with Adam – not to start an affair with... with Pukey Luke. He was grumpy, arrogant, obnoxious and... I lowered my hands to his chest and pushed him away. Forget Lady Chatterley's lover, instead I could just see this headline in Infamous: "Lady Cupcakey's Lover – Kimmy Spurns Adam for Hunky Handyman."

'Why did you, I mean, we...It's not right...' I stuttered and, in a most unladylike manner, wiped my mouth with the back of my hand.

There was no reply, just the feeling of his strong arms around me again. My mouth opened in anticipation. Talk about random. Luke and I didn't get on, right? He was big-headed, patronising... Yet, I couldn't resist his lips, ever so gently teasing mine as my fingers traced the line of his spine.

Adam. I ought to think of Adam. Sensible. Protective. Reassuring. But it was no good, I felt dizzy when Luke and I kissed. And his interest in my business – how Luke took my dreams seriously – was a huge aphrodisiac. Increasingly lately, I'd been asking myself whether Adam was the right man for me. Yes, he offered me all the security I'd never enjoyed as a child, but was that stifling my ambition? I felt so confused and now occasionally questioned the point of my mission to win him back.

With tender confidence, Luke kissed me deeper, and my mind emptied of thoughts about Luton, CountryHouse

Potatoes, my latest cupcake recipe, the universe… Like a returning tide, it refilled with nothing but an overpowering, flowing, luxuriating warmth.

As he trailed intense kisses up and down my neck, I let out a gasp. An X-rated Facebook status flashed before my eyes. Walter Carmichael was a gentleman by all accounts. I had to trust his eyes were firmly shut!

CHAPTER 22

'Impressive. That is an absolutely enormous willy.'

I grinned at Melissa.

'For such a small cake,' she continued, having popped by, just before the prospective buyers were due to arrive. She was ogling the cupcakes I'd made for Saffron's party. 'Those glittery pink ones with hearts on are pretty. And are those liquorice whips?' The corner of her rosebud mouth twitched. 'So, how did last night go?' She looked up. 'Did SpiritShooters find anything? And where's that whistling coming from… is luscious Luke still here?'

'Luscious Luke?'

'Isn't that what you think of him?'

I turned away to the kettle, so that she couldn't see me blush. Guilt twisted my stomach, at the thought of that kiss, which was stupid – Adam had broken things off with me, after all. I was single, so had done nothing wrong. Yet that lush snog went against everything I'd strived for in the last few days – namely, winning back my ex.

Not that the lust stuff had gone further than a bit of lip-on-lip action. Just as I'd thought about Walter watching us last night, Jess had appeared on the landing and headed for the bathroom – the cue for Luke and me to jump apart and go to our own rooms. By the time I'd got up this morning, he and Jess had left. However, Luke came back by nine as promised, which left one hour for us to tidy up.

'He offered to keep an eye on things whilst the visitors –
a Mr and Mrs Stedman – were here.'

'Uh huh…' She eyed me closely. 'Did you two shag?'

'Melissa!' I turned around, cheeks hotter than my body
had felt, last night, wrapped in Luke's arms.

She removed her sunglasses and laughed. I was glad to
note that her eyes weren't all blotchy and red. She wore the
most gorgeous tangerine orange halter-neck jumper with
a tight red skirt, like a kind of sexy Velma out of Scooby
Doo. Disappointingly, the snow had melted and turned to
slush overnight, hence her funky animal print wellington
boots.

'Only asking,' she said, and picked up one of the
hen party cupcakes. She pulled off the marzipan willy
and sucked the end. 'Must say your hair is perfectly
straightened this morning, darling, and I haven't seen that
lacy top before; it could almost pass for genuine vintage.
Seems like someone's trying to make an impression.'

'Stop it,' I snorted and grabbed the Tupperware box from
her. I re-sealed the lid.

'Mmm,' oozed her velvety voice, 'this is the sweetest
di–'

'I'll just check that the front garden is looking its best,'
interrupted Luke as his head appeared around the kitchen
door. Limp willy between her teeth, Melissa beamed at
him. Suddenly obsessed with my nails (okay, freshly
painted this morning in a cool purple colour), I examined
them closely. His footsteps left and I looked up again.
Melissa took the marzipan out of her mouth.

'You couldn't look him in the eye, that's all the evidence
I need,' she said. 'Come on, tell me everything! What
happened last night?' She peeked under the table. 'I'm
amazed you're not wearing those shoes I gave you. Talk
about dolled up…'

'I, um, thought I'd better look smart for the Stedmans.'

'Don't take me for a fool! Was there a kiss? Something more? He'd be pretty buff with the right clothes and grooming products. I can tell you're mad for him.'

'Am not!' I hissed and swallowed the wrong way which led to a coughing fit. *He* kissed *me*, right? I could barely escape. In fact, what a good thing Jess had interrupted us… I sighed. Oh God. Melissa was right. Try as I might, I hadn't been able to stop thinking about his skin pressed against mine – about his hands firmly following the curve of my back. Did he really like me or was he arrogantly making the most of what he considered to be my "crush"?

'By the way,' I said, 'SpiritShooters didn't find a ghost.'

'Don't change the subject, Kimmy.'

I pursed my lips.

'All right.' Melissa smiled. 'I get the message – it's a subject off-limits. So, those guys didn't exorcise some lost soul or evil demon?'

For one second I had an out-of-body revelation. Here I was, joking with Melissa Winsford, celebrity and DVD queen extraordinaire, as if she were one of the girls at the bakery or any old neighbour. I'd always believed there was something different about anyone who appeared on the telly or in a magazine. However, she was simply a better styled version than the rest of us. She still worried about her man, what the future held and her weight.

In answer to her question, I shook my head. It was just typical that the hooded thing didn't show up last night. 'They think someone is playing a joke – or has a grudge against either Mike Murphy or the estate agents. The only strange thing to happen was that a coin moved across a piece of paper and we don't know how.' I looked at my watch. Five minutes. 'What if the house gets messed up again? I know Luke is here, but he can't keep an eye on every room. And

I don't care what those investigators say – I did see a strange face in that front bedroom, that night.'

Melissa shrugged. 'I haven't got to get back, for a while. Jonny's taking me out to lunch later. Why don't I stay?'

'Everything still okay… you know – between you and him?'

'He's treating me like a princess.' Her voice warmed. 'The spring tournaments will be upon us before we know it, and things are going to get hectic. So, he's suggested we take a break – get away from it all, beforehand. He's booked a week in the Maldives.'

'Wow.'

'Fab, isn't it? Usually there's some hidden agenda, like our honeymoon in Bali where our hotel just happened to be next to the most amazingly scenic golf courses. There was the time we went to Sri Lanka… That course even had a steam train running through it. The worst was our trip to Southern Australia where he'd promised to only play one round of golf. Little did I know he'd chosen the longest course in the world which, at eight hundred and fifty miles, took most of the holiday to play. He's sworn that the only strokes he'll be interested in on this holiday belong to his hand rubbing sun cream all over my back.' She beamed. 'So, I'm in a good mood. Let me hang around with Luke. I'll keep an eye on all the rooms– make myself indiscreet, guarantee nothing disastrous happens…'

'This place still doesn't spook you?'

'I'm the youngest of five children. When you've spent your childhood being teased and having practical jokes played on you twenty-four seven, it takes a lot to make you jump as an adult. It was good training for the celebrity life. Really, I should be used to no privacy.' She opened her huge crocodile handbag. 'Before I forget… Give that to Jess. I… don't think I'll need it for a while.'

I took the book. 'A Guide to Pregnancy.'

She adjusted her top. 'I guess Jonny and me, we need to work on our relationship first, before…' She cleared her throat. 'I'm just lucky to have him.'

The doorbell chimed and I hurried into the hallway.

'Chill! It'll go fine,' Melissa called after me.

I opened the door. It was a middle-aged couple. Where on earth was Luke? Hopefully he'd keep Groucho from barking, as I'd locked him out in case the prospective buyers didn't like dogs. The woman held out her hand. I shook it, and then the man's.

'Do come in. My name's Kimmy.' I stood back. They both gasped at the magnificent chandelier. This was a good start. In fact everything went as well as it could, whilst they explored downstairs. The man – Mr Stedman – loved the Games Room and teased his wife that she'd never get him out of there. She fell in love with the kitchen and hot tub, whilst they both cooed over the summerhouse. Recently they'd come into an inheritance and had five-year-old twins. I could tell they thought Mistletoe Mansion and its location were perfect. As we went upstairs I crossed my fingers, as Melissa paced up and down the landing. I had a good feeling about this couple. Sad as I'd be to leave, maybe I was getting near to selling this place; completing the task I was set, being responsible.

Because I still wanted to impress Adam. Definitely. Snogging Luke didn't mean a thing. It had nothing to do with the extra care I took to shave my bikini line this morning; nothing to do with me getting up extra early to jog around the garden.

'Where's Luke?' I hissed to Melissa, as the Stedmans explored the mint bathroom. I'd introduced her and they'd chatted briefly about the tranquillity of Badgers Chase.

Poor them. They'd be in for a shock living here with all the long lenses and dodgy-looking journos.

'No idea,' Melissa said and sniffed. 'Just as well I'm here. I think we've got a bit of a problem.'

That familiar sweet smell wafted into my nostrils. Oh God. I shivered. Smoke drifted down the landing towards my bedroom. And there was that wind rushing sound.

'Leave this to me,' whispered Melissa. 'You keep them the other side of the landing as long as you can.'

She teetered along to the bedroom at the front and rattled the door. It was locked. I smiled nervously at the Stedmans and bundled them back into the bathroom. I managed to talk for a couple of minutes about the bidet and they were well impressed with the waterproof telly. Then I walked them along to the office. What was Melissa doing?

Tentatively, I entered the office, in my high shoes. Phew. No knocked over chairs or scattered papers like the time Deborah was here. I glanced at the laptop and swore I'd update my Facebook status that afternoon. Plus Ashton Kutcher might have noticed my absence on Twitter.

'Um… back in a minute…' I said. 'Do look out of the window. From up here, you'll see just how magnificent the back garden is.'

I strolled out of the room and then darted to Melissa. She was bending over, hairpin in the keyhole, jiggling the door handle.

'Where did you learn to do that?' I asked.

'My older sisters used to lock me in my bedroom for a joke. We moved house a lot. I learnt to pick lots of different types of locks. There.' She stood up and replaced the pin into her swept up blonde hair. 'After you,' she said. I took a deep breath and pushed open the door.

Melissa followed me in. Wow. There were paintings, random bits of furniture, a couple of sets of golf clubs and sheets draped over various items – a large ceramic plant stand by the looks of it and a fancy-looking needle box. I picked up a glass swan and ran my hand along its contours. There was an intricately engraved cutlery set, a knitting machine and a gorgeous purple upholstered rocking chair. I could see why Luke was protective of these rooms. Walter and Lily had some really posh stuff.

'Well, there's no bogeyman in here,' I muttered, minutes later. What an anti-climax. 'Come on. I'd better get back to the Stedmans.'

But Melissa stared at the far wall which backed onto my bedroom. 'Something moved,' she mouthed and put a finger to her lips. She slipped off her squeaky rubber boots and tiptoed over, picking up the glass swan on her way as she navigated various objects. Finally she stopped. We looked at each other, as her hand was poised over a sheet. She brandished the swan and in one swift move, yanked the material away, like a magician revealing a rabbit.

'Luke?' I raised my eyebrows. He was no rabbit, but certainly looked as if he'd been caught in the headlights.

He stood up. 'Um… Hi. I thought I smelt smoke, so I came in here to have a look.'

'Why lock yourself in?' said Melissa, the glass swan now by her side.

He ran a hand through his hair. 'If, um, there was anyone in here, I didn't want them to escape and cause you lot trouble.'

'Why not let us know you were here, when you heard our voices?' I said, an uneasiness stirring in my stomach. I made my way over, any awkwardness about last night forgotten. I bent down behind him but he pulled me back up.

'No! Don't look there! I mean… I knocked something over. There's broken glass. You might hurt yourself.'

But flexible Melissa had already ducked behind his legs. She pulled out what looked like a cross between a fan heater and a huge old-fashioned camcorder. She examined it for a moment and then straightened up. Her generously mascara-ed eyes narrowed.

'I used one of these for a party once,' she said. 'It's a smoke machine.'

Something else caught my eye. I moved another sheet, near to me. Underneath was a CD player. I pressed "play". The spooky wind-rushing noise swept around the room.

'*You*?' I said to him. 'The face in the window? The hooded figure? No wonder you've not taken long to get here every time I've called for help. You've already been in the house!' My stomach churned.

'I don't know what you're talking about,' he said with a shrug. 'Anyone could have set this up.'

'You've got the keys to get in,' I said, a waver in my voice. 'Haven't you at least got the guts to own up?'

'It's not like that,' said Luke and reached out to touch me. 'Let me explain.'

I shook him off.

'Helloooo?' called a voice from the landing.

'It's all right,' said Melissa. 'I'll finish the viewing – they've nearly seen everything by now, right?'

'Yes.' I mumbled, without moving my gaze from Luke's face as I heard her pick up her boots and leave the room. Tears pricked my eyes and a wave of nausea backed up my throat. Walter. The thuds. The White Christmas music – no doubt that was his idea of a joke as well. How could I have been so stupid? I glanced down. How ridiculous I was, with my lacy top, poker-straight hair and glossy nails. Fancy going to all that effort for such a slimeball.

'Why do this?' I said. 'Why don't you want the house to sell? The locked doors, turning the lights off… Did you think it was funny?'

'No. I–'

'All week this has been going on. Right from the first day I got here. Last Saturday night, the spooky face in the window – you did that? How? Just dumped the dressmaking doll in your car and then let yourself back in to Mistletoe Mansion and waited for me to come back from walking Groucho?' Heart racing now, I headed for the window, lifting up sheet after sheet, rummaging through boxes. Something fell onto the ground and smashed. It was a glass dolphin.

'Stop!' shouted Luke. 'Don't damage Walter and Lily's stuff.' He strode over. 'Okay, okay, I'll show you.' He reached behind the curtain and pulled out a circle of tracing paper. It had two eye shapes drawn on it and a mouth and nose. 'Light this up with a torch behind it,' he said, in a quiet voice, 'and–'

My hands flew up to cover my eyes. I'd been a prize idiot. 'Then the next day, when you were over to mend the chandelier and my dripping shower – you never went home, did you?' I took my hands away from my face. 'The smoke, locking me in, you must have pretended to leave and instead gone right upstairs and into the front room, whilst I was still in the kitchen, and waited for me to come up.'

'I'll do anything to stop this place selling, Kimmy.'

'And that evening you stayed over,' I continued, running over the last week, hardly listening to his mutterings. '…You were the hooded figure who grabbed my leg on the bed.' My voice wavered. 'You scared the shit out of me, you bastard.'

'As I told you before, none of this is personal.'

'Oh, here we go with the cryptic comments again. Have you any idea how stupid I feel? All the conversations I've had with Walter – you thudding out the replies, treating me like some imbecile, playing me Bing Crosby music, shooting gusts of cold air. I bet you nearly died with laughter.'

He frowned. 'I don't know what you're talking about. What thuds and music? I haven't heard you say anything to Walter.'

'Oh, please! Next you'll be telling me that it wasn't you who messed up the house when the last viewers came round.'

His eyes widened. 'No. All I've tried to do is scare off the housesitters. A couple have been really untidy, letting Deborah down at viewings. I just assumed that the mess this week, well… was your fault.'

'Stop lying!'

'I'm not! And it's not a criticism,' he said in an exasperated voice. 'I'm not the most orderly of people, myself. That's why I was originally asked to move out, at the beginning, because I never kept the place smart enough.'

'And what about the night before last,' I continued. 'When Terry and Melissa were here? You pushed me into the cupboard.'

'I… didn't mean to hurt you,' he reached out to touch my cheek, but I stepped back.

'And you scratched that desk,' I said, my voice breaking.

'It was old. Walter wouldn't have minded.'

'And last night? That coin?'

'I moved it with a snooker cue.'

'Why didn't you do more? Make the pictures crooked again? Throw my make-up against the walls?'

'What are you talking about?' he muttered. 'The smoke, the windy noise, locking the doors, turning out the lights – yes, okay, hands up. But I told you – I've never messed up the rooms. And as for last night, I kind of got distracted.'

His eyes crinkled at the corners. Those moss green eyes. Just below his sexily tousled hair. Just above those irresistibly bristly cheeks. A lump hurt my throat.

'You and me, Kimmy. That kiss. It threw me right off track.'

I snorted. 'Don't act now as if it meant anything. All that talk about my business, about my mum – be honest, you really couldn't give a toss. It was just a ploy to make me think you cared, to let you hang around this morning and "help" so you could ruin things, just like you have for previous housesitters.' A sob rose in my chest and I held my breath for a few seconds, determined to keep it down. 'Well, for your information,' I muttered, eventually, 'that kiss meant nothing to me either.'

'I've wanted to wrap my arms around you from the first night we met,' he murmured.

Tears pricked my eyes. 'Liar. You were rude and obnoxious.'

'And you were adorable, with your attitude and that honeysuckle behind your ear. From the first moment I met you, I sensed a… a kindred spirit.'

'Don't bother with the sweet-talk.'

'It's not like that, Kimmy. You've got to believe me. And any deception on my part – it's because I'm trying to put things right. Something's wrong with the will–'

I snorted again. 'Yeah. Fell for that hook, line and sinker didn't I, during my conversation with "Walter"? Was it fun pretending to be a dead man? Do you think Walter would approve?'

A car door slammed shut on the driveway. The Stedmans must have left. Hopefully they'd put in an offer and I could get out of Harpenden. How dense was I, thinking I was special enough to talk to a spirit; special enough to have been chosen by a nice old gent, to sort out his problems?

'I don't know what you've got against Mike Murphy,' I said, 'but he's Walter's closest relative and entitled to inherit.'

'Not in my opinion,' said Luke and a muscle flinched in his cheek. 'I knew the Carmichaels a lot better than he did.'

'Oh my God. So that's behind all of this – you're jealous? Mad that the house wasn't left to you instead?' A sneer crept over my face. 'But you're nothing but the handyman.' I swallowed. Why did I say that? But then he hadn't worried about my feelings when he'd snogged the face off me, just to get into my good books.

'Hand over your keys!' I said, voice trembling.

'You've got it all wrong,' he said, in a measured voice.

I stretched out my hand, willing it not to shake.

He dug his hand into his pocket and pulled out a bunch of keys, then dropped it into my palm. 'I can see you've decided what my motives were, so there's no point trying to explain.' He shut the door behind him and I collapsed to the floor, finally releasing that sob. I was nothing but a silly little girl who believed in spirits; who believed she could one day be a successful business woman. Luke had only taken an interest in KimCakes Ltd so that I wouldn't suspect him of doing the spooky stuff. Deep down, he probably had as little faith in my entrepreneurial skills as Adam.

My eye caught sight of the tracing paper face on the floor by the window. Adam would never scare me witless or bruise my back or kid me that I was communicating with the dead. A sudden shiver ran from my head to my toes and, eyes blurred with tears, I stumbled out of the room – telling myself I was mad to think I'd just that minute felt cold and heard the comforting notes of White Christmas…

CHAPTER 23

Sorry to let you down at the last minute, Saffron, but KimCakes Ltd is no longer in business. I've given up my stupid dreams. Adam was right…

I'd even dialled Saffron's number, this speech ready, me prepared to throw all the girly cupcakes into the bin. But when it came to it I just couldn't let her down. With a heavy heart I decided to get through the hen night, this evening – my last as a professional caterer. Luke's ghostly trick had confirmed what I should have known all along: Stupid Kimmy Jones was not meant for the Big Time. A factory job in Luton… That was the sensible option.

You couldn't miss Saffron's house with the pink shimmer curtain hanging over the front door. Plus the "Girls Only" road sign on the tree in the middle of the lawn. And surely that wasn't a naked blow-up hunk in the front window? A group of teenagers scooted past, on bikes. They stopped for a few moments and jeered at the blow-up doll. I parked on the other side of the street and waited for the clock to turn to seven.

My old Fiesta wasn't too out of place in the street full of modest semi-detached houses. Steve and Saffron's place was smartly maintained and the front garden even had a little fountain. It would have been paradise for Adam and me, although it was the poor relative to Melissa's house. On the drive was a small red car with pink dice hanging in the windscreen – just like mine. Next to it stood a grey metallic saloon – pretty impressive, but nothing like Jonny's Bugatti. The clock ticked to seven and I clambered out into the chilly air and opened the boot. I took a deep breath.

So what if Luke had only pretended to believe in my business idea, I told myself bravely. My eyes welled for a second. How could I ever face that man again? He must have had a right laugh over the last week. My little brother, Tom, always said I was gullible, especially when I'd jumped at his fake spiders or hurtled into the kitchen every time he burnt toast on purpose, to set off the smoke alarm. Well, no more. Cynic was my new middle name.

Two large plastic laundry bags filled with Tupperware boxes and the silver cakestands filled the boot. After Luke had revealed all and left this morning, I'd paced around wringing my hands and knew there was only one thing that would calm me down. So I'd jumped in the car and gone to the supermarket. I needed to bake. A new recipe from one of Terry's coffee table magazines had caught my imagination – and would provide an extra batch for the hen party. It was perfect for health-conscious Saffron: low-fat Green Tea cupcakes.

Carefully, I'd added the cooked green tea liquid to the rest of the ingredients, after steeping the tea bags in boiling water. Then I'd piped on the green frosting. Those cakes were elegant, and counteracted the boobs and willies and whips. Then I'd ironed my apron – the one that silly me had previously believed Walter had left out.

Time for my happy face. I slammed shut the boot and dragged my bags across the street, up to the pink shimmer curtain. Three times I knocked loudly, glad of my gold parka as cold, white breath escaped my lips. Giggles rippled from inside and footsteps approached that could only belong to killer heels. I must have looked as plain as Madeira cake, but hadn't felt in the mood for even a smudge of foundation or rouge.

'Hello, Kimmy. This way,' said Saffron. Her backcombed hair would have made Jackie Collins proud. She wore high white stilettos, a matching tight dress and her skin was impossibly bronzed. Whatever she'd used had left streaks up her ankle. I stumbled through the shimmer curtain and carried the heavy bags into the kitchen. A curvy woman sat at the small kitchen table, in front of a hand mirror, applying glitzy eyeshadow.

'This is my big sis, Amy,' said Saffron.

I smiled at the woman's dark mousy hair and pale skin. No doubt she represented a natural version of Saffron, without the peroxide and bottled tan. But then to be fair, I'd almost forgotten what my natural colour was.

'Nice to meet you, Kimmy,' she said. 'I've heard all about your cupcakes. They sound fab.'

'Really?' I gave a half-smile. 'Thanks. Um… Congratulations on your engagement.'

'Better move out the way, Amy, babes,' said Saffron. 'Kimmy needs to set up. This party's going to be mental.' As her sister disappeared into the next room, mirror and a bottle of Lambrini in hand, Saffron took a sip of her drink and ate a single cheese puff. 'Plates are in here.' She pointed to a cupboard. 'I've set the buffet out in the lounge but thought we'd leave the alcohol and cakes in the kitchen.' She glanced at me. 'Of course, I haven't got as much room as Melissa.'

'Nice house, though.'

Her face smoothed out, as if she'd had Botox at Melissa's after all.

'How many guests are coming?' I said.

'Fifteen, at the last count.'

I took out the boxes and set out the stands. Nervously I lifted a lid. I'd show her the innocent girly ones first.

'They're so pretty,' she cooed. 'I'm loving that glitter buttercream icing and the way you've spelt Amy's name out. Nothing could look classier than that. Are they full fat?'

A smile spread across my face. 'Yes. Every woman deserves a treat once in a while.' For me, translate that as at least once a day. In fact I might just wolf down a cake when she left me alone. My smile broadened at Saffron's sparkling eyes, as she oohed and aahed over my detailed decorations and use of colouring.

'Me and Amy are rubbish at baking,' said Saffron. 'The last cake I done looked more like some sponge frisbee. You're really clever.'

I felt all warm inside. You know what? Maybe she was right. I had talent. At least, I don't think a Simon Cowell of the culinary world would say 'My trousers rise higher than your sponge.'

'These ones are low-calorie,' I said and took the lid off another box. 'Green Tea cupcakes – they're the very height of fashion. Elegant, healthy – your friends should be well impressed.'

Saffron shook back her big hair. 'Fab – I saw those in a magazine at the hairdresser's. And what's in the other boxes?'

'Um…. This is a hen party, right? You ladies intend to have fun?' Slowly I prised off the lid. Saffron gasped.

'Are they for real…? I mean…'

'Every last inch is edible.' I held my breath.

'Amy, babes! Come here!' she squealed.

Her sister came in, only one eye made-up, and stopped dead as Saffron lifted up one of the willy cupcakes. The two sisters burst out laughing and within seconds tears streamed down Amy's cheeks. Saffron was disciplined enough not to ruin her mascara, whereas her sister would have to apply her whole face once again.

'I'm loving these,' said Saffron, and held up a cake decorated with a mini handcuffs. 'Isn't Kimmy amazing?'

A lump welled in my throat. You know what? Thanks to Saffron for making good the temporary knock to my confidence. Blow Adam – and Luke – I was born to cook cupcakes and nothing would stand in my way. They were the stupid ones for not believing in me.

My chest tightened as I knew this declaration could only mean one thing: my ex should remain my ex… He was never going to approve of, or respect, my baking ambitions. I swallowed at the memory of feeling safe, wrapped up in his arms. Is that how people felt when their mum hugged them? I didn't know. In my childhood house I'd been the one giving support and comfort – the parent/ child relationship, more often than not, had been turned around.

Question was, could I resist running back into Adam's secure, protective arms? My cheeks flushed as Luke's strong embrace infiltrated these thoughts. I shook myself. Better concentrate on the job at hand.

When the two sisters eventually stopped giggling, Saffron went upstairs. Someone put on music in the lounge and humming, I set out the plates. I called up to Saffron to ask where to find the dessert forks, but the chick flick medley was playing too loud. So, I went up and knocked on a door which was shut – presumably with her inside.

There was no reply, so I went in to face a double bed and a pair of men's jeans draped over a chair. Saffron was on the phone and immediately ended the call. She picked something off her dressing table and shoved it in the desk's drawer.

'Just asking Steve for some last minute advice about my speech – it's a big night for Amy.' She stood up and inspected her dress for fluff. 'And public speaking is very important. Who knows when I'll need it and wished I'd practiced.'

'Um… yes… right… Sorry for barging in, but I couldn't find all the dessert forks.'

The doorbell rang.

'Could you get that, ta?' she said. 'It'll be the first guests. I'll be down in a minute.'

And so went the evening – Saffron enjoying every moment of bossing me about, as if I were a butler, waitress and doorman rolled into one. I just kept repeating to myself "The Customer is King." Or Queen. Or perhaps spoilt princess.

'You okay?' I asked as I nipped into the kitchen to see if there were anymore sausage rolls. Saffron was searching through the drawers and lifted a pile of celebrity gossip magazines from the worktop. I hoped she didn't notice my buttercream icing fingerprints on them – I hadn't been able to resist a quick peek.

'No!' she squeaked. 'I've lost my speech. That was going to be the best part of the evening for everyone.'

Really? From what I'd seen, her girlfriends were more interested in competing to eat their cupcake in the most suggestive way. They weren't slaves to calorie counting like Saffron, who'd eaten little more than one mini hotdog (I was sure I'd spotted some BargainMarket boxes in the bin) and a cherry tomato.

'Where did you last have it?' I asked.

'If I knew that, there wouldn't be a problem.'

'Jane! Your turn next!' screamed a voice.

'Coming, babes,' called Saffron – or was that *Jane*? She blushed and cleared her throat.

'Saffron's not your real name?' I said.

'So?' Her bottom lip jutted out. 'Everyone likes it. I was always destined for classy things and needed a name to match. Know what I mean?'

'Didn't your parents mind?'

'Mum's always said I was different; special. She paid for me to change it by deed poll – said it was the least she could do, seeing as she could never afford for me to go to stage school. Anyway, hardly any celebs use the name they were born with.'

'True. Ashton Kutcher's real name is Christopher.'

'Lady GaGa's is Stefani,' said Jane – I mean, Saffron.

'I'll look for your speech,' I said. 'You go and see to your guests. It can't be far. It's probably somewhere silly like on top of the toilet cistern.'

Saffron frowned. 'Okay. Ta.'

'And then I'll pack up and head off,' I said.

Saffron nodded and went to a drawer. She pulled out a cheque. 'Thanking you for your services, Kimmy,' she said, as if she'd been practicing her mistress-of-the-manor voice.

I tried to contain my excitement, as if earning money like this was an everyday occurrence. A quick glance at the signature revealed Steve's name. I tucked the cheque into my apron pocket as she tippy-toed out of the kitchen in her catwalk heels. They had two mini bows on the back and I recognised them instantly from my favourite online shoe shop – designer copies, of course.

First I checked in the fridge because at a certain time of the month, I did things like put my shoes in the tumble dryer or store ketchup under the sink. Then I stuck my head in the cupboard under the stairs. A vacuum cleaner and ironing board stood side by side like a pair of models, waiting for a photo to be taken. After a hunt around the dining room, I headed upstairs and checked the bathroom –

nothing unusual there. Then it struck me. Of course! When I'd barged in on Saffron earlier, she'd been chatting to Steve on the phone and quickly shoved something in her drawer when I startled her. That had to be it! I snuck into her bedroom.

Wow. Top-notch beauty products crowded her dressing table. How could she afford Clarins? I sat down and slid open the drawer. Oh. There was no speech there. Just a hairbrush, a small photoframe and... I lifted out a pretty charm necklace – not one of those Pandora ones, but an old-fashioned silver chain. Hanging from it was a small heart and a mini Eiffel Tower. Something stirred inside my chest. Where had I seen that before? I gasped. In a flash, it came to me – the picture of Jonny in the paper with that blonde woman... She'd worn a bracelet just like this.

I studied the heart. Turned it over. OMG, it was engraved with the head of an *eagle*. A wave of nausea washed over me – that was Jonny's golfing nickname.

CHAPTER 24

'What you doing in here?' screeched a voice.

Shit. I dropped the bracelet back into the drawer. It fell on a pile of cut out magazine photos of reality stars.

'Saffron…' I stuttered. 'When I came in earlier, you shoved something in this drawer after your phone call. I thought it might be the missing speech.'

She stumbled towards me and glanced down at the bracelet and photos.

'I should grass you to the feds,' she squeaked. 'Is this your game? Robbing people whilst they eat your cupcakes?' Her lips pursed. 'You'd better leave.'

I lifted out the bracelet and pointed to the eagle.

A muscle twitched in her cheek. 'Did that stuck-up bitch Melissa send you?'

'Melissa hasn't got a clue.'

Saffron's tan suddenly looked paler. 'Don't tell her,' she stuttered. 'Jonny'll go mad.'

I stared at her. 'You weren't on the phone to *Steve*, were you?'

'That stupid newspaper… Everything was brill 'til they printed that photo.' She took the bracelet from me and fingered the heart charm. 'He gave me that on my birthday, last month. And the Eiffel Tower… He loves me, you know…'

'Don't tell me,' I scoffed, 'he took you to Paris.'

A triumphant smile flickered across her face.

'Oh my God,' I said. 'So how long have you been seeing him?'

'Long enough to know how bored he is with Melissa. I make him feel young again.'

'Melissa's hardly drawing her pension.'

'She's thirty next year.' Saffron shuddered.

'He bought her those boobs, you know.' I looked pointedly at her flat chest.

'Not nothing wrong with that. Anyway, Jonny says I'm perfect.'

I stared at the cut-out photos in the drawer.

'Don't think you're any better than me,' said Saffron. 'I saw the way you handled Melissa's fine china and admired the golden birdcage. You and me, we both want fancy stuff like that. Other people have managed it, like the contestants off Big Brother. That's all I've wanted ever since I can remember – nice things; people to know who I am; the paparazzi to take my photo. Remember Stella out of Sleeping Booty and Ashley out of Vajazzlers Versus Vets? Then there was Tracy out of Look-a-Like Lock-Up… They're all famous now.'

I squirmed. She was right. For years I'd craved that kind of life. 'But wouldn't it be better to become famous by achieving something, with a great voice, or business idea or sports skill?'

She swivelled her petite body. 'I've got the skills to get Jonny to marry me. He's done it twice already – proves he believes in the institution of marriage. I've tried the clubs in London where footballers hang out, but there's too much competition there to hook anyone really well-known. Then I met Steve. I thought his golf was stupid until he talked about Jonny. It got me thinking. Golfers – they're the new footballers, take it from me, babes.'

'But you're engaged!'

Saffron sneered. 'Steve's just a stepping stone.'

My mouth fell open.

'Do you really thing I'd waste this body on someone who worked in an office?' she said. 'He's lucky to have had a girl like me on his arm for a few months. It's a win win situation for both of us. I done nothing wrong.'

I shook my head, stood up.

'I was shortlisted to appear on Blonde, Blingin' and Beautiful last year, you know?'

Ignoring her, I opened the bedroom door.

'She won't appreciate you telling her,' said Saffron, following me. 'Not nothing going to be achieved by that. You wouldn't want to hurt Steve, would you?'

I hurried downstairs, along the hallway and into the kitchen. The music was louder than ever. Quickly I packed away the cakestands and empty plastic boxes and slipped on my gold parka jacket.

'Aren't you going to wash those plates up before you go?' asked Saffron in a tight voice. She stood at the kitchen door, clutching her phone. Her hand shook.

'Goodbye Saffron.' I pushed past her and stopped at the front door to open it.

'I'm just trying to make something of myself,' she shouted above the R&B beat.

I swung around and glared. 'By sleeping with someone else's husband? How clever is that?'

Saffron folded her arms. 'It's her fault. She shouldn't keep nagging him about having kids. Jonny's life is busy enough. He's a star. Melissa ought to remember she'd be a nobody without him. Not nothing she does makes him feel like a man anymore.'

'Is that what he told you? They're still sleeping together, you know? I saw them, my first night in the cul-de-sac. It was pretty wild by the looks of it…'

'He don't love her anymore,' Saffron snapped.

'But you can't split them up! The Winsfords... they're a brand.' I lowered my voice. 'Saffron – it'll tear Melissa apart.'

She snorted. 'And what about me? Don't I deserve a taste of the good life? I want the best beauty treatments, exotic holidays abroad. I want a tan that comes from a far-away island, not a bottle. I want people to stare at me in the street. A life like that would be mental.'

Everything stood still for a moment and an uneasy sensation shifted in my stomach. That speech sounded so familiar. Saffron sounded just like me.

'Don't tell me you wouldn't do anything for a bit of the celebrity lifestyle,' she crowed.

'I don't break up marriages to achieve my goals,' I said. 'I work bloody hard at my business. And what do you think Jonny's going to do when *you* approach thirty and start using Botox – that's assuming you're still together.'

'I bet you're not this critical of your new best friend Melissa,' she sneered.

'Melissa's nothing like you. She never even knew he was famous when they first got together,' I muttered.

'Then she don't deserve him.' Saffron's eyes narrowed. 'Any woman with half a brain does her research before giving a bloke the glad eye. I don't waste my assets on just anyone.'

With a sigh I pulled open the front door and, bags and cakestands bumping against my legs, hurtled down the drive. Music poured out of the house, onto the quiet dark road. I crossed to my car, unlocked it and threw my stuff in the boot. Ignoring Saffron's high-pitched insults, I got in the front seat and drove off.

Five minutes later, several streets away, my heart still raced. Listening to her... It was like someone playing back the speeches I'd made to Adam over the last few months. Shallow, materialistic... A surge of heat filled my face.

'Watch where you're going, bimbo!' shouted a voice as a pair of headlights screeched out of Badgers Chase. I swerved, pulled up and just caught the outline of a Bugatti. My mouth went dry. One guess as to where Jonny was going.

Chest tightening, I parked at Mistletoe Mansion before dragging my feet towards the Winsfords' place. I really didn't want to go in, but I'd promised to call on Melissa and give her the low-down on my evening. Nervously, I rapped the eagle knocker, kind of hoping that no one would answer. But no such luck. The door opened and there stood Melissa, in a gorgeous pink tracksuit. Should I tell her about her husband's affair? My stomach scrunched into a ball. How could I? It would devastate my celebrity friend and knock that already fragile confidence. Yet if I didn't, Jonny was making a fool of her. She deserved the truth.

'She's in here, Kimmy darling,' said Melissa, and puzzled, I followed her into her lush lounge. Ah. There was Jess, perched on the plum sofa. The velvet red curtains were pulled and on the coffee table fragrant candles burned, next to bowls of potpourri.

'I did leave a note for you,' said Jess.

'Listen to you two – you're like an old married couple,' said Melissa. Her eyes looked a bit red. Her voice sounded quieter than usual.

'Melissa insisted I come round,' continued Jess. 'For these magazines...' She lifted one up. It had a photo of a naked pregnant woman on the front page.

'Champagne?' Melissa said to me as she headed back to the hallway. 'I've done my best to stick to non-alcoholic drinks with the pregnant lady around. But seeing as you're here I may as well indulge myself. Then you can tell me all about sulky Saffron and how her hen party went.'

She beckoned to me and I darted back into the hallway. 'How are you?' she said, in low tones. 'After this morning?'

'I'm fine,' I said, stomach even tighter than before. Melissa's concern made me almost reveal her husband's affair then and there. Yet I couldn't bear to see her hurt. Perhaps, instead, I should have a word with Jonny – tell him if he didn't 'fess up, I'd do it for him...

With a feeble smile, I exchanged looks with my glamorous pal. Melissa understood. I didn't want to talk about Luke. Not yet. Whilst she got the drinks, I went back into the lounge and sat down next to Jess. 'Didn't think you liked our golfing friend that much,' I whispered.

Jess tucked a strand of red hair behind her ear. 'She's okay, actually. Did you know there's a compost bin at the bottom of her garden? And she orders her make-up from the same online company as me, the one that only uses natural products.' At the end of her cold now, Jess wiped her nose. 'I feel sorry for her – look at all this stuff Melissa's collected to do with babies. She's decided to put her pregnancy plans on hold and has given me a bucket-load of folic acid tablets.'

'You'd think she wouldn't want to talk about babies, what with Jonny dragging his feet.'

'I know. She's like an encyclopaedia when it comes to information about getting pregnant – did you know the first ever contraceptive used in Ancient Egypt was crocodile dung?'

I pulled a face. 'Just the smell would be enough, like that fertiliser you sell. Talking of which, how was work today?' I said, dying to tell Jess about Saffron, but worried Melissa might overhear.

'I told Dana – about… my condition.'

'Oh my God – did the Dalek threaten to exterminate you?'

'It was dead weird. She didn't say much; asked me about the father.'

'That's a bit of a cheek! Did you tell her?'

'No point in hiding it. The rest of the staff heard I'd broken up with my boyfriend, although they didn't know he was married. When Dana found out I was going to be on my own, she started muttering about maternity leave; wanted to know if I'd be going back to work.'

'And what did you say?'

'Yes. I mean, somehow…'

I squeezed her hand. 'We'll sort it out.'

Jess half-smiled. 'So. How was the hen party? Oh yes, and I must tell you about poor Melissa. You see–'

'Here – this is top stuff,' said Melissa, appearing with two glasses full of champagne. 'One of the sponsors gave it to Jonny.'

I took my glass as Melissa collapsed into an armchair, opposite.

'Was that him I saw, just now, zooming off in his car?' I asked, innocently.

'One minute he was playing darts, the next he shouted something about needing to check a rota at the club and vanished.' She bit her lip.

'What's the matter?' I asked softly. 'He was going pretty fast. That's why I came round – to check everything was all right.'

'Nothing… Everything…' Her voice sounded kind of strangled. 'He's furious. But it's not my fault.' She looked at Jess who nodded. 'I mean, I've got to trust some people. I can't go through life thinking the worst of every person I meet.'

'What's happened?'

'My agent contacted me. He'd had a call from a friend of his, a guy who works at Infamous. Word's got around that someone's sold a story on me. It's hitting the shelves tomorrow morning.'

'Who?'

Melissa's chin wobbled. 'I can't believe… How could she…?'

'Sandra,' said Jess. 'You met her, didn't you, Kimmy?'

'*Sandra*?' I put down my glass. That warm, cosy, mumsy woman I'd met at Melissa's coffee morning, who did Botox and nails? 'No way! There's got to be some mistake.'

Melissa swigged back her drink. 'All this interest in these photos of Jonny and that blonde… Sandra's obviously been waiting and has decided this is a good time to earn some bucks. Come to think of it, she recently mentioned how much she wanted a conservatory but couldn't afford it.' Her chin wobbled. 'Apparently she's said all sorts of things about me drinking and how she regularly has to chauffeur me around – that happened once! Then there's everything I've told her about how much I want a baby. Plus my cosmetic procedures and all the inside gossip I've given her about the other golfers' wives…' Melissa gulped. 'I feel like a teenager who's just had her diary stolen. I thought we were friends.'

'What a bitch,' I said. 'Can't you sue? Get… what do you call it… an injunction? Stop the article going to press?'

Melissa shrugged. 'Jonny reckons we wouldn't have a leg to stand on because there's probably some truth in what she's revealed. I trusted her.' Tears travelled down the contours of her perfect cheekbones. 'Jonny can't believe I've been so stupid.'

My fists curled. What a cheek when he'd been so stupid, with Saffron, himself.

'You'd think Jonny would be more sympathetic,' I said. 'People must have done the dirty on him.'

She nodded. 'I reminded him of how foolish he'd been a couple of years ago, when his mum was ill.'

'Cancer, wasn't it?' I said.

'Yes. When the papers announced it, she hadn't even had time to tell her best friend.'

'That's awful,' said Jess.

'Some journos hacked Jonny's phone. It was easy to tap into his voicemail because he'd chosen an obvious password. Me messing up has just brought it all back and made him feel bad again.' She sniffed. 'Anyway, darling, distract me. Tell me all about Saffron – and the buffet. Was there anything to eat apart from cottage cheese and low-fat crackers?'

'Where does this Sandra woman live?' I said, hardly listening. 'Let's go round. I'll pretend to be your lawyer. We could threaten all sorts. Tell her that… that by the time she's been through the courts, she won't be able to afford a cardboard box to sit in, let alone a conservatory.'

'Please, Kimmy,' she said in a small voice. 'I… I won't hold it together if I think about it anymore. You know what it's like…' She stared at me. 'Sometimes things are too painful to talk about.'

Wasn't that the truth. My eyes tingled as I thought of Luke and his smoke machine making a fool of me.

'Okay, um, Saffron, yes… the hen party.' I took a deep breath. Was now the moment to tell her? But with a look at her face, already hurting from her row with Jonny, I just couldn't do it. Not yet. 'The do wasn't bad – all the cupcakes went down a bomb.' Don't hint about the affair, I told myself. Tonight definitely wasn't the night to reveal all. 'What's this Steve like?'

'He's all right,' said Melissa. 'A hardworking type – he carries a lot of statistics around in his head. I had a bit of a funny phone call from him, actually, the week before you got here. He wanted to know if I'd seen Saffron, as if we were best friends or something; he didn't seem to want to get off the phone.'

'Sounds like he was checking up on her,' said Jess. 'Maybe she's up to no good.'

I spluttered and swallowed the wrong way. Jess thumped my back hard. I took another sip of champagne.

'Was it something I said?' Jess grinned. 'Here, have a stick of chewing gum, it'll calm you down.'

'No thanks,' I mumbled.

Melissa stared at me. 'Kimmy? Did you find out something juicy tonight? Don't say Jess is right... Is she playing away?'

'How... um... should I know?'

'Come on, spill,' she said.

'What makes you think there's anything to tell?' Oh no, I could feel my cheeks going red.

'Because that's exactly how you reacted when I asked you if you'd shagged Luke. You nearly choked to death.'

'What's that!' gasped Jess. 'Kimmy? You and Luke?'

'No!' I said, hotly. 'Melissa just got the wrong idea. As if Luke and me...' I knocked back another mouthful of fizz. 'Did he drop round to ours after work today, Jess?'

'You and Luke?' she repeated.

'It was only a kiss,' I said. 'We got carried away last night – it was dark, a bit spooky...'

Jess shook her head. 'I'd never have guessed. But he's, I mean... I can't even begin to make sense of it.'

'Well, it's all over now,' I rambled, 'not that there was anything really going on.'

Jess stared at me. 'I can't keep up. By the way – did you remember to ring Mr Murphy?'

'Yes – this afternoon. I wasn't sure what to say – just assured him that things were in hand and that the morning's viewing had gone well,' I said, hoping Melissa wouldn't ask me again about the hen party – but no such luck.

'Back to Saffron,' said Melissa. 'Give me some dirt so that next time I see her, I can wipe off that annoying smile. God knows she'll have enough ammunition against me after Sandra's articles are published.'

I put down my glass. 'Okay.' Breathe in, breathe out. I didn't need to tell the full story. Perhaps I could just drop a hint. 'For a start her real name is Jane.'

Melissa clapped her hands. 'I love it.'

'And is she seeing someone else?' asked Jess.

I squirmed as they both stared at me. The moment of truth. 'Yes.'

Melissa put down her glass. 'But she only got engaged about six months ago,' she said, voice all quiet again.

'Who is it?' asked Jess.

I opened my mouth and really tried to say the word Jonny, but nothing came out.

'Kimmy?' said Melissa.

'How did you find out?' asked Jess.

'I found something… in one of her drawers… I was helping her look for a piece of paper. She'd written a little speech for her sister's party.'

'What did you find?' asked Melissa, flatly.

'Look. It's late,' I stuttered. This was going too far. 'Why don't we discuss this tomorrow? After last night, I'm shattered.'

Melissa raised her perfectly tattooed eyebrows.

Aarggh! There was no way around this. And, deep down, I knew Melissa had a right to know. My hands felt all sweaty. 'A bracelet, with a heart charm and mini Eiffel Tower on it,' I mumbled, knowing that if I'd scoured that photo of Jonny with the blonde, Melissa would have certainly memorised every millimetre.

'Huh?' Jess put down her orange juice.

Melissa said nothing.

'Would someone mind telling me what this is all about?' said Jess.

I reached out and touched Melissa's arm. 'You had your suspicions, didn't you? I'm so sorry. I wasn't sure whether to mention it, but… well, we're friends and–'

'Friends?' Melissa stood up unsteadily. 'I'm not sure I know what those are anymore.'

'I know you're upset,' I said and got to my feet too. 'But surely it's best to find out sooner rather than later?'

'It's not true!' she said, loudly. 'Jonny loves me and Saffron's engaged to that finance nerd. Just because Luke's let you down, you want to ruin my happiness. I don't know why I've even bothered talking to you this last week.' Her velvety tones were gone. 'You're staff, for God's sake.'

A ball of coldness hit the centre of my chest. '*What* did you just say?' I shook off Jess's arm which was trying to guide me to the front door.

'Let's just say I've humoured you – done my bit for the little people. Let you experience a bit of the high life.' Melissa shuddered. 'It's the first and last time anything from Primark touches my sofa.'

'You've spent most of your time around at ours!' I said.

'*Yours*? I hardly think that house belongs to you, dear.'

'You didn't complain when I invited you to use the hot tub.'

'Yes – captivating it was, listening to your stories of going to the pub with Adam. Well wake up, darling, time to go back to your dull little life.' She wrinkled her nose. 'Did you really think Melissa Winsford would be anything but bored with a two bit cakemaker from Luton, whose boyfriend…' she winced, '… packs potatoes for a living? I eat caviar, drink Cristal champagne. I discuss bunker shots with Tiger Woods. Did you really believe I was interested in hearing about your dreary life and...' her voice wobbled, '...your self-delusional dream of making it big in the catering world?'

Melissa stuck her head in the air and went into the hallway. Followed closely by Jess, I strode past her and stormed out of the house, past the tinkling golf club fountain and along to the end of her drive.

'And unless you want Jonny's lawyers to screw *you*,' screeched Melissa, 'stay away and keep your dirty little suspicions to yourself!'

CHAPTER 25

"The Silky Prawn" sounded like something fun your boyfriend might present you with as a Valentine's gift. As it turned out it was a very posh Chinese restaurant I'd been dying to visit, on the outskirts of Luton. Turning into the tiny car park, around the back, my luck was in, and I drove into the last space. It was Saturday night. Frost glinted on the pavement. The weather couldn't make up its mind this week, veering between damp days and ones cold enough to freeze my car's engine – even though it now spent its nights in a fancy garage.

It was one week since I'd left Adam. This morning, after yesterday's fall-outs with Luke and Melissa, I'd phoned him. My Ex had listened and made reassuring noises, then to my amazement, asked me out to dinner. He hadn't said "to grab a bite" or "to hit the drive-thru" and I nearly fainted when the words came down the line "and blow the expense". Unless he was hoping I'd pay, after I told him about Saffron's cheque. Maybe Adam felt sorry for me, after I'd repeated Melissa's snotty comments. I didn't tell him about Luke taking me for a mug, by pretending to be the ghost.

I smoothed down my short tartan skirt, which looked kind of festive with the red jacket, and locked the car door. With a deep breath, I headed into the restaurant and stopped for a second to breath in the savoury aroma of deep-fried pork and soy sauce. Mmm. Lush.

Ahem. No, bad word – it reminded me of Melissa calling Luke *luscious*. He'd called round early this morning; shouted something about being sorry – I'd slammed the door in his face, before, armed with magazines, taking a long soak in the hot tub. Except it wasn't such fun any more, reading the juicy gossip; not since I'd seen how such stuff hurt Melissa.

I smiled at the smartly dressed waiter. When I gave him Adam's name, he led me past a small bar, at the front of which was an amazing fish tank. There was a folded up newspaper on a chair next to it and I caught the sports headlines on the back. It had been all over the news today – how golf's Golden Couple was torn apart by drink, affairs and negative pregnancy tests. Despite her nasty comments last night, I felt sick for Melissa and the way Sandra had portrayed herself as a loyal friend, who made out that she was only telling her story so that Melissa would "get help".

What a cute restaurant, with red and gold dragons painted across the walls. Orange pumpkin-like lanterns hung from the ceilings, and each table we passed was covered with a white tablecloth, on top of which stood a red candle and small vase containing a plastic orchid. The ceiling was jade green and pictures of mountains and animals hung here and there. The restaurant looked really festive, with the red and gold decor. By the bar stood an exquisite, twinkling Christmas tree, decorated with unusual baubles. Next to the cash till was a waving metallic Chinese lucky cat.

'Kimmy?'

I smiled at Adam as the waiter pulled out a chair. I sat down, in front of half a lager.

'I ordered your usual drink,' he said and returned my smile.

'Great,' I said and took a sip. The week had seemed so long, yet now it was as if we'd never been apart. Deep breath. No flighty comments. Talk only about money and responsibility and for God's sake don't mention the Games of Thrones Room, hot tub or champagne. Because even though I had my doubts about Adam, this was a last chance to see if we really had something special.

'You look nice,' he said.

'Thanks.' I said, telling myself it didn't matter that Adam had just pulled on a sports shirt. Luke's shirts hung a bit more loosely and left you to imagine what was underneath... In fact, like his hair, the handyman was altogether more laid back. I shook myself. I wasn't going to think about that lying, dishonest–

'Crispy duck pancakes to start?' said Adam. 'And lemon chicken and chilli beef with fried rice for the main?'

I nodded. We always had those dishes for take-away.

'Swanky, isn't it?' he said and gazed around. 'But I guess you're used to that, after a week in Harpenden.'

'I... I've been working too hard to really make the most of it. That day you visited, honestly, it was a one-off. Me and Jess, we're doing everything we can to get that place sold. We're the most reliable housesitters they've had – it's not been a popular job.' What with snobby neighbours and spooks...

Adam placed his hand over mine. 'What's up, babe? This Melissa really got to you, didn't she? When we first spoke after you'd moved in, you were so excited.'

'Yes, partly because I thought you'd be impressed that I'd got a job so quickly and made do with the first place I could find to live in.'

'*Made do*?' Adam snorted. 'Your new pad's smarter than any hotel and it's rent-free. Sorry, Kimmy, but I'd have been more pleased if you'd at least signed on at the Job Centre and got your CV sorted.'

'But what about the money I've earned from my business?'

'Business?' he took his hand away. 'Can you still not see that this madness is nothing but a hobby? You've made a couple of contacts, but those people aren't going to order off you, week in week out. And how are you going to meet any more people wealthy enough to pay through the nose for cakes, now that you've fallen out with this Winsford woman?'

'I'm thinking of doing a business course.' I said, voice wavering, as I slipped off my red jacket and hung it over the back of my chair.

'What, wasting more money? And you'd have to start from the bottom up – you don't even know the basics. Like the way you've randomly called yourself KimCakes Ltd – do you even know what the Ltd bit means?'

My cheeks flamed. Not exactly. But it sounded good didn't it? More professional.

'For a start, you have to register any Limited business under the Companies Act. Face it, Kimmy, you've not even considered the paper-pushing side of things yet. As Uncle Ron always says, working for yourself means bloody long hours with very little profit in the first few years. We'd never get any savings together.'

'Then why don't you have a word with Ron for me and get some advice? Or better still, invite him round for dinner – I could pick his brains. I've always thought how much he enjoyed being his own boss.'

'I don't want to see you disappointed, babe, when this bonkers project of yours fails.'

'You assume I won't succeed?' I thought of Luke. He hadn't doubted me. My jaw tightened. Not that I could trust anything that two-faced slimeball said.

At that moment the waiter appeared and Adam gave him our order. Nothing had changed in the last week. Just like Melissa, Adam thought I should know my place in life and stick to it. When the waiter bowed and left, Adam nipped to the toilet, giving me space to sigh.

'What's today's speciality?' said a familiar voice. 'Bang Bang Chicken? Yep. Plenty of noodles, please.'

What the…? I turned to the next table and glared at Luke, wearing a smart, sexy navy shirt that showed just the right amount of tanned chest. He'd even shaved – though an irritating, disloyal part of me crazily liked his rugged side and felt disappointed.

'Fancy seeing you.' He grinned.

'What are you doing here?' I hissed. Then I blushed. My eyes welled. No. I wasn't going to show him I was bothered or embarrassed about how he'd duped me.

'Free country, isn't it? I just fancied eating out. I know I'm *nothing but a handyman,* but I like to think my taste in food is cosmopolitan.'

'I didn't mean that,' I muttered. 'Not that I'm apologising – not after your behaviour.' I turned my attention to the menu.

'If you'd just let me explain…'

'Forget it.'

He sipped a beer. 'Your boyfriend's a bundle of laughs, isn't he?'

I turned back to him. 'He's not my boyfriend – I don't think. Anyway, at least he's honest, unlike someone I could mention. Just go away. Adam will be back in a minute.'

He stared at me. 'Maybe I'll join your table, if you aren't a couple. Unless, of course, you'll let me say my bit before he gets back. Then I'll leave.'

Aargh! Could he possibly be any more annoying? My fists curled under the table. I glanced over to the door of the men's toilets and then consulted my watch. 'You've got one minute and counting.' I didn't want to upset Adam.

He put down his drink. 'I think Mike Murphy has messed with Walter's will. Just before Lily died, the Carmichaels told me that they were leaving everything to their favourite charities.'

I eyed him closely. 'That was a while ago. People change their minds. Walter was close to his nephew in the end.'

'Not that close – I remember calling round, a couple of weeks before Walter passed on. Murphy rang him whilst I was there, said he was coming down on yet another business trip and would stop by. Walter pulled a face – said his nephew meant well but was tiring him out with all the well-meaning lunches and trips. He also mentioned that Murphy kept trying to save him money – he'd suggested new energy providers, a different television package and a new solicitor. But was the financial advice so that there'd be more left for him? Plus Walter was very independent and resented the interference. Murphy didn't sound to me like someone he'd want to leave loads of money to.'

'So?'

Luke folded his arms. 'I reckon Murphy got him to change solicitors and somehow forged a new will, making himself the major beneficiary. I overheard him once, a couple of months after Walter died. I was tidying up the garden whilst Murphy was on his phone, in the summerhouse. He talked about how he'd be able to buy a new car, bigger house and book a dream-of-a-lifetime trip to the States. So, the money he must be getting from the Carmichaels' estate must be considerable. Yet, Walter's charity work was always important to him, right up to the end – he wouldn't have them miss out.'

'You've been watching too many detective mysteries.' I said and looked at my watch.

He ran a hand through his thick, chestnut hair. 'The smoke, wind noise, light switches, dressing up in that hooded top… all I've ever intended was to scare off the housesitters and delay the sale of Mistletoe Mansion, until I can work out how Murphy managed to swindle Walter – and get proof.'

I shrugged. 'Any luck?'

'Not yet. I've searched through all the items in the locked rooms – there's a filing cabinet containing all the Carmichaels' paperwork. You know, mortgage stuff, health insurance, receipts, private health bills and so on – but nothing to do with a will. Murphy must have hidden it. Or worst, destroyed all the evidence.'

'So, where could it be?'

'I've still got to look through some of the loft. It's been difficult, what with housesitters around.'

I gazed at those moss green eyes. 'You seem to care an awful lot… Wasn't Walter just another client?'

Luke reddened. 'He and Lily – I'd have done anything for them. You see… I'm not going to pretend running your own business is easy. Adam is right. A few years ago I was struggling to make ends meet – when we had that really hot summer and everyone's lawns dried up and there were hosepipe bans. I lost a few customers for a while and I'd just bought some new equipment I had to pay off. Walter insisted on giving me a loan to tide me over. He trusted me implicitly.'

Out of the corner of my eye I saw Adam returning. 'Okay. Maybe I get it. I'll think it all over but for now, go away. Please.'

'Everything all right?' said Adam, as he sat down and the waiter appeared with our crispy duck and a plateful of pancakes.

'Uh huh.' I smiled, self-consciously. Please don't let him notice Luke, who was probably watching our every move. I spread the plum sauce on a pancake, added the cucumber strips and the duck. Adam had almost finished eating his first pancake.

'That job's still available,' he said, mouth full.

I sighed. 'Don't you ever give up?'

But suddenly eyes wide, he pointed his mouth.

'What's the matter? It's not spicy.'

Frantically, he pointed again.

'Try to cough!' ordered Luke, from the next table and jumped up. He caught my eye. 'He must have swallowed a bone – Adam's choking!'

CHAPTER 26

Adam made a gravelly noise and turned red in the face. Luke pulled him to his feet but my ex shoved him away, even though he was on course to beat Walter to the Pearly Gates. I blinked rapidly, our whole relationship flashing before my eyes.

'Let him help you, Adam!' I screeched and gazed frantically around the restaurant in hope of spotting someone stand up, claiming to be a doctor or nurse.

'Keep calm,' said Luke, 'there's no need to panic.' Hardly daring to breathe, I watched him gently open Adam's mouth. 'I can't see anything, it's too far down.' Quickly, he tilted Adam forwards, so that he bent from the hips. 'I'm going to whack you hard in between the shoulders, mate.'

Adam grimaced and I bit hard on my fist which had found its way into my mouth. Peanut couldn't die. All our differences aside, he'd been my mainstay for the last couple of years. For the first time ever I'd enjoyed a routine to my life for the basic things others took for granted, like paying bills and spending the night curled up, asleep instead of awake worrying about a drunk mum. However much our paths had separated, Adam, he… he meant so much.

With the heel of his hand, Luke hit him, from behind, then walked around and once again looked inside Adam's mouth. Again he hit him, whilst my teeth sunk further into my skin. Then again. Now a fourth time. Adam made a gurgly moaning noise and flapped his hands. Someone help! Come on Adam! I took my hand away and a desperate sob escaped. Everyone's eyes in the room were fixed on the drama. Someone screamed at the manager to ring the emergency services.

'One last blow and then I'll try something else,' said Luke. There was a loud slap. Oh God... Thank you, thank you, thank you... Something small and brown had shot out of Adam's mouth.

Poor Adam. Tears streamed down his face as he leant on the table.

'You saved his life...' I muttered, heart still pounding, eyes wet, as everyone in the room cheered.

I dashed up to Adam and gave him a big hug, but he pushed me away, still recovering from the shock, his body racked with deep breaths. Whilst the manager fussed over my ex, Luke told the waiter to fetch a glass of water and then took me to one side.

'After the way he spoke to you, I quite enjoyed hitting your ex,' he said. 'Believe the worst of me if you want, Kimmy, but I meant every word I said about KimCakes Ltd and you giving it a go. Don't abandon your dream. Don't give it all up for this narrow-minded bozo.'

I was still staring at Adam, relief surging through my veins. I couldn't meet Luke's gaze. Our kiss in the dark... The spurts of desire he'd raised in me... I... I couldn't think of that at the moment – my head was all over the place. He tossed a twenty pound note down on his table and was about to go when Adam called him over. Now he was recovering remarkably quickly, no doubt fuelled by the prospect of a free meal, which he was already discussing with the manager.

'Stay away from Kimmy,' he snapped at Luke, in a croaky voice. 'She's off-limits.'

'It was my pleasure, mate, no need to thank me,' said Luke, with a smirk. 'And the Kimmy I know can speak for herself.'

Adam lunged at him and I darted in between the two men. I wasn't sure whether to be more pleased that Adam was jealous, or upset that he hadn't thanked Luke.

'Please, gentlemen,' said the manager.

Adam backed off, then glanced around us. He apologised to some nearby customers. 'Sit down, Kimmy,' he muttered. He looked at Luke. 'Thanks for what you did,' he growled, 'but just stay away from my girlfriend.' As he turned back to me, his grey eyes looked more metallic and steely than ever.

My girlfriend? Did he really say that? Not that I approved of him speaking on my behalf. Luke left and I sat down, waiting for butterflies to flutter in my stomach because Adam had seen off a love-rival. But they didn't. Why couldn't I get excited about proof that Adam might want me back?

In fact, as we sat drinking free drinks, courtesy of the management, an unsettling sensation washed over me; the realisation that I was sooo relieved Adam was okay, but still unsure that he was the man for me.

'What was that jerk doing here?' Adam's mouth set in a firm line.

'Dunno,' I said. 'Let's not talk about him. Tell me instead – what you just called me… your girlfriend… Does that mean…?'

Adam rubbed his throat. 'I've missed you, Kimmy. Maybe I was a bit rash about asking you to leave. Why don't you move back? We could work something out?'

'What about the factory job?'

'I still feel the same about that; still want us to start planning a future.' He stared into the bottom of his glass. 'But what if I'm not enough for you any more, babe? When I saw you in that Mistletoe Mansion, I could tell you felt right at home. Not like me. Posh houses and motors, they just aren't my bag. In the end, I'd probably let you down.'

'Oh, Adam…' I leant forwards and kissed him on lips. Mmm. That was… nice. After all these years, I couldn't expect eye-popping passion, could I?

A couple of hours later, I was still mulling over that kiss, when pulling into Mistletoe Mansion's cul-de-sac. Adam must have been in shock after almost choking to death. That's the only thing that could have explained him talking as if things had about-turned – and now apparently it was me who wouldn't want him. I'd followed him in my car, back to the flat and helped him find the painkillers as his throat and back hurt.

'S'pose my gaff looks tiny now,' he'd muttered.

'If only you'd support my dreams, I'd happily live in a shoe.'

'But it would have to be designer, right?' he'd said and squeezed my shoulder.

'Too right,' I'd replied and smiled.

Then I'd left; said we'd talk again soon; decided we weren't quite boyfriend and girlfriend again, yet. My gentle giant hugged me well tight; swamped me in his embrace. He'd never risk hurting me like hooded Luke had. When we'd first started dating I'd brace myself, expecting to be crushed. But he'd always cuddle as if he thought I were made of egg-shell. Perhaps that was the problem. He didn't think I was tough enough to make it in the business world, unlike Luke who had no doubts that I could give it a good go.

I parked and, legs feeling shaky for a moment, stayed in the car. If Adam had died, tonight would have been the worst night in my world. And yet that world of mine was changing and now featured new territories I longed to explore. My chest felt all funny as I realised, even more, that perhaps safe, reliable Adam just wasn't the person to accompany me on that journey.

I shook myself and got out of the car. A note hung out of the letterbox. I'd recognise that fancy handwriting anywhere – it was from Melissa: "Please come around to mine, however late it is."

What a cheek! Her summoning me, as if I really was on her payroll. Yet the edges were all wet and curled up – because of tears? Nah, vodka more like. No doubt she was going to present me with a load of evidence to prove Jonny was innocent of any affair. Yet what if something was wrong... and why did I even care? Shivering slightly in the arctic December air, I teetered around to her house in the platforms she'd given me, avoiding icy patches. After hesitating, I rapped the eagle brass knocker.

Eventually the door opened. There stood Melissa, in a plum jogging suit and wearing unusually little make-up. She held up a basket.

'Did you want something?' I asked, 'because I'm not interested in more insults.' On closer inspection, her cheeks were blotchy and her eyes bloodshot. She handed over the basket. I lifted up the tea towel lying over the top. There, underneath, were five small, unevenly shaped cupcakes with gritty-looking yellow butter icing on top. Crowning each one was a letter made from raisins. All together, they spelt the word "SORRY".

'*You* made these?' I asked. As far as I could tell from her kitchen cupboards, Melissa's culinary skills, at best, stretched to heating a tin of soup.

'I didn't have any other edible decorations,' she mumbled. 'I had to pick those raisins out of Jonny's muesli. Jess let

me pinch your flour, sugar and eggs.' She cleared her throat.
'I suppose you'd better come in.'

'Now wait a minute! You asked me to come round.'

Her chin trembled.

'Only for a few minutes,' I muttered and followed her
into the amazing lounge, past the gold birdcage and out
to the conservatory. In the garden, on one of the mini golf
greens, a bonfire was burning.

'You're just in time,' she said and led me onto the lawn.
Next to the fire was something silky and white, all torn into
pieces. I could just make it out from the flickers of fire.

I gasped. Not her wedding dress? I remembered the
pictures of it in *Infamous*, with its train longer than my
duvet and the bodice studded with crystals. She ripped
off one sleeve and tossed it into the flames. Whilst I stood
mesmerised, she disappeared and came back with two
garden chairs and blankets. We sat down. She held a long
bit of cane and every now and again poked the fire. As a
charcoaled tuft of lace fluttered into the air, a bat swooped
past. Not sure what to say, I simply listened for a moment,
to the comforting crackle of burning twigs. It was going to
be hard to move back to the noisy, smelly bustle of Luton.

I set down the basket and lifted out a cupcake. It had
reached a reasonable height. Yet the buttercream icing
looked lumpy. The icing sugar clearly hadn't been sieved.
I took a small bite. Mmm, a surprisingly good textured
sponge with chewy raisins to finish off.

'Not bad.' I glanced sideways at Melissa. 'You could be
onto something here – the breakfast cupcake, perhaps with
wholemeal flour instead and a yogurt topping with various
cereal sprinkles.'

'Feel free to hijack the idea,' she mumbled.

'You won't report me to the police? Say you've got a
thief on the staff?'

'Sorry about that,' she said, in a small voice. 'I didn't mean to call you that. And I don't think KimCakes Ltd is a silly idea. You should definitely enter the cake competition this weekend. I'll ring the organiser tomorrow, pull in some favours. I was just mouthing off... I was upset.'

'You knew I was right, didn't you? About Saffron?'

She nodded.

'You've confronted Jonny?'

'He's moved out.' Her voice cracked. 'He finally admitted that he couldn't resist the thrill of the chase and the adrenalin-rush from all that creeping around. That's the thing with Jonny, that's what sets him apart from other players. As well as great skill he's got golf-bags of nerve and likes taking risks. That's what's needed to win tournaments.' She cleared her throat. 'I suppose this is what they call karma. Now I know how his first wife, Jeanie, felt. She must have loved reading the newspapers today.'

I put my arms around her and didn't let go until she hugged me back.

'You know the strangest thing...' she said, eventually pulling away to wipe her nose with a torn piece of wedding dress, '...Vivian and Denise – they both rang me; asked if there was any way they could help. Vivian said no one really liked Saffron anyway and Denise really came up trumps. She offered to take me to Alcoholics Anonymous; said she'd get all the details from work.' Melissa half-smiled. 'Of course, I explained that two-faced Sandra had exaggerated my situation, in the papers, but Denise was really sweet – said if I ever needed to talk she was the person to choose because she was used to keeping things confidential, what with her responsible job.' Her eyes glistened. 'I thought they'd laugh at me.'

'See – you have got friends after all. What will you do? Stay around here?'

'For the time being, yes. Whilst he was packing, Jonny reminded me of our agreement – that if we split, I'd keep this house as long as he kept the flat in Scotland and the villa in Florida. Although I told him to shove his stinking money, that I had my DVD earnings and could earn my own living, thank you very much.'

'You didn't!'

'What's the point of wearing expensive clothes and injecting my lips with fat from my bum if I'm all by myself?' She put down the cane and turned to me. 'You've been a good friend, Kimmy. I think I'd forgotten what one of those was. Let me apologise properly – how about a Brazilian blow dry, my treat? It'll keep your curly hair straight for three months.'

'Oh Melissa… I hope I did the right thing by telling you.'

She stood up and threw the crystal-studded bodice onto the fire. 'No question about that.'

My phone bleeped. I took it out of my handbag. It was a text. From Luke.

"Did u dump him?" it said.

Of all the arrogant, big-headed… "None your business," I texted back.

'Let me guess,' said Melissa. 'A certain handyman?'

I shrugged.

'Have you sorted things out?'

'I've just had dinner with Adam, actually. Sometimes it's better the devil you know…'

I was still staring at that last text message, a couple of hours later in Lily's four poster oak bed. Melissa and I had drunk several double espressos each. For some reason, now the worst had happened, Melissa didn't feel like getting tipsy. She'd kept quizzing me about Luke. Funny that she hardly knew who he was one week ago. Then we'd finished off with a tiramisu coffee. Wow. I was buzzing on caffeine. Jess was asleep. I had no one to talk to so, with a sigh, I sat up further in bed. Of course, there was one person who might like to chat. I cleared my throat. Luke had promised he wasn't Walter. Could I believe him? There was only one way to test it out.

'Walter?' I said. 'Are you there?'

Nothing.

'Luke's on your side, you know. I could ask him over, we could look through any stuff left in the loft.'

No reply.

'Let's sort out this mess together; get you to those Pearly Gates before you know it. Let me know you understand.'

There were three low thuds. A lump rose in my throat and my eyes felt wet. Walter's ghost *was* real.

'Is Luke right?' I whispered, heart racing a little. 'Are you worried about the charities not getting your money?'

Three low thuds again. Wow. Mike *had* swindled his uncle. I reached for my phone and texted Luke:

"Come round 2mro. U and me – look in loft. Mst sort out Walter's will."

A few minutes later my phone bleeped.

"K. C U then."

Sensing a sudden cold gust, I put my phone back on the bedside table and snuggled down under the crimson duvet and silk sheets. Good old Walter. I felt all warm and fuzzy inside. Our friendship did exist. Bing Crosby's well-known tune began to play softly and despite the espressos, my eyes drooped and eventually closed tight. I drifted into a well weird dream with Luke on a white horse, brandishing a giant prawn cracker as a shield and a huge chopstick as a spear, when… What was that? I sat up. The music had stopped to be replaced by a loud creak. I jumped out of bed and ran onto the landing. Was someone creeping out of the front door? That could only mean… What a fool I was. Luke must have got hold of another set of keys and been up to his old tricks again.

'I should have known!' I shouted. 'Still think it's funny, do you, pretending to be a ghost, with your Christmas music and thuds? To think, I believed your excuses in the Silky Prawn, you complete bastard!'

The chandelier flicked on and I gasped in horror. I'd just sworn at a flabbergasted Mike Murphy.

CHAPTER 27

'Hands off my bottom!'

I glared down at Luke who'd just pushed me up into the loft.

'Needs must. Don't read anything into it,' he said and clambered up the ladder, behind me.

Since I'd let slip what I'd shouted at Mike last night, Luke was back to his frosty old self. He said I still believed the worst in him, despite the effort he'd made to explain his actions by following me to the Silky Prawn. So, to make up for it – not that I owed him anything – I finally told him about my contact with Walter's ghost.

Wow. What a surprise. He didn't laugh, and stared into the distance for a while. We both agreed immediate action was necessary as Mistletoe Mansion had actually sold. That's why Mike Murphy was back – the Stedman couple had put in an offer. I'd had to spend a good ten minutes explaining to Walter's nephew that his unexpected arrival had caught me yelling in the middle of a nightmare about being burgled. He'd said not to worry – all things considered, it wasn't surprising after the highjinks I'd had to put up with since moving in.

A switch clicked and I balanced carefully on the loft's wooden beams. The roof space lit up to reveal a maze of dustbin bags and cardboard boxes. There was little room to move.

'This'll take ages!' I said.

Luke stood up crazily close to me and every molecule of my body jumped to attention as if just having been given an electrical shock. 'I installed this light up here a couple of years ago and helped Walter sort through some of the stuff. A lot of it's labelled – old records, Lily's cross-stitching pieces, photo albums, crock–'

'Photo albums? Where?' I gushed, trying not to think of his athletic limbs. Anyway, I loved looking at people's holiday and wedding snaps – probably because it was something I'd never seen as a child. Mum wasn't the most organised person. Only occasionally did she buy a disposable camera for birthdays and then always said we didn't have the money to develop the film. Only a handful of photos from Christmases and holidays existed, not that we ever went abroad. If we were lucky, Mum took us to stay with a mate of hers in Bournemouth, which was fun – me and Tom paddling, Mum laughing like she never did back in Luton.

Luke hauled a black dustbin bag over from the left hand side and set it at my feet. I sat on a bulging cardboard box.

'It used to be a lot more orderly up here,' he said. 'But the first time I came up, after Walter died, there were bags everywhere. I reckon Murphy's been looking for something… Talking of which, how long do you think we've got before he's back?'

'A while. Melissa's persuaded him to take her out to lunch. After that it's back to hers for coffee. She'll try and find out when his appointment is with Walter's solicitor. He's down here to tie up all the loose ends from the sale. Then we thought we could follow him…'

'In your little Fiesta? It's hardly Miami Vice.'

'Don't diss the car!' I glared. 'Have you got a better idea?'

He shrugged. 'For Walter's sake, I'd offer to drive but my gardening van is too conspicuous. You should get a taxi.'

'That might not be such a bad plan,' I said. 'The driver will know Harpenden better than me. Mr Murphy won't ever suspect. If you're right about him, he'll think he fooled everyone months ago.'

'Get the taxi to park somewhere away from here, like by the Royal Oak pub, down the road. There are more paparazzi in Badgers Chase than ever at the moment – no doubt still fussing about the affair.'

'Haven't you heard? Now Jonny's moved out. For once, though, Melissa seems glad to see the cameras and was all glammed up when she called on Mr Murphy. They strolled down the drive, arm-in-arm. I guess she's kind of determined to show Jonny what he's lost.'

'Moved out? Really? The man's a prat. I read about this Saffron woman – can't believe he's taken it one stage further and chosen her over his wife.'

I nodded. 'So be nice tonight. She said to go over if we find anything out. We can study the whole situation properly then, without Walter's nephew breathing down our necks.' I picked up a dusty album.

'So, he's accepted those people's offer on the house?' Luke said.

'Yep. Luckily he's agreed me and Jess can stay put for Christmas. The Stedmans won't move in until the New Year.'

'You two won't be going home for the twenty-fifth?' Luke eyed me curiously.

I bit my lip. Mum had done okay lately – but Christmas always saw her fall off the sober wagon. Tom and I had long ago given up hoping for quality family time during the festive season. 'Tom has a good mate whose parents are brill and have always asked him around for a turkey dinner and sleepover. Mum's latest boyfriend, Rick, will no doubt help her celebrate the festive season. It's never been a family day for her – not unless you include Miss Gin and Mr Tonic as blood relatives.'

Luke's brow softened. 'And what about Jess? Surely you won't be here all alone?'

What about Jess, indeed. I shrugged. 'Dunno. I've got pals who would have me around, no problem, but what with splitting with Adam… I kind of fancy a lazy, indulgent day on my own. Groucho will keep me company.'

I turned my attention back to the album's stiff black paper pages. Sepia and black and white photos were neatly stuck on, throughout, although a couple were crooked and one had fallen out. It was of a young couple sitting on a sand dune, their arms around each other. The woman had curly set hair and wore a blouse and knee-length skirt. The man had an Elvis kiss curl and looked smart with a cravat. I turned the photo over – "Walter and Lily, Brighton, 1950". I flicked further through the album, gazing at pictures in back gardens, them sitting on deckchairs with older relatives. The last was of them both outside a barracks style building, Walter in some uniform, Lily wrapped up in a stylish coat with a beret and gloves.

'Walter was in the army,' I muttered.

'Yeah. It was one of his big regrets that he was colour blind and couldn't get into the RAF.'

I picked up another album which was bright red and much more modern. Stuck on the front was a small piece of paper saying "Lily's Creations." I turned the first page, and behind plastic sheets was photo after photo of stitched cushions and embroidered rugs. A bit further on were snaps of cake after cake… Wow. Just look at that intricate icing. There were gateaux decorated with fruit and piped whipped cream, and themed birthday cakes – a golfing one, of course, another was the shape of a handbag and next to it a teddy bear... Lilian could have made some awesome Pinterest boards.

'This looks promising,' said Luke and carried over a cardboard box. He lifted the lid for me. Stashed inside were files, loose paperwork and a large zipped-up leather pouch. I pulled it out, slid open the zip and peeked inside, before tipping the contents on top of another box. Two passports and various certificates tumbled out, as well as several loose papers, their driving licences and bundles of old letters.

'Look at these,' I said. 'Must be love notes.'

'Thing of the past, they are,' he said. 'Now everyone emails or texts.'

He was right. Come to think of it, all I had left of Adam's and my relationship, on paper, were the Valentine's Day cards I'd kept.

'What about these?' I said and unfolded two important-looking sheets of paper.

Luke crouched down next to me and took one of them. 'At last! The will. It's dated 1960.' He scanned the writing. 'Nothing out of the ordinary... they leave each other everything and if they both die, Mr and Mrs Colin Murphy – Walter's sister and her husband, Mike Murphy's parents – receive the lot.'

I shook the other sheet. 'This one is an updated version, dated 1990. It doesn't name the Murphys, instead on both of Lily and Walter's deaths, two charities are to inherit the bulk of the estate.'

'I knew it!' Luke punched the air. 'Don't tell me! The charities are some children's home and Wildlife Watch? They were always talking about them.'

'The solicitors for both wills are called Dean and Brothers, in Harpenden,' I said and took the older will from him. 'Wonder why the Murphys weren't mentioned in the latest. Perhaps there was some fall-out.'

Luke examined the small print again. 'They are, right at the end – Walter and Lily wanted them to have all the antique furniture, the various ornament collections and… There's mention of an Eleanor Goodman. She was Lily's best friend. They left her a diamond necklace and earrings. Also, a Shirley Cooke is due to receive Lily's Cartier watch.'

I glanced over his shoulder. 'Hmm, and Walter wanted his paintings to be auctioned off and the money given to Harpenden Twilight Years care home. I looked up. 'Get this bit – they put aside twenty thousand pounds for their only nephew, Mike.'

'So how did the greedy bastard get the will changed so he got more?'

'Good question.' At that moment my mobile rang. 'What? Slow down. Okay. Thanks for the warning.' Quickly I stuffed everything back into the leather pouch. 'Hurry up! That was Melissa – Mr Murphy's not feeling well and they're on their way back.'

Luke stuck the zipbag in the cardboard box and then made his way down the ladder. 'Pass it to me,' he said, once on the landing.

I dragged the box towards the hatch and he stretched up as I let it slide down. I glanced around the loft. Everything looked more or less as we'd found it. This detective work was so cool! Starsky and Hutch… Cagney and Lacey… Move over! There's a new pair of fab cop buddies in the building, please meet Butler and Jones!

I switched off the light.

'What's wrong with Murphy?' said Luke as I climbed down and he dragged the box along the landing. His arm muscles flexed and his shirt rose as he bent over to reveal a smooth tanned back and the waistband of tight trunks…

'Sounds like bad indigestion,' I said and averted my eyes. 'But then he did insist on eating two of my latest cupcakes for breakfast.'

'Which were?'

'A disaster.' I sighed. 'I'm experimenting – trying to come up with something innovative for the cake competition at the Christmas fair on Saturday.'

'Innovative is a big word,' he said with a half-smile. Finally he was thawing.

I raised my fist and met his gaze. 'So is "knuckle-sandwich".'

'What flavour are they?'

'Ginger and black treacle topped with salted caramel butter icing. Very rich and I'm not sure they work. I did think about creating a Christmas recipe, but I bet everyone will do something festive. I want to stand out.'

'I'm always up for a challenge. Sounds like they'd go perfectly with a strong coffee. Meet you outside in the summerhouse in a few minutes?'

'Summerhouse?' I shook my head, 'It'll be freezing.'

He shrugged. 'We can wrap up. I'm an outdoorsy kind of guy.'

Unlike Adam, who was never happier than when holed up in the flat.

'Okay – but why can't you come now? What are you up to?'

'Don't worry – I'm not going to set up any more tricks.'

'I didn't mean–'

'If you must know, I'm going to close the hatch and hide this box in the front bedroom. We need to work out how I'm going to smuggle it to Melissa's tonight, without Murphy noticing.'

My phone bleeped – a text this time. They'd just left the village and were about ten minutes away.

'I won't be long,' said Luke and breathed heavily as he heaved the box along another metre.

I raced down to put the kettle on and had just set up the tray when the front door clicked open. Mr Murphy was back. Luke appeared in the kitchen, opened the patio doors and took the tray from me. Quickly I followed him and his whistling across the lawn, to the summerhouse, me having grabbed my gold parka. Groucho followed and once we'd sat down, sprawled at our feet.

'That's very gentlemanly of you,' I said, as Luke passed me the plate of cakes. I took one and then we both pulled the wicker chairs forward and out of the shade.

Eyes twinkling, he lifted up one of the cakes. 'Glad you made it to the summerhouse in one piece and didn't get attacked by that hose again.'

Ignoring him, I bit into the ginger cake. The overall flavour was too strong and not sweet enough. The heavy consistency of the sponge meant I'd used too much treacle.

'Could you make me a batch of these,' said Luke. 'I could do with some filler for my stone wall.'

'That's better – you insulting me.'

A warmth surged through my chest as we grinned at each other.

'Sorry I thought you were up to your old tricks again last night. But you can't blame me. This has been the most random week of my life.'

'Fair enough. Guess it's not every week you befriend a ghost and develop a mammoth-sized crush.' He put down his coffee and flexed an arm.

'Idiot.'

'So, you've got plenty of time to practise for the competition, seeing as you won't be showing any more prospective buyers around.'

'True – although I've got a week of tidying ahead of me. Mr Murphy is getting in house clearers and has already arranged for the antique furniture and ornaments to be driven up to his parents, before Christmas.' I gave a wry smile. 'The place might look quite empty by the twenty-fifth.'

'What about the rest of the stuff?' said Luke, with a frown. 'All the personal bits – Lily's sewing, the photos, and Walter had collected some amazing golf memorabilia over the years.'

'He's getting rid, I suppose.'

Luke's eyes flashed. 'Quite the caring nephew, isn't he?'

'He goes back to Manchester on Wednesday – something about a sales convention.'

Luke shook his head.

'Walter and Lily will be together again soon, that's the main thing,' I said softly, 'once we put the last pieces of this puzzle together and find out exactly how Mr Murphy's swindled Walter.'

'Did you, um…' Luke cleared his throat. '…have a long conversation with Walter's spirit… the ghost, last night then?'

I waited for his mouth to twitch but unlike Adam, whether Luke believed my story about the ghost or not, he didn't make me feel ridiculous.

'Not really,' I smiled. 'He's a man of few thuds.'

Luke nodded. 'So… the Harpenden Christmas Market…'

'According to Melissa, whoever wins that cake competition gets lots of promotion in the local paper. Last year's winner now sells her cakes to several local cafés.'

'What does Adam think to all this? Will you move back in with him?'

I hadn't told anyone this yet, but – deep breath – regardless of whether Adam and I got back together... 'No. After this week, I couldn't live in his flat again.'

'Wow. Used to the high life now, are we?' Luke teased.

I pulled a face. 'There's a bedsit above a chip shop near where I once lived. I rang up to enquire. The landlord doesn't care if I'm not in regular work, as long as the rent gets paid, and said I can move in after Christmas.'

'Big decision.'

I swallowed. Yes. It was a bold move.

'So... Have you told Adam?'

I shook my head. And it should have felt wrong that Luke knew first, but for some reason it didn't. It was time to own my life again – be in charge of my own destiny. No one would be able to throw me out again, unless I failed to pay the rent... Adam could always come around for a meal, after work, if we were still going out. I bit my lip. The trouble was, why couldn't I imagine that happening? Instead, when I pictured my new home, it was cluttered with Tupperware boxes full of cakes, with eggshells and flour trails littering the kitchen units; me singing to some girly music or watching TV that Adam would have called "crap".

'And Jess?'

'She's managed to wangle an invite to crash on the sofa of a girl she gets on well with, at work, once Mr Murphy asks us to leave. I made a few enquiries, to see if we could find somewhere together, but it looks like anything bigger will be too expensive. Anyway, my new landlord seems pretty laidback. I doubt he'll visit often so I thought Jess could discreetly stay at my new place if she ever needs to, until she finds somewhere permanent. I... I'd like to look out for her, you see…' I glanced sideways at him. 'She's, um, pregnant.'

Luke let out a low whistle. 'Not the best time to be looking for a new gaff.'

'A few months' time and she'll need to plan a nursery. To be honest, I think she's still in denial; not used to the idea of being a mum yet.' My eyes tingled.

'You're worried about her?'

I nodded. 'She talks about the pregnancy and birth but not much after that.'

'I'm good at building furniture. You tell Jess I can knock up a cot any time she likes.'

'Thanks, Luke. That'd be great.' I blushed. 'Melissa's been helpful as well.'

'Yeah. Now I've got to know her, for a celebrity, she's pretty cool. So…' He brushed crumbs off his shirt. 'Let's brainstorm and come up with a winning recipe for this competition.'

'Really?'

'Shh! I'm thinking. Don't interrupt the master at work!' His eyes closed for a few minutes. I glanced towards the house and saw Mr Murphy, back, in the kitchen drinking a glass of water. Then he disappeared, no doubt for a lie-down.

'First of all,' Luke said. 'It's the judges you've got to please – who are they?'

'One of the local vicars, um, a teashop owner from the village and a lady from the Woman's Institute.'

'Okay. Well, that says to me that you need to keep things fairly traditional. Nothing too outlandish – like marzipan whips and handcuffs. Can you think of a local theme? What do we know about Harpenden?'

'That it's expensive, so I could, say, decorate my cakes with diamonds and pearls. The only other thing I know about this place is that it's where Eric Morecambe used to live…'

My voice trailed off, as a sudden thought entered my head. Oh my God, this was the wackiest idea in the world. Morecambe & Wise – they were huge once, weren't they? Every Brit's favourite comedy duo? And they were known for a certain song… 'What about "Bring Me Sunshine" cupcakes?' I said, cautiously.

'Huh? After that tune Eric and Ernie always sang?'

'The judges sound old enough to have loved them. The flavour could be lemon… perhaps lemon cheese or meringue, with bright yellow buttercream icing piped on top in swirls… Such a summery colour will really stand out.'

'I like it,' he said. 'And on the top, just for a bit of fun, you could have a pair of black Eric Morecambe glasses made out of liquorice or whatever you used for those whips and handcuffs.'

'You're a star!' My smile dropped for a moment. 'Do you think they'll find it funny? Or tasteless? A joke too far? You said they'd like something traditional.'

'Everyone loves nostalgia. They'll love it, Kimmy. Trust me. Those cakes will look really cheerful.'

We looked at each other. 'Will… you be at the market?'

'I'll try. A local customer has just bought two semis in Brighton. He's a property developer; wants me to do them up. It's good money. I've no ties here, so I'll be busy packing on Saturday. Straight after Boxing Day I'll be leaving for a month.'

'Oh. I mean… Good for you.' My stomach twisted. It was still pinching half an hour later when I went to my room to fetch my purse for a speedy ingredients shopping spree, which was mad? How could I think I was going to miss someone I hardly knew yet?

Humming myself out of such thoughts, I planned to make up a batch of those sunshine cakes and take them over to Melissa's tonight. Luke had just left to take the box over to hers. If Mr Murphy noticed, he would say it was full of my belongings as Melissa had said I could store some stuff in her house. With a heavy heart, I pushed open my bedroom door and looked around. Now where had I left my purse?

A cold breeze tickled my neck and lifted my hair, as I sat down on the plush bedcovers. A smile crept onto my face. Something rustled and I felt underneath my thighs – I'd sat down on a faded piece of paper and lifted it to my face. It smelt musty and looked as if it had been torn from a book. I studied the neat, old-fashioned writing. Listed were the ingredients for… *Sunny Lemon Cakes*. The hairs stood up on the back of my neck. This must have belonged to Lily. Walter had left out the perfect recipe to win the competition!

CHAPTER 28

'Apparently he's missing me,' said Jess, with a smile, whilst I sat down at the breakfast table with a glass of juice. Outside strands of dark cloud hung low – sadly not thick or white enough for the promise of snow.

'Start from the beginning,' I said. Jess was off work today and I hadn't seen her the night before, having got back late from Melissa's. She seemed chirpier than she had been for days. More like the old Jess.

For a second, she stopped chewing her gum. 'Ryan's girlfriend – the one I walked in on, you know, all boobs and Brazilian – she came into work yesterday. He actually told her that his place wasn't the same without me.'

'Yeah,' I scoffed, 'it's knee-high in dust, you mean.'

Jess smiled. 'We both know my brother's an emotional desert. But even if he just misses my cleaning skills, that's quite an admission. This woman – Julie – has actually been seeing Ryan for a while. When I burst in, that was the first time she'd slept over and guess what?'

I raised my eyebrows.

'He even makes her breakfast.'

Wow. This was the commitment-phobe who boasted that he'd never once met a girlfriend's parents. Usually, he'd get rid of the previous night's conquest in the morning by slathering his face with Jess's body oil and feigning a feverish illness. And as for breakfast, he only ever made himself a pint of Alka-Seltzer dissolved in cola, let alone cater for someone else.

'Why didn't he visit you himself then?'

Jess's eyes crinkled. 'Julie *gets* Ryan. She knows he'd never publicly admit his feelings. She's dead sick of his new roommate, or rather beer-buddy...'

'So she realised it'll be down to her to get you back.' I swallowed a mouthful of cereal. Queasy, that's how I felt, and it was all down to last night and Melissa's cocktails. She and Terry had spent half the evening working on some concoction they promised would go with my trial batch of "Bring Me Sunshine" cupcakes. Eventually, I was served with a tall glass of something yellow and icky, containing obscene amounts of advocaat. 'So, what's the plan? You're prepared to live with him again, after everything he said?'

She shrugged. 'That's brothers and sisters for you. Remember the time you forgave Tom for refilling your tub of moisturiser with hair removal cream?'

I shuddered. A face full of fuzzy regrowth and peeling skin was not a good look.

'And there's not just me to think about now; he's not just my brother anymore. He's going to be an uncle.' She chewed manically for a moment. 'Julie's taking him shopping, in Luton, at the weekend. We've agreed that Ryan and I will "accidentally" meet up.'

I squeezed her arm. 'I'm glad you're making plans for the two of you. That is, you and–'

'Stieg Six?' She gave a wry grin.

'You seem more... not resigned to it all but–'

'Melissa's been great,' she said, voice quieter. 'What with her pregnancy magazines and vitamin tablets, I guess she's helped me face reality. And your support... It's meant everything to know I won't be on my own. If I get to move back in with Ryan at least I can start making plans. The baby could have the small box room.'

'So, how do you feel about… well, this cute bump becoming a screaming, pooing bundle of fun?'

'You make it sound so appealing…' Jess ran a finger around the top of her juice glass. 'I…' Her voice broke. 'All I want is to be a decent mum. What if I screw up and can't cope?'

'Jess, you are one of the most capable people I know! Who put that collapsed pensioner, in the street, into the recovery position, last month?'

Her cheeks tinged pink.

'And remember when a colleague of yours had a raging stomach ache and you insisted they go to the hospital? Their appendix was about to burst. You practically saved their life.' I folded my arms. 'You, my girl, are going to be one awesome mother.'

Jess's cheeks flushed even redder. 'You reckon?'

'Yep – in fact, here's more proof. Remember that computer game at school, where you had to look after a virtual animal – you know, feed it, play with it, take it for walks…? Mine always died within two days. You held the school record at twenty-one weeks.'

'Wonder if I'll manage a child for eighteen years,' she muttered, though I could see a small sparkle in her eyes.

'Do you feel any of that maternal instinct yet, that people talk about?' I shot her a curious glance.

A smile crossed her face, its warmth making her eyes even twinklier. 'I can't wait to meet the baby, Kimmy,' she whispered. 'And hold it in my arms…'

We smiled at each other. This was good. Time – and Melissa – were helping Jess come to terms with becoming a mum.

'Luke said he'd build you a cot if you like. Um, hope you don't mind me telling him.'

'Guess it's not like I'm going to be able to hide it much longer.'

'Have you been tempted to ring, you know, the, um dad – Phil?'

'No!' Jess sat more upright. 'Okay, yes. But I'm over that. You know what stopped me? I won't have him treating this kid the way he treats his others. When we split up, he let slip that our affair wasn't his first. It won't be his last. I'm not prepared to see this baby right at the bottom of a list topped by previous children, his wife and other mistresses.'

'See – you've already got the good mum factor… But what about money?'

'As long as I don't lose my job, I'll muddle on by. Dana's been acting dead strange lately. I just hope she's not trying to find a way to sack me.' Jess shoulders sagged and she sipped her tea. 'So? Yesterday? Did you find the will?'

'I'm always here if you need to talk, you know,' I mumbled. 'Or if you want to throw food colouring and flour at anyone, I'm your gal.'

'Thanks, Kimmy. You're the best.' Her mouth upturned. 'Melissa has already insisted on throwing me a baby shower.'

'Great American tradition, that,' I said and smiled.

'Hmm, a giddy mix of presents, cake and talk about stretch marks and sore nipples... Anyway. Back to the business in hand – what did you find in the loft?'

'Two wills and the latest, from 1990, said the bulk of the estate was to be split between two charities. Me and Luke went through the rest of the paperwork round at Melissa's last night and couldn't find any new one that made Mr Murphy the main beneficiary.' I grinned. 'Luke was so funny, he…' Jess gazed hard at me, whilst I chatted.

'Kimmy!' she finally said. 'Melissa was right, you *do* like him!'

'No! I mean... Okay... Maybe... I didn't think so, but...' My voice steadied. 'He's going away for a month, anyway, so what's the point? Then there's Adam. My good, solid Adam...'

Jess's shoulders bobbed up and down. 'Sometimes, you can have too much of a good thing.'

'And Adam *is* good, isn't he, Jess? It's just, he doesn't get me and my business dreams *at all*.' I shook my head. 'I'm so confused. Anyway. As I said, we didn't find a later will, so it looks like it's plan B – following Mr Murphy to his appointment with the solicitor. Melissa found out that it's at eleven o'clock this morning...' I looked at my watch. 'In fact, I'd better go and call for her now. Could you stay here? It might look odd if we both bunk out of tidying this place. Me and Melissa are catching a taxi near the Royal Oak pub.'

'Did I hear my name?' boomed a voice. Mike Murphy strolled in, a newspaper under his arm. He wore smart jeans which hung below his rounded belly and a black turtle neck jumper. Around his wrist was a prominent gold chain bracelet. 'The house clearers are due this afternoon. If the quote's good enough, they'll take a lot of the stuff then and there. Tomorrow some man's coming to look at Walter's gardening equipment. I'm going to be in and out, so I'm assuming one of you delightful girls will be around?'

'I've, um, got errands to run too,' I said, 'but Jess will be here today and I'll make sure I'm in tomorrow.'

'Guess you've got to get another job lined up... If you ever need a reference...? After all, you've both done a cracking job here, what with all the shenanigans. You girls have got steel...' He glanced at his watch and disappeared into the hallway. A few seconds later, the Games Room door creaked shut.

'See you later,' I muttered to Jess and raced upstairs to fetch my fake leopard-skin handbag – it matched my leopard print headband. I rushed back down and out of the front door. At the bottom of the drive I ran into Terry and Frazzle. In a pink Pringle jumper, under a blush anorak and white plus fours, he was talking to a young woman wearing huge black sunglasses. Short black hair poked out from underneath a cap. She wore faded jeans cut off just below the knee, fingerless gloves and a hooded sweatshirt saying "I love London". A load of photographers hung outside the Winsfords' house.

'Kimmy! How are you feeling?' Terry said and kissed me on either cheek.

'Not the best. What did you and Melissa put in those cocktails last night?' I asked, glad I'd thrown my second drink out of the window. If only I'd brought a bottle of water with me – although I could always borrow the Evian face mist Melissa kept in her handbag and spray it onto my tongue instead of my cheeks.

'Advocaat of course, vodka, lime cordial and a squirt of champers, probably. I can't remember the rest... Have to admit, I'm feeling a bit delicate too.' He chuckled. 'And talking of Melisssa, I bumped into her earlier – she'll meet you by the Royal Oak.'

I nodded and glanced at the woman in the cap. Who was she? A friend of his? A niece? We headed for Terry's house.

'Where are my manners!' he said. 'Kimmy, this is Becca. I've got so many all-day tournaments on over the next few weeks, I've decided to hire someone to walk Frazzle. She and I are just taking a stroll, so that they can get to know each other. In fact we may as well go a bit further, and accompany you to the pub.'

'Hello,' I smiled at her. 'Do you walk many micro-pigs?'

'Dogs are my usual bag,' she said, with a strong Luton twang as we carried on towards the end of the cul-de-sac. 'But how different can a pig be? Food still goes in one end and comes out the other, right? And mud baths sound wicked.' In fact, she didn't stop talking as we headed down the long, winding road to the Royal Oak. I heard all about her last client who insisted she read a story to their dogs before they lay down for a nap. Her make-up looked a bit full on for a dog walker. She must have earned lots as she was wearing a pair of designer trainers. Wishing I'd put on gloves, as well, I bent down to tickle Frazzle between the ears, before saying goodbye.

'Can't see Melissa,' I said and stared at the bearded taxi driver, waiting in his car by the pub. There was no one sitting in the back.

Terry sniggered. So did Becca.

'What's so funny?' I said.

'It's me, you big doofus,' said the girl, leaning forward to whisper in my ear.

I stood back as she pulled down her sunglasses and wiggled them Eric Morecambe style. I pushed her shoulder and grinned. 'Cool hair! You're quite the actress, Melissa!'

'Well, I did take a drama course for a few weeks last year – thought it might help my confidence, presenting my exercise DVD.' She pushed her glasses back on. 'I had to avoid the paparazzi outside the house, somehow. Hopefully the bloodsuckers will get bored and go bother Jonny and Saffron.'

We got in the back of the taxi, as Terry waved goodbye and went off with Frazzle. It was a saloon car, nothing conspicuous. Melissa pulled a face as she sat inside, having brushed down the seat before she parked her perfect bottom on it.

'Where to?' muttered the driver, as rain started to spit against the windows. Low-volume rock music emanated from his radio and a half-eaten sandwich sat on the front seat, on top of a newspaper. He looked in his rear view mirror. 'The meter's running.'

'We're not quite sure,' I said, 'you see…'

'Look, it's been a long night, love. Do you want to go somewhere or not?'

Melissa took off her cap and sunglasses and smiled broadly towards the rear view mirror. The man almost choked.

'You're… Jonny Winsford's wife… I mean…' He flushed purple. 'Bad week for you. What with the papers…'

'This trip could be a nice earner for you if you don't ask too many questions,' she said.

He brushed crumbs from his greying beard and winked in the mirror. 'Say no more.'

At that moment Mr Murphy's black car loomed into view. Melissa pointed at it with a perfectly manicured finger – a detail that would have eventually given away her dog-handling disguise.

'Follow that car!' she said.

Damn! I'd always wanted to say that!

Whilst we pulled away, Melissa and me ducked down. After a few seconds we sat back up. The black car was just about visible in the distance.

'Don't lose him,' said Melissa.

'No problems, Mrs Winsford. Is it your husband?'

'Remember what I said – less you know, the better,' she said.

'So, he's heading for St Albans,' I muttered. 'We could go to the precinct afterwards. Have a coffee. Discuss our findings.'

But Melissa wasn't listening; she was too busy looking behind us to see if the paparazzi were following. This was the first trip she'd taken out since the news of Jonny and Saffron broke. But she needn't have worried and some twenty minutes later we found ourselves in the centre of St Albans, well away from the lenses and snide comments. The taxi driver tailed Mr Murphy down a side road and pulled up about fifty metres behind him as the black car stopped outside a row of businesses and shops.

'Where that car's stopped, is a solicitor's,' said the driver, looking at us from his rear view mirror. 'I used to go to the chiropodist on the top floor. Great little Indian take-away next door to it, if you're in the mood for something hot.'

Mr Murphy went inside.

'We'll just sit here until that man comes out again,' said Melissa, to the driver.

'But the meter's running,' I whispered.

'My treat,' she whispered back.

For half an hour we sat there– me playing games on my phone, Melissa answering various texts as rain now pelted down. Suddenly, the driver turned around.

'That bloke's just come out of the building, ladies,'

He was by his car and a woman with short brown curly hair, in a black trouser suit, was talking to him under a large navy brolly. Awkwardly, he kissed her on the cheek. Melissa took out her purse, tapped the driver's shoulders and thrust several twenty pound notes into his hand.

'That's, um, very generous,' he said, revealing a bit of tomato stuck in between two of his teeth.

'Remember,' she said. 'Confidentiality is paramount. Keep this to yourself and I'll use you again.'

'Thanks for paying,' I said as he drove off and we hid for a moment, behind a post box. Melissa pulled down her cap, whilst I put up my parka hood.

'It's all for a good cause,' she said. 'Plus it takes my mind off Jonny and his bit of fluff. Do you know, Infamous rang me this morning? Apparently Saffron's doing a double spread with them about her and Jonny's "deep love". They wondered if I wanted a page to myself to retaliate; said they could set me up with some hunky model and take some snaps that would drive Jonny wild.'

'What did you say?' I remembered in the past tit-for-tat articles between celebrity couples who'd split. Good reading they were, trying to guess who was the most upset and which couple were actually fake. Except now it concerned the real lives of people I actually knew – and it seemed nothing but... sad.

'David Khan is represented by my agency and–'

'Isn't he that hot new soap actor who won all those newcomer awards last month?'

She nodded. 'Just think how mad Jonny would be if we did an interview together – me saying what a support he'd been. How we'd been friends for a long time and how my break-up with Jonny had sparked something between us. We might "accidentally" get papped going out to dinner together.' She smiled. 'Where's the harm? It'll do wonders for David's career.'

'Wouldn't it be better to just lay low for a while?'

'No. Because my side of the story needs to be heard.' She glanced at me. 'Guess you think I'm a hypocrite? One minute moaning about a lack of privacy, the next selling my marriage breakdown? But you said yourself, people like celebrities to mess up. It makes them feel human, right?'

My cheeks burned. 'I reckoned they couldn't complain as, at the end of the day, whatever happened, they had a fancy home to go back to or could swan off to Barbados. Those magazines used to make me feel that whatever the problem, I'd rather face it with loads of money in my pocket than sitting eating a supermarket value pizza in a one-bedroom flat. Break-ups, drug problems, affairs... They almost look glamorous, set out on a page, in between adverts for liposuction and the latest designer handbag. Yet since I've got to know you...' I shrugged. 'Dunno – reckon it's all just as painful, however much money you've got.'

Melissa nodded. 'Money doesn't stop you being miserable. It doesn't stop you wanting revenge or making a fool of yourself. All it does is play out your desperation in front of a massive audience.' Her voice wobbled. 'You know what I really miss? When we first got together, Jonny used to tell me he loved me most of all, because I "kept him right" – in other words, kept his feet on the ground. He was so frightened of losing me he did all that he could – like visit my parents, and he never stayed out for the whole night. Jonny would cook at weekends and encouraged me to get an agent and make the most of my own talents. But lately, he's slipped into the old habits and is more like the Jonny his first wife described, when she sold her story, after their divorce.' She sniffed loudly. 'I reckon these photos with David Khan will make him realise how he took me for granted.'

'You're better off without him.'

A tear rolled from behind her glasses – or was it a raindrop? 'It'll take some getting used to. What's my life if I'm not Melissa Winsford? I'm a nobody. Seeing myself in the papers, it reminds me that I've made something of my life.'

'You don't need a man to be someone, Melissa.'

'But it was more than that – being married to The Eagle. It was my job, like working for some exclusive brand.'

'But you've got loads going for you – you could be a personal trainer or… or beautician.'

'You're sweet.' She gave me a smile straight from her eyes. 'Come on. Deep breaths. Let's get on with this mission – and get out of this rain.'

I gave her a quick hug and glanced over to the road. Mr Murphy's car had left. 'Okay. So… We need to find some new will; see if Mr Murphy has legitimately inherited everything. But we mustn't be too obvious. He seemed well friendly with that solicitor – she might be in on it.'

'So, what's the plan?'

We looked at each other and approached the solicitor's front door. Hopefully inspiration would strike at the right time. A gold plaque to the right of the glass white-framed door was engraved with the words, "Chapman Solicitors, Legal Service Professionals." We entered and turned left into a reception area. I pushed back my hood. A young woman was on the phone, in a smart navy blouse, hair pinned up in a bun. Past the receptionist's desk was a dark corridor which presumably led to the solicitors' offices.

'Can I help you?' said the girl, as she put down the receiver. She eyed Melissa – or rather Becca – closely. It wasn't the best wig. Or hat. In fact, she looked highly suspicious. Which could mean only one thing – it was time to blag.

'Good morning,' I said, crisply, and held out my hand. 'My name's Kimmy. This is Becca. We'd like to see a solicitor. It's, um, private business.'

She stared at both of us a minute longer and then nonchalantly consulted her computer. 'I'm sorry. We are very busy for the next few weeks.'

'There must be something!' I said. 'Please. It's urgent. You come highly recommended.'

The girl sighed. 'How about next Tuesday?'

'We were hoping to see someone today,' I said and linked my arm through Melissa's. 'We, um, forgot all about a pre-nup, you see. I've come into an inheritance and Becca here, bless her, insists that I protect my fortune.' I kissed my disguised neighbour. 'The wedding's tomorrow,' I told the receptionist. 'Isn't it exciting? We're getting married!'

CHAPTER 29

I almost wet myself at the look on Melissa's face.

'Oh. Erm…' the receptionist smiled awkwardly. 'You could always try another solicitor's, there's one–'

'Please,' said Melissa, who'd recovered enough to put on a strong Geordie accent. 'I cannee marry me girl without a pre-nup. Don't make us cancel the wedding, lassie. Money's no object… You wouldn't get in the way of a young couple's love, now, would ya?'

Wow. Cheryl Cole eat your heart out.

The girl consulted her computer again and sighed. 'Ms Chapman is very busy but at a pinch, I mean I'd have to check with him, Mr Hurst could fit you in–'

'Oh no!' Melissa said and sucked in her breath. 'It would have to be a lass, like. No offence, but we want someone on our wavelength.'

At that moment the woman in the trouser suit, whom we'd seen with Mr Murphy, appeared out of the corridor. A file in her hand, she wore gold-rimmed glasses which magnified dark circles under her eyes. Two deep vertical lines between her eyebrows made her look as grumpy as Adam when the rent was due and we couldn't afford to go to the pub. By the lines around her mouth I could tell that, like Mum, she smoked more than Groucho Marx.

'Is everything all right, here?' she asked. 'I'm Beth Chapman.'

'Please, say you can fit us in today,' I said. 'We're in desperate need of a pre-nup and...'

She smiled tightly. 'Today's out of the question, I'm afraid. I might have an opening in the next week or so.'

'Don't be daft, lass. A solicitor can always fit in extra business! If I could just have a wee word in private,' said Melissa, and before I knew it she'd grabbed the astonished Ms Chapman by the elbow and steered her into the dark corridor. Minutes later, a beaming Ms Chapman emerged.

'Hold all my calls until I tell you otherwise,' she said to the receptionist. She nodded towards me. 'Follow me, please.'

Blimey! That was a bit of a turn around. We entered the second door on the left and I found myself in a large office where Melissa stood, minus her glasses and wig. There was a black leather sofa, two swivel chairs facing an oak desk and several shelves of reference books and weird framed sketches, no doubt some sort of modern art. There were no plants or photos, nothing much personal, except a cross-stitched cushion of an owl which looked totally out of place on one of the office chairs. In the corner, by the window, were two enormous grey filing cabinets.

Ms Chapman pointed us both to the swivel chairs. 'Coffee?' she asked.

We shook our heads and sat down.

'I was just explaining to Beth,' said Melissa to me, 'that it was necessary to come in disguise because of the paparazzi.'

'Absolutely understandable,' said Ms Chapman and sat behind her desk. 'So, Mrs Winsford – you're looking for someone to represent you in the divorce?'

Ms Chapman's eyes glinted like the diamonds she clearly hoped she'd be able to buy with the money she'd make from this potential wealthy client.

'Please. Call me Melissa,' she said and swivelled in her chair. 'No doubt you've seen the tabloids, Beth. You know what a pickle I'm in. But before I can even consider using you, there is one thing: Kimmy is my Life Guide and must soak up the aura from your work space immediately.'

And I thought I was a blagger extraordinaire!

'A Life Guide?' Ms Chapman frowned.

'All the celebrities have them, darling.' Melissa beamed. 'If you and I could just leave Kimmy to it for ten minutes, she'll do a mental sweep of your room; decide whether you are right for me.'

'I don't know. That's not the normal procedure, first of all I need some details and…'

Melissa put on her most velvet tones. 'Beth. Would you like to know how much Jonny earned last year after tax?' She stood up. 'What about that coffee. Why don't you and I find somewhere else to talk business?'

Ms Chapman stared at me and then smiled. 'Of course. Come this way. What harm can ten minutes do?'

On my knees, I pressed my hands together and bowed my head, like some mystical guru. Way to go, Melissa! The door clicked shut and I jumped up. Where to search first, the computer or filing cabinet? I checked my watch and went over to the window. Damn, the cabinet's drawers were all locked. I went back to the oak desk. Its drawer was locked too. Where would she hide her keys? I looked under the desk. There was a plain brown handbag. Taking a deep breath, I knelt down, zipped it open and rummaged around inside.

Bingo! I pulled out a bunch of keys. I tried the smallest in the desk drawer. No good. Then I shot over to the window and tried the cabinet. At that moment the office door opened. Shit! I folded my arms to hide the keys and started humming, swaying to and fro.

'Would you like a drink?' asked a voice. I recognised it as belonging to the receptionist.

'No,' I said, without opening my eyes. 'Please, don't interrupt me again.'

The door clicked closed and I stopped swaying. Phew. I slotted in the key and turned it. Thank God it worked.

A… B… C for Carmichael… Nope. Nothing there. I sighed. Perhaps it was filed under M for Murphy. K… L… M… No. Pursing my lips, I locked the cabinet back up and returned the keys to the bag.

I looked at my watch. Five more minutes. Perhaps there was something on the computer. I pushed a file out of the way to grab the mouse and just happened to notice… Of course! The file on the desk said Carmichael. Mr Murphy had only just visited – she wouldn't have had time to put it away yet. I opened it and flicked through the paperwork until… Finally! I lifted out the will and a similar looking document attached, underneath it, crossed with a great big red line of biro. I closed the folder.

There was no time to find a photocopier so, reluctantly, I stuffed the two documents into my leopard print handbag. Then I rushed around the desk and knelt on the floor, just as the door opened.

'Kimmy?' It was Melissa, holding a business card.

I stood up and pretended to shake off a deep trance.

'Have I passed?' asked Ms Chapman, politely.

I smiled. 'Must speak with my client first.'

Melissa pushed her blonde hair up into her wig then put on the glasses and cap. She held out her hand. 'Thank you, Beth. I'll be in touch.'

I bowed to the solicitor. 'May… the breeze of eternity be with you.'

As quickly as we could we scuttled out of the building, turned immediately left, and walked out of view. I burst out laughing.

'What the hell is the breeze of eternity?' said Melissa.

I snorted.

'Any success?' she asked as we slowed down outside a newsagent's.

'I've got the will,' I said. 'Well, two versions, I think.'

'You stole them!'

'Borrowed! What else could I do?'

'I think we deserve some chocolate after that, Miss Marple. Or I do at least, for making conversation with that woman for ten minutes.'

'Hard work?' I said.

'She could hardly contain her excitement when I hinted at how much Jonny earns.' She showed me the business card. 'Look what she jotted on the back: "When you've decided ring me. Have a nice day. Best, Beth." Melissa pulled a face. 'She obviously thinks the American personal touch will swing it.'

I grinned. 'A family-sized bar for you, then! You wait out here and ring for a taxi.' Which she did – thank goodness, as the first thing I spotted inside the shop was Saffron in a bra and suspenders on the front of a tabloid. A grown-up paper (that's what I called the big ones) had a smaller headline saying that some family-orientated sponsors were thinking of dropping Jonny Winsford. As quick as I could, I chose two bars of chocolate. My hand skimmed over a Snickers bar, which reminded me of Adam and the question mark still sort of hanging over our relationship. What was I going to do about him?

Standing by a black bin, Melissa read the two documents, one with a red line through. Whilst she unwrapped her bar, I took them and scanned the details. At a first glance, they looked identical and they were newer versions than the ones from the attic, both with the same date from this year. Sure enough, a large part of the estate – about half – was left to Murphy. As I read further, it appeared that the rest, four hundred thousand pounds, was to be split between the two charities mentioned in the other will – Bluebells Children's Home and Wildlife Watch UK. So, according to this, Mr Murphy was entitled to more than the twenty thousand in the 1990 will, but not every single penny.

I examined the small print again. 'Like in the earlier 1990 will, there's mention of Lily's best friend, Eleanor Goodman on both of these – she's still been left a diamond necklace and earrings. The paintings are still to be auctioned off and the money given to Harpenden Twilight Years care home…'I shrugged at Melissa. 'I don't understand. Okay, so this will does entitle Mr Murphy to a lot more than previously – a massive amount of money – but not the whole estate, like we assumed, and those charities are more than well catered for. Plus the smaller requests are still mentioned. So what's wrong? Why isn't Walter happy?'

She glanced sideways at me. 'Apart from the fact you fancy the pants off him, why are you so convinced that Luke's right about Mike somehow fiddling Walter?'

'There's nothing going on between us now,' I muttered.

'And doesn't that bother you? He's pretty hot.'

'You thought he was gay!'

'I've always thought he had an amazing bottom.' She shrugged. 'And his eyes, kind of consume you – like you're the most important person in the world... What if he got together with someone else? You're not bothered?'

I shrugged. 'He's not interested in me. Now, can we change the subject? You asked why I think Mr Murphy's fiddling Walter?'

She nodded.

I caught her eye. 'Promise not to laugh?'

She snorted. 'In recent years I've seen and heard it all.'

I took a deep breath. 'During the last week, I've, um, been communicating with old Mr Carmichael.'

Her face was deadpan. 'How?'

'He plays me music – that tune White Christmas; he knocks three times to reply; I always feel a cold gust of air when he's around. Then he's left useful things out for me – an apron, a cake stand, a recipe for the cake competition… He made it quite clear that he's not happy with the will. I didn't tell the paranormal investigators about him because I knew he needed to hang around a bit longer, to sort things out. I was just hoping they'd get rid of the other violent spirit – the one who grabbed me and made that smoke. That was before I knew it was Luke.' I gave a half-smile. 'Do I sound bonkers?'

'Trust me, I've heard more bonkers things, since mingling on the celebrity circuit – so Luke definitely isn't pretending to be the old man?'

I shook my head. 'Do you believe me?'

'Several of my friends have had paranormal experiences. It's nothing to be ashamed of. But thanks,' she said and popped a small square of chocolate into her mouth.

'What for?'

She put an arm around my shoulder. 'For making my life seem a little saner.'

I grinned. 'Lily's waiting for him, you know. They had an agreement, that whoever went first would wait for the other at the Pearly Gates.'

'That's so romantic.'

'You don't think I'm completely mad, thinking a ghost has told me he's unhappy with the way his estate is being executed?'

She took one of the documents off me and held it up. 'No, and I'll show you why. Take a look at Walter's signature on the one without the red line through it. Do you think it looks like all the ones we saw on all that paperwork last night?'

I studied it. 'Yes – a big upright W and then Carmichael scribbled and leaning to the left.

'But something's missing,' she said. 'And I should know about these things as a calligraphist.'

'You said you only did a short course!'

'Seriously, Kimmy, can't you spot the difference?'

I looked again and shook my head.

'The top ends of the W are curled slightly inwards,' she said. 'Walter curled his ends the opposite way. There's also no full stop after Carmichael. Yet on every single signature I saw last night, from all the paperwork in that cardboard box, there was. I notice details like that. He wouldn't change the habit of a lifetime all of a sudden, for one document.' She shook the piece of paper. 'I'd say that the other one, slashed with red pen, was actually signed by Walter. This one wasn't. No wonder the old boy's not happy. It's forged.'

CHAPTER 30

'Shh! I'm concentrating!'

Luke, Melissa and I rolled our eyes at each other as Jess sat under the chandelier at the black circular breakfast table in Melissa's kitchen. She stared hard at the two documents, like we all had, determined to find a difference between them.

'We're at a dead end, darlings,' said Melissa. 'Let's face it – we haven't enough to prove that there's anything dodgy going on.'

She bit into a savoury cupcake. When we'd got back I'd quickly made up a batch using cheese and juicy tomatoes from the fridge. The topping was cream cheese, sprinkled with chopped basil. The house clearers had arrived soon after, along with Mr Murphy. His errands hadn't taken as long as he'd expected, so he gave me and Jess the afternoon off. Apparently his solicitor, a Ms Chapman he said, was coming around later. She was a huge fan of cross-stitch and he'd promised her the pick of Lily's threads, fabrics and needles.

Jess passed a hand over her stomach. 'It could be nothing, but all I can find is a discrepancy in the name of the charities. On the red-slashed document, with Walter's proper signature, they are called Bluebell Children's Home and Wildlife Watch and exactly match the charities mentioned on the 1990 will. On the other document they read as Bluebell*s* Children's Home and Wildlife Watch *UK*.'

'Worth checking out,' said Luke and pulled off the black wig a giggling Melissa had placed on his head. 'Aren't solicitors supposed to be meticulous about that sort of thing?'

'You'd think so, for the amount they charge,' said Melissa. 'Jonny's set his pre-nup out in minute detail – although it wasn't exactly straightforward.'

'Why?' I asked.

'After his first divorce, Jonny was wary, wanted to protect his assets. And who can blame him? Jeanie still puts in a claim every time he has a big win; says she supported him when he was just starting out, put her own career to one side, so deserves a cut of his winnings for life. I wasn't bothered about what I got if we split up – I was never in this marriage for the money. But for fun, I suggested taking a leaf out of Catherine Zeta-Jones's book; she receives a "bonus" if the marriage is ended by her husband cheating.' She sighed. 'Little did I know that if it actually happened, the last thing I'd want was money earned directly from him shagging another woman.'

Jess opened Walter's laptop, which we'd smuggled out of Mistletoe Mansion, and Googled the charities and their different names.

'Interesting,' said Luke to her and she nodded.

'There are four websites to go with the four charities,' she said. 'The children's homes ones look very similar, as do the wildlife ones – apart from the contact details.'

'Which sites were created first?' I said.

'Yeah, can you find out when the websites were registered?' said Luke.

Jess duly clicked the mouse several times, jumping to and fro between computer windows.

'Now we're getting somewhere,' she said. 'The website for Bluebell Children's Home, mentioned on the 1990 will, was registered in 1996. Wildlife Watch's site was registered in 2001. Whereas the two charities from this most recent will, with slightly different names and Walter's funny signature, they were both registered... just under six months ago. No doubt soon after Walter died.'

We all looked at each other.

'Where are their headquarters?' I said. 'Googlemap the addresses.'

Melissa fiddled with her coffee machine and got us all to select a disc beverage pod, whilst Jess and Luke searched the different locations.

'Bingo,' said Luke finally.

'The earlier websites look kosher,' said Jess. 'But the ones registered this year... their contact addresses are the same and belong to a random burger bar in Luton.'

Melissa slid her mobile out of her pocket. 'Let me dial those phone numbers,' she said. 'This is getting more and more weird.'

Ten minutes later we all sat in silence, drinking coffee. The charities mentioned in the 1990 will had answered professionally. The other two numbers linked to the random burger joint address never rang out; they didn't exist. They were phoney.

'Looks like someone has forged this will without the red biro, then – presumably the one considered kosher,' I said, eventually, 'with Mr Murphy still getting half of the estate but the other half going to fake charities. Do the websites give the names of the charities' founders?' I asked Jess.

She clicked the mouse a few times. 'Yes – in dead tiny print at the bottom. Let's see... Both the fake ones were set up by the same person – an E. Chapman. Of course!'

Luke let out a low whistle.

'The solicitor. E for Eliza*beth* Chapman. But why would she risk her reputation like this?' said Melissa. 'It doesn't make sense.'

'She and Mr Murphy must be in on it together,' said Jess. 'But why would Walter's nephew push to get even more money? He's already due a decent share.'

Melissa went to one of the kitchen drawers, rummaged around and pulled out a card. 'I thought so,' she said. 'Look at Beth's business card and what she wrote on the back.' She put it on the table and we read the message: "When you've decided ring me. Have a nice day. Best, Beth."

'The capital W' said Luke. 'Well spotted. You're quite good at this detective lark.'

'Thank you,' said Melissa and her cheeks tinged pink. 'See everyone, the top ends slightly curl in, like on Walter's forged signature.'

'Ms Chapman – Beth – is coming round to see Mr Murphy this afternoon,' I said and jumped up. 'Come on – we don't want to miss her.

'I'll ring the police,' said Luke and grinned at Melissa. 'Keep that wig – if I ever need something investigating I know who to call on.'

Melissa giggled. My stomach pinched. I'd been in on it too. Why didn't his moss green eyes twinkle at me?

'I'll keep the cameras hanging around,' said Melissa. 'If she – or Mike – denies everything, we can always threaten to go public.'

When we got back to Mistletoe Mansion, a sensible-looking, new, saloon car was parked outside. Jess and I let ourselves in. Mr Murphy had just come off the phone. I looked around. It was so sad to see Walter's home stripped of many pieces of furniture. Even the little hallway desk was missing. But the paintings were still up. I cleared my throat as footsteps came into the hall.

'Hello, girls,' said Mr Murphy. 'I'm just making my solicitor, Beth Chapman, a coffee. She's waiting for me in the lounge.' He smiled at us. 'Actually, I've a favour to ask. Um… there's quite a lot of personal stuff left. I couldn't let the house clearers take it all.' He fiddled with the end of his tie. 'Would you two go through my uncle's address book and invite round any friends to take an item they might like – you know, to remember him by. I've held onto Walter's golf memorabilia, the ornaments, Lily's jewellery and lot of books. There's also a fur coat and some top-notch crockery and cooking equipment. It's something I should have done before.'

'Er, of course,' said Jess.

Maybe he did have a heart after all. And yet that time in the Games Room, when Melissa was there and he'd been mouthing off about how close he'd been to Walter, my spooky friend made it clear that his nephew wasn't telling the truth.

'You must miss your uncle,' I said, and eyed him closely.

At that moment, quick, abrupt footsteps entered the hallway. Ms Chapman appeared. She stopped dead. 'Kimmy, isn't it? Mrs Winsford's Life Guide? You know Mike?'

'Didn't you know, Melissa Winsford lives next door?' I ignored Mr Murphy's puzzled expression. 'We were just talking about Mr Carmichael. I'm sure he'd be pleased that his estate was finally being sorted out.' A cold gust of wind blew around my shoulders.

'What the hell is a Life Guide?' asked Mr Murphy.

'Um… it's…' I cleared my throat and turned my attention to Ms Chapman. 'I'd like you to meet Jess,' I said. 'She's a private detective. Like me, actually. We have reason to believe that the Carmichaels' latest will has been forged.'

'I am?' said Jess. 'I mean… Yes. We've just been examining the evidence.'

'Private detectives?' Mr Murphy snorted. 'Yes, girlies, and I'm Donald Trump.'

I held out the two wills, hoping (probably too late) that I wouldn't end up in jail for theft.

'I wondered where they'd gone,' said Ms Chapman and quickly reached out.

'Not so fast,' said Jess and pulled them away. 'We've examined both documents. We know you've forged Walter's signature on a second will and set up two bogus charities. The four hundred thousand pounds designated for Bluebell Children's Home and Wildlife Watch is going to go straight to you.'

'How dare you suggest such a thing!' said Mr Murphy, purple in the face. 'Beth Chapman is one of the most respected solicitors in Harpenden. This is slander.'

'So you know nothing about it?' I said to him. 'The fake charity websites and contact details, set up in an E. Chapman's name? A calligraphist we know has confirmed that Walter's signature had been faked. We're sure our… our contacts in the police will confirm the same…'

'Why did you get Walter to change solicitors?' said Jess to Mr Murphy.

'To save him money. Not that it's any business of yours. We became very close and…ow!'

He jumped, as if he'd been poked in the ribs. Naughty Walter!

'Look…' I said, quietly. 'Don't ask me how I know, but own up – you and Walter weren't exactly best buddies. I'm not saying you didn't become fond of him, but talk about going over the top… Why make all that stuff up?'

'You can't speak to me like that!'

'Well, he hasn't left you a single personal item,' said Jess. 'That's dead odd. And you haven't even put aside… I dunno, that painting of him for yourself.'

'That proves nothing!'

'Why did you get Walter to change solicitors?' she repeated.

His face shone with beads of sweat. 'All right... Look, we might not have been like father and son but I wanted the best for him. Beth is an old friend. I knew she'd give us a good deal on writing up the new will and selfishly, seeing as it was going to be me involved with sorting everything out after Uncle snuffed it, I wanted someone I knew was going to be easy to work with and professional. I'm a busy man.' He shrugged. 'And I'm not a total moron. I know what everyone thinks – that I've only been interested in Walter's money. But that's wrong. When he fell ill I felt kind of guilty that I'd not visited more often since Auntie Lily died – especially as they'd had no kids. And I think, in his own way, Walter appreciated it – even though I could tell I irritated him. We didn't have a huge amount in common. But we got closer.'

'So it was his idea to leave a good amount of his estate to you?' asked Jess.

He nodded. 'I asked him to think about it. I mean, sure, the money's welcome but as my bank accounts would prove, I'm doing very well for myself, thank you. I don't need Uncle Walter's inheritance.' He half-smiled. 'Although it'll be nice to book a dream-of-a-lifetime trip to the States... But it's not like I've even got a shopaholic wife and sprogs to support. I think Walter was hoping that one day I'd settle down and have the kids he never could, even though I told him that was unlikely. Plus, as part of the deal, he made me promise to give regularly to my own charities.' He pulled a face. 'That was the hardest bit but I've looked around and there's one up in Manchester I'm going to donate to, for professionals who end up homeless.' He shuddered. 'I can't think of anything worse. Just imagine if…'

Whilst he was rambling, Ms Chapman's eyes had glazed over. In fact, she'd been suspiciously quiet.

'You said Beth was an old friend?' I interrupted.

'We used to… She's an ex-girlfriend,' he muttered and loosened his tie.

'I was a bit more than that, Mikey,' she said in a tight voice. 'We almost put down roots together, at one point.'

'Why didn't you?' I asked. They seemed well-matched and both were business people who clearly still got on.

'Mike wasn't ready to settle down – didn't want to commit… But that was a long time ago,' she said and forced a laugh.

'How long?' asked Jess.

'Eight years,' said Mike.

'And five months,' she snapped.

Wow. Talk about bitterness in her voice. Perhaps Mike had an affair...

'No one else was involved,' said Mike, as if he'd read my mind. 'I just didn't want the whole wedding and kids package – still don't.' He shrugged. 'These things happen,' said Mike. 'I did us both a favour in the long run.'

'You've not met anyone since?' I asked her.

She sniffed. 'No one wants a dried-up career woman who can't have kids.'

'But we never wanted children!' he said.

Her cheeks flushed purple. 'You never were good at reading in between the lines. You were my last shot, Mikey,' she hissed. 'When we got engaged I could feel my body gearing up for the menopause. I thought if I told you how I really felt – that I was desperate for a baby – it would have put you off and I'd lose my last chance.' She pulled off her glasses, yanked out a tissue from her trouser pocket and cleaned them until they shone.

'Beth? The fake will… Do you know what these two are talking about? I thought the break-up was behind us – all these years, you've never mentioned it again.' He shook his head. 'What were you going to do if we'd stayed together? Accidentally get pregnant?'

'I thought you'd come around to the idea.'

'You always were good at winning arguments,' he muttered. 'These charities… the four hundred thousand… Why, Beth? Jess and Kimmy are right, aren't they? I mean, you're obsessive about detail, I remember how you used to check just your phone bill a dozen times. Any apparent "mistakes" on a document like that, drawn up by you, like charity names, that wouldn't be accidental.'

We all jumped as the knocker rapped loudly on the front door. I went to open it. Luke and Melissa were there, her arm linked in his.

'The police are on their way,' said Luke.

'You of all people should understand,' said Beth in a small voice, to Melissa. 'I bet you'll take your husband to the cleaners, now he's done the dirty on you.'

'It was a long time ago,' said Mr Murphy. 'Beth – you need to move on.'

'That's precisely what I intended to do. Amongst other things, that money was going to pay for fertility treatment. I've spent all my savings and so far it's failed. This is my only hope.' She shook her fist.

Poor Beth – despite her sneering attitude, I felt sorry for her. At that moment the police arrived and a male officer hurried forwards and stood in between the former love birds.

'Folks, let's all calm down,' he said.

'Calm down?' Beth screeched. 'I've waited years to call in this debt. He ruined my life! Giving me a few measly grand is the least he can do.'

As a female officer steered Beth firmly into the lounge, I hurried into the kitchen, put on the kettle and glanced around… Thank goodness the baking utensils I needed were still left. I grabbed a mixing bowl and my silicone cupcake moulds. Sponge and chocolate, that's what everyone needed, to induce a friendlier mood.

'We did it, Walter,' I whispered and tipped sugar onto the scales. 'Everything will be in order soon. Now you'll soon be at those Pearly Gates. Lily won't have to wait anymore.' My chest squeezed. The house would feel strange without him – although I had a busy week ahead. A week today was Monday the twenty-fifth. Apart from anything else, I had Christmas food to buy.

A gust of cold air gently tickled my neck and I heard three very light, skippity-jumppity thuds – plus the faint sound of the familiar White Christmas music. My cheeks glowed. So what if Mistletoe Mansion was bare and I might spend next Monday just with Jess? I had new friends. A great career ahead of me. Things could have been a lot worse.

Something bleeped and I reached for my phone. It was a text.

"Had 2 go – Melissa wants me 2 look at her guttering – but got surprise 4 U at market on Sat. U'll never guess wot. Luke."

CHAPTER 31

Oh my. Talk about white Christmasses. As the week progressed, the air became crisper than a Pringle from a newly opened tube. It was Saturday, the day of the Harpenden Christmas Market, and yay! Me and Jess had woken up to a carpet of sparkling snow. The impossible had happened – it made Badgers Chase look even prettier than usual. This would be great in the future, I told Jess, when she had the little one – it would give us an excuse to play in the snow.

Jess must have been feeling better, cos she'd chortled and said 'Who needs an excuse?' Cue both of us, outside in our boots and dressing gowns, pounding each other with snowballs. I know. Mature or what? But deep snow only came around now and again. If only we had a sledge to slide across the garden on. Mind you, in Jess's condition that wouldn't be wise. Perhaps, instead, I could pull my cakes along on it, for the walk into town.

Fortunately, however, Luke had offered to drive me in. I grinned at him, as we pushed our way through what looked like the entire population of Harpenden, crowded around the entrance to the town hall, in the high street. I loved how the fresh snow squeaked under our boots, without the slightest hint of slush. Fairy lights lined the road and everyone was well wrapped up in hats, scarves and wellington boots. Stalls served aromatic mulled wine and warm mince pies... I spotted hot chocolate stands and farmers' cheese tables in all sorts of cute flavours like cranberry and Port... Mmm, breakfast suddenly seemed like a long time ago.

'Now, tell me now what that text and my surprise is all about, or the dog gets it.' I carried my Tupperware box of cakes carefully, as if it contained the unseen manuscript to JK Rowling's next novel. Luke had offered to drive me into town "as a last favour" because I'd been paranoid that the box would fall over in my car, if the wheels had slid on the snow.

'I mean it,' I said and looked down menacingly at Groucho, who wore a cute navy waterproof jacket. I'd bought it for him this week, as the arctic air had descended, and amazingly Luke didn't object. Just as well, cos Groucho now belonged to him – Luke had adopted the dog as Mr Murphy's only other option would be to hand him over to the animal rescue centre. Two chocolate button eyes stared up at me and Groucho yapped. 'Only joking, matey,' I cooed at my canine friend.

'I've told you all week – you'll see your surprise once your cakes are laid out,' said Luke, with one of his teasing smiles.

We headed towards a grand tent ahead, outside a wine shop, near the town hall. A banner was hung across the top of it saying "Harpenden Christmas Market Cake Competition". 'What time do they announce the winner?' he asked.

'After lunch. I've got to be back on the stall at two o'clock.' Jess had the day off but was shopping in Luton this morning to "accidentally" bump into Ryan. She hoped to make it back in time for the announcement of the winners.

A few metres in front of the stall, Luke and I stopped. Several competitors were already there, wearing aprons and fussing over buttercream icing or glazed nuts. 'Those entries all look so sensible,' I muttered. 'Maybe I should have left off the liquorice Eric Morecambe glasses.'

Luke squeezed my shoulder and tiny patches of pleasure burst into life, all over my body.

'They'll love your cakes,' he said, looking particularly hot in a jacket as green as his eyes. 'The flavour's fantastic. Really outstanding.' He groaned. 'I should know.'

Poor Luke. And Terry. Plus Jess and Melissa. All week I'd worked to perfect the recipe and they must have each put on half a stone. Although Melissa had gone back to her habit of spitting each mouthful out or discreetly passed chunks under the table to Luke. Then, at the end of the week she'd cried off my tasting sessions, sounding really cheerful, with the only explanation that she was "busy" and vague talk about some sort of trip. Luke wasn't around as much either, although they'd both been brill on Thursday, helping out with the Carmichaels' friends when they'd come over to look through the personal items. Not that Luke had acted remotely romantically towards me, which was probably sensible. My stomach scrunched at the thought of him leaving for Brighton soon.

Okay! I admit it! Me and Luke… It felt so… right. He was exasperating and smug, yet ambitious and funny all in equal measure. But most importantly – yes, even more important than his hot bristly cheeks and tight embrace – he believed in me and in taking risks. A smile spread across my face. After the start we'd had, nothing surprised me more than how much we actually had in common. As for his deep, oh so tender kisses… my pulse quickened just at the thought of his tantalising lips on mine.

I nodded to the other competitors. One had visited Mistletoe Mansion on Thursday… Eleanor Goodman, that was it, Lily's best friend, who'd been mentioned in the will.

How carefully she'd searched through all of the bookcases, muttering about Lily's coveted recipe book.

'Good luck,' said Luke. 'And ta dah! Here's your surprise – open this once you've set up.' He thrust a small, flat package into my open handbag. 'I've got time for a quick Christmas cinnamon hot chocolate and Stollen slice before I go home to pack. Meet you by the drinks stall in half an hour, if you like. Otherwise… Well. I don't like goodbyes.'

Before I knew it… before we could, maybe, tell each other how we felt… he and his whistling disappeared into the crowd. I bit my lip. Couldn't blame him. Most of the time I'd acted as if he and I gelled together as well as a cake mixture that had curdled. Perhaps he didn't like me so much, after all? But this package… I glanced down. It was wrapped in silver paper. Surely this was proof that he liked me; that our random kissing hadn't just been a one-off because I'd been spooked and he'd been hyped and we'd both been alone in the dark? I couldn't remember the last time Adam had kissed me like that. Not even when we had that power cut last month and he'd ignored my suggestion of a candle-lit early night. Instead, he'd strapped a torch to the front of his head. The potholer look was not his most flattering.

I sighed for a second. The last day or two, when I thought about Adam and me, all I could recall was the negatives. I took a deep breath and, emptying my mind of men for a moment, made my way into the tent. A white-haired woman in a salmon skirt and postbox red fleece came up to me. She held what looked like a list of names.

'You are…?'

'Kimberley Jones – my entry is "Bring Me Sunshine" cakes.' I set my box down on a table and rummaged in my handbag. 'Here's the list of ingredients you requested. Sorry I'm a bit late.'

'Better late than never. Thank you, dear.' She nodded over to where Eleanor was standing. 'You set up on that table over there.'

I headed over. Eleanor gave a tight smile.

'You were lucky, getting a place in this competition,' she said. 'The rest of us had to register over two months ago. Friends in high places obviously help. Although your neighbour has obviously lowered her standards.'

My brow furrowed.

Eleanor passed me a newspaper from under her table. 'Take a look at page three when you've got a moment. Mrs Winsford may not be in a social position to pull many strings next year if she moves in with her new beau.'

What was she going on about? I stuck the paper under my arm and glanced at her traditional Christmas cake, decked with Brazil nuts and cherries. She must have been referring to those photos Melissa had taken with... What was that model called? David Khan.

'Mine's a classic recipe, of course,' she continued and puffed out her chest, 'with a special homemade orange marmalade glaze on top... I strive for perfect depth and immaculate lines.'

Hmm. Those rows of nuts sure were, indeed, symmetrical.

Eleanor glanced across as I put out my cupcakes with the luminous yellow butter icing and black liquorice glasses on top. 'Simplicity. Class. Good food suited to a given time of year. That's what Harpenden judges admire.' She smirked. 'How unusual. Competitors don't often enter children's fairy cakes that also have nothing to do with Christmas.'

'They aren't for kids.' I said brightly. 'Cupcakes are big business nowadays and anything goes. I felt something different might go down well.'

'How… inventive,' she said, with a dismissive wave of her hand, before wandering off to steal a look at the other cakes on show. My gaze followed her and rested on a perfect chocolate log, with what looked like a marzipan robin on top. The woman standing behind it had a grey perm and wore sensible slacks with a hiker's anorak. She blew on her red hands and smiled at me as I admired her cake's cylindrical shape. Next to her was a young man plating up a gorgeous sponge with swirls of white buttercream icing on top, covered in a delicate array of tiny edible Christmas decorations – small sugar bells, green holly leaves, sparkly baubles – the effect was classy and subtle, completed with a silver ribbon tied around the sides.

I scoured the other tables, feeling less confident by the second, as each and every one had something to do with Christmas – but there had been nothing about that in the rules. There was a golden coloured Stollen log, dusted with snowy icing powder. Plus another fruit cake decorated with royal icing. Then a sponge in the shape of Santa which would be a huge hit with any kid.

I put down the newspaper and filled in the small name card, writing "Bring Me Sunshine cakes" in my neatest handwriting.

'Clever. A nod to Morecambe and Wise, no?' said a voice next to me. I glanced up at a woman, probably around my age, with short auburn hair. She wore a white apron and looked very professional. 'Been making cupcakes long?' she said and held out her hand. 'I'm Ruth.'

'Um… Kimmy.' I shook her hand.

'Love the colour of that buttercream icing. Have you got a website?'

'I'm, um, in the process of setting one up.' I smiled. 'Where's your entry?'

She jerked her head towards a table a couple of rows behind. Wow. There on a miniature cake stand sat the most amazing chocolate cakes, with green buttercream icing swirled upwards into a pyramid, on each one, to look like Christmas tree. Then tiny sparkly sugar balls had been pressed into the sides, to look like baubles. A gold star topped each one.

'Awesome,' I muttered and sniffed. 'Mint icing?'

'Yes – these are "After Dinner Muffins"!'

'What a fabulous concept.'

The woman shrugged. 'I came third last year. I'm keeping everything crossed this time. Good luck to you, though.' She lowered her voice. 'Nice to see someone else daring to enter something less predictable.'

We smiled at each other then she zipped up her duffle coat, grabbed her handbag and disappeared into the crowds. I took one last look at my cakes and headed off to meet Luke at the hot chocolate stall. Delicate snowflakes had started to fall – the first of the day. I reached into my bag to put my gloves back on. Ah ha! I'd almost forgotten – at last I could open my surprise. I stopped for a minute by a candyfloss stall and fumbled with the silver wrapping. Inside, tied with a little silver bow, was a pile of small white, gilt-edged cards. Printed on each was a watercolour sketch of a cupcake and in gold italic letters it said: "Let KimCakes bring you sunshine. For uniquely delicious cakes, made with the finest ingredients, contact Kimberley Jones on…" and there was my mobile number.

Wow. My very first business cards. Tears pricked my eyes. I couldn't believe Luke had gone to such trouble. This was the ultimate gesture of confidence in me. Lovingly I stroked the surface of one, feeling more certain than ever that a future in the baking business was for me. Carefully, I slipped them into my bag, grabbed the newspaper and pushed my way through the crowd, towards the hot chocolate stall.

Luke. I had to find Luke. To kiss that flirty mouth – to breathe in his musky smell. I passed tables of Christmas decorations – wooden toys for the tree, festive wreaths and garlands… Luke had even knocked off the "Ltd" on those cards because he knew my business wasn't yet off the ground. But that made it seem all the more real, and I liked using my full name for once.

My brow furrowed for a second. For God's sake, this was the twenty-first century. Why had I waited all week for Luke to kiss me again? Why hadn't I made the first move? In the distance I saw Melissa, wearing an amazing white Russian fur hat, with a matching fur-trimmed white coat and jeans. That reminded me. I was curious about the page three Eleanor had been banging on about. Quickly I stopped, turned over the front page of the newspaper… A report on the rising price of petrol, the fattest dog in the world… and right at the bottom, a photo of… A shard of hurt pierced the centre of my chest. I gulped for air. No. Could it really be Melissa and… Luke? They were facing each other, him staring deep into her eyes and running his fingers through her hair.

My chin trembled and I loosened the top of my coat. No wonder she'd kept asking me how I'd feel if he met someone else. Unlike me, he couldn't have… clearly hadn't tingled after our kiss. This explained why Melissa had really cheered up the last day or two. And "the trip" – she must be travelling to Brighton with him. I looked back over the last week – them laughing together over that wig; her arm linked with his. My throat ached. Stupid, stupid me. I'd paved the way for their relationship, insisting every time she asked that I felt nothing for Luke and that our snog was a one-off. Vision blurry, I sniffed and tossed the newspaper into a nearby bin.

'Kimmy! Darling!' called velvety tones.

I stopped in my tracks. Took a deep breath. Turned around.

'Wow. You, um, look fab,' I said to Melissa in a flat voice. A ponytail trailed out of her hat and was an impossbily creamy blonde. Her skin glowed and the white outfit contrasted her caramel tan. A silver designer bag was slung casually over one shoulder. She looked every inch the celebrity – a happy one, at that.

I turned back around and pushed through the crowd again. No. I couldn't face talking to her. Bowing my head, away from tiny snowflakes, I walked away as quickly as I could.

'Hey, you,' said a voice and a strong hand curled around my arm. I raised my head. Unintentionally, I'd ended up at the drinks stall. The aroma of spiced chocolate teased my nostrils.

'You must have a thirst on you, at that pace,' said Luke and let go.

'I… um… yes. Thanks for the cards… They look very… professional.'

'No problem.' His eyes crinkled. 'So, after meeting the other competitors, do you need something strong, like a pint of mulled wine?'

'I can't stay,' I said. 'You must be busy anyway – things to do before your trip. Thanks though, for… for everything.' I forced myself to smile and bent down to give Groucho a goodbye stroke.

'You haven't got time for even one drink?' His eyebrows knotted. No doubt he was hoping to pump me for information about his latest conquest.

'Enjoy Brighton,' I mumbled. 'See you around.'

'Right. It's just that we won't, will we? See each other, I mean. Those cards, it was my way of saying…'

Saying what? Sorry for making a fool of you again? 'It's been fun, Luke. I've got to go.' I barked and swivelled around, almost skidding on a patch of flat snow. If only real life were like Facebook and I could just delete him and block all contact. He took my arm to steady me.

'What's the matter? The cards, I hoped they'd show you that…'

'Yadda yadda. They aren't really my style – too twee by half.' Throat aching, I shook him off and headed through the throng of people, hoping he hadn't heard the wobble in my voice. Quickly, I past the Belgian chocolate stall, resisting the urge to buy comfort food.

'Kimmy!'

I stopped and turned around. 'Jess?'

'Jess?' said someone else, at the same time, and my friend and I both stared at a short, squat, middle-aged woman. She had a sensible, short hairstyle and was with a teenage boy who was trying hard to look bored.

'Dana,' said Jess. 'I wasn't expecting to see you here. Who's running things back at Nuttall's?'

The Dalek had taken a Saturday off work?

'Andrew,' said Dana. 'It's time he got used to a bit of responsibility.'

Jess paled. I knew what my best mate was thinking – surely Dana hadn't come all this way to let her go? To tell her that she was priming someone else – Jess's colleague Andrew – to take her job? The Dalek nodded at the teenager.

'Off you go, Will. I'll meet you by the raffle stall in ten minutes.'

'Whatever.' The boy ambled off.

'I'd better get going.' I cleared my throat and glanced again at my watch.

'No! I mean…' Jess frowned and clutched my parka sleeve. I got it. If the Dalek was going to terminate her, she wanted me around to pick up the pieces. I really didn't feel like company, right at that moment, but she was my best mate.

'I was wondering if we could have a quick chat,' said Dana. 'In private.'

Jess took out a pack of gum and pushed two tabs in her mouth. 'I don't keep anything from Kimmy,' she said.

'Fine. Your future at Nuttall's. That's what I want to talk about.'

Jess nodded and I slipped my arm through hers.

Dana folded her arms. 'I'm making Andrew supervisor.'

'But that's my job!' said Jess, top lip quivering. 'I mean… I've got rights, you know. You just can't get rid of me because I'm pregnant. It won't affect my work, honestly. I need the money, don't–'

'Have you quite finished?' she said. 'I'm not going to fire you. I want you to manage the garden centre. Andrew will be your second in command.'

Jess's mouth fell open. 'What about you?'

Dana smiled and immediately looked years younger. 'You know the big run-down greenhouses out the back? I've got planning permission to extend the garden centre onto that land. I'll be running our new pet and aquatics shop. And a café.'

'Pet and aquatics?' I said. 'Nice move. All the best garden centres have one now.' And a café? She'd be needing cupcakes for that.

'You… I mean… So…' Jess stuttered. 'You'll be taking on extra staff?'

'Yes.' said Dana. 'Of course, it'll be months before it's all up and running, but the garden centre's been doing so well I came up with a sound business plan. I just wanted

you to know, I mean…' She cleared her throat. 'You're
a hard worker, Jess. There'll be a pay rise with your new
role. Enough, I would have thought, to pay for child care.'

Wow. For a moment I even forgot all about Luke Butler.
I nudged a speechless Jess.

'Thanks,' she stuttered.

'You seem surprised?' said Dana.

'I am,' replied Jess. 'I didn't think… You've been…'

Dana bit her lip. 'I know. Probably harder on you than
usual. I was upset for you, that's all. I know how hard it
is. I was left to bring up my son as a single mother. I've
been there, Jess. You're such a sensible girl, I figured you'd
do things the right way – you know, engagement, marriage,
then get pregnant, all in that order.'

'Who's to say what's right, nowadays,' Jess muttered.

Dana nodded. 'I know. And I wouldn't change a thing.
But I hated myself for years. Felt so stupid for getting
myself into that situation. Guess you getting pregnant
brought all of that back.'

'But you've done so well,' I said. 'Nuttall's – it's one of
the most popular garden centres around here.'

'Thank you,' said Dana. 'But it's been bloody hard.
I used to take Will into work with me when he was a
toddler, when I first got my parents' inheritance and started
things up. It wasn't easy.' She smiled at the teenager who
had wandered back. 'Talk of the devil.'

Will sloped up. 'Got any money for a cola, Mum?'

'So, see you first thing tomorrow, Jess?' said Dana.

Jess nodded. 'Yes. Thanks.' She waited a minute until
her boss had disappeared into the crowds. 'Am I dreaming?
That's the most that woman has opened up to me in the last
three years.'

I grabbed her hands and Jess's face crumpled into
a smile.

'I can't take so much good news in one day!' she said.

'Why? What else? How did it go with Ryan?'

Tears filled her eyes. Blimey. Hormones again.

'Julie stage-managed it perfectly.' She sniffed. 'Ryan and me bumped into each other and ending up having a latte in the Spoon & Sausage – just the two of us, brother and sister.'

'What did he say?'

'That he missed me. Well, I had to translate that from Ryan-speak of course. I think his actual words were "it would be nice to dare to sit down on the toilet seat again".'

'Yuck!'

'Then I told him – about the baby.'

I nodded, on tenterhooks to hear about Ryan's reaction. Once I'd got over the shock, butterflies had been building in my stomach at the prospect of becoming some sort of auntie. No, kids weren't on my own agenda yet, but that didn't mean I couldn't wait to get my mitts on a gorgeous baby. Over the last few days, I'd hugged my knees at the prospect of trips to the park with Jess's little kiddie. When I was younger I'd always loved babysitting. Plus I liked the warm sense of responsibility this auntie business gave me. Like my decision to go all out to start my own business. This was grown-up stuff, which felt so different – so much better – than the responsibility I used to carry, as a child, for a mum who was often drunk. What's more, it was my version of being mature, not Adam's…

'And?' I said, eyebrows raised.

'This Julie… He's smitten with her. Apparently she's a single mum. He's been to toddlers group and Mothercare and started telling me about the time this kid accidentally called him "Dad".' She squeezed my hands. 'Even though he wanted to "go around and sort Phil out" he's one hundred percent supportive and insisted I had to move back

in, right away. In any case, the bloke who was sharing with
him is leaving, because of a new job. Julie doesn't want to
move in at the moment because her kid is dead settled –
they live at her parents' house.'

I hugged her. 'Our plan worked, Jess! Well… kind of.
You get to move back with Ryan.'

'Of course, I'm spending Christmas with you at
Mistletoe Mansion.'

'No, don't be sil–'

Jess's eyes had narrowed and I knew better than to argue
with that look.

'Anyway,' she said, 'hasn't Terry invited us both over for
a Boxing Day drinks party he's hosting?'

I grinned. 'Yes – he's super excited because someone's
bringing a blind date along for him, who loves pets and
golf.'

'And Luke… What's he doing?' Jess eyed me closely.

I shrugged. 'Who knows?' I couldn't dampen her spirits
with my tale of woe. I checked my watch again. 'Better
get off. See you later. But yay! I'm so pleased for you.'
I hurtled through the crowd, desperate for a few seconds
on my own. I needed to pull myself together. Tickling tears
were still threatening, at the backs of my eyes.

'Yoo hoooo! Kimmy! Don't run off this time!'

Aargh! I glanced to my right.

'Hello, Melissa,' I said as she loomed into view. A trail
of photographers followed her. She stopped right in front of
me, brushed down her clothes and stood in a model pose.

'Luke was over at the hot chocolate stall last time I saw
him.' I mumbled and nodded towards the cameras. 'They
probably want a photo of you both.'

'What *are* you going on about?' She lifted my chin.
'Why the sad eyes? This is your day. I've every confidence
you're going to win. And why on earth would the paparazzi

want to snap me with Luke, when...' Her mouth fell open. 'Oh my God! Kimmy! You've seen that photo. Don't tell me you took it at face value? After all your years of reading gossip magazines, you still can't spot a fake shot?'

'Huh?'

Melissa shook her head. 'Luke. He's been clearing out our guttering all week. One bit was damaged from that storm and when Luke touched it, it fell down and hit my eye. Luke brushed my hair out of the way and checked for mud and dirt. Surprise, surprise, a long lens was waiting.' She bit her lip. 'You must have thought me a prize bitch.'

'No! Of course not!' My insides tied into tight knots as I recalled how rude I'd been to Luke about the cards. Urgh! Had I got it wrong? They weren't an item? She wasn't off with him to Brighton?

My heart raced. Now I've messed everything up. 'It wouldn't have been your fault even if you and Luke were together,' I stuttered. 'I mean, you asked me often enough how I felt about him and I denied having any feelings.'

She chuckled. 'You didn't fool me. I've been trying to make you face your emotions for days, before it's too late...'

'That's why you kept asking me how I'd feel if he met someone else?'

She wiped a snowflake off her nose and nodded.

Desperately, I searched the crowd of faces – for moss green eyes and bedroom hair. Would Luke forgive me, if I could ever find him?

CHAPTER 32

'There's a jolly good reason Luke and I aren't together anyway.' Melissa beamed, as blossom petals of snow stopped falling. She pointed to the left. Jonny was surrounded by a posse of kids, signing autographs. I told myself I hadn't just seen him look down the cleavage of a young mum. Melissa's eyes shone.

'You're not back with him?' I said. 'What about Saffron? He cheated on you. I thought you agreed, life was better without him around.'

'Infamous let slip to Jonny about the planned photo spread with me and David Khan. Apparently he went mad – said that I was the sexiest golfer's wife on the planet and, I quote, "out of that dickhead's league".'

'He was jealous?'

'Don't sound so surprised!'

'I'm not, it's just… with the spring tournaments here before we know it… you don't think he's–'

'Doing this for appearances' sake?' she interrupted.

I nodded.

She fiddled with her yellow diamond ring. 'No. I truly believe he's sorry. And well, me without… Jonny…' She cleared her throat. 'I'm giving him one more chance. Anyway, what more proof could I need when he suggested – wait for this – that we renew our vows!'

'What?'

'Fabulous, isn't it? I always knew I was the love of his life.' She caught my eye. 'I have to believe that. Jonny and I were meant to be. Just you wait and see.'

I stared over at The Eagle again, women fluttering around him like moths around the Christmas lights back at Badgers Chase. 'But you've burnt your wedding dress.'

She grinned and shrugged. 'Infamous have offered us a ridiculous amount of money for the pictures. And guess what Jonny suggested I spent it on?'

'Um… bigger boobs? Not that you need them,' I hurriedly added.

She shook her head.

'Adopting a baby from abroad?'

'No! But we have discussed making our own little Winsford. Jonny's promised to seriously consider it over the next year. He's whisking me off to the Caribbean, after Christmas, so that we can have lots of one-on-one time.'

So that was her trip – Barbados, not Brighton.

'He'd only been with Saffron five minutes and apparently she was already requesting the new soft top Audi and a nose job. He's realised I'm not as high maintenance as he thought; that maybe asking for kids is more about "us" and less about what I want.'

'Um, congratulations,' I said. 'So, spill…' Time was ticking. I had to catch Luke. 'What does Jonny think you should spend the money on?'

'My own business as a party organiser! I'm always putting on get-togethers and have a book full of contacts, such as photographers, florists and musicians. And the best bit?'

I shrugged.

'Name me a party that doesn't need a cake? There isn't one.' She clapped her hands. 'You and me – we could go into this venture together!'

My jaw dropped. 'You're not serious.'

'We're the perfect combination. My glamour coupled with your practical skills…'

'But what about when you start a family?'

'Mere details! We'd cope with that when it happened. So, what do you say?'

Surely this was everything I'd dreamed of? With Melissa's contacts, I'd be cooking for celebrities within the month. Within the year I'd have that shiny van and pedigree dog called Chico that I'd always dreamed of. I'd be someone. People would love me. Want my photo. Ask for my autograph. I could afford to buy my kids anything they wanted. Give them the childhood I never had. Take them on cool holidays. Buy my daughter a brand new first bra of her own.

I gazed at Melissa's beautiful face and she winked at me as she struck a pose for the impatient photographers. She waved across to Jonny. The paparazzi had homed in by now. Dads pushed their young sons up to him with bits of paper to sign. Women giggled nervously in his presence and fiddled with their hair. Two weeks ago I'd have jumped at this chance. But now…? I still wanted to make money – still wanted to succeed, but I didn't want to live in a world where strangers thought they knew me and supposed friends did the dirty. I thought of Luke and how he'd built up his business on his own, from scratch.

'Melissa?'

'Kimmy?'

'I really appreciate the offer. I can't thank you enough.'

She stopped posing for a moment. 'But?'

'I want to run my own business. Be independent. Know that I've created something successful by myself.' Without relying on a friend or boyfriend. Without relying on state hand-outs, like Mum.

Her face dropped. 'Are you sure? We could bring out a cookery DVD together.'

'Maybe one day – you could work out a fitness routine based around beating batter and squeezing icing bags.'

We both smiled.

'And we'll stay in touch,' I said. 'I can always do the cakes for your parties now and again.'

'Well no arguments, you're doing the cake for our vows ceremony. With publicity like that, your business will be made. Did you, um, see Saffron in the papers today?'

I pulled a face. 'What a predictable kiss 'n' tell. Bet she had chicken fillets in that bikini top.'

'She won't be heard of after her five minutes of fame.'

'Her fiancé dumped her and gave his side of the story in another paper. Apparently…'

'Shh!' Melissa smiled. 'A good friend knows when to stay quiet. And, um, that's what you are. The best. Don't be a stranger. I'm counting on you to invent the calorie-free cupcake.'

I hugged her.

'Not too tight,' she said and backed off. 'I'll crease.'

I grinned.

'Did I tell you Jess is going to redesign the back garden for me?' she said. 'Help get rid of those bloody golf holes and bunkers. And guess what? Jonny's putting in planning permission – if our team wins the Ryder Cup this year, he's promised to build me an indoor swimming pool and get rid of that shed-cum-clubhouse. I think it scared him – a couple of days with Saffron. She reminded him of his first wife. Me telling him to shove his stinking money made him realise how much I love him, not his bank balance.' She rolled her eyes. 'Honestly, men! I let him have a mini-golf course in the back garden – that alone should have proved that he means the world to me. Anyway, all this business should make me more independent than ever – my agent rang today to say there's a perfume deal in the pipeline for me to bring out a scent called "Forgiveness".

'That's awesome,' I said and looked at my watch.

'Not keeping you, am I?' Melissa grinned. 'Don't tell me – the handyman's somewhere about.'

Probably in the car park. If I hurried, I might just catch him.

She shooed me. 'Go on, girl, go. No! Stop a minute.' She searched her bag. 'Stand still. Dehydrated is not a good look.' She sprayed Evian all over my face. I hoped it wouldn't freeze. 'You two are a good match. He only fooled you about that haunting for a good purpose. He wasn't trying to do you out of money or sell you drugs or…' she shuddered, '…worst of all, sleep with you and cut out one of your kidneys whilst you slept. That happened to a friend of Jonny's; it got sold on the blackmarket.'

'Well, if you put it like that…'

'Tomorrow night I'm throwing a small Christmas Eve cocktail party and counting on you and Jess to come. I've asked Terry, as well.'

Then she air-kissed me! So, it was official! I'd been accepted into the world of celebritydom! Except it didn't mean so much to me now. I didn't look around in the hope that we'd been photographed. I wasn't even conjuring up a headline in my mind. Nor an impressive Facebook status.

'And now,' said a voice through a megaphone, 'we are proud to announce the winner of this year's baking competition. Please, everyone, congregate around the cake stall.'

Oh no! Was it that time already?

'You can catch him later,' said Melissa and linked her arm in mine. 'This is far more important.'

'Nervous?' muttered a friendly voice as we reached the cake stall. It was Ruth, the "After Dinner Muffin" contestant. I nodded and stole a glance at Eleanor who stood smugly behind her nutty fruit cake. I positioned myself behind my blindingly yellow cupcakes.

'Ladies and Gentlemen,' said a voice – the vicar. 'Thank you for your patience. It has been a very difficult decision this year. The quality of the entries has been outstanding. How heart-warming it is, to have so much interest in this traditional element of the Christmas market.'

At the word "traditional", Eleanor looked even smugger. Perhaps she was right – maybe quirky cupcakes were no contest for her good old-fashioned entry.

'We have marked the entries on several different levels,' said the vicar. 'Taste, texture, appearance, level of skill and overall enjoyment. With no further ado, here are the top three winners. In third place is last year's third place winner yet again, Ruth Hodgkiss with her sensational Christmas tree muffins – such exquisite presentation and flavour to match. Well done!'

Ruth gave me a wry smile before she went up to shake hands and collect her envelope.

I breathed in and out deeply for a moment and took a hopeful look around the crowd. My heart sank. Luke was nowhere to be seen. Who could blame him?

'It was very hard to decide between the runner up and this year's winner,' said the vicar, when the clapping stopped. 'Both showed a considerable degree of skill. Both tasted fantastic. But, eventually, we came to a decision and the runner up prize has been awarded to… Eleanor Goodman for her deliciously moist and tastily glazed Christmas fruitcake. Come up here Eleanor. Well done!'

Oh my God! I was sure she was going to win it! Her eyes glazed over for a moment before, through gritted teeth, she said her thanks.

So, the winner... Was there a chance? I swallowed hard. The local press were there, ready with their cameras. I had my business cards ready to hand out... But who was I kidding? That chocolate log cake with the marzipan robin had looked mouthwatering.

'When choosing the winner, the overall enjoyment factor was high on the agenda. Of course, to win top prize, the cake has to be perfect when it came to flavour and texture. Its appearance has to be seamless. There needs to be a certain degree of skill employed to achieve all of this. And the winner we have chosen, like many of the other entries, fulfilled all of these criteria. But what bowled us over was something extra.' He smiled. 'I think it's what Simon Cowell would call the "X Factor".'

Why was he lifting up my plate and holding it in front of the crowd?

'The "Bring Me Sunshine" cupcakes,' he continued, 'on top of everything else, made us all laugh. Eric Morecambe would have been proud, with their sunny colour and his glasses on the top. They embody everything about Christmas – the feel-good factor and ability to bring sunshine into people's lives – just like the money raised from our entrants' fees when it is handed over to our various good causes. So please, give a big round of applause to this year's winner, Kimberley Jones!'

Melissa shrieked and Jess cheered. I'd done it! Me! Little Kimmy from Luton! As the cameras clicked I took my envelope. I didn't even know what the prize was.

'Well done!' Ruth winked and passed me her card. 'Give me a ring some time. We'll have to meet up and compare ingredients.'

'I knew you could do it, darling!' called Melissa.

'Go, Kimmy!' Jess punched my shoulder.

'Beginner's luck,' sniffed Eleanor. 'Did you by any chance find Lily's recipe book?'

'Did she like Eric Morecambe?' I asked, politely.

'Didn't everyone? Gimmicks won't win every year though.' She sighed and half-smiled at me. 'I dare say I get rather competitive. Well done, dear.'

'You were friends with Lily?'

'Yes. Lovely woman,' she said, softly. 'I miss her terribly. She used to cheer me on during this competition; remind me that it was all for fun and ticked me off for taking it so seriously.'

I smiled. 'There's always next year.'

'Yes, you'd better watch out. I've a year to practise baking cupcakes.' She patted my shoulder, then started to pack up.

By the time the crowd had cleared, my throat was hoarse and I'd almost run out of business cards. The local health shop was interested in some of my ideas. Some reporter wanted to do an article on me and said it would inspire readers, in these hard times, to see a young person set up their own business. Then Vivian turned up and said the golf club could do with a good dessert-maker and that she'd put my name forward! I'd be catering for Melissa and Jonny's vows ceremony... I could have jumped up and down on the spot!

The prize turned out to be a very welcome cheque for one hundred pounds. That would buy me some new silicone cake moulds. How impressed Adam would be that I wasn't going to blow it on a new bag or pair of shoes.

'See you back at the ranch,' said Jess. 'Melissa's giving me a lift. Sure you won't come with us, now?'

I shook my head. The vicar's wife was waiting to talk to me. 'See you later,' I said. 'I knew we could do it. You... me... Mistletoe Mansion.'

Jess nodded. 'It's been one hell of a two weeks. Feels like a lifetime.'

'Yeah – you're pregnant, I've kick-started my business...' And fallen in love. There. I'd admitted it. I sighed. As I packed up my Tupperware box, someone tapped me on the shoulder. My heart leapt. Was it possible that...?

'Adam? What are you doing here?' Blimey. He'd put on his smartest jeans and gelled his hair.

He kissed me on the cheek. 'I'm here... to support you. Well done for winning. Mum's around somewhere.' He half-smiled. 'She misses you – almost as much as I do.'

I blushed.

'Move back in, Kimmy. I've thought a lot since that Chinese restaurant – almost choking like that, it's made me realise what's really important. Forget the factory job. We're still only young. And... and who knows, maybe this cake business will take off. You've worked hard, I can see that. Mum says you can use her kitchen any time. She's even got one of those fancy mixers.'

'Oh Adam...' I took his hand. A fortnight ago I'd have been on cloud nine to hear a speech like that. My eyes felt wet. 'I'm sorry but...' My throat ached. This was hard. Adam was a decent bloke. 'I don't feel the same any more. About us. Your dream is security, building up a pension, saving for a mortgage. I'm not wired that way, never will be. I want the security of money, but I don't want to spend our life – my life – ducking every risk. It could be years before my cakes make any real money. Would you really wait that long?'

'I'd try.'

'But that's not fair on either of us. You'd end up hating me, and your mum would have bought hundreds of wedding outfits by then.'

'Think about it?' he asked, his voice unsteady.

'I already have. I was going to ring you, once today was over. I... don't want to hurt you. You don't deserve that.' Just then a group of children ran past, throwing snowballs, and almost knocked me over. Adam put out a protective arm.

'You okay?' he muttered.

'Thanks, Adam.

'What for?'

'Caring. No one's ever looked out for me the way you have, all this time. I'll never forget.'

He nodded. A muscle flinched in his cheek before he turned around. My tears distorted Adam's outline as he disappeared into the crowd.

'No need to cry. I'm here,' said a tender voice from my left.

'Luke?' My heart leapt.

He came over. 'I believe congratulations are in order.'

'Huh?'

'The competition – I knew you'd do it.'

'Oh, yes, um... Couldn't have come this far without you. Thanks for all the support. What I said about the cards... I didn't mean it. The cake motif is really sweet.'

He grinned. 'I'll take that as an apology.'

'How come you're still here?'

He looked himself up and down. 'You gave this body the brush off. I knew something had to be seriously wrong.'

'Don't flatter yourself!' I said, but couldn't help my mouth upturning into a huge smile.

'Groucho picked up a newspaper on the way out. Tore most of it to bits. When I finally pulled it away I caught sight of a photo. You must have thought...'

'No! Don't be silly. As if I'd fall for a shot like that!' I cleared my throat.

'Of course not. So. It was just your nerves, right? A psychotic episode because of the pressure of competing?'

'Something like that.'

'You and Adam okay? I know it's an off-limits topic but…'

'We've split up.' Deep breath. Wipe eyes dry. Today was a winning day and right now I knew exactly what other prize I wanted. 'When you get back from Brighton… perhaps we could meet up.'

'You won't throw a Christmas tree at me? You now believe I'm not a murderer nor conman nor two-timing–'

'Idiot!'

'An idiot who has found his kindred spirit,' he murmured and took my hand.

'Erm, I'm not sure that's a compliment!' I said, heartbeat accelerating as he squeezed my fingers gently.

'If it's compliments you want, Kimmy, I could stand here for hours, listing everything about you that appeals – like your feisty attitude, your ambition, the way you stick by your mates and that cute little sunspot just to the left of your nose. Plus–'

I leant forwards and pressed my lips hard against his.

'Stay at my pad whilst I'm away, once you've left Mistletoe Mansion, if you want,' he whispered, when we finally surfaced from the most delectable, spine-tingling kiss in the world. 'I've got a thing for housesitters…' Those moss green eyes crinkled at the corners and he touched my hair, which had frizzed in the snow. 'I couldn't read you this week; wasn't sure how you felt; didn't want to risk making a move and ruining our recently-found friendship.'

'Our truce, more like.' I grinned. 'Anyway, didn't you know? Risks are good.'

He grinned. 'Housesit for me, then.'

'Thanks,' I said, 'but no... I can't let my new landlord down. But maybe when you get back, you could help me with my business plan? Will I see you over Christmas?'

'Just try keeping me away – why don't I visit after lunch? Spend the rest of the day annoying you and Jess with my penchant for playing charades? Mum and Dad's place is full to the rafters Christmas afternoon, with nieces and nephews and neighbours – they won't mind, as long as I'm there for the turkey.'

I nodded, thinking it was just as well hearts couldn't sing, as mine would be breaking glass. 'And, um, will you ring me whilst you're away?'

'I'll write. You know, in the old-fashioned way – not with a keyboard, but paper and pen. You could write down your new address for me on one of those cards. Unless you'd rather I communicate with a ghostly smoke signal.'

I swatted him with my bag before once again slipping my arms around his neck.

'I'm already looking forward to the homecoming cake you'll make me,' he mumbled.

Mmm, me too, and I didn't think I'd need the recipe I used for my old postie, with sweet basil as an aphrodisiac.

Someone coughed behind us and reluctantly, we drew apart. It was the vicar's wife, beaming at us. I knelt down to ruffle Groucho's ears before Luke winked and with a cheerful whistle, headed off. I could still smell his musky aftershave whilst having a celebratory cup of tea with the judges. I was still tingling from those kisses when I got back to Mistletoe Mansion.

Jess stood in the kitchen making an omelette, just like I had on our first night there. Keen to freshen up before eating, I made my way upstairs. My head was full. Me and Luke... Luke and me... I chuckled as I remembered the dressmaking doll. To think I'd once thought him capable of murder. What a day. What a fortnight.

I opened my bedroom door, stopped dead for a moment and stared at the bed. Amongst the cushions was a spray of winter honeysuckle and a tattered book. A lump welled in my throat. I sat down and lifted the bouquet to my nose. That light, floral smell would always remind me of Harpenden.

I took the spray of flowers and slipped it behind my ear, then picked up the book. Hands shaking, I leant back on the bed. As I suspected, it was Lily's famous recipe collection. Avoiding the odd grease stain, I ran my finger over the lists of ingredients.

'Walter?' I whispered. 'Thank you… I'll treasure this; do Lily well proud.'

Silence.

'Are you there? Have you already gone to meet her at the Pearly Gates?' Straining to listen for thuds, I sat up and gazed around the room. Me and Walter, we were mates, weren't we? Mates didn't leave without saying goodbye.

My chest tightened as I put down the book. Throat hurting, eyes all watery, I squished back against the pillows. Who could blame him? He and Lily had waited long enough to see each other again. But then suddenly, a tickling sensation spread from the heel of my foot to the toes. I sniffed and grinned. A gust of cold wind brushed my neck and lifted my hair. I sat bolt upright and let out a giggle. On cue, the dreamy White Christmas music wafted across the room.

'It was my pleasure,' I said, voice wobbling slightly, as this was no doubt the last time I'd talk to my paranormal pal. 'The police have charged Ms Chapman, and Mistletoe Mansion is in good hands; the Stedmans seem like a great couple. So go! Meet Lily. In time for Christmas!' (Er, okay, they probably didn't celebrate it up there). 'But just one more thing, Walter…'

There were three faint thuds.

'I'd really love to know if you see Elvis or Michael Jackson.'

With a squeal, I jumped as something gently poked me in the ribs, then the Christmas music stopped.

'Take care,' I murmured, then shook myself and bounced off the bed. A big smile across my face, I scooted downstairs to show Jess my awesome new recipe book.

If you loved MISTLETOE MANSION
Turn the page for more from Samantha Tonge in
DOUBTING ABBEY

LORD EDWARD'S E-DIARY

Welcome to this blog. Your visit is appreciated. May I introduce myself—I am Lord Edward, the son of the Earl of Croxley. Our home, Applebridge Hall, is in the final of the *Million Dollar Mansion* competition. For regular updates of our progress, please do grace this blog with your presence.

Monday 27th August

7p.m. Good evening, readers. Finally I write my first entry. Do bear with me, as I am new to blogging, which I see as a modern twist on my ancestors' habit of keeping journals. The programme-makers insist you will be interested in my thoughts on the competition, so I shall attempt to bring honesty and some perspective to this diary.

Honest thought number one? Chaos has descended. The film crews arrived again today—cue a refresher course on camera and sound procedures. A national tabloid interviewed Father. To my irritation, the photographer suggested we both wore monocles and borrowed a cluster of the Queen's corgis. Regardless of the fact I don't know Her Majesty, my response equalled 'over my dead body'.

Some perspective? I await a phone call from my, um, dear cousin, Abigail Croxley who, I'm sure, will confirm her intention to join us imminently. How we intend to beat the other finalist, the Baron of Marwick Castle, is still top secret. However, here is an exclusive clue: my cousin's cooking knowledge will be an instrumental part of our tactics. I am very much looking forward to seeing her.

Best bit of today? Right now, sitting by myself in our tranquil library.

Worst? Gaynor, the director, handing me a DVD of *Pride and Prejudice*, along with a frilly white shirt and breeches. I made it quite clear that I am a down-to-earth gentleman who will *never*, under any circumstances, resemble some sort of romantic hero like Mr Darcy.

CHAPTER 1

Abbey was born to sophistication, whereas I was more Barbara than Buckingham Palace Windsor. The two of us had just got back from a goodbye lunch with our Pizza Parlour colleagues, and were standing in front of the bathroom mirror. Having toasted each of our redundancies, I felt a bit tiddly, but still sharp enough to realize this idea was bonkers.

'Look, Abbey, I don't know what's behind this plan, but seriously…' I smiled '…wise up. I could never trick people into thinking I was you, a member of the aristocracy. Ask me to mimic a…a pop star or footballer's wife, then I'd give it a shot, but even then I dunno if I could live a lie for very long.' With a grin, I shrugged. 'Run this idea past me again.' Perhaps I'd misheard.

Abbey's bottom lip quivered. 'It's…um, no joke, Gemma— please, pretend to be me. Just for two weeks.' Her cheeks flushed. 'Who else could I trust with such a mission?'

My jaw dropped. 'Are you out of your mind? You know I'd flog all my make-up and fave shoes on eBay if it meant helping you get out of a scrape… But this? Abbey, mate…' My eyes narrowed for a second. 'Marcus next door hasn't given you one of his funny-smelling cigarettes has he?'

'Goodness, no!' Abbey's face broke into a smile. 'Honestly, I quite understand your apprehension, but…'

She fiddled with the waistband of her skinny white trousers. 'It'd only be for a fortnight and it is in a good cause.' She took my hands and squeezed them. 'Oh, please, Gemma. You're the only person in the world who can pull this off. Remember when Laurence, the son of one of Mummy's friends, stayed over a few weeks ago?'

Ooh, yeah. Hotter than Dad's chilli con carne, he was, in that white scarf and tux.

'He caught you fresh-faced in the morning,' she said, 'and insisted we looked terribly alike. If you dyed your brunette hair blonde, he joked we could pass as sisters, what with the same shape nose and blue eyes.'

'He must have still had his beer goggles—or champers shades—on.' I let my hands drop from her grip and looked down at my skimpy skirt, the streak of fake tan and high-heeled shoes. 'Mind you…' I giggled '…remember my first day at work?'

Abbey leant towards me and joined in the laughter. My chest glowed, glad to have cheered her up—but then it *was* funny, me being mistaken for her. Several members of staff had thought that Abbey—who already worked there—had suffered some sort of identity crisis and undergone a chavvy makeover. Or, in their opinion, make*under*. I should have been insulted at their relief when she'd turned up looking her usual sophisticated self.

'Even the regular customers were fooled.' I turned to the bathroom mirror for a moment. Personally, I couldn't see a strong resemblance but time had taught me that the world at large occasionally considered us each other's doppelgänger.

Abbey's grey-haired aunt came in, picked up a bottle of cleanser and passed it to me. 'Do hurry up, Gemma—we only have ten days to complete your transformation.'

A bubble of laughter tickled the inside of my chest. Really? I mean, *really*? This wasn't a wind-up? To humour them, I removed the make-up from half of my face. Minus one false eyelash and a cheek of bronzer, I resembled an unsymmetrical Picasso portrait.

I leant towards Abbey and whispered, 'Come on, spill— tell me what this is really about and what *she*'s actually doing here.'

'*She* has a name,' said the old dear, who clearly had bionic hearing and a strict dinner lady stare.

'How rude of me not to introduce my aunt formally,' said Abbey with a sheepish smile at the old dear. 'Gemma, this is Lady Constance Woodfold, my mother's sister—she used to run her own finishing school.'

'I'm sure you'll look delightful without all that bronzer, Gemma,' said Lady C (posh titles were too long to say in full, unless you were Lady Gaga). 'Surely your mother would prefer to see your skin au naturel?'

'No idea. She um…' I cleared my throat '…Mum got ill when I was little and…'

Lady C's cheeks tinged pink. 'Do accept my apologies. Of course. Abigail told me of her demise.' Her wrinkled face softened. 'Was there no female relative on hand during your formative years?'

I almost chuckled. Didn't people only speak like that on old BBC news reels?

'Auntie Jan's cool. If it wasn't for her, I'd know nothing about clothes and make-up. People always mistook me for a boy, as a kid. When I hit the teen years, she intervened and even bought my first chicken fillets.'

'She's a proficient cook?' said Lady C, brow furrowed.

I grinned. 'They're the inedible kind that you stick down your bra, to up the cup size.'

Lady C pursed her lips. 'Those fake appendages must disappear, along with your heavy eye-liner. Then we can concentrate on the more important things you need to learn, like the art of good conversation and table manners.'

Huh? What *was* all this about?

The old woman glanced at Abbey. 'Does Gemma not know yet that your Uncle James is in the final of *Million Dollar Mansion*?'

'*Whaaat*?' I almost choked on the word. 'Your dad's brother? The one who inherited the family home—Apple…?'

'Applebridge Hall?' said Abbey. 'Yes. That's him.'

'Amaaaaaazin'! I saw a clip of that programme! Castles and Tudor mansions and all sorts competing against each other to win a million dollars to set their place up as… what did they call it? *A going concern*… The dosh is up for grabs from some American billionaire obsessed with *Downton Abbey*. But how…? What…?'

'All you need to know at this stage, dear,' said Lady C, 'is that Abigail is expected to help out with some catering project—no doubt serving cream teas in some shop they've probably constructed within a converted part of the estate. With its exciting armoury and dungeons, the Earl believes the opposition, Marwick Castle, could win. The Croxleys have owned Applebridge Hall since the sixteenth century, so must build on its strength of history, tradition and… family values.' She stood up straighter. 'Abbey is unable to go. That's where you come in.'

'Me? On the telly?' Wow. So it wasn't a joke. I bit my thumbnail. 'Much as I love reality shows, the last thing I'd want is to be on screen. It's bad enough in real life, worrying about spots and bad hair days, let alone in front of the whole nation.'

'But people won't know it's you,' said Abbey. 'Not even my uncle, who hasn't seen me since I was nine, when he and Daddy had words. My parents will be away on a cruise and my friends don't watch such programmes. Even if they do, more than once, people have mistaken us for each other. It's a foolproof plan.'